Henry Du

by

Mary Elizabeth Braddon

edited with an introduction and notes
by Anne-Marie Beller

Victorian Secrets 2010

Published by

Victorian Secrets Limited
32 Hanover Terrace
Brighton BN2 9SN

www.victoriansecrets.co.uk

Henry Dunbar by Mary Elizabeth Braddon
First published in 1864
This Victorian Secrets edition 2010

Introduction and notes © 2010 by Anne-Marie Beller
This edition © 2010 by Victorian Secrets

Composition and design by Catherine Pope
Cover photo © iStockphoto.com/duncan1890

A catalogue record for this book is available from the British Library.

ISBN 978-1-906469-15-3

Contents

Introduction

> "[A] book without a murder, a divorce, a seduction, or a bigamy,
> is not apparently considered worth either writing or reading, and
> a mystery and a secret are the chief qualifications of the modern
> novel."[1]

The following commentary reveals important aspects of the plot. Readers new to the novel might wish to treat this introduction as an afterword.

Sensation fiction

When Mary Elizabeth Braddon's eighth acknowledged novel, *Henry Dunbar*, was published in 1864, she had already secured a reputation as the "queen of the circulating libraries" and was considered the chief proponent, with Wilkie Collins, of sensation fiction.[2] Throughout the 1860s, sensation novels were the focus of a vociferous critical campaign, conducted chiefly in the highbrow quarterly journals and certain sections of the middle-class press. Readers of all classes, however, were captivated by the genre, and its extreme popularity with this broad spectrum of the reading public accounts, in part, for the critics' anxiety. For not only were large numbers of "vulnerable" readers (particularly respectable middle-class women) being exposed to supposedly immoral plots involving murder, bigamy and madness, but the huge sales of such novels also heightened concerns for the status of literary art. Many critics betrayed fears that an increased commercialisation was leading to the contamination and "cheapening" of literature, and the sensation novelists seemed to exemplify this tendency toward the lowering of literary standards, in their bid to pander to the less sophisticated, newly literate reader.

Given the enormous popularity of Braddon's novels, it is unsurprising that she became a key focus for these anxieties, and through-

---

[1] Anon., "The Popular Novels of the Year", *Frasers Magazine* LXIII (Aug. 1863): 262.
[2] Previous novels, in order of publication, were: *Three Times Dead* (subsequently republished as *The Trail of the Serpent*), *The Lady Lisle*, *The Captain of the Vulture*, *Lady Audley's Secret*, *Aurora Floyd*, *Eleanor's Victory*, and *John Marchmont's Legacy*. Braddon had also published anonymous serials for the halfpenny and penny press—including *The Black Band*, *The Octoroon*, *The White Phantom*—and a novelette, *Ralph the Bailiff*, which was serialized between April and June 1861 in the *St. James's Magazine*, and later published in three volumes with short stories.

out the 1860s her work was subjected to strident attacks by a number of outraged critics. One of the most hostile of these was W. Fraser Rae, who comprehensively attacked the morality, tone, and aesthetic value of Braddon's novels in a lengthy review essay published in 1865. Among the many faults he identified in her fiction, Rae found Braddon's insistent focus on crime and criminals particularly abhorrent. He claimed:

> According to Miss Braddon, crime is not an accident, but it is the business of life. She would lead us to conclude that the chief end of man is to commit murder, and his highest merit to escape punishment; that women are born to attempt to commit murders, and to succeed in committing bigamy.[3]

The sensation novelist's habitual tendency to place crime at the centre of their plots was, indeed, a frequent source of objection to the genre. Even the Archbishop of York was moved to discourse on sensation fiction, claiming indignantly from his pulpit that such novelists "want to per-suade people that in almost every one of the well-ordered houses of their neighbours, there is a skeleton shut up in some cupboard".[4] The refer-ence to "well-ordered houses" points to the real source of complaint, that sensation novels disturbed comfortable middle-class notions that criminality was located in the lower sections of society. For most Victorians the idea of crime was firmly associated with the East End slums, and not with the drawing-rooms of Belgravia. The fact that novelists such as Braddon invariably depicted crime as occurring within the sanctum of the respectable middle- and upper-class home was in-tolerable to some, while evidently titillating to the many readers of sensation fiction. If the Newgate novel, popular in the 1830s and 40s, had offered middle-class readers the voyeuristic opportunity to enjoy the spectacle of crime in a vicarious manner, reassured by the class "otherness" of the criminal, then the 1860s sensation novel turned this scrutiny inwards, inviting the reader to question fundamental beliefs about the nature of middle-class values.

Crime and detective fiction

Another source of criticism, and one in which *Henry Dunbar* was

---

[3] W.Fraser Rae, 'Sensation Novelists: Miss Braddon', *North British Review* XLIII (Sept. 1865): 104.
[4] "The Archbishop of York on works of fiction", *The Times* 2 November 1864: 9.

perceived to be a prime offender, was the sensation novel's typical evasion of the conventional channels of criminal justice. Despite committing a brutal murder and perpetrating an audacious masquerade, Joseph Wilmot is nevertheless allowed to escape police capture, live out his natural span of life, finally repent of his crime, and ultimately find peace. For many contemporary reviewers this resolution was not merely unacceptable, but potentially subversive, particularly since the death penalty was the subject of fervent debate at this time. In the same year that *Henry Dunbar* was published, a Royal Commission on Capital Punishment was set up, chaired by the Duke of Richmond. The initial report of the Commission was published in 1865, and widely reported in the press.[5] Though their verdict was not unanimous and the report included suggestions for some reform, the overall recommendation was to retain capital punishment, a decision which seems to have reflected the general mood of the country during that decade.[6]

In *Henry Dunbar*, Braddon exhibits a distinctly pro-abolition stance on this issue, primarily through the narration of Clement Austin who, with regard to Joseph Wilmot's fate, declares himself "deeply thankful that Providence had suffered him to escape that hideous earthly doom which is supposed to be the wisest means of ridding society of a murderer" (340).[7] Given the limited public support for the abolitionists during the 1860s, Braddon's treatment of her murderer was unlikely to be popular and arguably goes some way to explain the antagonism of many reviewers. The *Athenaeum* critic, for instance, found the ending of *Henry Dunbar* preposterous, and derisively commented: "He was sorry for what he had done! There's a moral for you!"[8] W. Fraser Rae was similarly disgusted by Joseph Wilmot's liberty to enjoy the fruits of his crime and observed that "few other novelists could have invented anything so diabolical as the murder or have depicted, with seeming complacency, the after-life of the criminal. The impression made is, that the murderer was a clever man, and was very hardly used."[9] What Rae deliberately ignores in this assessment is Braddon's emphasis on how little pleasure Wilmot actually derives from the riches and status acquired through his crime, due to his nightmarish feeling of imprisonment in "those splendid rooms, whose grandeur had been more hideous to him than the blank

---

5 See "Capital Punishment", *The Times,* Thursday, Dec 28, 1865: 8.
6 For a discussion of British attitudes to capital punishment in the period see Philip Collins, *Dickens and Crime* 3rd ed. (London: Macmillan, 1994): 245-253.
7 All references are to this edition of *Henry Dunbar* and page numbers are given parenthetically in the text.
8 "Henry Dunbar", *Athenaeum*, 21 May 1864: 703.
9 Rae, "Sensation Novelists: Miss Braddon", 189.

walls of a condemned cell" (306). Wilmot is constantly haunted by appalling memories of the murder and remains in a persistent state of paranoia that his crime will be detected.

Sensation novels played a vital role in shaping the genre of detective fiction, which achieved immense popularity towards the end of the nineteenth century. *Henry Dunbar* was not the first novel by Braddon to include a professional detective, or indeed a female amateur detective. *The Trail of the Serpent* (1861) and *Aurora Floyd* (1863) had both contributed memorable examples with Joseph Peters and Joseph Grimstone respectively. And in *Eleanor's Victory* (1863), Braddon presented an early, if not particularly effective, female detective in Eleanor Vane. In *Henry Dunbar*, Mr. Carter of Scotland Yard anticipates Wilkie Collins's Sergeant Cuff in *The Moonstone* (1868). Both were important precursors of the police detective who would become a staple of later crime fiction, but they also engaged with contemporary debates over the efficacy and desirability of the relatively recently established police detective corps.[10] Though he ultimately fails to bring the murderer to justice, Carter is shown to be an able and clever detective, despite his chagrin at being hoodwinked by the heroine, Margaret Wilmot. In fact, as in many other novels by Braddon, the downfall and fate of the criminal is attributed more to the workings of Providence, than it is due to the investigative work of the amateur or professional detectives. The train crash, which prevents Wilmot's first attempt at escape, is just one of many examples in this novel of circumstance overriding individual agency: "No man could have been more completely a prisoner than this man had become by the result of the fatal accident near Rugby. 'Providence has thrown him into my power,' Margaret said" (232). Carter's consolation upon losing the chance to capture Wilmot lies in his similar belief that "there's a Providence that lies in wait for wicked men" (289).

Class and the literary marketplace

Crime as a subject for literature tended to be associated with lower forms of entertainment, such as the Newgate calendar, penny bloods, and sensational journalism, all of which were seen primarily as catering to the debased and unsophisticated tastes of the working classes. When sen-

---

[10] The Metropolitan Police Force was founded by Sir Robert Peel in 1829. Twelve years later that the Detective division was established in London (in 1842), but this remained a small operation until after the middle of the century. 1856 saw the London police model replicated throughout the country, with a plain clothes detective branch at Scotland Yard following in 1878.

sation novels began to dominate the literary marketplace in the early years of the 1860s, many cultural commentators feared that "low" reading habits were spreading upwards and contaminating middle-class cultural practices. The threat to traditional class distinctions, implied by these cross-class reading habits, contributed significantly to concerns over sensational reading, as Rae implied when he accused Braddon of "making the literature of the kitchen the favourite reading of the Drawing-room".[11] Braddon, perhaps more than any of the other sensation novelists, embodied this sense of a shared literary taste by writing simultaneously for both markets. In an 1862 letter to her literary mentor, Edward Bulwer-Lytton, she admitted, "I do an immense deal of work which nobody ever hears of, for Halfpenny and penny journals. This work is most piratical stuff, and would make your hair stand on end, if you were to see it."[12] Braddon is here referring to her anonymous serials, such as *The Black Band* and *The White Phantom*, both of which appeared in publications aimed specifically at the working classes, but these unsigned productions were not the full extent of her links with the penny fiction market. *Lady Audley's Secret* and *Aurora Floyd* appeared in the *London Journal*, a penny fiction weekly, though both had appeared previously in three-volume form. *The Outcasts*, however, was written specifically for that magazine, later being reshaped for a middle-class readership as *Henry Dunbar*. Braddon seems to have been keenly aware of the different expectations and requirements of the two markets, and she took time to significantly revise *The Outcasts* before it was allowed to appear in three volumes.[13]

The revisions Braddon made to her story, before its release as *Henry Dunbar*, were all designed to make the three volume novel less melodramatic and more suited to middle-class tastes. In *The Doctor's Wife* (1864) Braddon introduced Sigismund Smith, a penny fiction author whose entertaining views on the literary marketplace offer an interesting insight into those of his creator. Smith enjoys his work, producing sensational reading for the masses, though he ruefully admits that "the penny public require excitement", a predilection which means "you're obliged to have recourse to bodies". By contrast, he tells us, the middle-class market is satisfied with one corpse, and it is Smith's ambition to become the author of "a legitimate three-volume romance, with all the

---

[11] Rae, "Sensation Novelists: Miss Braddon", 105.

[12] Robert Lee Wolff, "Devoted Disciple: The Letters of Mary Elizabeth Braddon to Sir Edward Bulwer-Lytton, 1862-1873", *Harvard Library Bulletin* XXII: 1 (Jan. 1974): 11.

[13] See Braddon's letter to Edward Tinsley, quoted in Robert Lee Wolff, *Sensational Victorian: The Life and Fiction of Mary Elizabeth Braddon* (London: Garland, 1979): 136.

interest concentrated on one body".[14] Interestingly, in turning her penny serial into a "legitimate" triple-decker, Braddon follows Smith's prescriptions to the letter. By eliminating a prominent subplot of the serialized version, involving a secret marriage, the murder of an unwanted wife, and the kidnapping of the young heir to an earldom, Braddon ensures that in the "respectable" three-volume *Henry Dunbar*, the focus is all on "one body".

The increasing fluidity of Victorian class distinctions, apparent in Braddon's reissuing of a penny serial as a three-volume novel, is also present as a thematic concern within *Henry Dunbar*. Indeed, the performativity of class is crucial to the plot, since the story hinges on Wilmot's ability to successfully pass for a man of Dunbar's superior social position. A key episode in this respect is Wilmot's initial transformation from outcast to gentleman: "The man's manner was as much altered as his person. He had entered the shop at eight o'clock that morning a blackguard as well as a vagabond. He left it now a gentleman; subdued in voice, easy and rather listless in gait, self-possessed in tone" (37). The shop-boy who serves Wilmot is at first openly suspicious of his customer's ragged appearance, leading the outcast to remark that "he's like the rest of the world, and he thinks if a man wears a shabby coat, he must be a scoundrel" (35). However, when he dons the apparel of a gentleman, Wilmot also assumes the bearing appropriate to his new appearance, and the formerly hostile shop-boy informs him "you look like a dook" (33).

While Braddon implies that class may be no more than an outward assumption, she also plays with her readers' preconceptions and prejudices, since despite Wilmot's successful transformation into a respectable "gentleman" and his protestations regarding society's presumptions, he remains, in fact, the very "scoundrel" that he was initially suspected to be. Braddon's own class prejudices may be implicit in the fact that the true nobility somehow sense that Wilmot is not quite "right": he "did the honours of his house with a certain haughty grandeur, which was a little stiff and formal as compared to the easy friendly grace of his high-bred visitors. People shrugged their shoulders, and hinted that there was something of the 'roturier' in Mr. Dunbar" (126). Braddon's critique of class privilege is most trenchant when it highlights the prevailing double standard in perceptions of criminality and the practical ways in which these assumptions influence the judicial process:

---

[14] Mary Elizabeth Braddon, *The Doctor's Wife*, ed. Lyn Pykett (Oxford: OUP, 1998): 47; 187.

If Henry Dunbar had been some miserable starving creature, who, in a fit of mad fury against the inequalities of life, had lifted his gaunt arm to slay his prosperous brother for the sake of bread—detectives would have dogged his sneaking steps, and watched his guilty face, and hovered round and about him till they tracked him to his doom. But because in this case the man to whom suspicion pointed had the supreme virtues comprised in a million of money, Justice wore her thickest bandage, and the officials, who are so clever in tracking a low-born wretch to the gallows, held aloof, and said respectfully, 'Henry Dunbar is too great a man to be guilty of a diabolical crime.'" (281)

Performing female identities

If Braddon is interested in class discrimination in this novel, then she is also concerned with issues of gender. Through the character of Margaret Wilmot Braddon explores, what Lyn Pykett terms, "the complexities and contradictions of women's conflicting familial roles as daughters, wives, and mothers".[15] The centrality of Margaret Wilmot was signalled by the subtitle used by Tom Taylor, when he successfully dramatised Braddon's novel in 1865: *Henry Dunbar; Or, a Daughter's Trials* effectively sums up the ordeals suffered by Braddon's heroine in her various identities as daughter, detective, and fiancée. Margaret is initially presented as a rather stoic figure, devoted to her unworthy father and resigned to the hardships of her life, a direct result of his past transgressions. Like her predecessor Eleanor Vane, Margaret's life is transformed by the (apparent) death of her father, and she embarks on a quest to avenge his murder. However, Margaret's detection leads to the horror of discovering her father to be the murderer and not the victim as she had assumed, a cataclysmic event which overturns everything she had previously believed.

Margaret's encounter with her "dead" father evokes a temporary paralysis of selfhood, followed by a forced reconstruction of her personal identity. Braddon emphasizes this paralysis at the textual level by an abrupt dislocation of the narrative, which reflects the dislocation of Margaret's identity:

"Mr. Dunbar!" cried Margaret, in a clear, resolute voice; "awake! it is I, Margaret Wilmot, the daughter of the man who was murd-

---

[15] Lyn Pykett, *The Sensation Novel: From The Woman in White to The Moonstone* (Plymouth: Northcote, 1994): 53.

ered in the grove near Winchester!" The man lifted his head, and looked at her. Even the fire seemed roused by the sound of her voice! for a little jet of vivid light leapt up out of the smouldering log, and lighted the scared face of the banker. (236)

The ensuing encounter between father and daughter is not described. At this point of imminent discovery, the narrative is suspended and the viewpoint shifts abruptly to Clement Austin, waiting outside the house for his fiancée. This thematic emphasis on secrecy and misapprehension provokes a crisis in the main characters' understanding of their own and each others' identities. Thus, when Margaret refuses to confide her discovery to Austin, he is unable to understand her sudden transformation from a gentle, affectionate girl to the unstable, transgressive woman she becomes with the knowledge of Wilmot's guilt. The detection process has destabilized Margaret, in terms of her sense of her own identity and in her social relations to others. Such a destabilization would seem to highlight dramatically the incompatibility of the detective role with conventionally constructed femininity: for whereas the detective figure is expected to display cool rationalism and detached intellect, at the climax of Margaret's investigation, she gives way to "feminine" frailty and emotionality. Lucy Sussex suggests that this type of debilitation is characteristic of "early Victorian female detectives of the heroine ilk (whose sleuthing success is usually followed by physical or mental breakdowns, from which they emerge suitably chastised for their 'unwomanliness' and ready to marry the hero)".[16]

Arguably, these displays of feminine weakness following an incursion into the male realm operate to stabilize the disordered gender roles that the female detective has generated. By submitting to emotional collapse at this crucial moment, the female detective protects her "womanly" credentials, which thus allows her to retain the position of heroine. Braddon's text adopts similar strategies but resists the complete retreat into dominant stereotypes that Sussex implies. Although Margaret's successful detective work has confronted her with a debilitating knowledge about her father (and thus, herself), Braddon undercuts Margaret's "weakness" by inflecting it with connotations of strength of mind and purpose. The doctor, brought in by Austin to treat Margaret, comments: "If she were an ordinary person, she would cry, and the relief of tears would have a most advantageous effect upon her mind. Our patient is by

---

[16]Lucy Sussex, "The Detective Maidservant: Catherine Crowe's *Susan Hopley*", *Silent Voices: Forgotten Novels by Victorian Women Writers*. Ed. Brenda Ayres (London: Praeger, 2003): 57–66. 61.

no means an ordinary person. She has a very strong will." "Margaret has a strong will!" exclaimed Clement, with a look of surprise; "why, she is gentleness itself." "Very likely; but she has a will of iron, nevertheless." (244) Not only does Margaret reject such signs of femininity as crying or swooning, she also refuses to confide in her fiancé or allow him to provide comfort or aid. On finding Margaret after her inexplicable flight from the supposed Henry Dunbar's house, Austin is "startled by the blank whiteness of her face, the fixed stare of her dilated eyes" (241); "his gaze was fascinated by the girl's awful pallor, and the strange expression of her eyes," which later he describes as being "still fixed in the same deathlike stare" (242). The images of "whiteness," "pallor," and the "deathlike stare" arguably represent a figurative death, the demise, or at least suspension, of Margaret's identity as a devoted, loving daughter. Moreover, like Laura Fairlie in Wilkie Collins's *The Woman in White*, Margaret is significantly linked with whiteness and blankness, indicative not only of an erasure of identity but more generally, the absence of an independent social identity for the Victorian woman.

It is perhaps appropriate that Margaret's crisis is evoked through the detection of her father's true and assumed identities. Because Victorian female identity was defined and shaped by women's relationships to men (as daughters, sisters, wives), Margaret's sense of herself is dependent on the fixed, stable identity of her father. However, Margaret's act of detection reveals that Joseph Wilmot no longer "exists": He is neither dead (as officially believed) nor really "alive" in the sense of existing in the world under his own name and identity. By stealing an identity that is not his, Wilmot has, in effect, rendered his daughter "nameless," particularly as Margaret also discovers that the name she has borne all her life—Wentworth—is actually an assumed one. The detective quest, in this respect, becomes a search for origins and self-knowledge. Margaret's "blankness," then, is not only suggestive of her position as a woman in Victorian society, that is, as a cipher; she is also "blank" because she can no longer properly be defined in relation to men. Not only has she lost her father but the guilty knowledge of his crime separates her from her fiancé as well. Such a position naturally causes Margaret distress and confusion, but in one sense, her "blankness" may be read as liberating, as an opportunity to "write" her own story. As Heidi Johnson has suggested, "the 'sensational' daughter of the Victorian detective plot proffers a paradigm for the transformation [. . .] into selfhood".[17]

---

[17] Heidi Johnson, "Electra-fying the Female Sleuth: Detecting the Father in *Eleanor's Victory* and *Thou Art the Man*." *Beyond Sensation: Mary Elizabeth Braddon in Context*. Ed. Marlene Tromp, Pamela K. Gilbert, and Aeron Haynie (Albany: State University of New

Whereas Margaret begins the novel defined as a daughter and ends it defined as a wife, during the period of her "blankness" and her adoption of the role of detective, Margaret is autonomous.

Throughout the novel, Margaret moves through a series of names (Wentworth, Wilmot, Betty the housemaid, Wilson, Austin), suggesting the unstable and fluid nature of identity. The act of detection aims to contain this fluidity yet, at the same time, is the catalyst for exposing it. That is, by embarking on her detective quest, the "wholeness" of Margaret's identity is gradually exposed as an illusion with each successive discovery she makes. In the early parts, she is Margaret Wentworth, devoted daughter of James Wentworth, the assumed name under which Wilmot is living. The events surrounding the supposed murder of her father induce Margaret to investigate her family's past and lead to the discovery of his (and thus, her) true name, which she finds written on her father's old transportation documents. Accordingly, the revelation of Wilmot's true identity consists of his daughter learning, simultaneously, both his name and his criminal nature. The female detective's inherent tendency to disruption thus leads directly to an exposure of the fallibility of the father. At the end of the novel, after Wilmot's death, Margaret has become Mrs. Austin and "a new existence has begun for her as wife and mother" (358). The conventional ending, with Margaret safely returned to a "proper" feminine role, may be read as an attempt to reinscribe appropriate gender norms following the temporary disruption caused by Wilmot's crime and Margaret's foray into the field of amateur detection. Yet Margaret remains elusive in the final pages of *Henry Dunbar*. "Covered" by Clement Austin's name and his narration, she recedes from our view, her voice and independent identity lost to us.

Although Margaret "performs" different identities in the novel, her definitive identity is as a daughter, in a novel that is principally concerned with the effects of a father's crime on daughters. Johnson, with reference to mid- and late-Victorian novels of crime and detection, has noted the "frequently recapitulated scenario of the daughter who detects to discover the secret of her father's death or, conversely, whose detection reveals his culpability".[18] Such plots, Johnson suggests, offer an archetype for the negotiation of female desire and autonomy: "What the female sleuth seeks is the secret of the father's power, as her act of detection demystifies his primacy and allows her to reinaugurate through her own agency a process of psychosexual growth arrested by her protracted attachment to the father" (256). Although the nominal victim

---

York Press, 2000): 255–75. 256.
[18] Johnson, "Electra-fying the Female Sleuth", 256.

in *Henry Dunbar* is the rich banker, Braddon's narrative is influenced most directly by the daughters of the two men, whose positions throughout the plot are interchanged in a similar manner to that of their fathers. Margaret suffers grief for the loss of a father, unaware that he is, in fact, alive. Laura Dunbar, by contrast, has truly lost a father but believes that he has been newly restored to her. Both Margaret and Laura adhere closely to contemporary ideals of femininity and embody the role of the self-sacrificing, devoted daughter. Laura desires to be "a loving companion, a ministering angel" (135), while Margaret believes her father "to be the noblest and most gifted of men," for whom "it was no grief to her to toil" (17). Interestingly, it is this very embodiment of the ideal that leads to Margaret embarking on the role of detective, through which gender norms are threatened. Only with Wilmot's death at the end of the novel can conventional gender relations be reestablished, through Margaret's assimilation as "wife and mother" (358). Appropriately, this resolution is only made possible by Austin's reclamation of the role of detective. Unable to find Margaret, who has exiled herself with her criminal father, Austin employs the methods of the sleuth, tracking her down through a stationer's mark: "Could it be really possible that in this sheet of paper I had found a clue which would help me to trace my lost love?" (353). That the final piece of detective work is carried out by the male hero, motivated by a desire to locate and marry the erstwhile female detective, would seem to signify the end of Margaret's autonomy and the reinstatement of conservative gender values.

Critical reception

As discussed above, many of the contemporary reviews were scathing. Rae's vitriolic attack was echoed in the views articulated by the author of "Kitchen Literature", who deemed *Henry Dunbar* "the worst class of what is called 'sensation' literature".[19] Elsewhere, however, there were more nuanced responses, as the reviews included in the appendices of the present volume aim to illustrate. Curiously, the *Spectator*, who were usually scathing of Braddon's fiction, thought it her best novel to date, and similar approbation was bestowed by both the *Era* and the *Times*, despite their reservations regarding certain aspects of the work. Notwithstanding the critical reservations, *Henry Dunbar* was one of the most financially successful of Braddon's novels,[20] and it deserves to be

[19] Anon., "Kitchen Literature", *Examiner* (25 June 1864): 404-6. 406. (See Appendix A in this edition)
[20] Wolff, *Sensational Victorian*, 158.

read today, not only as an interesting story in its own right, but also as a fascinating commentary on mid-Victorian ideas about class, gender, and crime.[21]

Biographical note

Mary Elizabeth Braddon's long life spanned the period of Queen Victoria's reign and she was, in many ways, a typical Victorian. Her industry and energy, which generated an extraordinarily prolific output, are characteristic of contemporaries as diverse as Charles Dickens, Margaret Oliphant, and Anthony Trollope, who all testify to the inexhaustible productivity of the mid-Victorian novelist. At the same time, however, Braddon was also atypical, particularly when measured against the dominant expectations of middle-class female behaviour in the mid-nineteenth century. Her courageous decisions—to become an actress in the 1850s, to carve out a literary career for herself within the competitive world of periodical publishing in the 1860s, and above all her resolve to live outside of convention with a married man—mark her out as an extraordinary woman.

Born in Soho, London, in 1835, Mary was the youngest child of Henry Braddon, an unsuccessful solicitor from a well-to-do family, and his wife Fanny. Their marriage, marked by a series of financial crises, was not a happy one, and they separated in 1840, when Fanny discovered evidence that Henry's general unreliability also included infidelity. Braddon's older sister, Maggie, lived with her paternal grandparents in Cornwall at this time, and their brother, Edward, was away at school, so after the separation of her parents, Braddon alone moved to East Sussex with her mother. They later returned to London, living in a series of rented houses, before moving again to Hampstead when Braddon was six years old. Despite the early upheaval to family life, Braddon's childhood seems to have been a happy one, and she remained devoted to her mother, sharing her life and home with her until Fanny's death in 1868. This loss devastated Braddon and she suffered a breakdown, followed by a long period of convalescence during which, for the only time in her adult life, she wrote nothing.

In 1852, Braddon made the decision to embark on an acting career,

---

[21] Part of this introduction appeared in an article entitled "Detecting the Self in the Sensation Fiction of Wilkie Collins and Mary Elizabeth Braddon". This article was originally published in *Clues*, Vol. 26, No. 1, 2007 by McFarland & Company, Inc., Publishers.

an unconventional and potentially shocking course of action for a middle-class girl of this period. With her mother's support and constant chaperonage, Braddon's stage career (conducted under the name Mary Seyton) lasted for eight years and included engagements at a series of London and provincial theatres.[22] During her time on the stage, Braddon had continued to develop her early interest in literature, publishing poems in a number of newspapers through the late 1850s. By 1859 she had met John Gilby, a wealthy Yorkshire gentleman who became Braddon's benefactor, and offered to financially support her in writing a volume of poetry, the lead poem to be on the subject of Giuseppe Garibaldi's Sicilian campaign. At the same time, Braddon worked on her first novel, *Three Times Dead: or, The Secret of the Heath* (1860), which was published in weekly penny numbers by William Empson, in Beverley, Yorkshire. This novel was later successfully republished, in 1861, under the title *The Trail of the Serpent*.

In 1860, Braddon met John Maxwell, a contractor of advertisements and proprietor of a number of short-lived magazines, including at this point the *Welcome Guest*. Maxwell was married with children, but separated from his wife, Mary Anne, who was mentally unstable. Braddon began to contribute stories to the *Welcome Guest* and soon became involved with Maxwell on a more personal level. By 1861 they were living together and Braddon was expecting their first child. Gerald, born in March 1862, was the first of six children Braddon bore Maxwell, although Francis, born in 1863, did not survive his fourth year. Braddon also took on the role of stepmother to Maxwell's six children from his marriage, and she maintained good relationships with them all throughout her life.[23] Maxwell was finally able to marry Braddon when his wife died in 1874.

Although Braddon's early novels made money, it was the spectacular success of *Lady Audley's Secret* that brought her instant fame. With Wilkie Collins's *The Woman in White* and Mrs. Henry Wood's *East Lynne*, it helped to establish the sensation novel as the most popular mode of fiction throughout the 1860s and beyond. Sensation fiction delighted readers and outraged conservative critics by presenting scandalous and melodramatic plots of murder, bigamy, adultery, and mystery within an otherwise realist and contemporary middle-class setting. The novels

---

[22] Jennifer Carnell, *The Literary Lives of Mary Elizabeth Braddon* (Hastings: Sensation Press, 2000): 13. See chapter one particularly for extensive information on Braddon's stage career.

[23] John Maxwell and Mary Anne Maxwell had seven children. One seems to have died prior to Maxwell's relationship with Braddon and another, Kate (or Katie) also died young. See Carnell, *Literary Lives*, 140-1.

which rapidly followed *Lady Audley's Secret*, at the rate of two and some-times even three a year in this early period, secured her wealth and notoriety in equal measure. In 1867, Maxwell founded *Belgravia* magazine and Braddon took on the editorship. This periodical provided a ready channel for her own fiction, and the serializations of most of her novels were published in *Belgravia* for the next seven years. In 1873 Braddon entered into an agreement with Tillotson's Newspaper Literature Syn-dicate, and her novels subsequently appeared first in serial form in various newspapers, beginning with *Taken at the Flood*. *Joshua Haggard's Daughter* was the final novel to be serialized in *Belgravia* before Braddon relinquished her position as editor. Maxwell then sold the magazine to Chatto and Windus in 1876.

Though she suffered at the hands of the critics during the controversy over sensation fiction in the 1860s, Braddon's popularity and sales remained unaffected. Through most of the 1870s, she was still publishing two novels a year, most of them in the sensational style that had made her famous, but also increasingly experimenting with other genres. Her work includes examples of realism, supernatural tales, sen-sationalism, detective fiction, social problem novels, Naturalistic studies, and many excellent ghost stories. Despite the irregularity of their early union, and the scandal this caused in some quarters, Braddon remained happy with Maxwell until his death in 1895. She survived him by twenty years and, by the time of her own death in 1915, was the author of over eighty novels, as well as numerous short stories, plays, and poems.

Chronology of Braddon's Life and Writing

1835 Mary Elizabeth born at 2 Frith Street, Soho, London, the youngest child of Henry Braddon, an unsuccessful solicitor, and Fanny Braddon, née White.

1840 Fanny Braddon finds compromising letters, which suggest Henry's adultery. She initiates a separation. Braddon moves to East Sussex with her mother.

1845 Spends some time as a pupil at Dartmouth Lodge, a boarding school in London.

1852 Embarks on a stage career and spends the next 8 years acting and touring with provincial companies.

1860 Meets John Maxwell at the offices of his magazine the *Welcome Guest*. He is married and unable to divorce his wife, who suffers from mental instability.

Three Times Dead, Or the Secret of the Heath published by Empson in Beverley, Yorkshire, and by W. & M. Clark in London. Braddon's play, *The Loves of Arcadia*, staged at the Strand theatre. Begins to contribute short stories to Maxwell's magazines.

1861 Braddon begins to live with John Maxwell. *Garibaldi and Other Poems* published. *The Lady Lisle* published serially in the *Welcome Guest*. *Ralph the Bailiff* serialized in *St. James's Magazine*.

Lady Audley's Secret begins serialization in *Robin Goodfellow*. Despite the popularity of the story, the magazine collapses after 13 issues. The novel resumes publication in the *Sixpenny Magazine*. *Aurora Floyd* has already begun its serial run in *Temple Bar*. *The Black Band, Or The Mysteries of Midnight* begins serialization in Maxwell's new venture, *The Halfpenny Journal: A Magazine for All Who Can Read*, under the pseudonym Lady Caroline Lascelles. Maxwell reissues *Three Times Dead* as *The Trail of the Serpent*, and records that 1000 copies are sold in 7 days.

1862 First child of Braddon and Maxwell, Gerald Maxwell, born in March. *Lady Audley's Secret* published in 3 volumes. *The White Phantom* serialized anonymously from May in *The Halfpenny Journal*. *Ralph the Bailiff and Other Tales* published.

1863 Two more children born in the same year: Francis in January and Fanny in December. *Aurora Floyd, Eleanor's Victory* and *John Marchmont's Legacy* all appear in three volume form, published by Tinsley.

1864 *Henry Dunbar* and *The Doctor's Wife*. Maxwell attempts to scotch rumours about his relationship with Braddon by inserting a notice of their "marriage" in the newspapers. This makes matters worse as Maxwell's wife's brother-in-law, Richard Brinsley Knowles, immediately publishes statements contradicting the claims.

1865 *Only a Clod* and *Sir Jasper's Tenant*.

1866 *The Lady's Mile*. Maxwell founds *Belgravia Magazine*, which would be edited by Braddon for the next ten years, featuring many of her novels as serials. Braddon's son, Francis, dies and a period of depression follows, although she continues to work. Another son, the future novelist William Babington Maxwell (Will), is born in June.

1867 *Rupert Godwin, Birds of Prey,* and *Ralph the Bailiff and Other Tales* republished with four new stories. Braddon and Maxwell move to Lichfield House in Richmond, where they will live for the rest of their lives. The *Pall Mall Gazette* accuses Braddon of plagiarism in *Circe*, published under the pseudonym Babington White.

1868 *Charlotte's Inheritance, Dead Sea Fruit* and *Run to Earth*. Braddon's sister, Maggie, dies in October, followed a month later by her mother, Fanny. Braddon, in the late stages of pregnancy, has a nervous breakdown, which is complicated by the difficult birth in December of Winifred Rosalie (known to the family as "Rosie"). This is followed by puerperal fever and postnatal depression. A long period of convalescence ensues and Braddon doesn't publish another novel until 1871.

1870 Braddon's last child, Edward Henry Harrington Maxwell (Ted), is born in December.

1871 *Fenton's Quest* and *The Lovels of Arden*.

1872 *Robert Ainsleigh* and *To the Bitter End*.

1873 *Milly Darrell, Lucius Davoren,* and *Strangers and Pilgrims*.

1874 *Taken at the Flood* and *Lost for Love*. Mary Anne Maxwell dies in Dublin and Richard Knowles places prominent notices of her death in the major newspapers, designed to highlight Maxwell and Braddon's unconventional relationship. The servants at Lichfield House all walk out. Braddon and Maxwell finally marry on 2nd October 1874 in London. They then leave Richmond for a period, leasing a house in Chelsea while the scandal dies down.

1875 *A Strange World* and *Hostages to Fortune*.

1876 *Dead Men's Shoes* and *Joshua Haggard's Daughter*. Resigns as editor of *Belgravia*, but retains her editorship of the Christmas annual *Mistletoe Bough*.

1877 *Weavers and Weft*.

1878 *An Open Verdict*.

1879 *Vixen* and *The Cloven Foot*.

1880 *The Story of Barbara* and *Just As I Am*.

1881 *Asphodel*.

1882 *Mount Royal*.

1883 *The Golden Calf* and *Phantom Fortune*.

1884 *Ishmael* and *Flower and Weed*. Braddon and Maxwell buy a second home, Annesley Bank near Lyndhurst in Hampshire.

1885 *Wyllard's Weird*.

1886 *One Thing Needful*, *Cut by the County*, and *Mohawks*. *Under the Red Flag* written for *Mistletoe Bough*.

1887 *Like and Unlike*.

1888 *The Fatal Three*.

1889 *The Day Will Come*.

1890 *One Life, One Love.*

1891 *Gerard.* Rosie Maxwell marries Robert Lachlan.

1892 *The Venetians.* A son, Lucien (known as Austin), born to Rosie and Robert Lachlan.

1893 *All Along the River.*

1894 *Thou Art the Man.* The *Christmas Hirelings* written for *Mistletoe Bough.*

1895 John Maxwell dies at Annesley Bank. *Sons of Fire*, Braddon's last three-decker.

1896 *London Pride.*

1897 *Under Love's Rule.*

1898 *In High Places* and *Rough Justice.*

1899 *His Darling Sin.* Braddon's youngest daughter, Rosie, dies and is buried in Richmond cemetery.

1900 *The Infidel.*

1901 Queen Victorian dies.

1903 *The Conflict.* Braddon's youngest son, Ted, marries Maud Hudson. In December their first child, Marjorie, is born.

1904 *A Lost Eden.* Edward Braddon dies.

1905 *The Rose of Life.*

1906 *The White House.* Will Maxwell marries Sidney Brabazon Moore on July 25th. They live at Lichfield House with Braddon.

1907 *Dead Love has Chains* and *Her Convict.* Will and Sidney Maxwell's daughter, Barbara, born on March 25th. Braddon suffers a stroke, which leaves her with some temporary paralysis.

1908 *During Her Majesty's Pleasure.*

1909 *Our Adversary*. Will and Sidney Maxwell's son, Henry, born on March 11th.

1910 *Beyond These Voices*.

1911 *The Green Curtain*.

1912 Braddon in Brighton. Her journal records that she spent a few days reading a play with Arthur Conan Doyle.

1913 *Miranda*. Braddon attends the screening of a film adaptation of *Aurora Floyd*.

1914 With the outbreak of World War I, Braddon's son Will joins up, as well as her grandson "Austin" (Lucien Lachlan). Braddon does her bit by becoming interested in the plight of Belgian refugees, taking in a family to live with her at Lichfield House.

1915 Following another stroke, Braddon dies on the 4th of February at Lichfield House. She is buried in Richmond Cemetery next to her daughter Rosie.

1916 *Mary* published posthumously.

Suggestions for further reading

Jeanne F. Bedell, "Amateur and Professional Detectives in the Fiction of Mary Elizabeth Braddon", *Clues: A Journal of Detection* 4:1 (1983): 19-34.

Anne-Marie Beller, *A Mary Elizabeth Braddon Companion* (Jefferson: McFarland, 2010).

Anne-Marie Beller, *Mary Elizabeth Braddon: Writing in the Margins* (Aldershot: Ashgate, 2011).

Anne-Marie Beller, "Detecting the Self in the Sensation Fiction of Wilkie Collins and M. E. Braddon", *Clues: A Journal of Detection* 26.1 (2007): 49-61.

Thomas Boyle. *Black Swine in the Sewers of Hampstead: Beneath the Surface of Victorian Sensationalism* (London: Hodder & Stoughton, 1990).

Jennifer Carnell, *The Literary Lives of M. E. Braddon* (Sussex: Sensation Press, 2000).

Alberto Gabriele, *Reading Popular Culture in Victorian Print: Belgravia and Sensationalism* (Basingstoke: Palgrave Macmillan, 2009).

Pamela K. Gilbert, ed. *A Companion to Sensation Fiction* (Oxford: Blackwell, 2011).

Winifred Hughes, *The Maniac in the Cellar: Sensation Novels of the 1860s* (New Jersey: Princeton University Press, 1980).

Elizabeth Langland, *"Nobody's Angels": Middle-Class Women and Domestic Ideology in Victorian Culture* (Ithaca & London: Cornell University Press, 1995).

Andrew Mangham, *Violent Women and Sensation Fiction* (Basingstoke: Palgrave Macmillan, 2007).

Jennifer Phegley, *Educating the Proper Woman Reader: Victorian Family Literary Magazines and the Cultural Health of the Nation* (Columbus: Ohio State University Press, 2004).

Lyn Pykett, *The Sensation Novel: From The Woman in White to The Moonstone* (Plymouth: Northcote, 1994).

Lyn Pykett, *The Improper Feminine: The Women's Sensation Novel and the New Woman Writing* (London: Routledge, 1992).

Elaine Showalter, "'Desperate Remedies': Sensation Novels of the 1860s", *Victorian Newsletter* 49 (Spring 1976): 1-5.

Saverio Tomaiuolo, *In Lady Audley's Shadow: Mary Elizabeth Braddon and Victorian Literary Genres* (Edinburgh: Edinburgh University Press, 2010).

Anthea Trodd, *Domestic Crime in the Victorian Novel* (London: Macmillan, 1989).

Anthea Trodd, 'The Policeman and the Lady: Significant Encounters in Mid-Victorian Fiction', *Victorian Studies* 27 (Summer 1984): 435-460.

Marlene Tromp, Pamela K. Gilbert, & Aeron Haynie (eds.), *Beyond Sensation: Mary Elizabeth Braddon in Context* (New York: State University of New York Press, 2000).

Robert Lee Wolff, *Sensational Victorian: The Life and Fiction of Mary Elizabeth Braddon* (London & New York: Garland, 1979).

A Note on the Text

Henry Dunbar: The Story of an Outcast was first published in 3 volumes by John Maxwell, London, in 1864. It had previously appeared as a serial in *The London Journal* under the title *The Outcasts: Or, the Brand of Society*. This ran from 12 September 1863 to 26 March 1864. A second serialization ran almost parallel in the newspaper *The Golden Era*, from 25 October 1863 to 8 May 1864, under the same title, *The Outcasts: Or the Brand of Society*, by Miss M. E. Braddon.

Before the novel appeared in three volumes as *Henry Dunbar*, Braddon carried out significant revisions. The most important of these changes is the elimination of a key subplot in the serialized version, involving Laura Dunbar's husband, Philip Jocelyn. In *The Outcasts*, Jocelyn is a more prominent character. He is also the heir to an Earldom, and in the course of the serialization becomes Lord Haughton. The rather melodramatic subplot involves Jocelyn's secret first marriage and the murder of his wife on the eve of his marriage to Laura Dunbar. Jocelyn does not commit the murder himself, which is carried out by his gamekeeper, Humphrey Melwood, but he is implicated in guilt nevertheless. The young son of this ill-fated former marriage is stolen, and restored to his father in time to be identified as the rightful heir to the Earldom, before Philip Jocelyn dies. At the end of the serial, the reader is informed that Laura Dunbar (the Countess of Haughton) has married the solicitor Arthur Lovell. Lovell, of course, is doomed to unrequited love in the later novel. Braddon cut the entire subplot concerning Philip Jocelyn's first marriage and his stolen son, and later used it for her short story, "Lost and Found".[1] Other variations include the character of Major Vernon who, in the serial, uses the more comically melodramatic pseudonym Herr Von Volterchoker, and is responsible for hiding Lord Haughton's son, while blackmailing the Earl over his first wife's murder.

There were numerous later editions of *Henry Dunbar*. Maxwell published a revised fifth edition in 1865, but the revisions are minor. A sixth and seventh edition by Maxwell appeared the same year. The Tauchnitz edition was published in 1864, as volumes 722 and 723 of the "Tauchnitz collection of British Authors" (Leipzig). There were also American editions and a number of translations. *Henry Dunbar* remained in print

---

[1] Published in *Ralph the Bailiff and Other Tales* (London: Ward, Lock and Tyler, no date [1867]): 213-382.

throughout the century, and other editions I have consulted include the yellowback edition by Simpkin, Marshall, Kent, and co. (circa 1898) and an early twentieth-century reprint by Simpkin, Marshall, Kent, and Co. (circa 1904).

This text is based on the first three volume edition by Maxwell (1864), with only one minor deviation, which is detailed in the footnotes. Chapter numbers in this single volume edition are sequential, but in the original volume one ended with chapter 17, and volume two with chapter 34. Arabic numbers have replaced the roman numerals in the original text for ease of reference. The spelling of the original edition has also been retained, for example, in following Braddon's practice of spelling grey as "gray".

Acknowledgements

I would like to thank Catherine Pope for her unfailing enthusiasm, energy, and good humour, which make her a delight to work with. Thanks are also due to friends and colleagues, particularly Janice Allan, Carol Bolton, Nick Freeman, Andrew Mangham, and Julian Wolfreys, for their generous help and advice at various points, and I am especially grateful to Robert Maidens for shedding light on an obscure reference that had me utterly baffled. My greatest debt of gratitude is to Alan Fletcher and I would like to dedicate this edition to him.

Part of the introduction to the present volume previously appeared in an article, "Detecting the Self in the Sensation Fiction of Wilkie Collins and Mary Elizabeth Braddon", published in *Clues: A Journal of Detection*, volume 26, no. 1, 2007. I am grateful to McFarland for permission to reproduce this material.

About the editor

Anne-Marie Beller is a lecturer in the department of English and Drama at Loughborough University. Her publications include *Mary Elizabeth Braddon: Writing in the Margins* for Ashgate's 19th century series, and also *A Mary Elizabeth Braddon Companion* for McFarland. Anne-Marie has published articles and chapters on Wilkie Collins and Ellen Wood, as well as Braddon, and has contributed chapters on Amelia B. Edwards and Braddon's *Joshua Haggard's Daughter* to the forthcoming *Blackwell Companion to Sensation Fiction*.

Henry Dunbar

Contents

- CHAPTER 1 -

AFTER OFFICE HOURS IN THE HOUSE OF DUNBAR, DUNBAR, AND BALDERBY

The house of Dunbar, Dunbar, and Balderby, East India bankers, was one of the richest firms in the city of London—so rich that it would be quite in vain to endeavour to describe the amount of its wealth. It was something fabulous, people said. The offices were situated in a dingy and narrow thoroughfare leading out of King William Street, and were certainly no great things to look at; but the cellars below their offices—wonderful cellars, that stretched far away underneath the church of St. Gundolph, and were only separated by party-walls from the vaults in which the dead lay buried—were popularly supposed to be filled with hogsheads of sovereigns, bars of bullion built up in stacks like so much firewood, and impregnable iron safes crammed to overflowing with bank bills and railway shares, government securities, family jewels, and a hundred other trifles of that kind, every one of which was worth a poor man's fortune.

The firm of Dunbar had been established very soon after the English first grew powerful in India.[1] It was one of the oldest firms in the City; and the names of Dunbar and Dunbar, painted upon the door-posts, and engraved upon shining brass plates on the mahogany doors, had never been expunged or altered: though time and death had done their work of change amongst the owners of that name.

The last heads of the firm had been two brothers, Hugh and Percival Dunbar; and Percival, the younger of these brothers, had lately died at eighty years of age, leaving his only son, Henry Dunbar, sole inheritor of his enormous wealth.

That wealth consisted of a splendid estate in Warwickshire; another estate, scarcely less splendid, in Yorkshire; a noble mansion in Portland Place; and three-fourths of the bank. The junior partner, Mr. Balderby, a good-tempered, middle-aged man, with a large family of daughters, and a handsome red-brick mansion on Clapham Common, had never poss-

---

[1] A significant British presence in India dates back to the early 17th century, but Braddon's reference to when "the English first grew powerful" probably alludes to the mid-eighteenth century, when Robert Clive's military victories consolidated the East India Company's power in the country.

essed more than a fourth share in the business. The three other shares had been divided between the two brothers, and had lapsed entirely into the hands of Percival upon the death of Hugh.

On the evening of the 15th of August, 1850, three men sat together in one of the shady offices at the back of the banking-house in St. Gundolph Lane.

These three men were Mr. Balderby, a confidential cashier called Clement Austin, and an old clerk, a man of about sixty-five years of age, who had been a faithful servant of the firm ever since his boyhood.

This man's name was Sampson Wilmot.

He was old, but he looked much older than he was. His hair was white, and hung in long thin locks upon the collar of his shabby bottle-green great coat. He wore a great coat, although it was the height of summer, and most people found the weather insupportably hot. His face was wizen and wrinkled, his faded blue eyes dim and weak-looking. He was feeble, and his hands were tremulous with a perpetual nervous motion. Already he had been stricken twice with paralysis, and he knew that whenever the third stroke came it must be fatal.

He was not very much afraid of death, however; for his life had been a joyless one, a monotonous existence of perpetual toil, unrelieved by any home joys or social pleasures. He was not a bad man, for he was honest, conscientious, industrious, and persevering.

He lived in a humble lodging, in a narrow court near the bank, and went twice every Sunday to the church of St. Gundolph.

When he died he hoped to be buried beneath the flagstones of that City church, and to lie cheek by jowl with the gold in the cellars of the bank.

The three men were assembled in this gloomy private room after office hours, on a sultry August evening, in order to consult together upon rather an important subject, namely, the reception of Henry Dunbar, the new head of the firm.

This Henry Dunbar had been absent from England for five-and-thirty years, and no living creature now employed in the bank, except Sampson Wilmot, had ever set eyes upon him.

He had sailed for Calcutta five-and-thirty years before, and had ever since been employed in the offices of the Indian branch of the bank; first as clerk, afterwards as chief and manager. He had been sent to India because of a great error which he had committed in his early youth.

He had been guilty of forgery. He, or rather an accomplice employed by him, had forged the acceptance of a young nobleman, a brother officer of Henry Dunbar's, and had circulated forged bills of accommodation to the amount of three thousand pounds.

These bills were taken up and duly honoured by the heads of the firm. Percival Dunbar gladly paid three thousand pounds as the price of his son's honour. That which would have been called a crime in a poorer man was only considered an error in the dashing young cornet of dragoons,[2] who had lost money upon the turf, and was fain to forge his friend's signature rather than become a defaulter.

His accomplice, the man who had actually manufactured the fictitious signatures, was the younger brother of Sampson Wilmot, who had been a few months prior to that time engaged as messenger in the banking-house—a young fellow of nineteen, little better than a lad; a reckless boy, easily influenced by the dashing soldier who had need of his services.

The bill-broker who discounted the bills speedily discovered their fraudulent nature; but he knew that the money was safe.

Lord Adolphus Vanlorme was a customer of the house of Dunbar and Dunbar; the bill-brokers knew that *his* acceptance was a forgery; but they knew also that the signature of the drawer, Henry Dunbar, was genuine.

Messrs. Dunbar and Dunbar would not care to see the heir of their house in a criminal dock.

There had been no hitch, therefore, no scandal, no prosecution. The bills were duly honoured; but the dashing young officer was compelled to sell his commission, and begin life afresh as a junior clerk in the Calcutta banking-house.

This was a terrible mortification to the high-spirited young man.

The three men assembled in the quiet room behind the bank on this oppressive August evening were talking together of that old story.

"I never saw Henry Dunbar," Mr. Balderby said; "for, as you know, Wilmot, I didn't come into the firm till ten years after he sailed for India; but I've heard the story hinted at amongst the clerks in the days when I was only a clerk myself."

"I don't suppose you ever heard the rights of it, sir," Sampson Wilmot answered, fumbling nervously with an old horn snuff-box and a red cotton handkerchief, "and I doubt if any one knows the rights of that story except me, and I can remember it as well as if it all happened yesterday—ay, that I can—better than I remember many things that really did happen yesterday."

"Let's hear the story from you, then, Sampson," Mr. Balderby said. "As Henry Dunbar is coming home in a few days, we may as well know

---

[2] Cornet: a commissioned officer rank in a cavalry troop, once the bearer of the Troop's flag or Cornet. Dragoons were originally mounted infantry, but by the time in which *Henry Dunbar* is set, the dragoons had evolved into conventional light cavalry regiments.

the real truth. We shall better understand what sort of a man our new chief is."

"To be sure, sir, to be sure," returned the old clerk. "It's five-and-thirty years ago,—five-and-thirty years ago this month, since it all happened. If I hadn't good cause to remember the date because of my own troubles, I should remember it for another reason, for it was the Waterloo year, and city people had been losing and making money like wildfire.[3] It was in the year '15, sir, and our house had done wonders on 'Change.[4] Mr. Henry Dunbar was a very handsome young man in those days—very handsome, very aristocratic-looking, rather haughty in his manners to strangers, but affable and free-spoken to those who happened to take his fancy. He was very extravagant in all his ways; generous and open-handed with money; but passionate and self-willed. It's scarcely strange he should have been so, for he was an only child; he had neither brother nor sister to interfere with him; and his uncle Hugh, who was then close upon fifty, was a confirmed bachelor,—so Henry considered himself heir to an enormous fortune."

"And he began his career by squandering every farthing he could get, I suppose?" said Mr. Balderby.

"He did, sir. His father was very liberal to him; but give him what he would, Mr. Percival Dunbar could never give his son enough to keep him free of gambling debts and losses on the turf. Mr. Henry's regiment was quartered at Knightsbridge, and the young man was very often at this office, in and out, in and out, sometimes twice and three times a week; and I expect that every time he came, he came to get money, or to ask for it. It was in coming here he met my brother, who was a handsome lad—ay, as handsome and as gentlemanly a lad as the young cornet himself; for poor Joseph—that's my brother, gentlemen—had been educated a bit above his station, being my mother's favourite son, and fifteen years younger than me. Mr. Henry took a great deal of notice of Joseph, and used to talk to him while he was waiting about to see his father or his uncle. At last he asked the lad one day if he'd like to leave the bank, and go and live with him as a sort of confidential servant and amanuensis, to write his letters, and all that sort of thing. 'I shan't treat you altogether as a servant, you know, Joseph,' he said, 'but I shall make quite a companion of you, and you'll go about with me wherever I go.

---

[3] Napoleon Bonaparte was defeated at the Battle of Waterloo in 1815. Rumours of Napoleon's imminent defeat had been circulating since the year prior to Waterloo, creating a significant impact on stock values. The "du Bourg hoax" of February 1814, for instance, was a deliberate conspiracy to manipulate the London stock market through false reports of Napoleon's capture.

[4] Common abbreviation for the London Stock Exchange.

You'll find my quarters a great deal pleasanter than this musty old banking-house, I can tell you.' Joseph accepted this offer, in spite of everything my poor mother and I could say to him. He went to live with the cornet in the January of the year in which the fabricated bills were presented at our counter."

"And when were the bills presented?"

"Not till the following August, sir. It seems that Mr. Henry had lost five or six thousand pounds on the Derby.[5] He got what he could out of his father towards paying his losses, but he could not get more than three thousand pounds; so then he went to Joseph in an awful state of mind, declaring that he should be able to get the money in a month or so from his father, and that if he could do anything just to preserve his credit for the time, and meet the claims of the vulgar City betting fellows who were pressing him, he should be able to make all square afterwards. Then, little by little, it came out that he wanted my brother, who had a wonderful knack of imitating any body's handwriting, to forge the acceptance of Lord Vanlorme. 'I shall get the bills back into my own hands before they fall due, Joe,' he said; 'it's only a little dodge to keep matters sweet for the time being.' Well, gentlemen, the poor foolish boy was very fond of his master, and he consented to do this wicked thing."

"Do you believe this to be the first time your brother ever committed forgery?"

"I do, Mr. Balderby. Remember he was only a lad, and I dare say he thought it a fine thing to oblige his generous-hearted young master. I've seen him many a time imitate the signature of this firm, and other signatures, upon a half-sheet of letter-paper, for the mere fun of the thing: but I don't believe my brother Joseph ever did a dishonest action in his life until he forged those bills. He hadn't need have done so, for he was only eighteen at the time."

"Young enough, young enough!" murmured Mr. Balderby, compassionately.

"Ay, sir, very young to be ruined for life. That one error, that one wicked act, was his ruin; for though no steps were taken against him, he lost his character, and never held his head up in an honest situation again. He went from bad to worse, and three years after Mr. Henry sailed for India, my brother, Joseph Wilmot, was convicted, with two or three others, upon a charge of manufacturing forged Bank of England notes,

---

[5] The Derby Stakes is an annual flat horserace run at Epsom Downs in Britain, named after the twelfth Earl of Derby. It was inaugurated on 4 May 1780 and is one of the five "Classics" of the racing calendar.

and was transported for life."[6]

"Indeed!" exclaimed Mr. Balderby; "a sad story,—a very sad story. I have heard something of it before, but never the whole truth. Your brother is dead, I suppose."

"I have every reason to believe so, sir," answered the old clerk, producing a red cotton handkerchief and wiping away a couple of tears that were slowly trickling down his poor faded cheeks. "For the first few years of his time, he wrote now and then, complaining bitterly of his fate; but for five-and-twenty years I've never had a line from him. I can't doubt that he's dead. Poor Joseph!—poor boy!—poor boy! The misery of all this killed my mother. Mr. Henry Dunbar committed a great sin when he tempted that lad to wrong; and many a cruel sorrow arose out of that sin, perhaps to lie heavy at his door some day or other, sooner or later, sooner or later. I'm an old man, and I've seen a good deal of the ways of this world, and I've found that retribution seldom fails to overtake those who do wrong."

Mr. Balderby shrugged his shoulders.

"I should doubt the force of your philosophy in this case, my good Sampson," he said; "Mr. Dunbar has had a long immunity from his sins. I should scarcely think it likely he would ever be called upon to atone for them."

"I don't know, sir," the old clerk answered; "I don't know that. I've seen retribution come very late, very late; when the man who committed the sin had well nigh forgotten it. Evil trees bear evil fruit,[7] Mr. Balderby: the Scriptures tell us that; and take my word for it, evil consequences are sure to come from evil deeds."

"But to return to the story of the forged bills," said Mr. Austin, the cashier, looking at his watch as he spoke. He was evidently growing rather impatient of the old clerk's rambling talk.

"To be sure, sir, to be sure," answered Sampson Wilmot. "Well, you see, sir, one of the bills was brought to our counter, and the cashier didn't much like the look of my lord's signature, and he took the bill to the inspector, and the inspector said, 'Pay the money, but don't debit it against his lordship.' About an hour afterwards the inspector carried the bill to Mr. Percival Dunbar, and directly he set eyes upon it, he knew that Lord Vanlorme's acceptance was a forgery. He sent for me to his room;

---

[6] Transportation to the colonies began in Britain in the 17th century. By the 19th century, penal transportation was mainly to Australia and Tasmania (then called Van Diemen's Land). Convicted criminals could be sentenced to transportation for a wide array of offences, and could vary from specific periods of time to life sentences.
[7] Matthew 7.18; also Luke 6.43.

and when I went in, he was as white as a sheet, poor gentleman. He handed me the bill without speaking, and when I had looked at it, he said—

"'Your brother is at the bottom of this business, Sampson. Do you remember the half-sheet of paper I found on a blotting-pad in the counting-house one day; half a sheet of paper scrawled over with the imitation of two or three signatures? I asked who had copied those signatures, and your brother came forward and owned to having done it, laughing at his own cleverness. I told him then that it was a fatal facility, a fatal facility, and now he has proved the truth of my words by helping my son to turn forger and thief. That signature must be honoured, though I should have to sacrifice half my fortune to meet the demands upon us. Heaven knows to what amount such paper as that may be in circulation. There are some forged bills that are as good as genuine documents; and the Jew who discounted these knew that. If my son comes into the bank this morning send him to me.'"

"And did the young man come?" asked the junior partner.

"Yes, Mr. Balderby, sir; in less than half an hour after I left Mr. Percival Dunbar's room, in comes Mr. Henry, dashing and swaggering into the place as if it was his own.

"'Will you please step into your father's room, sir?' I said; 'he wants to see you very particular.'

"The cornet's jaw dropped, and his face turned ghastly white as I said this; but he tried to carry it off with a swagger, and followed me into Mr. Percival Dunbar's room.

"'You needn't leave us, Sampson,' said Mr. Hugh, who was sitting opposite his brother at the writing-table. 'You may as well hear what I have to say. I wish somebody whom I can rely upon to know the truth of this business, and I think we may rely upon you.'

"'Yes, gentlemen,' I answered, 'you may trust me.'

"'What's the meaning of all this?' Mr. Henry Dunbar asked, pretending to look innocent and surprised; but it wouldn't do, for his lips trembled so, that it was painful to watch him. 'What's the matter?' he asked.

"Mr. Hugh Dunbar handed him the forged bill.

"'This is what's the matter,' he said.

"The young man stammered out something in the endeavour to deny any knowledge of the bill in his hand; but his uncle checked him. 'Do not add perjury to the crime you have already committed,' he said. 'How many of these are in circulation?'

"'How many!' Mr. Henry repeated, in a faltering voice. 'Yes,' his uncle answered; 'how many—to what amount?' 'Three thousand

11

pounds,' the cornet replied, hanging his head. 'I meant to take them up before they fell due, Uncle Hugh,' he said. 'I did, indeed; I stood to win a hatful of money upon the Liverpool Summer Meeting,[8] and I made sure I should be able to take up those bills: but I've had the devil's own luck all this year. I never thought those bills would be presented; indeed, I never did.'

"'Henry Dunbar,' Mr. Hugh said, very solemnly, 'nine men out of ten, who do what you have done, think what you say you thought: that they shall be able to escape the consequences of their deeds. They act under the pressure of circumstances. They don't mean to do any wrong—they don't intend to rob any body of a sixpence. But that first false step is the starting point upon the road that leads to the gallows; and the worst that can happen to a man is for him to succeed in his first crime. Happily for you, detection has speedily overtaken you. Why did you do this?'

"The young man stammered out some rambling excuse about his turf losses, debts of honour which he was compelled to pay. Then Mr. Hugh asked him whether the forged signature was his own doing, or the work of any body else. The cornet hesitated for a little, and then told his uncle the name of his accomplice. I thought this was cruel and cowardly. He had tempted my brother to do wrong, and the least he could have done would have been to try to shield him.

"One of the messengers was sent to fetch poor Joseph. The lad reached the banking house in an hour's time, and was brought straight into the private room, where we had all been sitting in silence, waiting for him.

"He was as pale as his master, but he didn't tremble, and he had altogether a more determined look than Mr. Henry.

"Mr. Hugh Dunbar taxed him with what he had done.

"'Do you deny it, Joseph Wilmot?' he asked.

"'No,' my brother said, looking contemptuously at the cornet. 'If my master has betrayed me, I have no wish to deny anything. But I dare say he and I will square accounts some day.'

"'I am not going to prosecute my nephew,' Mr. Hugh said; 'so, of course I shall not prosecute you. But I believe that you have been an evil counsellor to this young man, and I give you warning that you will get no character from me. I respect your brother Sampson, and shall retain him in my service in spite of what you have done; but I hope never to see your face again. You are free to go; but have a care how you tamper with other men's signatures, for the next time you may not get off so easily.'

---

[8] Liverpool Summer Meeting probably refers to a horse racing fixture at Aintree Racecourse, where the Grand National has been held since 1839.

"The lad took up his hat and walked slowly towards the door.

"'Gentlemen—gentlemen!' I cried, 'have pity upon him. Remember he is little more than a boy; and whatever he did, he did out of love for his master.'

"Mr. Hugh shook his head. 'I have no pity,' he answered, sternly: 'his master might never have done wrong but for him.'

"Joseph did not say a word in answer to all this; but, when his hand was on the handle of the door, he turned and looked at Mr. Henry Dunbar.

"'Have you nothing to say in my behalf, sir?' he said, very quietly; 'I have been very much attached to you, sir, and I don't want to think badly of you at parting. Haven't you one word to say in my behalf?'

"Mr. Henry made no answer. He sat with his head bent forward upon his breast, and seemed as if he dare not lift his eyes to his uncle's face.

"'No!' Mr. Hugh answered, as sternly as before, 'he has nothing to say for you. Go; and consider this a lucky escape.'

"Joseph turned upon the banker, with his face all in a crimson flame, and his eyes flashing fire. 'Let *him* consider it a lucky escape,' he said, pointing to Mr. Henry Dunbar,—'let *him* consider it a lucky escape, if when we next meet he gets off scot free.'

"He was gone before any body could answer him.

"Then Mr. Hugh Dunbar turned to his nephew.

"'As for you,' he said, 'you have been a spoilt child of fortune, and you have not known how to value the good things that Providence has given you. You have begun life at the top of the tree, and you have chosen to fling your chances into the gutter. You must begin again, and begin this time upon the lowest step of the ladder. You will sell your commission, and sail for Calcutta by the next ship that leaves Southampton. To-day is the 23rd of August, and I see by the *Shipping Gazette* that the *Oronoko* sails on the 10th of September. This will give you little better than a fortnight to make all your arrangements.'

"The young cornet started from his chair as if he had been shot.

"'Sell my commission!' he cried; 'go to India! You don't mean it, Uncle Hugh; surely you don't mean it. Father, you will never compel me to do this.'

"Percival Dunbar had never looked at his son since the young man had entered the room. He sat with his elbow resting upon the arm of his easy-chair, and his face shaded by his hand, and had not once spoken.

"He did not speak now, even when his son appealed to him.

"'Your father has given me full authority to act in this business,' Mr. Hugh Dunbar said. 'I shall never marry, Henry, and you are my only nephew, and my acknowledged heir. But I will never leave my wealth to

13

a dishonest or dishonourable man, and it remains for you to prove whether you are worthy to inherit it. You will have to begin life afresh. You have played the man of fashion, and your aristocratic associates have led you to the position in which you find yourself to-day. You must turn your back upon the past, Henry. Of course you are free to choose for yourself. Sell your commission, go to India, and enter the counting-house of our establishment in Calcutta as a junior clerk; or refuse to do so, and renounce all hope of succeeding to my fortune or to your father's.'

"The young man was silent for some minutes, then he said, sullenly enough—

"'I will go. I consider that I have been harshly treated; but I will go.'"

"And he did go?" said Mr. Balderby.

"He did, sir," answered the clerk, who had displayed considerable emotion in relating this story of the past. "He did go, sir,—he sold his commission, and left England by the *Oronoko*. But he never took leave of a living creature, and I fully believe that he never in his heart forgave either his father or his uncle. He worked his way up, as you know, sir, in the Calcutta counting-house, and by slow degrees rose to be manager of the Indian branch of the business. He married in 1831, and he has an only child, a daughter, who has been brought up in England since her infancy, under the care of Mr. Percival."

"Yes," answered Mr. Balderby, "I have seen Miss Laura Dunbar at her grandfather's country seat. She is a very beautiful girl, and Percival Dunbar idolized her. But now to return to business, my good Sampson. I believe you are the only person in this house who has ever seen our present chief, Henry Dunbar."

"I am, sir."

"So far so good. He is expected to arrive at Southampton in less than a week's time, and somebody must be there to meet him and receive him. After five-and-thirty years' absence he will be a perfect stranger in England, and will require a business man about him to manage matters for him, and take all trouble off his hands. These Anglo-Indians are apt to be indolent, you know, and he may be all the worse for the fatigues of the overland journey. Now, as you know him, Sampson, and as you are an excellent man of business, and as active as a boy, I should like you to meet him. Have you any objection to do this?"

"No, sir," answered the clerk; "I have no great love for Mr. Henry Dunbar, for I can never cease to look upon him as the cause of my poor brother Joseph's ruin; but I am ready to do what you wish, Mr. Balderby. It's business, and I'm ready to do anything in the way of business. I'm only a sort of machine, sir—a machine that's pretty nearly worn out, I fancy, now—but as long as I last you can make what use of me you like, sir. I'm ready to do my duty."

"I am sure of that, Sampson."

"When am I to start for Southampton, sir?"

"Well, I think you'd better go to-morrow, Sampson. You can leave London by the afternoon train, which starts at four o'clock. You can see to your work here in the morning, and reach your destination between seven and eight. I leave everything in your hands. Miss Laura Dunbar will come up to town to meet her father at the house in Portland Place. The poor girl is very anxious to see him, as she has not set eyes upon him since she was a child of two years old. Strange, isn't it, the effect of these long separations? Laura Dunbar might pass her father in the street without recognizing him, and yet her affection for him has been unchanged in all these years."

Mr. Balderby gave the old clerk a pocket-book containing six five-pound notes.

"You will want plenty of money," he said, "though, of course, Mr. Dunbar will be well supplied. You will tell him that all will be ready for his reception here. I really am quite anxious to see the new head of the house. I wonder what he is like, now. By the way, it's rather a singular circumstance that there is, I believe, no portrait of Henry Dunbar in existence. His picture was painted when he was a young man, and exhibited in the Royal Academy; but his father didn't think the likeness a good one, and sent it back to the artist, who promised to alter and improve it. Strange to say, this artist, whose name I forget, delayed from day to day performing his promise, and at the expiration of a twelve-month left England for Italy, taking the young man's portrait with him, amongst a lot of other unframed canvases. This artist never returned from Italy, and Percival Dunbar could never find out his whereabouts, or whether he was dead or alive. I have often heard the old man regret that he possessed no likeness of his son. Our chief was handsome, you say, in his youth?"

"Yes, sir," Sampson Wilmot answered, "he was very handsome—tall and fair, with bright blue eyes."

"You have seen Miss Dunbar: is she like her father?"

"No, sir. Her features are altogether different, and her expression is more amiable than his."

"Indeed! Well, Sampson, we won't detain you any longer. You understand what you have to do?"

"Yes, sir, perfectly."

"Very well, then. Good night! By the bye, you will put up at one of the best hotels at Southampton—say the Dolphin—and wait there till the *Electra* steamer comes in. It is by the *Electra* that Mr. Dunbar is to arrive. Once more, good evening!"

The old clerk bowed and left the room.

"Well, Austin," said Mr. Balderby, turning to the cashier, "we may prepare ourselves to meet our new chief very speedily. He must know that you and I cannot be entirely ignorant of the story of his youthful peccadilloes, and he will scarcely give himself airs to us, I should fancy."

"I don't know that, Mr. Balderby," the cashier answered; "if I am any judge of human nature, Henry Dunbar will hate us because of that very crime of his own, knowing that we are in the secret, and will be all the more disagreeable and disdainful in his intercourse with us. He will carry it off with a high hand, depend upon it."

- CHAPTER 2 –

MARGARET'S FATHER

The town of Wandsworth is not a gay place. There is an air of old-world quiet in the old-fashioned street, though dashing vehicles drive through it sometimes on their way to Wimbledon or Richmond Park.

The sloping roofs, the gable-ends, the queer old chimneys, the quaint casement windows, belong to a bygone age; and the traveller, coming a stranger to the little town, might fancy himself a hundred miles away from boisterous London; though he is barely clear of the great city's smoky breath, or beyond the hearing of her myriad clamorous tongues.

There are lanes and byways leading out of that humble High Street down to the low bank of the river; and in one of these, a pleasant place enough, there is a row of old-fashioned semi-detached cottages, standing in small gardens, and sheltered by sycamores and laburnums from the dust, which in dry summer weather lies thick upon the narrow roadway.

In one of these cottages a young lady lived with her father; a young lady who gave lessons on the piano-forte, or taught singing, for very small remuneration. She wore shabby dresses, and was rarely known to have a new bonnet; but people respected and admired her, notwithstanding; and the female inhabitants of Godolphin Cottages, who gave her good-day sometimes as she went along the dusty lane with her well-used roll of music in her hand, declared that she was a lady bred and born. Perhaps the good people who admired Margaret Wentworth would have come nearer the mark if they had said that she was a lady by right divine of her own beautiful nature, which had never required to be schooled into grace or gentleness.

She had no mother, and she had not even the memory of her mother, who had died seventeen years before, leaving an only child of twelve months old for James Wentworth to keep.

But James Wentworth, being a scapegrace and a reprobate, who lived by means that were a secret from his neighbours, had sadly neglected this only child. He had neglected her, though with every passing year she grew more and more like her dead mother, until at last, at eighteen years of age, she had grown into a beautiful woman, with hazel-brown hair, and hazel eyes to match.

And yet James Wentworth was fond of his only child, after a fashion of his own. Sometimes he was at home for weeks together, a prey to a fit of melancholy; under the influence of which he would sit brooding in silence over his daughter's humble hearth for hours and days together.

At other times he would disappear, sometimes for a few days, sometimes for weeks and months at a time; and during his absence Margaret suffered wearisome agonies of suspense.

Sometimes he brought her money; sometimes he lived upon her own slender earnings.

But use her as he might, he was always proud of her, and fond of her; and she, after the way of womankind, loved him devotedly, and believed him to be the noblest and most brilliant of men.

It was no grief to her to toil, taking long weary walks and giving tedious lessons for the small stipends which her employers had the conscience to offer her; they felt no compunction about bargaining and haggling as to a few pitiful shillings with a music mistress who looked so very poor, and seemed so glad to work for their paltry pay. The girl's chief sorrow was, that her father, who to her mind was calculated to shine in the highest station the world could give, should be a reprobate and a pauper.

She told him so sometimes, regretfully, tenderly, as she sat by his side, with her arms twined caressingly about his neck. And there were times when the strong man would cry aloud over his blighted life, and the ruin which had fallen upon his youth.

"You're right, Madge," he said sometimes, "you're right, my girl. I ought to have been something better; I ought to have been, and I might have been, perhaps, but for one man—but for one base-minded villain, whose treachery blasted my character, and left me alone in the world to fight against society. You don't know what it is, Madge, to have to fight that battle. A man who began life with an honest name, and fair prospects before him, finds himself cast, by one fatal error, disgraced and broken, on a pitiless world. Nameless, friendless, characterless, he has to begin life afresh, with every man's hand against him. He is the outcast of society. The faces that once looked kindly on him turn away from him with a frown. The voices that once spoke in his praise are loud in his disfavour. Driven from every place where once he found a welcome, the ruined wretch hides himself among strangers, and tries to sink his hateful identity under a false name. He succeeds, perhaps, for a time, and is trusted, and being honestly disposed at heart, is honest: but he cannot long escape from the hateful past. No! In the day and hour when he is proudest of the new name he has made, and the respect he has won for himself, some old acquaintance, once a friend, but now an enemy, falls across his pathway. He is recognized; a cruel voice betrays him. Every hope that he had cherished is swept away from him. Every good deed that he has done is denounced as the act of a hypocrite. Because once sinned he can never do well. *That* is the world's argument."

"But not the teaching of the gospel," Margaret murmured. "Remember, father, who it was that said to the guilty woman, 'Go, and sin no more.'"

"Ay, my girl," James Wentworth answered, bitterly, "but the world would have said, 'Hence, abandoned creature! go, and sin afresh; for you shall never be suffered to live an honest life, or herd with honest people. Repent, and we will laugh at your penitence as a shallow deception. Weep, and we will cry out upon your tears. Toil and struggle to regain the eminence from which you have fallen, and when you have nearly reached the top of that difficult hill, we will band ourselves together to hurl you back into the black abyss.' That's what the *world* says to the sinner, Margaret, my girl. I don't know much of the gospel; I have never read it since I was a boy, and used to read long chapters aloud to my mother, on quiet Sunday evenings; I can see the little old-fashioned parlour now as I speak of that time; I can hear the ticking of the eight-day clock, and I can see my mother's fond eyes looking up at me every now and then. But I don't know much about the gospel now; and when, you, poor child, try to read it to me, there's some devil rises in my breast, and shuts my ears against the words. I don't know the gospel, but I *do* know the world. The laws of society are inflexible, Madge; there is no forgiveness for a man who is once found out. He may commit any crime in the calendar, so long as his crimes are profitable, and he is content to share his profits with his neighbours. But he mustn't be found out."

Upon the 16th of August, 1850, the day on which Sampson Wilmot, the banker's clerk, was to start for Southampton, James Wentworth spent the morning in his daughter's humble little sitting-room, and sat smoking by the open window, while Margaret worked beside a table near him.

The father sat with his long clay pipe in his mouth, watching his daughter's fair face as she bent over the work upon her knee.

The room was neatly kept, but poorly furnished, with that old-fashioned spindle-legged furniture which seems peculiar to lodging-houses. Yet the little sitting-room had an aspect of simple rustic prettiness, which is almost pleasanter to look at than fine furniture. There were pictures,—simple water-colour sketches,—and cheap engravings on the walls, and a bunch of flowers on the table, and between the muslin curtains that shadowed the window you saw the branches of the sycamores waving in the summer wind.

James Wentworth had once been a handsome man. It was impossible to look at him and not perceive as much as that. He might, indeed, have been handsome still, but for the moody defiance in his eyes, but for the half-contemptuous curve of his finely-moulded upper lip.

He was about fifty-three years of age, and his hair was grey, but this grey hair did not impart a look of age to his appearance. His erect figure, the carriage of his head, his dashing, nay, almost swaggering walk, all belonged to a man in the prime of middle age. He wore a beard and thick moustache of grizzled auburn. His nose was aquiline, his forehead high and square, his chin massive. The form of his head and face denoted force of intellect. His long, muscular limbs gave evidence of great physical power. Even the tones of his voice, and his manner of speaking, betokened a strength of will that verged upon obstinacy.

A dangerous man to offend! A relentless and determined man; not easily to be diverted from any purpose, however long the time between the formation of his resolve and the opportunity of carrying it into execution.

As he sat now watching his daughter at her work, the shadows of black thoughts darkened his brow, and spread a sombre gloom over his face.

And yet the picture before him could have scarcely been unpleasing to the most fastidious eye. The girl's face, drooping over her work, was very fair. The features were delicate and statuesque in their form; the large hazel eyes were very beautiful—all the more beautiful, perhaps, because of a soft melancholy that subdued their natural brightness; the smooth brown hair rippling upon the white forehead, which was low and broad, was of a colour which a duchess might have envied, or an empress tried to imitate with subtle dyes compounded by court chemists. The girl's figure, tall, slender, and flexible, imparted grace and beauty to a shabby cotton dress and linen collar, that many a maid-servant would have disdained to wear; and the foot visible below the scanty skirt was slim and arched as the foot of an Arab chief.

There was something in Margaret Wentworth's face, some shade of expression, vague and transitory in its nature, that bore a likeness to her father; but the likeness was a very faint one, and it was from her mother that the girl had inherited her beauty.

She had inherited her mother's nature also: but mingled with that soft and womanly disposition there was much of the father's determination, much of the strong man's force of intellect and resolute will.

A beautiful woman—an amiable woman; but a woman whose resentment for a great wrong could be deep and lasting.

"Madge," said James Wentworth, throwing his pipe aside, and looking full at his daughter, "I sit and watch you sometimes till I begin to wonder at you. You seem contented and most happy, though the monotonous life you lead would drive some women mad. Have you no ambition, girl?"

"Plenty, father," she answered, lifting her eyes from her work, and looking at him mournfully; "plenty—for you."

The man shrugged his shoulders, and sighed heavily.

"It's too late for that, my girl," he said; "the day is past—the day is past and gone—and the chance gone with it. You know how I've striven, and worked, and struggled; and how I've seen my poor schemes crushed when I had built them up with more patience than perhaps man ever built before. You've been a good girl, Margaret—a noble girl; and you've been true to me alike in joy and sorrow—the joy's been little enough beside the sorrow, poor child—but you've borne it all; you've endured it all. You've been the truest woman that was ever born upon this earth, to my thinking; but there's one thing in which you've been unlike the rest of your sex."

"And what's that, father?"

"You've shown no curiosity. You've seen me knocked down and disgraced wherever I tried to get a footing; you've seen me try first one trade and then another, and fail in every one of them. You've seen me a clerk in a merchant's office; an actor; an author; a common labourer, working for a daily wage; and you've seen ruin overtake me whichever way I've turned. You've seen all this, and suffered from it; but you've never asked me why it has been so. You've never sought to discover the secret of my life."

The tears welled up to the girl's eyes as her father spoke.

"If I have not done so, dear father," she answered, gently, "it has been because I knew your secret must be a painful one. I have lain awake night after night, wondering what was the cause of the blight that has been upon you and all you have done. But why should I ask you questions that you could not answer without pain? I have heard people say cruel things of you; but they have never said them twice in my hearing." Her eyes flashed through a veil of tears as she spoke. "Oh, father,—dearest father!" she cried, suddenly throwing aside her work, and dropping on her knees beside the man's chair, "I do not ask for your confidence if it is painful to you to give it; I only want your love. But believe this, father,—always believe this,—that, whether you trust me or not, there is nothing upon this earth strong enough to turn my heart from you."

She placed her hand in her father's as she spoke, and he grasped it so tightly that her pale face grew crimson with the pain.

"Are you sure of that, Madge?" he asked, bending his head to look more closely in her earnest face.

"I am quite sure, father."

"Nothing can tear your heart from me?"

"Nothing in this world."

"What if I am not worthy of your love?"

"I cannot stop to think of that, father. Love is not mete out in strict proportion to the merits of those we love. If it were, there would be no difference between love and justice."

James Wentworth laughed sneeringly.

"There is little enough difference as it is, perhaps," he said; "they're both blind. Well, Madge," he added, in a more serious tone, "you're a generous-minded, noble-spirited girl, and I believe you do love me. I fancy that if you never asked the secret of my life, you can guess it pretty closely, eh?"

He looked searchingly at the girl's face. She hung her head, but did not answer him.

"You can guess the secret, can't you, Madge? Don't be afraid to speak, girl."

"I fear I can guess it, father dear," she murmured in a low voice.

"Speak out, then."

"I am afraid the reason you have never prospered—the reason that so many are against you—is that you once did something wrong, very long ago, when you were young and reckless, and scarcely knew the nature of your own act; and that now, though you are truly penitent and sorry, and have long wished to lead an altered life, the world won't forget or forgive that old wrong. Is it so, father?"

"It is, Margaret. You've guessed right enough, child, except that you've omitted one fact. The wrong I did was done for the sake of another. I was tempted to do it by another. I made no profit by it myself, and I never hoped to make any. But when detection came, it was upon *me* that the disgrace and ruin fell; while the man for whom I had done wrong—the man who had made me his tool—turned his back upon me, and refused to utter one word in my justification, though he was in no danger himself, and the lightest word from his lips might have saved me. That was a hard case, wasn't it, Madge?"

"Hard!" cried the girl, with her nostrils quivering and her hands clenched; "it was cruel, dastardly, infamous!"

"From that day, Margaret, I was a ruined man. The brand of society was upon me. The world would not let me live honestly, and the love of life was too strong in me to let me face death. I tried to live dishonestly, and I led a wild, rackety, dare-devil kind of a life, amongst men who found they had a skilful tool, and knew how to use me. They did use me to their heart's content, and left me in the lurch when danger came. I was arrested for forgery, tried, found guilty, and transported for life. Don't flinch, girl! don't turn so white! You must have heard something of this whispered and hinted at often enough before to-day. You may as well know the whole truth. I was transported, for life, Madge; and for thirteen years I toiled amongst the wretched, guilty slaves in Norfolk Island[9]— that was the favourite place in those days for such as me—and at the end of that time, my conduct having been approved of by my gaolers, the governor sent for me, gave me a good-service certificate, and I went into a counting-house and served as a clerk. But I got a kind of fever in my blood, and night and day I only thought of one thing, and that was my chance of escape. I did escape,—never you mind how, that's a long story,—and I got back to England, a free man; a free man, Madge, *I* thought; but the world soon told me another story. I was a felon, a gaol-bird; and I was never more to lift my head amongst honest people. I couldn't bear it, Madge, my girl. Perhaps a better man might have persevered in spite of all till he conquered the world's prejudice. But *I* couldn't. I sank under my trials, and fell lower and lower. And for every disgrace that has ever fallen upon me—for every sorrow I have ever suffered—for every sin I have ever committed—I look to one man as the cause."

Margaret Wentworth had risen to her feet. She stood before her father now, pale and breathless, with her lips parted, and her bosom

---

[9] Established as a penal settlement in 1788, Norfolk Island lies between Australia and New Zealand and is today part of Australia's external territories. It was temporarily abandoned by the British government in 1814, but resettled as a penal colony in 1824 and used particularly for the detention of serious criminals. Conditions were extremely harsh and bleak, with horrifying levels of violence against convicts, leading in 1834 to a mutiny.

heaving.

"Tell me his name, father," she whispered; "tell me that man's name."

"Why do you want to know his name, Madge?"

"Never mind why, father. Tell it to me—tell it!"

She stamped her foot in the vehemence of her passion.

"Tell me his name, father," she repeated, impatiently.

"His name is Henry Dunbar," James Wentworth answered, "and he is the son of a rich banker. I saw his father's death in the paper last March. His uncle died ten years ago, and he will inherit the fortunes of both father and uncle. The world has smiled upon him. He has never suffered for that one false step in life, which brought such ruin upon me. He will come home from India now, I dare say, and the world will be under his feet. He will be worth a million of money, I should fancy; curse him! If my wishes could be accomplished, every guinea he possesses would be a separate scorpion to sting and to torture him."

"Henry Dunbar," whispered Margaret to herself—"Henry Dunbar. I will not forget that name."

- CHAPTER 3 -

THE MEETING AT THE RAILWAY STATION

When the hands of the little clock in Margaret's sitting-room pointed to five minutes before three, James Wentworth rose from his lounging attitude in the easy-chair, and took his hat from a side-table.

"Are you going out, father?" the girl asked.

"Yes, Madge; I'm going up to London. It don't do for me to sit still too long. Bad thoughts come fast enough at any time; but they come fastest when a fellow sits twirling his thumbs. Don't look so frightened, Madge; I'm not going to do any harm. I'm only going to look about me. I may fall in with a bit of luck, perhaps; no matter what, if it puts a few shillings into my pocket."

"I'd rather you stayed at home, father dear," Margaret said, gently.

"I dare say you would, child. But I tell you, I can't. I *can't* sit quiet this afternoon. I've been talking of things that always seem to set my brain on fire. No harm shall come of my going away, girl; I promise you that. The worst I shall do is to sit in a tavern parlour, drink a glass of gin-and-water, and read the papers. There's no crime in that, is there, Madge?"

His daughter smiled as she tried to arrange the shabby velvet collar of his threadbare coat.

"No, father dear," she said; "and I'm sure I always wish you to enjoy yourself. But you'll come home soon, won't you?"

"What do you call 'soon,' my lass?"

"Before ten o'clock. My day's work will be all over long before that, and I'll try and get something nice for your supper."

"Very well, then, I'll be back by ten o'clock to-night. There's my hand upon it."

He gave Margaret his hand, kissed her smooth cheeks, took his cane from a corner of the room, and then went out.

His daughter watched him from the open window as he walked up the narrow lane, amongst the groups of children gathered every here and there upon the dusty pathway.

"Heaven have pity upon him, and keep him from sin!" murmured Margaret Wentworth, clasping her hands, and with her eyes still following the retreating figure.

James Wentworth jingled the money in his waistcoat-pocket as he walked towards the railway station. He had very little; a couple of six-pences and a few halfpence. Just about enough to pay for a second-class return ticket, and for his glass of gin-and-water at a London tavern.

He reached the station three minutes before the train was due, and took his ticket.

At half-past three he was in London.

But as he was an idle, purposeless man, without friends to visit or money to spend, he was in no hurry to leave the railway station.

He hated solitude or quiet; and here in this crowded terminus there was life and bustle and variety enough in all conscience; and all to be seen for nothing: so he strolled backwards and forwards upon the plat-form, watching the busy porters, the eager passengers rushing to and fro, and meditating as to where he should spend the rest of his afternoon.

By-and-by he stood against a wooden pillar in a doorway, looking at the cabs, as, one after another, they tore up to the station, and disgorged their loads.

He had witnessed the arrival of a great many different travellers, when his attention was suddenly arrested by a little old man, wan and wizen and near-sighted, feeble-looking, but active, who alighted from a cab, and gave his small black-leather portmanteau into the hands of a porter.

This man was Sampson Wilmot, the old confidential clerk in the house of Dunbar, Dunbar, and Balderby.

James Wentworth followed the old man and the porter.

"I wonder if it *is* he," he muttered to himself; "there's a likeness—there's certainly a likeness. But it's so many years ago—so many years—I don't suppose I should know him. And yet this man recalls him to me somehow. I'll keep my eye upon the old fellow, at any rate."

Sampson Wilmot had arrived at the station about ten minutes before the starting of the train. He asked some questions of the porter, and left his portmanteau in the man's care while he went to get his ticket.

James Wentworth lingered behind, and contrived to look at the portmanteau.

There was a label pasted on the lid, with an address, written in a business-like hand—

> "MR. SAMPSON WILMOT,
>   PASSENGER TO SOUTHAMPTON."

James Wentworth gave a long whistle.

"I thought as much," he muttered; "I thought I couldn't be mistaken!"

He went into the ticket-office, where the clerk was standing amongst the crowd, waiting to take his ticket. James Wentworth went up close to him, and touched him lightly on the shoulder.

Sampson Wilmot turned and looked him full in the face. He looked, but there was no ray of recognition in that look.

"Do you want me, sir?" he asked, with rather a suspicious glance at the reprobate's shabby dress.

"Yes, Mr. Wilmot, I want to speak to you. You can come into the waiting-room with me, after you've taken your ticket."

The clerk stared aghast. The tone of this shabby-looking stranger was almost one of command.

"I don't know you, my good sir," stammered Sampson; "I never set eyes upon you before; and unless you are a messenger sent after me from the office, you must be under a mistake. You are a stranger to me!"

"I am no stranger, and I am no messenger!" answered the other. "You've got your ticket? That's all right! Now you can come with me."

He walked into a waiting-room, the half-glass doors of which opened out of the office. The room was empty, for it only wanted five minutes to the starting of the train, and the passengers had hurried off to take their seats.

James Wentworth took off his hat, and brushed his rumpled grey hair from his forehead.

"Put on your spectacles, Sampson Wilmot," he said, "and look hard at me, and then tell me if I am a stranger to you."

25

The old clerk obeyed, nervously, fearfully. His tremulous hands could scarcely adjust his spectacles.

He looked at the reprobate's face for some moments and said nothing. But his breath came quicker and his face grew very pale.

"Ay," said James Wentworth, "look your hardest, and deny me if you can. It will be only wise to deny me; I'm no credit to any one—least of all to a steady respectable old chap like you!"

"Joseph!—Joseph!" gasped the old clerk; "is it you? Is it really my wretched brother? I thought you were dead, Joseph—I thought you were dead and gone!"

"And wished it, I dare say!" the other answered, bitterly.

"No, Joseph,—no!" cried Sampson Wilmot; "Heaven knows I never wished you ill. Heaven knows I was always sorry for you, and could make excuses for you even when you sank lowest!"

"That's strange!" Joseph muttered, with a sneer; "that's very strange! If you were so precious fond of me, how was it that you stopped in the house of Dunbar and Dunbar? If you had had one spark of natural affection for me, you could never have eaten their bread!"

Sampson Wilmot shook his head sorrowfully.

"Don't be too hard upon me, Joseph," he said, with mild reproachfulness; "if I hadn't stopped at the banking-house your mother might have starved!"

The reprobate made no answer to this; but he turned his face away and sighed.

The bell rang for the starting of the train.

"I must go," Sampson cried. "Give me your address, Joseph, and I will write to you."

"Oh, yes, I dare say!" answered his brother, scornfully; "no, no, *that* won't do. I've found you, my rich respectable brother, and I'll stick to you. Where are you going?"

"To Southampton."

"What for?"

"To meet Henry Dunbar."

Joseph Wilmot's face grew livid with rage.

The change that came over it was so sudden and so awful in its nature, that the old clerk started back as if he had seen a ghost.

"You are going to meet *him*?" said Joseph, in a hoarse whisper; "he is in England, then?"

"No; but he is expected to arrive almost immediately. Why do you look like that, Joseph?"

"Why do I look like that?" cried the younger man; "have you grown to be such a mere machine, such a speaking automaton, such a living tool of the men you serve, that all human feeling has perished in your breast? Bah! how should such as you understand what I feel? Hark! the bell's ringing—I'll come with you."

The train was on the point of starting: the two men hurried out to the platform.

"No,—no," cried Sampson Wilmot, as his brother stepped after him into the carriage; "no,—no, Joseph, don't come with me,—don't come with me!"

"I will go with you."

"But you've no ticket."

"I can get one—or you can get me one, for I've no money—at the first station we stop at."

They were seated in a second-class railway carriage by this time. The ticket-collector, running from carriage to carriage, was in too great a hurry to discover that the little bit of pasteboard which Joseph Wilmot exhibited was only a return-ticket to Wandsworth. There was a brief scramble, a banging of doors, and Babel-like confusion of tongues; and then the engine gave its farewell shriek and rushed away.

The old clerk looked very uneasily at his younger brother's face. The livid pallor had passed away, but the strongly-marked eyebrows met in a dark frown.

"Joseph—Joseph!" said Sampson, "Heaven only knows I'm glad to see you, after more than thirty years' separation, and any help I can give you out of my slender means I'll give freely—I will, indeed, Joseph, for the memory of our dear mother, if not for love of you; and I do love you, Joseph—I do love you very dearly still. But I'd rather you didn't take this journey with me—I would, indeed. I can't see that any good can come of it."

"Never you mind what comes of it. I want to talk to you. You're a nice affectionate brother to wish to shuffle me off directly after our first meeting. I want to talk to you, Sampson Wilmot. And I want to see *him*. I know how the world's used *me* for the last five-and-thirty years; I want to see how the same world—such a just and merciful world as it is—has treated my tempter and betrayer, Henry Dunbar!"

Sampson Wilmot trembled like a leaf. His health had been very feeble ever since the second shock of paralysis—that dire and silent foe, whose invisible hand had stricken the old man down as he sat at his desk, without one moment's warning. His health was feeble, and the shock of meeting with his brother—this poor lost disgraced brother—whom he had for five-and-twenty years believed to be dead, had been almost too much for him. Nor was this all—unutterable terror took possession of him when he thought of a meeting between Joseph Wilmot and Henry

Dunbar. The old man could remember his brother's words:

"Let him consider it a lucky escape, if, when we next meet, he gets off scot free!"

Sampson Wilmot had prayed night and day that such a meeting might never take place. For five-and-thirty years it had been delayed. Surely it would not take place now.

The old clerk looked nervously at his brother's face.

"Joseph," he murmured, "I'd rather you didn't go with me to Southampton; I'd rather you didn't meet Mr. Dunbar. You were very badly treated—cruelly and unjustly treated—nobody knows that better than I. But it's a long time ago, Joseph—it's a very, very long time ago. Bitter feelings die out of a man's breast as the years roll by—don't they, Joseph? Time heals all old wounds, and we learn to forgive others as we hope to be forgiven—don't we, Joseph?"

"*You* may," answered the reprobate, fiercely; "I don't!"

He said no more, but sat silent, with his arms folded over his breast.

He looked straight before him out of the carriage-window; but he saw no more of the pleasant landscape,—the fair fields of waving corn, with scarlet poppies and deep-blue corn flowers, bright glimpses of sunlit water, and distant villages, with grey church-turrets, nestling among trees. He looked out of the carriage-window, and some of earth's pleasantest pictures sped by him; but he saw no more of that ever-changing prospect than if he had been looking at a blank sheet of paper.

Sampson Wilmot sat opposite to him, restless and uneasy, watching his fierce gloomy countenance.

The clerk took a ticket for his brother at the first station the train stopped at. But still Joseph was silent.

An hour passed by, and he had not yet spoken.

He had no love for his brother. The world had hardened him. The consequences of his own sins, falling very heavily upon his head, had embittered his nature. He looked upon the man whom he had once loved and trusted as the primary cause of his disgrace and misery, and this thought influenced his opinion of all mankind.

He could not believe in the goodness of any man, remembering, as he did, how he had once trusted Henry Dunbar.

The brothers were alone in the carriage.

Sampson watched the gloomy face opposite to him for some time, and then, with a weary sigh, he drew his handkerchief over his face, and sank back in the corner of the carriage. But he did not sleep. He was agitated and anxious. A dizzy faintness had seized upon him, and there was a strange buzzing in his ears, and unwonted clouds before his dim eyes. He tried to speak once or twice, but it seemed to him as if he was powerless to form the words that were in his mind.

Then his mind began to grow confused. The hoarse snorting of the engine sounded monotonously in his ears: growing louder and louder with every moment; until the noise of it grew hideous and intolerable—a perpetual thunder, deafening and bewildering him.

The train was fast approaching Basingstoke, when Joseph Wilmot was suddenly startled from his moody reverie.

There was an awful cause for that sudden start, that look of horror in the reprobate's face.

- CHAPTER 4 -

THE STROKE OF DEATH

T he old clerk had fallen from his seat, and lay in a motionless heap at the bottom of the railway carriage.

The third stroke of paralysis had come upon him; inevitable, no doubt, long ago; but hastened, it may be, by that unlooked-for meeting at the Waterloo terminus.

Joseph Wilmot knelt beside the stricken man. He was a vagabond and an outcast, and scenes of horror were not new to him. He had seen death under many of its worst aspects, and the grim King of Terrors had little terror for him. He was hardened, steeped in guilt, and callous as to the sufferings of others. The love which he bore for his daughter was, perhaps, the last ray of feeling that yet lingered in this man's perverted nature.

But he did all he could, nevertheless, for the unconscious old man. He loosened his cravat, unfastened his waistcoat, and felt for the beating of his heart. That heart did beat: very fitfully, as if the old clerk's weary soul had been making feeble struggles to be released from its frail tabernacle of clay.

"Better, perhaps, if this should prove fatal," Joseph muttered; "I should go on alone to meet Henry Dunbar."

The train reached Basingstoke; Joseph put his head out of the open window, and called loudly to a porter. The man came quickly, in answer to that impatient summons.

"My brother is in a fit," Joseph cried; "help me to lift him out of the carriage, and then send some one for a doctor."

The unconscious form was lifted out in the arms of the two strong men. They carried it into the waiting-room, and laid it on a sofa. The bell rang, and the Southampton train rushed onward without the two travellers.

In another moment the whole station was in commotion. A gentleman had been seized with paralysis, and was dying. The doctor arrived in less than ten minutes. He shook his head, after examining his patient.

"It's a bad case," said he; "very bad; but we must do our best. Is there anybody with this old gentleman?"

"Yes, sir," the porter answered, pointing to Joseph; "this person is with him."

The country surgeon glanced rather suspiciously at Joseph Wilmot. He looked a vagabond, certainly—every inch a vagabond; a reckless, dare-devil scoundrel, at war with society, and defiant of a world he hated.

"Are you—any—relation to this gentleman?" the doctor asked, hesitatingly.

"Yes, I am his brother."

"I should recommend his being removed to the nearest hotel. I will send a woman to nurse him. Do you know if this is the first stroke he has ever had?"

"No, I do not."

The surgeon looked more suspicious than ever, after receiving this answer.

"Strange," he said, "that you, who say you are his brother, should not be able to give me information upon that point."

Joseph Wilmot answered with an air of carelessness that was almost contemptuous:

"It is strange," he said; "but many stranger things have happened in this world before now. My brother and I haven't met for years until we met to-day."

The unconscious man was removed from the railway station to an inn near at hand—a humble, countrified place, but clean and orderly. Here he was taken to a bed-chamber, whose old-fashioned latticed windows looked out upon the dusty road.

The doctor did all that his skill could devise, but he could not restore consciousness to the paralyzed brain. The soul was gone already. The body lay, a form of motionless and senseless clay, under the white counterpane; and Joseph Wilmot, sitting near the foot of the bed, watched it with a gloomy face.

The woman who was to nurse the sick man came by-and-by, and took her place by the pillow. But there was very little for her to do.

"Is there any hope of his recovering?" Joseph asked eagerly, as the doctor was about to leave the room.

"I fear not—I fear there is no hope."

"Will it be over soon?"

"Very soon, I think. I do not believe that he can last more than four-and-twenty hours."

The surgeon waited for a few moments after saying this, expecting some exclamation of surprise or grief from the dying man's brother: but there was none; and with a hasty "good evening" the medical man quitted the room.

It was growing dusk, and the twilight shadows upon Joseph Wilmot's face made it, in its sullen gloom, darker even than it had been in the railway carriage.

"I'm glad of it, I'm glad of it," he muttered; "I shall meet Harry Dunbar alone."

The bed-chamber in which the sick man lay opened out of a little sitting-room. Sampson's carpet-bag and portmanteau had been left in this sitting-room. Joseph Wilmot searched the pockets in the clothes that had been taken off his brother's senseless form. There was some loose silver and a bunch of keys in the waistcoat-pocket, and a well-worn leather-covered memorandum-book in the breast-pocket of the old-fashioned coat. Joseph took these things into the sitting-room, closed the door between the two apartments, and then rang for lights.

The chambermaid who brought the candles asked if he had dined.

"Yes," he said, "I dined five hours ago. Bring me some brandy."

The girl brought a small decanter of spirit and a wine-glass, set them on the table, and left the room. Joseph Wilmot followed her to the door, and turned the key in the lock.

"I don't want any intruders," he muttered; "these country people are always inquisitive."

He seated himself at the table, poured out a glass of brandy, drank it, and then drew one of the candles towards him.

He had put the money, the keys, and the memorandum-book, in one of his own pockets. He took out the memorandum-book first, and examined it. There were five Bank of England notes for five pounds each in one of the pockets, and a letter in the other.

The letter was directed to Henry Dunbar, and sealed with the official seal of the banking-house. The name of Stephen Balderby was written on the left-hand lower corner of the envelope.

"So, so," whispered Joseph Wilmot, "this is the junior partner's letter of welcome to his chief. I'll take care of that."

He replaced the letter in the pocket of the memorandum-book, and then looked at the pencil entries on the different pages. The last entry was the only memorandum that had any interest for him.

It consisted of these few words—

"H.D., expected to arrive at Southampton Docks on or about the 19th inst., per steamer Electra; *will be met by Miss Laura D. at Portland Place."*[10]

"Who's Laura D.?" mused the spy, as he closed the memorandum-book. "His daughter, I suppose. I remember seeing his marriage in the papers, twenty years ago. He married well, of course. Fortune made *everything* smooth for him. He married a lady of rank. Curse him!"

Joseph Wilmot sat for some time with his arms folded upon the table before him, brooding, brooding, brooding; with a sinister smile upon his lips, and an ominous light in his eyes. A dangerous man always—a dangerous man when he was loud, reckless, brutal, violent: but most of all dangerous when he was most quiet.

By-and-by he took the bunch of keys from his pocket, knelt down before the portmanteau, and examined its contents. There was very little to reward his scrutiny—only a suit of clothes, a couple of clean shirts, and the necessaries of the clerk's simple toilet. The carpet-bag contained a pair of boots, a hat-brush, a night-shirt, and a faded old chintz dressing-gown.

Joseph Wilmot rose from his knees after examining these things, and softly opened the door between the two rooms. There had been no change in the sick chamber. The nurse still sat by the head of the bed. She looked round at Joseph, as he opened the door.

"No change, I suppose?" he said.

"No, sir; none."

"I am going out for a stroll, presently. I shall be in again in an hour's time."

He shut the door again, but he did not go out immediately. He knelt down once more by the side of the portmanteau, and tore off the label with his brother's name upon it. He tore a similar label off the carpet-bag, taking care that no vestige of the clerk's name was left behind.

When he had done this, and thrust the torn labels into his pocket, he began to walk up and down the room, softly, with his arms folded upon

---

[10] Braddon's choice of the name *Electra* for the steamer is significant, given the thematic focus on a daughter's vengeance and the centrality of the relationship between fathers and daughters. Electra, in Greek mythology, was the daughter of Agamemnon and Clytemnestra. In the plays by both Sophocles and Euripedes, Electra conspires with her brother to avenge their father's murder. In psychoanalytic theory, the Electra complex explains female sexual development as dependent on the daughter's psychosexual attachment to the father. The term was coined by Carl Jung as the female equivalent to Freud's Oedipus complex.

his breast.

"The *Electra*, is expected to arrive on the nineteenth," he said, in a low, thoughtful voice, "on or about the nineteenth. She may arrive either before or after. To-morrow will be the seventeenth. If Sampson dies, there will be an inquest, no doubt: a post-mortem examination, perhaps: and I shall be detained till all that is over. I shall be detained two or three days at least: and in the mean time Henry Dunbar may arrive at Southampton, hurry on to London, and I may miss the one chance of meeting that man face to face. I won't be balked of this meeting—I won't be balked. Why should I stop here to watch by an unconscious man's death-bed? No! Fate has thrown Henry Dunbar once more across my pathway: and I won't throw my chance away."

He took up his hat—a battered, shabby-looking white hat, which harmonized well with his vagabond appearance—and went out, after stopping for a minute at the bar to tell the landlord that he would be back in an hour's time.

He went straight to the railway station, and made inquiries as to the trains.

- CHAPTER 5 -

SINKING THE PAST

The train from London to Southampton was due in an hour. The clerk who gave Joseph Wilmot this information asked him how his brother was getting on.

"He is much better," Joseph answered. "I am going on to South-ampton to execute some important business he was to have done there. I shall come back early to-morrow morning."

He walked into the waiting-room, and stopped there, seated in the same attitude the whole time: never stirring, never lifting his head from his breast: always brooding, brooding, brooding: as he had brooded in the railway carriage, as he had brooded in the little parlour of the inn. He took his ticket for Southampton as soon as the office was open, and then stood on the platform, where there were two or three stragglers, waiting for the train to come up.

It came at last. Joseph Wilmot sprang into a second-class carriage, took his seat in the corner, with his hat slouched over his eyes, which were almost hidden by its dilapidated brim.

It was late when he reached Southampton; but he seemed to be acquainted with the town, and he walked straight to a small public-house by the river-side, almost hidden under the shadow of the town wall.

Here he got a bed, and here he ascertained that the *Electra* had not yet arrived.

He ate his supper in his own room, though he was requested to take it in the public apartment. He seemed to shrink from meeting any one, or talking to any one; and still brooded over his own black thoughts: as he had brooded at the railway station, in the parlour of the Basingstoke inn, in the carriage with his brother Sampson.

Whatever his thoughts were, they absorbed him so entirely that he seemed like a man who walks in his sleep, doing everything mechanically, and without knowing what he does.

But for all this he was active, for he rose very early the next morning. He had not had an hour's sleep throughout the night, but had lain in every variety of restless attitude, tossing first on this side and then on that: always thinking, thinking, thinking, till the action of his brain became as mechanical as that of any other machine, and went on in spite of himself.

He went downstairs, paid the money for his supper and night's lodging to a sleepy servant-girl, and left the house as the church-clock in an old-fashioned square hard by struck eight.

He walked straight to the High Street, and entered the shop of a tailor and general outfitter. It was a stylish establishment, and there was a languid young man taking down the shutters, who appeared to be the only person on the establishment just at present.

He looked superciliously enough at Joseph Wilmot, eyeing him lazily from head to foot, and yawning as he did so.

"You'd better make yourself scarce," he said; "our principal never gives anything to tramps."

"Your principal may give or keep what he likes," Joseph answered, carelessly; "I can pay for what I want. Call your master down: or stay, you'll do as well, I dare say. I want a complete rig-out from head to heel. Do you understand?"

"I shall, perhaps, when I see the money for it," the languid youth answered, with a sneer.

"So you've learned the way of the world already, have you, my lad?" said Joseph Wilmot, bitterly. Then, pulling his brother's memorandum-book from his pocket, he opened it, and took out the little packet of bank-notes. "I suppose you can understand these?" he said.

The languid youth lifted his nose, which by its natural conformation betrayed an aspiring character, and looked dubiously at his customer.

"I can understand as they might be flash uns," he remarked,

significantly.[11]

Mr. Joseph Wilmot growled out an oath, and made a plunge at the young shopman.

"I said as they *might* be flash," the youth remonstrated, quite meekly; "there's no call to fly at me. I didn't mean to give no offence."

"No," muttered Mr. Wilmot; "egad! you'd better *not* mean it. Call your master."

The youth retired to obey: he was quite subdued and submissive by this time.

Joseph Wilmot looked about the shop.

"The cur forgot the till," he muttered; "I might try my hand at that, if—" He stopped and smiled with a strange, deliberate expression, not quite agreeable to behold—"if I wasn't going to meet Henry Dunbar."

There was a full-length looking-glass in one corner of the shop. Joseph Wilmot walked up to it, looked at himself for a few moments in silent contemplation, and then shook his clenched hand at the reflected image.

"You're a vagabond!" he muttered between his set teeth, "and you look it! You're an outcast; and you look it! But who set the mark upon you? Who's to blame for all the evil you have done? Whose treachery made you what you are? That's the question!"

The owner of the shop appeared, and looked sharply at his customer.

"Now, listen to me!" Joseph Wilmot said, slowly and deliberately. "I've been down upon my luck for some time past, and I've just got a bit of money. I've got it honestly, mind you; and I don't want to be questioned by such a jackanapes as that shopboy of yours."

The languid youth folded his arms, and endeavoured to look ferocious in his fiery indignation; but he drew a little way behind his master as he did so.

The proprietor of the shop bowed and smiled.

"We shall be happy to wait upon you, sir," he said; "and I have no doubt we shall be able to give you satisfaction. If my shopman has been impertinent—"

"He has," interrupted Joseph; "but I don't want to make any palaver about that. He's like the rest of the world, and he thinks if a man wears a shabby coat, he must be a scoundrel; that's all. I forgive him."

The languid youth, very much in the background, and quite sheltered, by his master, might have been heard murmuring faintly—

"Oh, indeed! Forgive, indeed! Do you really, now? Thank you for nothing!" and other sentences of a derisive character.

---

[11] Flash uns: a slang term for stolen money, specifically bank notes.

"I want a complete rig-out," continued Joseph Wilmot; "a new suit of clothes—hat, boots, umbrella, a carpet-bag, half-a-dozen shirts, brush and comb, shaving tackle, and all the et-ceteras. Now, as you may be no more inclined to trust me than that young whipper-snapper of yours, for all you're so uncommon civil, I'll tell you what I'll do. I want this beard of mine trimmed and altered. I'll go to a barber's and get that done, and in the meantime you can make your mind easy about the character of these gentlemen."

He handed the tradesman three of the Bank of England notes. The man looked at them doubtfully.

"If you think they ain't genuine, send 'em round to one of your neighbours, and get 'em changed," Joseph Wilmot said; "but be quick about it. I shall be back here in half an hour."

He walked out of the shop, leaving the man still staring, with the three notes in his hand.

The vagabond, with his hat slouched over his eyes, and big hands in his pockets, strolled away from the High Street down to a barber's shop near the docks.

Here he had his beard shaved off, his ragged moustache trimmed into the most aristocratic shape, and his long, straggling grey hair cut and arranged according to his own directions.

If he had been the vainest of men, bent on no higher object in life than the embellishment of his person, he could not have been more particular or more difficult to please.

When the barber had completed his work, Joseph Wilmot washed his face, readjusted the hair upon his ample forehead, and looked at himself in a little shaving-glass that hung against the wall.

So far as the man's head and face went, the transformation was perfect. He was no longer a vagabond. He was a respectable, handsome-looking gentleman, advanced in middle age. Not altogether unaristo-cratic-looking.

The very expression of his face was altered. The defiant sneer was changed into a haughty smile; the sullen scowl was now a thoughtful frown.

Whether this change was natural to him, and merely brought about by the alteration in his hair and beard, or whether it was an assumption of his own, was only known to the man himself.

He put on his hat, still slouching the brim over his eyes, paid the barber, and went away. He walked straight to the docks, and made inquiries about the steamer *Electra*. She was not expected to arrive until the next day, at the earliest. Having satisfied himself upon this point, Joseph Wilmot went back to the outfitter's to choose his new clothes.

This business occupied him for a long time; for in this he was as difficult to please as he had been in the matter of his beard and hair. No punctilious old bachelor, the best and brightest hours of whose life had been devoted to the cares of the toilet, could have shown himself more fastidious than this vagabond, who had been out-at-elbows for ten years past, and who had worn a felon's dress for thirteen years at a stretch in Norfolk Island.

But he evinced no bad taste in the selection of a costume. He chose no gaudy colours, or flashily-cut vestments. On the contrary, the garb he assumed was in perfect keeping with the style of his hair and moustache. It was the dress of a middle-aged gentleman; fashionable, but scrupulously simple, quiet alike in colour and in cut.

When his toilet was complete, from his twenty-one shilling hat to the polished boots upon his well-shaped feet, he left the shady little parlour in which he had changed his clothes, and came into the shop, with a glove dangling loosely in one ungloved hand, and a cane in the other.

The tradesman and his shopboy stared aghast.

"If that turn-out had cost you fifty pound, sir, instead of eighteen pound, twelve, and elevenpence, it would be worth all the money to you; for you look like a dook;" cried the tailor, with enthusiasm.

"I'm glad to hear it," Mr. Wilmot said, carelessly. He stood before the cheval-glass, and twirled his moustache as he spoke, looking at himself thoughtfully, with a smile upon his face. Then he took his change from the tailor, counted it, and dropped the gold and silver into his waistcoat-pocket.

The man's manner was as much altered as his person. He had entered the shop at eight o'clock that morning a blackguard as well as a vagabond. He left it now a gentleman; subdued in voice, easy and rather listless in gait, haughty and self-possessed in tone.

"Oh, by the bye," he said, pausing upon the threshold of the door, "I'll thank you to bundle all those old things of mine together into a sheet of brown paper: tie them up tightly. I'll call for them after dark tonight."

Having said this, very carelessly and indifferently, Mr. Wilmot left the shop: but though he was now as well dressed and as gentlemanly-looking as any man in Southampton, he turned into the first by-street, and hurried away from the town to a lonely walk beside the water.

He walked along the shore until he came to a village near the river, and about a couple of miles from Southampton. There he entered a low-roofed little public-house, very quiet and unfrequented, ordered some brandy and cold water of a girl who was seated at work behind the bar, and then went into the parlour,—a low-ceilinged, wainscoted room,

whose walls were adorned here and there with auctioneers' announce-
ments of coming sales of live and dead stock, farm-houses, and farming
implements, interspersed with railway time-tables.

Mr. Joseph Wilmot had this room all to himself. He seated himself by
the open window, took up a country newspaper, and tried to read.

But that attempt was a most dismal failure. In the first place, there
was very little in the paper to read: and in the second, Joseph Wilmot
would have been unable to chain his attention to the page upon which
his eyes were fixed, though all the wisdom of the world had been
concentrated upon that one sheet of printed paper.

No; he could not read. He could only think. He could only think of
this strange chance which had come to him after five-and-thirty weary
years. He could only think of his probable meeting with Henry Dunbar.

He entered the village public-house at a little after one, and he stayed
there throughout the rest of the day, drinking brandy-and-water—not
immoderately: he was very careful and watchful of himself in that
matter—taking a snack of bread and cold meat for his dinner, and
thinking of Henry Dunbar.

In that he never varied, let him do what he would.

In the railway carriage, at the Basingstoke inn, at the station, through
the long sleepless night at the public-house by the water, in the tailor's
shop, even when he was most occupied by the choice of his clothes, he
had still thought of Henry Dunbar. From the time of his meeting the old
clerk at the Waterloo terminus, he had never ceased to think of Henry
Dunbar.

He never once thought of his brother: not so much even as to
wonder whether the stroke had been fatal,—whether the old man was
yet dead. He never thought of his daughter, or the anguish his prolonged
absence might cause her to suffer.

He had put away the past as if it had never been, and concentrated all
the force of his mind upon the one idea which possessed him like some
strong demon.

Sometimes a sudden terror seized him.

What if Henry Dunbar should have died upon the passage home?
What if the *Electra* should bring nothing but a sealed leaden coffin, and a
corpse embalmed in spirit?

No, he could not imagine that! Fate, darkly brooding over these two
men throughout half a long lifetime, had held them asunder for five-and-
thirty years, to fling them mysteriously together now.

It seemed as if the old clerk's philosophy was not so very unsound,
after all. Sooner or later,—sooner or later,—the day of retribution comes.

When it grew dusk, Joseph Wilmot left the little inn, and walked back to Southampton. It was quite dark when he entered the High Street, and the tailor's shop was closing.

"I thought you'd forgotten your parcel, sir," the man said; "I've had it ready for you ever so long. Can I send it any where for you?"

"No, thank you; I'll take it myself."

With the brown-paper parcel—which was a very bulky one—under his arm, Joseph Wilmot left the tailor's shop, and walked down to an open pier or quay abutting on the water.

On his way along the river shore, between the village public-house and the town of Southampton, he had filled his pockets with stones. He knelt down now by the edge of the pier, and tied all these stones together in an old cotton pocket-handkerchief.

When he had done this, carefully, compactly, and quickly, like a man accustomed to do all sorts of strange things, he tied the handkerchief full of stones to the whipcord that bound the brown-paper parcel, and dropped both packages into the water.

The spot which he had chosen for this purpose was at the extreme end of the pier, where the water was deepest.

He had done all this cautiously, taking care to make sure every now and then that he was unobserved.

And when the parcel had sunk, he watched the widening circle upon the surface of the water till it died away.

"So much for James Wentworth, and the clothes he wore," he said to himself as he walked away.

He slept that night at the village inn where he had spent the day, and the next morning walked into Southampton.

It was a little after nine o'clock when he entered the docks, and the *Electra* was visible to the naked eye, steaming through the blue water under a cloudless summer sky.

- CHAPTER 6 -

CLEMENT AUSTIN'S DIARY

"To-day I close a volume of the rough, careless, imperfect record which I have kept of my life. As I run my fingers through the pages of the limp morocco-covered volume, I almost wonder at my wasted labour;—the random notes, jotted down now and then, sometimes with long intervals between their dates, make such a mass of worthless literature. This diary-keeping is a very foolish habit, after all. Why do I keep this record of a most commonplace existence? For my own edification and improvement? Scarcely, since I very rarely read these uninteresting entries; and I very much doubt if posterity will care to know that I went to the office at ten o'clock on Wednesday morning; that I couldn't get a seat in the omnibus, and was compelled to take a Hansom, which cost me two shillings; that I dined *tête-à-tête*[12] with my mother, and finished the third volume of Carlyle's 'French Revolution' in the course of the evening. *Is* there any use in such a journal as mine? Will the celebrated New Zealander, that is to be, discover the volumes amidst the ruins of Clapham? and shall I be quoted as the Pepys of the nineteenth century?[13] But then I am by no means as racy as that worldly-minded little government clerk; or perhaps it may be that the time in which I live wants the spice and seasoning of that golden age of rascality in which my Lady Castlemain's white petticoats were to be seen flaunting in the wind by any frivolous-minded lounger who chose to take notes about those garments.[14]

"After all, it is a silly, old-fogeyish habit, this of diary-keeping; and I think the renowned Pepys himself was only a bachelor spoiled. Just now, however, I have something more than cab-drives, lost omnibuses, and the perusal of a favourite book to jot down, inasmuch as my mother and myself have lately had all our accustomed habits, in a manner, disorganized by the advent of a lady.

"She is a very young lady, being, in point of fact, still at a remote distance from an epoch to which she appears to look forward as a grand and enviable period of existence. She has not yet entered what she calls her 'teens,' and two years must elapse before she can enter them, as she is only eleven years old. She is the only daughter of my only sister, Marian Lester, and has been newly imported from Sydney, where my sister Marian and her husband have been settled for the last twelve years. Miss Elizabeth Lester became a member of our family upon the first of July, and has since that time continued to make herself quite at home with my mother and myself. She is rather a pretty little girl, with very auburn plaits hanging in loops at the back of her head. (Will the New Zealander and his countrymen care to know the mysteries of juvenile coiffures in the nineteenth century?) She is a very good little girl, and my mother adores her. As for myself, I am only gradually growing resigned to the fact that I am three-and-thirty years of age, and the uncle of a

---

[12] Literally meaning "head to head", the phrase refers to a private conversation or meeting between two people, without the intrusion of a third person.

[13] Samuel Pepys, renowned diarist, 1633-1703.

[14] Barbara Villiers, Countess of Castlemaine (1640-1709). One of the most celebrated of Charles II's mistresses, Lady Castlemaine appears in many contemporary accounts of the period, including Pepys's diary.

bouncing niece, who plays variations upon 'Non più mesta.'[15]

"And 'Non più mesta' brings me to another strange figure in the narrow circle of my acquaintance; a figure that had no place in the volume which I have just closed, but which, in the six weeks' interval between my last record and that which I begin to-day, has become almost as familiar as the oldest friends of my youth. 'Non più mesta'—I hear my niece strumming the notes I know so well in the parlour below my room, as I write these lines, and the sound of the melody brings before me the image of a sweet pale face and dove-like brown eyes.

"I never fully realized the number and extent of feminine require-ments until a hack cab deposited my niece and her deal travelling-cases at our hall-door. Miss Elizabeth Lester seemed to want everything that it was possible for the human mind to imagine or desire. She had grown during the homeward voyage; her frocks were too short, her boots were too small, her bonnets tumbled off her head and hung forlornly at the back of her neck. She wanted parasols and hair-brushes, frilled and furbelowed mysteries of muslin and lace, copybooks, penholders, and pomatum[16], a backboard and a pair of gloves, drawing-pencils, dumb-bells, geological specimens for the illustration of her studies, and a hundred other items, whose very names are as a strange language to my masculine comprehension; and, last of all, she wanted a musical govern-ess. The little girl was supposed to be very tolerably advanced in her study of the piano, and my sister was anxious that she should continue that study under the superintendence of a duly-qualified instructress, whose terms should be moderate. My sister Marian underlined this last condition. The buying and making of the new frocks and muslin furbelows seemed almost to absorb my mother's mind, and she was fain to delegate to me the duty of finding a musical governess for Miss Lester.

"I began my task in the simplest possible way by consulting the daily newspapers, where I found so many advertisements emanating from ladies who declared themselves proficients in the art of music, that I was confused and embarrassed by the wealth of my resources: but I took the ladies singly, and called upon them in the pleasant summer evenings after office hours, sometimes with my mother, sometimes alone.

"It may be that the seal of old-bachelorhood is already set upon me, and that I am that odious and hyper-sensitive creature commonly called a 'fidget;' but somehow I could not find a governess whom I really felt inclined to choose for my little Lizzie. Some of the ladies were elderly

---

[15] An aria from the second act of *La Cenerentola*, an opera by Italian composer, Gioachino Antonio Rossini (1792-1868), based on the fairytale Cinderella.
[16] A perfumed ointment, used in dressing the hair.

and stern; others were young and frivolous; some of them were uncertain as to the distribution of the letter *h*. One young lady declared that
she was fonder of music than anything in the world. Some were a great
deal too enthusiastic, and were prepared to adore my little niece at a
moment's notice. Many, who seemed otherwise eligible, demanded a
higher rate of remuneration than we were prepared to give. So, somehow
or other, the business languished, and after the researches of a week we
found ourselves no nearer a decision than when first I looked at the
advertisements in the *Times* supplement.

"Had our resources been reduced, we should most likely have been
much easier to please; but my mother said, that as there were so many
people to be had, we should do well to deliberate before we came to any
decision. So it happened that, when I went out for a walk one evening, at
the end of the second week in July, Miss Lester was still without a
governess. She was still without a governess: but I was tired of
catechizing the fair advertisers as to their qualifications, and went out on
this particular evening for a solitary ramble amongst the quiet Surrey
suburbs, in any lonely lanes or scraps of common-land where the
speculating builder had not yet set his hateful foot. It was a lovely
evening; and I, who am so much a Cockney as to believe that a London
sunset is one of the grandest spectacles in the universe, set my face
towards the yellow light in the west, and walked across Wandsworth
Common, where faint wreaths of purple mist were rising from the
hollows, and a deserted donkey was breaking the twilight stillness with a
plaintive braying. Wandsworth Common was as lonely this evening as a
patch of sand in the centre of Africa; and being something of a day-
dreamer, I liked the place because of its stillness and solitude.

"Something of a dreamer: and yet I had so little to dream about. My
thoughts were pleasant, as I walked across the common in the sunset;
and yet, looking back now, I wonder what I thought of, and what image
there was in my mind that could make my fancies pleasant to me. I know
what I thought of, as I went home in the dim light of the newly-risen
moon, the pale crescent that glimmered high in a cloudless heaven.

"I went into the little town of Wandsworth, the queer old-fashioned
High Street, the dear old street, which seems to me like a town in a
Dutch picture, where all the tints are of a sombre brown, yet in which
there is, nevertheless, so much light and warmth. The lights were
beginning to twinkle here and there in the windows; and upon this July
evening there seemed to be flowers blooming in every casement. I
loitered idly through the street, staring at the shop-windows, in utter
absence of mind while I thought—

"What could I have thought of that evening? and how was it that I did not think the world blank and empty?

"While I was looking idly in at one of those shop-windows—it was a fancy-shop and stationer's—a kind of bazaar, in its humble way—my eye was attracted by the word 'Music;' and on a little card hung in the window I read that a lady would be happy to give lessons on the piano-forte, at the residences of her pupils, or at her own residence, on very moderate terms. The word 'very' was underscored. I thought it had a pitiful look somehow, that underscoring of the adverb, and seemed almost an appeal for employment. The inscription on the card was in a woman's hand, and a very pretty hand—elegant but not illegible, firm and yet feminine. I was in a very idle frame of mind, ready to be driven by any chance wind; and I thought I might just as well turn my evening walk to some account by calling upon the proprietress of the card. She was not likely to suit my ideas of perfection, any more than the other ladies I had seen; but I should at least be able to return home with the consciousness of having made another effort to find an instructress for my niece.

"The address on the card was, 'No. 3, Godolphin Cottages.' I asked the first person I met to direct me to Godolphin Cottages, and was told to take the second turning on my right. The second turning on my right took me into a kind of lane or by-road, where there were some old-fashioned, semi-detached cottages, sheltered by a row of sycamores, and shut in by wooden palings. I opened the low gate before the third cottage, and went into the garden,—a primly-kept little garden, with a grass-plat and miniature gravel-walks, and with a grotto of shells and moss and craggy blocks of stone in a corner. Under a laburnum-tree there was a green rustic bench; and here I found a young lady sitting reading by the dying light. She started at the sound of my footsteps on the crisp gravel, and rose, blushing like one of the cabbage-roses that grew near her. The blush was all the more becoming to her inasmuch as she was naturally very pale. I saw this almost immediately, for the bright colour faded out of her face while I was speaking to her.

"'I have come to inquire for a lady who teaches music,' I said; 'I saw a card, just now, in the High Street, and as I am searching for an instructress for my little niece, I took the opportunity of calling. But I fear I have chosen an inconvenient time for my visit.'

"I scarcely know why I made this apology, since I had omitted to apologize to the other ladies, on whom I had ventured to intrude at abnormal hours. I fear that I was weak enough to feel bewildered by the pensive loveliness of the face at which I looked, and that my confidence ebbed away under the influence of those grave hazel eyes.

"The face is so beautiful,—as beautiful now that I have learned the trick of every feature, though even now I cannot learn all the varying changes of expression which make it ever new to me, as it was that evening when it beamed on me for the first time. Shall I describe her,— the woman whom I have only known four weeks, and who seems to fill all the universe when I think of her?—and when do I not think of her? Shall I describe her for the New Zealander, when the best description must fall so far below the bright reality, and when the very act of reducing her beauty into hard commonplace words seems in some manner a sacrilege against the sanctity of that beauty? Yes, I will describe her; not for the sake of the New Zealander, who may have new and extraordinary ideas as to female loveliness, and may require a blue nose or pea-green tresses in the lady he elects as the only type of beautiful womanhood. I will describe her because it is sweet to me to dwell upon her image, and to translate that dear image, no matter how poorly, into words. Were I a painter, I should be like Claude Melnotte, and paint no face but hers.[17] Were I a poet, I should cover reams of paper with wild rhapsodies about her beauty. Being only a cashier in a bank, I can do nothing but enshrine her in the commonplace pages of my diary.

"I have said that she is pale. Hers is that ivory pallor which sometimes accompanies hazel eyes and hazel-brown hair. Her eyes are of that rare hazel, that soft golden brown, so rarely seen, so beautiful wherever they are seen. These eyes are unvarying in their colour; it is only the expression of them that varies with every emotion, but in repose they have a mournful earnestness in their look, a pensive gravity that seems to tell of a life in which there has been much shadow. The hair, parted above the most beautiful brow I ever looked upon, is of exactly the same colour as the eyes, and has a natural ripple in it. For the rest of the features I must refer my New Zealander to the pictures of the old Italian masters—of which I trust he may retain a handsome collection;— for only on the canvases of Signori Raffaello Sanzio d'Urbino, Titian, and the pupils who emulated them, will he find that exquisite harmony, that purity of form and tender softness of outline, which I beheld that summer evening in the features of Margaret Wentworth.[18]

---

[17] Reference to *The Lady of Lyons* (1838), a romantic drama in five acts by Edward Bulwer, Braddon's literary mentor. When Pauline Deschappelles rejects the marriage proposal of the wealthy and aristocratic Beauséant, he tricks her into marrying Claude Melnotte, the son of a gardener. Melnotte is in love with Pauline and paints her image from memory. He declares to his mother that he "shall never be a painter", an art to which he aspires, because he "can paint no likeness but one, and that is above all art" (Act I, scene III).

[18] Italian painters of the High Renaissance period: Raffaello Sanzio da Urbino (1483-1520), referred to simply as Raphael; Tiziano Vecelli, known as Titian (Birthdate a matter of some controversy. Art historians have variously posited 1473, 1480, and 1490. Titian

"Margaret Wentworth,—that is her name. She told it me presently, when I had explained to her, in some awkward vague manner, who I was, and how it was I wanted to engage her services. Throughout that interview, I think I must have been intoxicated by her presence, as by some subtle and mysterious influence, stronger than the fumes of opium, or the juice of lotus flowers. I only know that after ten minutes' conversation, during which she was perfectly self-possessed, I opened the little garden-gate again, very much embarrassed by the latch on one hand, and my hat on the other, and went back out of that little paradise of twenty feet square into the dusty lane.

"I went home in triumph to my mother, and told her that I had succeeded at last in engaging a lady who was in every way suitable, and that she was coming the following morning at eleven o'clock to give her first lesson. But I was somewhat embarrassed when my mother asked if I had heard the lady play; if I had inquired her terms; if I had asked for references as to respectability, capability, and so forth.

"I was fain to confess, with much confusion, that I had not done any one of these things. And then my mother asked me why, in that case, did I consider the lady suitable,—which question increased my embarrassment by tenfold. I could not say that I had engaged her because her eyes were hazel, and her hair of the same colour; nor could I declare that I had judged of her proficiency as a teacher of the piano by the exquisite line of her pencilled eyebrows. So, in this dilemma, I had recourse to a piece of jesuitry, of which I was not a little proud. I told my dear mother that Miss Wentworth's head was, from a phrenological point of view, magnificent, and that the organs of time and tune were developed to an unusual degree.[19]

"I was almost ashamed of myself when my mother rewarded this falsehood by a kiss, declaring that I was a dear clever boy, and *such* a judge of character, and that she would rather confide in a stranger, upon the strength of my instinct, than, upon any inferior person's experience.

"After this I could only trust to the chance of Miss Wentworth's proficiency; and when I went home from the city upon the following afternoon, my mind was far less occupied with the business events of the day than with abstruse speculations at to the probabilities with regard to that young lady's skill upon the piano-forte. It was with an air of

---

died in 1576).

[19] Phrenology was a pseudo-science, popular in the nineteenth century, which posited that a person's character could be determined by the shape of their head. Phrenologists believed that individual mental faculties were located in specific areas of the brain, and therefore that the shape of the skull acted as a guide to the development of particular faculties.

supreme carelessness that I asked my mother whether she had been pleased with Miss Wentworth.

"'Pleased with her!' cried the good soul; 'why, she plays magnificently, Clement. Such a touch, such brilliancy! In my young days it was only concert-players who played like that; but nowadays girls of eighteen and twenty sit down, and dash away at the keys like a professor. I think you'll be charmed with her, Clem'—(I'm afraid I blushed as my mother said this; had I not been charmed with her already?)—'when you hear her play, for she has expression as well as brilliancy. She is passionately fond of music, I know; not because she went into any ridiculous sentimental raptures about it, as some girls do, but because her eyes lighted up when she told me what a happiness her piano had been to her ever since she was a child. She gave a little sigh after saying that; and I fancied, poor girl, that she had perhaps known very little other happiness.'

"'And her terms, mother?' I said.

"'Oh, you dear commercial Clem, always thinking of terms!' cried my mother.

"Heaven bless her innocent heart! I had asked that sordid question only to hide the unreasoning gladness of my heart. What was it to me that this hazel-eyed girl was engaged to teach my little niece 'Non più mesta'? what was it to me that my breast should be all of a sudden filled with a tumult of glad emotions, and thus shrink from any encounter with my mother's honest eyes?

"'Well, Clem, the terms are almost ridiculously moderate,' my mother said, presently. 'There's only one thing that's at all inconvenient, that is to say, not to me, but I'm afraid *you'll* think it an objection.'

"I eagerly asked the nature of this objection. Was there some cold chill of disappointment in store for me, after all?

"'Well, you see, Clem,' said my mother, with some little hesitation, 'Miss Wentworth is engaged almost all through the day, as her pupils live at long distances from one another, and she has to waste a good deal of time in going backwards and forwards; so the only time she can possibly give Lizzie is either very early in the morning or rather late in the evening. Now *I* should prefer the evening, as I should like to hear the dear child's lessons; but the question is, would *you* object to the noise of the piano while you are at home?'

"'Would I object? Would I object to the music of the spheres? In spite of the grand capabilities for falsehood and hypocrisy which had been developed in my nature since the previous evening, it was as much as I could do to answer my mother's question deliberately, to the effect that I didn't think I should mind the music-lessons *much*.

"'You'll be out generally, you know, Clem,' my mother said.

"'Yes,' I replied, 'of course, if I found the music in any way a nuisance.'

"Coming home from the City the next day, I felt like a schoolboy who turns his back upon all the hardships of his life, on some sunny summer holiday. The rattling Hansom seemed a fairy car, that was bearing me in triumph through a region of brightness and splendour. The sunlit suburban roads were enchanted glades; and I think I should have been scarcely surprised to see Aladdin's jewelled fruit hanging on the trees in the villa gardens, or the gigantic wings of Sinbad's roc[20] overshadowing the hills of Sydenham. A wonderful transformation had changed the earth to fairy land, and it was in vain that I fought against the subtle influence in the air around me.

"Oh, was I in love, was I really in love at last, with a young lady whose face I had only looked upon eight-and-forty hours before? Was I, who had flirted with the Miss Balderbys; and half lost my heart to Lucy Sedwicke, the surgeon's sister; and corresponded for nearly a year with Clara Carpenter, with the sanction of both our houses, and everything *en règle*,[21] only to be jilted ignominiously for the sake of an evangelical curate?—was I, who had railed at the foolish passion—(I have one of Miss Carpenter's long tresses in the desk on which I am writing, sealed in a sheet of letter-paper, with Swift's savage inscription, 'Only a woman's hair,' on the cover)—was I caught at last by a pair of hazel eyes and a Raffaellesque profile?[22] Were the wings that had fluttered in so many flames burnt and maimed by the first breath of this new fire? I was ashamed of my silly fancy in one moment, and proud of my love in the next. I was ten years younger all of a sudden, and my heart was all a-glow with chivalrous devotion for this beautiful stranger. I reasoned with myself, and ridiculed my madness, and yet yielded like the veriest craven to the sweet intoxication. I gave the driver of the Hansom five shillings. Had I not a right to pay him a trifle extra for driving me through fairy-land?

"What had we for dinner that day? I have a vague idea that I ate cherry tart and roast veal, fried soles, boiled custard, and anchovy sauce, all mixed together. I know that the meal seemed to endure for the

---

[20] A huge legendary bird of prey, encountered by Sinbad the Sailor on his fifth voyage. (Persian origin).

[21] Literally meaning "in rule"; everything done in the proper manner, in due order.

[22] Jonathan Swift (1667-1745), satirist and essayist, had a complicated relationship with Esther Johnson (known as "Stella"), beginning in her childhood, when Swift was employed as her tutor, and lasting until her death. After Swift's own death, a lock of hair, presumed to be Stella's, was found in an envelope, inscribed with the words "Only a woman's hair"; Raffaellesque: see footnote 18 above.

abnormal period of half-a-dozen hours or so; and yet it was only seven o'clock when we adjourned to the drawing-room, and Miss Wentworth was not due until half-past seven. My niece was all in a flutter of expectation, and ran out of the drawing-room window every now and then to see if the new governess was coming. She need not have had that trouble, poor child, had I been inclined to give her information; since, from the chair in which I had seated myself to read the evening papers, I could see the road along which Miss Wentworth must come. My eyes wandered very often from the page before me, and fixed themselves upon this dusty suburban road; and presently I saw a parasol, rather a shabby one, and then a slender figure coming quickly towards our gate, and then the face, which I am weak enough to think the most beautiful face in Christendom.

"Since then Miss Wentworth has come three times a week; and somehow or other I have never found myself in any way bored by 'Non più mesta,' or even the major and minor scales, which, as interpreted by a juvenile performer, are not especially enthralling to the ear of the ordinary listener. I read my books or papers, or stroll upon the lawn, while the lesson is going on, and every now and then I hear Margaret's— I really must write of her as Margaret; it is such a nuisance to write Miss Wentworth—pretty voice explaining the importance of a steady position of the wrist, or the dexterous turning over or under of a thumb, or something equally interesting. And then, when the lesson is concluded, my mother rouses herself from her after-dinner nap, and asks Margaret to take a cup of tea, and even insists on her accepting that feminine hospitality. And then we sit talking in the tender summer dusk, or in the subdued light of a shaded lamp on the piano. We talk of books; and it is wonderful to me to find how Margaret's tastes and opinions coincide with mine. Miss Carpenter was stupid about books, and used to call Carlyle nonsensical; and never really enjoyed Dickens half as much as she pretended. I have lent Margaret some of my books; and a little shower of withered rose-leaves dropped from the pages of 'Wilhelm Meister,' after she had returned me the volume.[23] I have put them in an envelope, and sealed it. I may as well burn Miss Carpenter's hair, by the way.

"Though it is only a month since the evening on which I saw the card in the window at Wandsworth, Margaret and I seem to be old friends. After a year Miss Carpenter and I were as far as ever—farther than ever,

---

[23] *Wilhelm Meister's Apprenticeship* (1795-6). Novel by the German author Johann Wolfgang von Goethe, popularly viewed as the archetypal *Bildungsroman*, a "novel of formation or development".

perhaps—from understanding each other; but with Margaret I need no words to tell me that I am understood. A look, a smile, a movement of the graceful head, is a more eloquent answer than the most elaborate of Miss Carpenter's rhapsodies. She was one of those girls whom her friends call 'gushing;' and she called Byron a 'love,' and Shelley an 'angel:' but if you tried her with a stanza that hasn't been done to death in 'Gems of Verse,' or 'Strings of Poetic Pearls,' or 'Drawing-room Table Lyrics,' she couldn't tell whether you were quoting Byron or Ben Jonson. But with Margaret—Margaret,—sweet name! If it were not that I live in perpetual terror of the day when the dilettante New Zealander will edit this manuscript, I think I should write that lovely name over and over again for a page or so. If the New Zealander should exercise his editorial discretion, and delete my raptures, it wouldn't matter; but I might furnish him with the text for an elaborate disquisition on the manners and customs of English lovers. Let me be reasonable about my dear love, if I can. My dear love—do I dare to call her that already, when, for anything I know to the contrary, there may be another evangelical curate in the background?

"We seem to be old friends; and yet I know so little of her. She shuns all allusion to her home or her past history. Now and then she has spoken of her father; always tenderly, but always with a sigh; and I fancy that a deepening shadow steals over her face when she mentions that name.

"Friendly as we are, I can never induce her to let me see her home, though my mother has suggested that I should do so. She is accustomed to go about by herself, she says, after dark, as well as in the daytime. She seems as fearless as a modern Una; and that would indeed be a savage beast which could molest such a pure and lovely creature."[24]

---

[24] In Book I of Edmund Spenser's *The Faerie Queene* (1590), Una travels with the Red-crosse Knight on a quest to save her parents from a dragon. She is representative of Truth. Braddon's reference to the "savage beast" probably alludes to the episode in which Una encounters a fierce lion. The lion is subdued by Una's innocence and beauty and relinquishes his intention to harm her, becoming instead her protector. Many of Braddon's readers may have been familiar with William Bell Scott's painting "Una and the Lion", which was exhibited in 1860.

- CHAPTER 7 -

AFTER FIVE-AND-THIRTY YEARS

Joseph Wilmot waited patiently enough, in all outward seeming, for the arrival of the steamer. Everybody was respectful to him now, paying deference to his altered guise, and he went where he liked without question or hindrance.

There were several people waiting for passengers who were expected to arrive by the *Electra*, and the coming of the steamer was hailed by a feeble cheer from the bystanders grouped about the landing-place.

The passengers began to come on shore at about eleven o'clock. There were a good many children and English nursemaids; three or four military-looking men, dressed in loose garments of grey and nankeen colour; several ladies, all more or less sunburnt; a couple of ayahs;[25] three men-servants; and an aristocratic-looking man of about fifty-five, dressed, unlike the rest of the travellers, in fine broadcloth, with a black-satin cravat, a gold pin, a carefully brushed hat, and varnished boots.

His clothes, in fact, were very much of the same fashion as those which Joseph Wilmot had chosen for himself.

This man was Henry Dunbar; tall and broad-chested, with grey hair and moustache, and with a haughty smile upon his handsome face.

Joseph Wilmot stood among the little crowd, motionless as a statue, watching his old betrayer.

"Not much changed," he murmured; "very little changed! Proud, and selfish, and cruel then—proud, and selfish, and cruel now. He has grown older, and stouter, and greyer; but he is the same man he was five-and-thirty years ago. I can see it all in his face."

He advanced as Henry Dunbar landed, and approached the Anglo-Indian.

"Mr. Dunbar, I believe?" he said, removing his hat.

"Yes, I am Mr. Dunbar."

"I have been sent from the office in St. Gundolph Lane, sir," returned Joseph; "I have a letter for you from Mr. Balderby. I came to meet you, and to be of service to you."

Henry Dunbar looked at him doubtfully.

"You are not one of the clerks in St. Gundolph Lane?" he said.

"No, Mr. Dunbar."

---

[25] Ayahs were Indian nurses hired by British colonialists in India to care for their children.

"I thought as much; you don't look like a clerk; but who are you, then?"

"I will tell you presently, sir. I am a substitute for another person, who was taken ill upon the road. But there is no time to speak of that now. I came to be of use to you. Shall I see after your luggage?"

"Yes, I shall be glad if you will do so."

"You have a servant with you, Mr. Dunbar?"

"No, my valet was taken ill at Malta, and I left him behind."

"Indeed!" exclaimed Joseph Wilmot; "that was a misfortune."

A sudden flash of light sparkled in his eyes as he spoke.

"Yes, it was devilish provoking. You'll find the luggage packed, and directed to Portland Place; be so good as to see that it is sent off immediately by the speediest route. There is a portmanteau in my cabin, and my travelling-desk. I require those with me. All the rest can go on."

"I will see to it, sir."

"Thank you; you are very good. At what hotel are you staying?"

"I have not been to any hotel yet. I only arrived this morning. The *Electra* was not expected until to-morrow."

"I will go on to the Dolphin, then," returned Mr. Dunbar; "and I shall be glad if you will follow me directly you have attended to the luggage. I want to get to London to-night, if possible."

Henry Dunbar walked away, holding his head high in the air, and swinging his cane as he went. He was one of those men who most confidently believe in their own merits. The sin he had committed in his youth sat very lightly upon his conscience. If he thought about that old story at all, it was only to remember that he had been very badly used by his father and his Uncle Hugh.

And the poor wretch who had helped him—the clever, bright-faced, high-spirited lad who had acted as his tool and accomplice—was as completely forgotten as if he had never existed.

Mr. Dunbar was ushered into a great sunny sitting-room at the Dolphin; a vast desert of Brussels carpet, with little islands of chairs and tables scattered here and there. He ordered a bottle of soda-water, sank into an easy-chair, and took up the *Times* newspaper.

But presently he threw it down impatiently, and took his watch from his waistcoat-pocket.

Attached to the watch there was a locket of chased yellow gold. Henry Dunbar opened this locket, which contained the miniature of a beautiful girl, with fair rippling hair as bright as burnished gold, and limpid blue eyes.

"My poor little Laura!" he murmured; "I wonder whether she will be glad to see me. She was a mere baby when she left India. It isn't likely she'll remember me. But I hope she may be glad of my coming back—I hope she may be glad."

He put the locket again in its place, and took a letter from his breast-pocket. It was directed in a woman's hand, and the envelope was surrounded by a deep border of black.

"If there's any faith to be put in this, she will be glad to have me home at last," Henry Dunbar said, as he drew the letter out of its envelope.

He read one passage softly to himself.

"If anything can console me for the loss of my dear grandfather, it is the thought that you will come back at last, and that I shall see you once more. You can never know, dearest father, what a bitter sorrow this cruel separation has been to me. It has seemed so hard that we who are so rich should have been parted as we have been, while poor children have their fathers with them. Money seems such a small thing when it cannot bring us the presence of those we love. And I do love you, dear papa, truly and devotedly, though I cannot even remember your face, and have not so much as a picture of you to recall you to my recollection."

The letter was a very long one, and Henry Dunbar was still reading it when Joseph Wilmot came into the room.

The Anglo-Indian crushed the letter into his pocket, and looked up languidly.

"Have you seen to all that?" he asked.

"Yes, Mr. Dunbar; the luggage has been sent off."

Joseph Wilmot had not yet removed his hat. He had rather an undecided manner, and walked once or twice up and down the room, stopping now and then, and then walking on again, in an unsettled way; like a man who has some purpose in his mind, yet is oppressed by a feverish irresolution as to the performance of that purpose.

But Mr. Dunbar took no notice of this. He sat with the newspaper in his hand, and did not deign to lift his eyes to his companion, after that first brief question. He was accustomed to be waited upon, and to look upon the people who served him as beings of an inferior class: and he had no idea of troubling himself about this gentlemanly-looking clerk from St. Gundolph Lane.

Joseph Wilmot stopped suddenly upon the other side of the table, near which Mr. Dunbar sat, and, laying his hand upon it, said quietly—

"You asked me just now who I was, Mr. Dunbar."

The banker looked up at him with haughty indifference.

"Did I? Oh, yea, I remember; and you told me you came from the office. That is quite enough."

"Pardon me, Mr. Dunbar, it is not quite enough. You are mistaken: I

52

did not say I came from the office in St. Gundolph Lane. I told you, on the contrary, that I came here as a substitute for another person, who was ordered to meet you."

"Indeed! That is pretty much the same thing. You seem a very agreeable fellow, and will, no doubt, be quite as useful as the original person could have been. It was very civil of Mr. Balderby to send some one to meet me—very civil indeed."

The Anglo-Indian's head sank back upon the morocco cushion of the easy-chair, and he looked languidly at his companion, with half-closed eyes.

Joseph Wilmot removed his hat.

"I don't think you've looked at me very closely, have you, Mr. Dunbar?" he said.

"Have I looked at you closely!" exclaimed the banker. "My good fellow, what do you mean?"

"Look me full in the face, Mr. Dunbar, and tell me if you see anything there that reminds you of the past."

Henry Dunbar started.

He opened his eyes widely enough this time, and started at the handsome face before him. It was as handsome as his own, and almost as aristocratic-looking. For Nature has odd caprices now and then, and had made very little distinction between the banker, who was worth half a million, and the runaway convict, who was not worth sixpence.

"Have I met you before?" he said. "In India?"

"No, Mr. Dunbar, not in India. You know that as well as I do. Carry your mind farther back. Carry it back to the time before you went to India."

"What then?"

"Do you remember losing a heap of money on the Derby, and being in so desperate a frame of mind that you took the holster-pistols down from their place above the chimney-piece in your barrack sitting-room, and threatened to blow your brains out? Do you remember, in your despair, appealing to a lad who served you, and who loved you, better perhaps than a brother would have loved you, though he *was* your inferior by birth and station, and the son of a poor, hard-working woman? Do you remember entreating this boy—who had a knack of counterfeiting other people's signatures, but who had never used his talent for any guilty purpose until that hour, so help me Heaven!—to aid you in a scheme by which your creditors were to be kept quiet till you could get the money to pay them? Do you remember all this? Yes, I see you do—the answer is written on your face; and you remember me—Joseph Wilmot."

53

He struck his hand upon his breast, and stood with his eyes fixed upon the other's face. They had a strange expression in them, those eyes—a sort of hungry, eager look, as if the very sight of his old foe was a kind of food that went some way towards satisfying this man's vengeful fury.

"I do remember you," Henry Dunbar said slowly. He had turned deadly pale, and cold drops of sweat had broken out upon his forehead: he wiped them away with his perfumed cambric handkerchief as he spoke.

"You do remember me?" the other man repeated, with no change in the expression of his face.

"I do; and, believe me, I am heartily sorry for the past. I dare say you fancy I acted cruelly towards you on that wretched day in St. Gundolph Lane; but I really could scarcely act otherwise. I was so harassed and tormented by my own position, that I could not be expected to get myself deeper into the mire by interceding for you. However, now that I am my own master, I can make it up to you. Rely upon it, my good fellow, I'll atone for the past."

"Atone for the past!" cried Joseph Wilmot. "Can you make me an honest man, or a respectable member of society? Can you remove the stamp of the felon from me, and win for me the position I *might* have held in this hard world but for you? Can you give me back the five-and-thirty blighted years of my life, and take the blight from them? Can you heal my mother's broken heart,—broken, long ago by my disgrace? Can you give me back the dead? Or can you give me pleasant memories, or peaceful thoughts, or the hope of God's forgiveness? No, no; you can give me none of these."

Mr. Henry Dunbar was essentially a man of the world. He was not a passionate man. He was a gentlemanly creature, very seldom demonstrative in his manner, and he wished to take life pleasantly.

He was utterly selfish and heartless. But as he was very rich, people readily overlooked such small failings as selfishness and want of heart, and were loud in praise of the graces of his manner and the elegance of his person.

"My dear Wilmot," he said, in no wise startled by the vehemence of his companion, "all that is so much sentimental talk. Of course I can't give you back the past. The past was your own, and you might have fashioned it as you pleased. If you went wrong, you have no right to throw the blame of your wrong-doing upon me. Pray don't talk about broken hearts, and blighted lives, and all that sort of thing. I'm a man of the world, and I can appreciate the exact value of that kind of twaddle. I am sorry for the scrape I got you into, and am ready to do anything reasonable to atone for that old business. I can't give you back the past; but I can give you that for which most men are ready to barter past, present, and future,—I can give you money."

"How much?" asked Joseph Wilmot, with a half-suppressed fierceness in his manner.

"Humph!" murmured the Anglo-Indian, pulling his grey moustaches with a reflective air. "Let me see; what would satisfy you, now, my good fellow?"

"I leave that for you to decide."

"Very well, then. I suppose you'd be quite contented if I were to buy you a small annuity, that would keep you straight with the world for the rest of your life. Say, fifty pounds a year."

"Fifty pounds a year," Joseph Wilmot repeated. He had quite conquered that fierceness of expression by this time, and spoke very quietly. "Fifty pounds a year—a pound a week."

"Yes."

"I'll accept your offer, Mr. Dunbar. A pound a week. That will enable me to live—to live as labouring men live, in some hovel or other; and will insure me bread every day. I have a daughter, a very beautiful girl, about the same age as your daughter: and, of course, she'll share my income with me, and will have as much cause to bless your generosity as I shall have."

"It's a bargain, then?" asked the East Indian, languidly.

"Oh, yes, it's a bargain. You have estates in Warwickshire and Yorkshire, a house in Portland Place, and half a million of money; but, of course, all those things are necessary to you. I shall have—thanks to your generosity, and as an atonement for all the shame and misery, the want, and peril, and disgrace, which I have suffered for five-and-thirty years—a pound a week secured to me for the rest of my life. A thousand thanks, Mr. Dunbar. You are your own self still, I find; the same master I loved when I was a boy; and I accept your generous offer."

He laughed as he finished speaking, loudly but not heartily—rather strangely, perhaps; but Mr. Dunbar did not trouble himself to notice any such insignificant fact as the merriment of his old valet.

"Now we have done with all these heroics," he said, "perhaps you'll be good enough to order luncheon for me."

- CHAPTER 8 -

THE FIRST STAGE ON THE JOURNEY HOME

Joseph Wilmot obeyed his old master, and ordered a very excellent luncheon, which was served in the best style of the Dolphin; and a sojourn at the Dolphin is almost a recompense for the pains and penalties of the voyage home from India. Mr. Dunbar, from the sublime height of his own grandeur, stooped to be very friendly with his old valet, and insisted upon Joseph's sitting down with him at the well-spread table. But although the Anglo-Indian did ample justice to the luncheon, and washed down a spatchcock and a lobster-salad with several glasses of iced Moselle, the reprobate ate and drank very little, and sat for the best part of the time crumbling his bread in a strange absent manner, and watching his companion's face. He only spoke when his old master addressed him; and then in a constrained, half-mechanical way, which might have excited the wonder of any one less supremely indifferent than Henry Dunbar to the feelings of his fellow-creatures.

The Anglo-Indian finished his luncheon, left the table, and walked to the window: but Joseph Wilmot still sat with a full glass before him.

The sparkling bubbles had vanished from the clear amber wine; but although Moselle at half-a-guinea a bottle could scarcely have been a very common beverage to the ex-convict, he seemed to have no appreciation of the vintage. He sat with his head bent and his elbow on his knee; brooding, brooding, brooding.

Henry Dunbar amused himself for about ten minutes looking out at the busy street—the brightest, airiest, lightest, prettiest High Street in all England, perhaps; and then turned away from the window and looked at his old valet. He had been accustomed, five-and-thirty years ago, to be familiar with the man, and to make a confidant and companion of him, and he fell into the same manner now, naturally; as if the five-and-thirty years had never been; as if Joseph Wilmot had never been wronged by him. He fell into the old way, and treated his companion with that haughty affability which a monarch may be supposed to exhibit towards his prime favourite.

"Drink your wine, Wilmot," he exclaimed; "don't sit meditating there, as if you were a great speculator brooding over the stagnation of the money-market. I want bright looks, man, to welcome me back to my native country. I've seen dark faces enough out yonder; and I want to see smiling and pleasanter faces here. You look as black as if you had committed a murder, or were plotting one."

The Outcast smiled.

"I've so much reason to look cheerful, haven't I?" he said, in the same tone he had used when he had declared his acceptance of the banker's bounty. "I've such a pleasant life before me, and such agreeable recollections to look back upon. A man's memory seems to me like a book of pictures that he must be continually looking at, whether he will or not: and if the pictures are horrible, if he shudders as he looks at them, if the sight of them is worse than the pain of death to him, he must look nevertheless. I read a story the other day—at least my girl was reading it to me; poor child! she tries to soften me with these things sometimes— and the man who wrote the story said it was well for the most miserable of us to pray, 'Lord, keep my memory green!'[26] But what if the memory is a record of crime, Mr. Dunbar? Can we pray that *those* memories may be kept green? Wouldn't it be better to pray that our brains and hearts may wither, leaving us no power to look back upon the past? If I could have forgotten the wrong you did me five-and-thirty years ago, I might have been a different man: but I couldn't forget it. Every day and every hour I have remembered it. My memory is as fresh to-day as it was four-and-thirty years ago, when my wrongs were only a twelvemonth old."

Joseph Wilmot had said all this almost as if he yielded to an un-controllable impulse, and spoke because he must speak, rather than from the desire to upbraid Henry Dunbar. He had not looked at the Anglo-Indian; he had not changed his attitude; he had spoken with his head still bent, and his eyes fixed upon the ground.

Mr. Dunbar had gone back to the window, and had resumed his contemplation of the street; but he turned round with a gesture of angry impatience as Joseph Wilmot finished speaking.

"Now, listen to me, Wilmot," he said. "If the firm in St. Gundolph Lane sent you down here to annoy and insult me directly I set foot upon British ground, they have chosen a very nice way of testifying their respect for their chief: and they have made a mistake which they shall repent having made sooner or later. If you came here upon your own account, with a view to terrify me, or to extort money from me, you have made a mistake. If you think to make a fool of me by any maudlin sentimentality, you make a still greater mistake. I give you fair warning. If you expect any advantage from me, you must make yourself agreeable to me. I am a rich man, and know how to recompense those who please me: but I will not be bored or tormented by any man alive: least of all by

---

[26] From Charles Dickens's novella, *The Haunted Man and the Ghost's Bargain* (1848). The last of Dickens's Christmas books.

you. If you choose to make yourself useful, you can stay: if you don't choose to do so, the sooner you leave this room the better for yourself, if you wish to escape the humiliation of being turned out by the waiter."

At the end of this speech Joseph Wilmot looked up for the first time. He was very pale, and there were strange hard lines about his compressed lips, and a new light in his eyes.

"I am a poor weak fool," he said, quietly; "very weak and very foolish, when I think there can be anything in that old story to touch your heart, Mr. Dunbar. I will not offend you again, believe me. I have not led a very sober life of late years: I've had a touch of *delirium tremens*,[27] and my nerves are not as strong as they used to be: but I'll not annoy you again. I'm quite ready to make myself useful in any way you may require."

"Get me a time-table, then, and let's see about the trains. I don't want to stay in Southampton all day."

Joseph Wilmot rang, and ordered the time-table; Henry Dunbar studied it.

"There is no express before ten o'clock at night," he said; "and I don't care about travelling by a slow train. What am I to do with myself in the interim?"

He was silent for a few moments, turning over the leaves of Bradshaw's Guide, and thinking.[28]

"How far is it from here to Winchester?" he asked presently.

"Ten miles, or thereabouts, I believe," Joseph answered.

"Ten miles! Very well, then, Wilmot, I'll tell you what I'll do. I've a friend in the neighbourhood of Winchester, an old college companion, a man who has a fine estate in Hampshire, and a house near St. Cross. If you'll order a carriage and pair to be got ready immediately, we'll drive over to Winchester. I'll go and see my old friend Michael Marston; we'll dine at the George, and go up to London by the express which leaves Winchester at a quarter past ten. Go and order the carriage, and lose no time about it, that's a good fellow."

Half an hour after this the two men left Southampton in an open

---

[27] *Delirium tremens* is a condition brought on by withdrawal from alcohol, where a person habitually consumes to excess. Symptoms typically include disorientation, confusion, and uncontrollable tremors. The condition appears extensively in Braddon's novels, for instance in *Eleanor's Victory* (1863), *The Golden Calf* (1883), and *Cut by the County* (1886), to name but a few.

[28] *Bradshaw's Railway Time Tables and Assistant to Railway Travelling* and, after 1840, *Bradshaw's Railway Companion*, was the world's first compilation of railway timetables. After 1841 it was issued monthly and cost sixpence. Throughout the Victorian period, and for most of the Edwardian period too, "Bradshaw" became the standard term for a railway timetable, regardless of the publisher.

carriage, with the banker's portmanteau, dressing-case, and despatch-box, and Joseph Wilmot's carpet-bag. It was three o'clock when the carriage drove away from the entrance of the Dolphin Hotel: it wanted five minutes to four when Mr. Dunbar and his companion entered the handsome hall of the George.

Throughout the drive the banker had been in very excellent spirits, smoking cheroots, and admiring the lovely English landscape, the spreading pastures, the glimpses of woodland, the hills beyond the grey cathedral city, purple in the distance.

He had talked a good deal, making himself very familiar with his humble friend. But he had not talked so much or so loudly as Joseph Wilmot. All gloomy memories seemed to have melted away from this man's mind. His former moody silence had been succeeded by a manner that was almost unnaturally gay. A close observer would have detected that his laugh was a little forced, his loudest merriment wanting in geniality: but Henry Dunbar was not a close observer. People in Calcutta, who courted and admired the rich banker, had been wont to praise the aristocratic ease of his manner, which was not often disturbed by any vulgar demonstration of his own emotions, and very rarely ruffled by any sympathy with the joys, or pity for the sorrows, of his fellow-creatures.

His companion's ready wit and knowledge of the world—the very worst part of the world, unhappily—amused the languid Anglo-Indian: and by the time the travellers reached Winchester, they were on excellent terms with each other. Joseph Wilmot was thoroughly at home with his patron; and as the two men were dressed in the same fashion, and had pretty much the same nonchalance of manner, it would have been very difficult for a stranger to have discovered which was the servant and which the master.

One of them ordered dinner for eight o'clock, the best dinner the house could provide. The luggage was taken up to a private room, and the two men walked away from the hotel arm-in-arm.

They walked under the shadow of a low stone colonnade, and then turned aside by the market-place, and made their way into the precincts of the cathedral. There are quaint old courtyards, and shadowy quad-rangles hereabouts; there are pleasant gardens, where the flowers seem to grow brighter in the sanctified shade than other flowers that flaunt in the unhallowed sunshine. There are low old-fashioned houses, with Tudor windows and ponderous porches, grey gables crowned with yellow stone-moss, high garden-walls, queer nooks and corners, deep window-seats in painted oriels, great oaken beams supporting low dark ceilings, heavy clusters of chimneys half borne down by the weight of the ivy that clings about them; and over all, the shadow of the great cathedral broods, like a sheltering wing, preserving the cool quiet of these cosy sanctuaries.

Beyond this holy shelter fair pastures stretch away to the feet of the grassy hills: and a winding stream of water wanders in and out: now hiding in dim groves of spreading elms: now creeping from the darkness, with a murmuring voice and stealthy gliding motion, to change its very nature, and become the noisiest brook that ever babbled over sunlit pebbles on its way to the blue sea.

In one of the grey stone quadrangles close under the cathedral wall, the two men, still arm-in-arm, stopped to make an inquiry about Mr. Michael Marston, of the Ferns, St. Cross.

Alas! Ben Bolt, it is a fine thing to sail away to foreign shores and prosper there; but it is not so pleasant to come home and hear that Alice is dead and buried; that of all your old companions there is only one left to greet you; and that even the brook, which rippled through your boyish dreams, as you lay asleep amongst the rushes on its brink, has dried up for ever![29]

Mr. Michael Marston had been dead more than ten, years. His widow, an elderly lady, was still living at the Ferns.

This was the information which the two men obtained from a verger, whom they found prowling about the quadrangle. Very little was said. One of the men asked the necessary questions. But neither of them expressed either regret or surprise.

They walked away silently, still arm-in-arm, towards the shady groves and spreading pastures beyond the cathedral precincts.

The verger, who was elderly and slow, called after them in a feeble voice as they went away:

"Maybe you'd like to see the cathedral, gentlemen; it's well worth seeing."

But he received no answer. The two men were out of hearing, or did not care to reply to him.

"We'll take a stroll towards St. Cross, and get an appetite for dinner," Mr. Dunbar said, as he and his companion walked along a pathway, under the shadow of a moss-grown wall, across a patch of meadow-land, and away into the holy quiet of a grove.

A serene stillness reigned beneath the shelter of the spreading branches. The winding streamlet rippled along amidst wild flowers and trembling rushes; the ground beneath the feet of these two idle wanderers was a soft bed of moss and rarely-trodden grass.

---

[29] *Ben Bolt* (1842) was a poem by Thomas Dunn English. It was set to music by the American composer Nelson Kneass, achieving great popularity as a song and spawning many parodies.

It was a lonely place this grove; for it lay between the meadows and the high-road. Feeble old pensioners from St. Cross came here sometimes, but not often. Enthusiastic disciples of old Izaak Walton now and then invaded the holy quiet of the place: but not often.[30] The loveliest spots on earth are those where man seldom comes.

This spot was most lovely because of its solitude. Only the gentle waving of the leaves, the long melodious note of a lonely bird, and the low whisper of the streamlet, broke the silence.

The two men went into the grove arm-in-arm. One of them was talking, the other listening, and smoking a cigar as he listened. They went into the long arcade beneath the over-arching trees, and the sombre shadows closed about them and hid them from the world.

- CHAPTER 9 -

HOW HENRY DUNBAR WAITED DINNER

The old verger was still pottering about the grey quadrangle, sunning himself in such glimpses of the glorious light as found their way into that shadowy place, when one of the two gentlemen who had spoken to him returned. He was smoking a cigar, and swinging his gold-headed cane lightly as he came along.

"You may as well show me the cathedral," he said to the verger; "I shouldn't like to leave Winchester without having seen it; that is to say without having seen it again. I was here forty years ago, when I was a boy; but I have been in India five-and-thirty years, and have seen nothing but Pagan temples."

"And very beautiful them Pagan places be, sir, bain't they?" the old man asked, as he unlocked a low door, leading into one of the side aisles of the cathedral.

"Oh yes, very magnificent, of course. But as I was not a soldier, and had no opportunity of handling any of the magnificence in the way of diamonds and so forth, I didn't particularly care about them."

They were in the shadowy aisle by this time, and Mr. Dunbar was looking about him with his hat in his hand.

"You didn't go on to the Ferns, then, sir?" said the verger.

"No, I sent my servant on to inquire if the old lady is at home. If I find that she is, I shall sleep in Winchester to-night, and drive over to-

---

[30] Izaak Walton (1593-1683), author of *The Compleat Angler* (1653). Braddon's reference suggests that the only visitors to the place are fishermen.

morrow morning to see her. Her husband was a very old friend of mine. How far is it from here to the Ferns?"

"A matter of two mile, sir."

Mr. Dunbar looked at his watch.

"Then my man ought to be back in an hour's time," he said; "I told him to come on to me here. I left him half-way between here and St. Cross."

"Is that other gentleman your servant, sir?" asked the verger, with unmitigated surprise.

"Yes, that gentleman, as you call him, is, or rather was, my confidential servant. He is a clever fellow, and I make a companion of him. Now, if you please, we will see the chapels."

Mr. Dunbar evidently desired to put a stop to the garrulous inclinations of the verger.

He walked through the aisle with a careless easy step, and with his head erect, looking about him as he went along: but presently, while the verger was busy unlocking the door of one of the chapels, Mr. Dunbar suddenly reeled like a drunken man, and then dropped heavily upon an oaken bench near the chapel-door.

The verger turned to look at him, and found him wiping the perspiration from his forehead with his perfumed silk handkerchief.

"Don't be alarmed," he said, smiling at the man's scared face; "my Indian habits have unfitted me for any exertion. The walk in the broiling afternoon sun has knocked me up: or perhaps the wine I drank at Southampton may have had something to do with it," he added, with a laugh.

The verger ventured to laugh too: and the laughter of the two men echoed harshly through the solemn place.

For more than an hour Mr. Dunbar amused himself by inspecting the cathedral. He was eager to see everything, and to know the meaning of everything. He peered into every nook and corner, going from monument to monument with the patient talkative old verger at his heels; asking questions about every thing he saw; trying to decipher half-obliterated inscriptions upon long-forgotten tombs; sounding the praises of William of Wykeham;[31] admiring the splendid shrines, the sanctified relics of the past, with the delight of a scholar and an antiquarian.

The old verger thought that he had never had so pleasant a task as that of exhibiting his beloved cathedral to this delightful gentleman, just returned from India, and ready to admire everything belonging to his

---

[31] William of Wykeham, Bishop of Winchester and Chancellor of England (1320-1404). Founded Winchester College and New College, Oxford.

native land.

The verger was still better pleased when Mr. Dunbar gave him half a sovereign as the reward for his afternoon's trouble.

"Thank you, sir, and kindly, to be sure," the old man cackled, gratefully. "It's very seldom as I get gold for my trouble, sir. I've shown this cathedral to a dook, sir; but the dook didn't treat me as liberal as this here, sir."

Mr. Dunbar smiled.

"Perhaps not," he said; "the duke mightn't have been as rich a man as I am in spite of his dukedom."

"No, to be sure, sir," the old man answered, looking admiringly at the banker, and sighing plaintively. "It's well to be rich, sir, it is indeed; and when one have twelve grand-children, and a bed-ridden wife, one finds it hard, sir; one do indeed."

Perhaps the verger had faint hopes of another half sovereign from this very rich gentleman.

But Mr. Dunbar seated himself upon a bench near the low doorway by which he had entered the cathedral, and looked at his watch.

The verger looked at the watch too; it was a hundred-guinea chronometer, a masterpiece of Benson's workmanship; [32] and Mr. Dunbar's arms were emblazoned upon the back. There was a locket attached to the massive gold chain, the locket which contained Laura Dunbar's miniature.

"Seven o'clock," exclaimed the banker; "my servant ought to be here by this time."

"So he ought, sir," said the verger, who was ready to agree to anything Mr. Dunbar might say; "if he had only to go to the Ferns, sir, he might have been back by this time easy."

"I'll smoke a cheroot while I wait for him," the banker said, passing out into the quadrangle; "he's sure to come to this door to look for me—I gave him particular orders to do so."

Henry Dunbar finished his cheroot, and another, and the cathedral clock chimed the three-quarters after seven, but Joseph Wilmot had not come back from the Ferns. The verger waited upon his patron's pleasure, and lingered in attendance upon him, though he would fain have gone home to his tea, which in the common course he would have taken at five o'clock.

"Really this is too bad," cried the banker, as the clock chimed the three-quarters; "Wilmot knows that I dine at eight, and that I expect him

---

[32] J. W. Benson of Ludgate Hill, London, established in 1837, were watchmakers to Queen Victoria and the Admiralty.

to dine with me. I think I have a right to a little more consideration from him. I shall go back to the George. Perhaps you'll be good enough to wait here, and tell him to follow me."

Mr. Dunbar went away, still muttering, and the verger gave up all thoughts of his tea, and waited conscientiously. He waited till the cathedral clock struck nine, and the stars were bright in the dark blue heaven above him: but he waited in vain. Joseph Wilmot had not come back from the Ferns.

The banker returned to the George. A small round table was set in a pleasant room on the first floor; a bright array of glass and silver glittered under the light of five wax-candles in a silver candelabrum; and the waiter was beginning to be nervous about the fish.

"You may countermand the dinner," Mr. Dunbar said, with evident vexation: "I shall not dine till Mr. Wilmot, who is my old confidential servant—my friend, I may say—returns."

"Has he gone far, sir?"

"To the Ferns, about a mile beyond St. Cross. I shall wait dinner for him. Put a couple of candles on that writing-table, and bring me my desk."

The waiter obeyed; he placed a pair of tall wax-candles upon the table; and then brought the desk, or rather despatch-box, which had cost forty pounds, and was provided with every possible convenience for a business man, and every elegant luxury that the most extravagant traveller could desire. It was like everything else about this man: it bore upon it the stamp of almost limitless wealth.

Mr. Dunbar took a bunch of keys from his pocket, and unlocked his despatch-box. He was some little time doing this, as he had a difficulty in finding the right key. He looked up and smiled at the waiter, who was still hovering about, anxious to be useful.

"I *must* have taken too much Moselle at luncheon to-day," he said, laughing, "or, at least, my enemies might say so, if they were to see me puzzled to find the key of my own desk."

He had opened the box by this time, and was examining one of the numerous packets of papers, which were arranged in very methodical order, carefully tied together, and neatly endorsed.

"I am to put off the dinner, then, sir?" asked the waiter.

"Certainly; I shall wait for my friend, however long he may be. I'm not particularly hungry, for I took a very substantial luncheon at Southampton. I'll ring the bell if I change my mind."

The waiter departed with a sigh; and Henry Dunbar was left alone with the contents of the open despatch-box spread out on the table before him under the light of the tall wax-candles.

For nearly two hours he sat in the same attitude, examining the papers one after the other, and re-sorting them.

Mr. Dunbar must have been possessed of the very spirit of order and precision; for, although the papers had been neatly arranged before, he re-sorted every one of them; tying up the packets afresh, reading letter after letter, and making pencil memoranda in his pocket-book as he did so.

He betrayed none of the impatience which is natural to a man who is kept waiting by another. He was so completely absorbed by his occupation that he, perhaps, had forgotten all about the missing man: but at nine o'clock he closed and locked the despatch-box, jumped up from his seat and rang the bell.

"I am beginning to feel alarmed about my friend," he said; "will you ask the landlord to come to me?"

Mr. Dunbar went to the window and looked out while the waiter was gone upon this errand. The High Street was very quiet, a lamp glimmered here and there, and the pavements were white in the moonlight. The footstep of a passer-by sounded in the quiet street almost as it might have sounded in the solemn cathedral aisle.

The landlord came to wait upon his guest.

"Can I be of any service to you, sir?" he asked, respectfully.

"You can be of very great service to me, if you can find my friend; I am really getting alarmed about him."

Mr. Dunbar went on to say how he had parted with the missing man in the grove, on the way to St. Cross, with the understanding that Wilmot was to go on to the Ferns, and rejoin his old master in the cathedral. He explained who Joseph Wilmot was, and in what relation he stood towards him.

"I don't suppose there is any real cause for anxiety," the banker said, in conclusion; "Wilmot owned to me that he had not been leading a sober life of late years. He may have dropped into some roadside public-house and be sitting boozing amongst a lot of country fellows at this moment. It's really too bad of him."

The landlord shook his head.

"It is, indeed, sir; but I hope you won't wait dinner any longer, sir?"

"No, no; you can send up the dinner. I'm afraid I shall scarcely do justice to your cook's achievements, for I took a very substantial luncheon at Southampton."

The landlord brought in the silver soup-tureen with his own hands, and uncorked a bottle of still hock, which Mr. Dunbar had selected from the wine-list. There was something in the banker's manner that declared him to be a person of no small importance; and the proprietor of the

George wished to do him honour.

Mr. Dunbar had spoken the truth as to his appetite for his dinner. He took a few spoonfuls of soup, he ate two or three mouthfuls of fish, and then pushed away his plate.

"It's no use," he said, rising suddenly, and walking to the window; "I am really uneasy about this fellow's absence."

He walked up and down the room two or three times, and then walked back to the open window. The August night was hot and still; the shadows of the queer old gabled roofs were sharply defined upon the moonlit pavement. The quaint cross, the low stone colonnade, the solemn towers of the cathedral, gave an ancient aspect to the quiet city.

The cathedral clock chimed the half-hour after nine while Mr. Dunbar stood at the open window looking out into the street.

"I shall sleep here to-night," he said presently, without turning to look at the landlord, who was standing behind him. "I shall not leave Winchester without this fellow Wilmot. It is really too bad of him to treat me in this manner. It is really very much too bad of him, taking into consideration the position in which he stands towards me."

The banker spoke with the offended tone of a proud and selfish man, who feels that he has been outraged by his inferior. The landlord of the George murmured a few stereotyped phrases, expressive of his sympathy with the wrongs of Henry Dunbar, and his entire reprobation of the missing man's conduct.

"No, I shall not go to London to-night," Mr. Dunbar said; "though my daughter, my only child, whom I have not seen for sixteen years, is waiting for me at my town house. I shall not leave Winchester without Joseph Wilmot."

"I'm sure it's very good of you, sir," the landlord murmured; "it's very kind of you to think so much of this—ahem—person."

He had hesitated a little before the last word; for although Mr. Dunbar spoke of Joseph Wilmot as his inferior and dependant, the landlord of the George remembered that the missing man had looked quite as much a gentleman as his companion.

The landlord still lingered in attendance upon Mr. Dunbar. The dishes upon the table were still hidden under the glistening silver covers.

Surely such an unsatisfactory dinner had never before been served at the George Hotel.

"I am getting seriously uncomfortable about this man," Mr. Dunbar exclaimed at last. "Can you send a messenger to the Ferns, to ask if he has been seen there?"

"Certainly, sir. One of the lads in the stable shall get a horse ready, and ride over there directly. Will you write a note to Mrs. Marston, sir?"

"A note? No. Mrs. Marston is a stranger to me. My old friend Michael Marston did not marry until after I left England. A message will do just as well. The lad has only to ask if any messenger from Mr. Dunbar has called at the Ferns; and if so, at what time he was there, and at what hour he left. That's all I want to know. Which way will the boy go; through the meadows, or by the high road?"

"By the high road, sir; there's only a footpath across the meadows. The shortest way to the Ferns is the pathway through the grove between here and St. Cross; but you can only walk that way, for there's gates and stiles, and such like."

"Yes, I know; it was there I parted from my servant—from this man Wilmot."

"It's a pretty spot, sir, but very lonely at night; lonely enough in the day, for the matter of that."

"Yes, it seems so. Send your messenger off at once, there's a good fellow. Joseph Wilmot may be sitting drinking in the servants' hall at the Ferns."

The landlord went away to do his guest's bidding.

Mr. Dunbar flung himself into a low easy-chair, and took up a newspaper. But he did not read a line upon the page before him. He was in that unsettled frame of mind which is common to the least nervous persons when they are kept waiting, kept in suspense by some unaccountable event. The absence of Joseph Wilmot became every moment more unaccountable: and his old master made no attempt to conceal his uneasiness. The newspaper dropped out of his hand: and he sat with his face turned towards the door: listening.

He sat thus for more than an hour, and at the end of that time the landlord came to him.

"Well?" exclaimed Henry Dunbar.

"The lad has come back, sir. No messenger from you or any one else has called at the Ferns this afternoon."

Mr. Dunbar started suddenly to his feet, and stared at the landlord. He paused for a few moments, watching the man's face with a thoughtful countenance. Then he said, slowly and deliberately,—

"I am afraid that something has happened."

The landlord fidgeted with his ponderous watch-chain, and shrugged his shoulders with a dubious gesture.

"Well, it is *strange*, sir, to say the least of it. But you don't think that——"

He looked at Henry Dunbar as if scarcely knowing how to finish his sentence.

"I don't know what to think," exclaimed the banker. "Remember, I am almost as much a stranger in this country as if I had never set foot on British soil before to-day. This man may have played me a trick, and gone off for some purpose of his own, though I don't know what purpose. He could have best served his own interests by staying with me. On the other hand, something may have happened to him. And yet what *can* have happened to him?"

The landlord suggested that the missing man might have fallen down in a fit, or might have loitered somewhere or other until after dark, and then lost his way, and wandered into a mill-stream. There was many a deep bit of water between Winchester Cathedral and the Ferns, the landlord said.

"Let a search be made at daybreak to-morrow morning," exclaimed Mr. Dunbar. "I don't care what it costs me, but I am determined this business shall be cleared up before I leave Winchester. Let every inch of ground between this and the Ferns be searched at daybreak to-morrow morning; let——"

He did not finish the sentence, for there was a sudden clamour of voices, and trampling, and hubbub in the hall below. The landlord opened the door, and went out upon the broad landing-place, followed by Mr. Dunbar.

The hall below was crowded by the servants of the place, and by eager strangers who had pressed in from outside; and the two men standing at the top of the stairs heard a hoarse murmur; which seemed all in one voice, though it was in reality a blending of many voices; and which grew louder and louder, until it swelled into the awful word "Murder!"

Henry Dunbar heard it and understood it, for his handsome face grew of a bluish white, like snow in the moonlight, and he leaned his hand upon the oaken balustrade.

The landlord passed his guest, and ran down the stairs. It was no time for ceremony.

He came back again in less than five minutes, looking almost as pale as Mr. Dunbar.

"I'm afraid your friend—your servant—is found, sir," he said.

"You don't mean that he is——"

"I'm afraid it is so, sir. It seems that two Irish reapers, coming from Farmer Matfield's, five mile beyond St. Cross, stumbled against a man lying in a little streamlet under the trees——"

"Under the trees! Where?"

"In the very place where you parted from this Mr. Wilmot, sir."

"Good God! Well?"

"The man was dead, sir; quite dead. They carried him to the

Foresters' Arms, sir, as that was the nearest place to where they found him; and there's been a doctor sent for, and a deal of fuss: but the doctor—Mr. Cricklewood, a very respectable gentleman, sir—says that the man had been lying in the water hours and hours, and that the murder had been done hours and hours ago."

"The murder!" cried Henry Dunbar; "but he may not have been murdered! His death may have been accidental. He wandered into the water, perhaps."

"Oh, no, sir; it's not that. He wasn't drowned; for the water where he was found wasn't three foot deep. He had been strangled, sir; strangled with a running-noose of rope; strangled from behind, sir, for the slip-knot was pulled tight at the back of his neck. Mr. Cricklewood the surgeon's in the hall below, if you'd like to see him; and he knows all about it. It seems, from what the two Irishmen say, that the body was dragged into the water by the rope. There was the track of where it had been dragged along the grass. I'm sure, sir, I'm very sorry such an awful thing should have happened to the—the person who attended you here."

Mr. Dunbar had need of sympathy. His white face was turned towards the landlord's, fixed in a blank stare. He had not seemed to listen to the man's account of the crime that had been committed, and yet he had evidently heard everything; for he said presently, in slow, thick accents,—

"Strangled—and the body dragged down—to the water. Who—who could—have done it?"

"Ah! that's the question, indeed, sir. It must all have been done for the sake of a bit of money, I suppose; for there was an empty pocket-book found by the water's edge. There are always tramps and such-like about the country at this time of year; and some of them will commit almost any crime for the sake of a few pounds. I remember—ah, as long ago as forty years and more—when I was a bit of a boy in pinafores, there was a gentleman murdered on the Twyford road, and they did say——"

But Mr. Dunbar was in no humour to listen to the landlord's reminiscences. He interrupted the man's story with a long-drawn sigh,—

"Is there anything I can do? What am I to do?" he said. "Is there anything I can do?"

"Nothing, sir, until to-morrow. The inquest will be held to-morrow, I suppose."

"Yes—yes, to be sure. There'll be an inquest."

"An inquest! Oh, yes, sir; of course there will," answered the landlord.

"Remember that I am a stranger to English habits. I don't know what steps ought to be taken in such a case as this. Should there not be some attempt made to find—the—the murderer?"

"Yes, sir; I've *no doubt* the constables are on the look-out already. There'll be every effort made, depend upon it; but I'm really afraid this is a case in which the murderer will escape from justice."

"Why so?"

"Because, you see, sir, the man has had plenty of time to get off; and unless he's a fool, he must be far away from here by this time, and then what is there to trace him by—that's to say, unless you could identify the money, or watch and chain, or what not, which the murdered man had about him?"

Mr. Dunbar shook his head.

"I don't even know whether he wore a watch and chain," he said; "I only met him this morning. I have no idea what money he may have had about him."

"Would you like to see the doctor, sir—Mr. Cricklewood?"

"Yes—no—you have told me all that there is to tell, I suppose?"

"Yes, sir."

"I shall go to bed. I'm thoroughly upset by all this. Stay. Is it a settled thing that this man who has been found murdered is the person who accompanied me to this house to-day?"

"Oh, yes, sir; there's no doubt about that. One of our people went down to the Foresters' Arms, out of curiosity, as you may say, and he recognized the murdered man directly as the very gentleman that came into this house with you, sir, at four o'clock to-day."

Mr. Dunbar retired to the apartment that had been prepared for him. It was a spacious and handsome chamber, the best room in the hotel; and one of the waiters attended upon the rich man.

"As you've been accustomed to have your valet about you, you'll find it awkward, sir," the landlord had said; "so I'll send Henry to wait upon you."

This Henry, who was a smart, active young fellow, unpacked Mr. Dunbar's portmanteau, unlocked his dressing-case, and spread the gold-topped crystal bottles and shaving apparatus upon the dressing-table.

Mr. Dunbar sat in an easy-chair before the looking-glass, staring thoughtfully at the reflection of his own face, pale in the light of the tall wax-candles.

He got up early the next morning, and before breakfasting he despatched a telegraphic message to the banking-house in St. Gundolph Lane.

It was from Henry Maddison Dunbar to William Balderby, and it consisted of these words:—

"*Pray come to me directly, at the George, Winchester. A very awful event has happened; and I am in great trouble and perplexity. Bring a lawyer with you. Let my daughter know that I shall not come to London for some days."*

All this time the body of the murdered man lay on a long table in a darkened chamber at the Foresters' Arms.

The rigid outline of the corpse was plainly visible under the linen sheet that shrouded it; but the door of the dread chamber was locked, and no one was to enter until the coming of the coroner.

Meanwhile the Foresters' Arms did more business than had been done there in the same space of time within the memory of man. People went in and out, in and out, all through the long morning; little groups clustered together in the bar, discoursing in solemn under-tones; and other groups straggled on the seemed as if every living creature in Winchester was talking of the murder that had been done in the grove near St. Cross.

Henry Dunbar sat in his own room, waiting for an answer to the telegraphic message.

- CHAPTER 10 -

LAURA DUNBAR

While these things had been happening between London and Southampton, Laura Dunbar, the banker's daughter, had been anxiously waiting the coming of her father.

She resembled her mother, Lady Louisa Dunbar, the youngest daughter of the Earl of Grantwick, a very beautiful and aristocratic woman. She had met Mr. Dunbar in India, after the death of her first husband, a young captain in a cavalry regiment, who had been killed in an encounter with the Sikhs a year after his marriage, leaving his young widow with an infant daughter, a helpless baby of six weeks old.

The poor, high-born Lady Louisa Macmahon was left most desolate and miserable after the death of her first husband. She was very poor, and she knew that her relations in England were very little better off than herself. She was almost as helpless as her six-weeks' old baby; she was heart-broken by the loss of the handsome young Irishman, whom she had fondly loved; and ill and broken down by her sorrows, she lingered in Calcutta, subsisting upon her pension, and too weak to undertake the perils of the voyage home.

It was at this time that poor widowed Lady Louisa met Henry Dunbar, the rich banker. She came in contact with him on account of

some money arrangements of her dead husband's, who had always
banked with Dunbar and Dunbar; and Henry, then getting on for forty
years of age, had fallen desperately in love with the beautiful young
widow.

There is no need for me to dwell upon the history of this courtship.
Lady Louisa married the rich man eighteen months after her first husband's death. Little Dorothea Macmahon was sent to England with a
native nurse, and placed under the care of her maternal relatives; and
Henry Dunbar's beautiful wife became queen of the best society in the
city of palaces, by the right of her own rank and her husband's wealth.

Henry Dunbar loved her desperately, as even a selfish man can
sometimes love for once in his life.

But Lady Louisa never truly returned the millionaire's affection. She
was haunted by the memory of her first and purest love; she was
tortured by remorseful thoughts about the fatherless child who had been
so ruthlessly banished from her. Henry Dunbar was a jealous man, and
he grudged the love which his wife bore to his dead rival's child. It was
by his contrivance the girl had been sent from India.

Lady Louisa Dunbar held her place in Calcutta society for two years.
But in the very hour when her social position was most brilliant, her
beauty in the full splendour of its prime, she died so suddenly that the
fashionables of Calcutta were discussing the promised splendour of a
ball, for which Lady Louisa had issued her invitations, when the tidings
of her death spread like wildfire through the city—Henry Dunbar was a
widower. He might have married again, had he pleased to do so. The
proudest beauty in Calcutta would have been glad to become the wife of
the sole heir of that dingy banking-house in St. Gundolph Lane.

There was a good deal of excitement upon this subject in the
matrimonial market for two or three years after Lady Louisa's death. A
good many young ladies were expressly imported from England by
anxious papas and mammas, with a view to the capture of the wealthy
widower.

But though Griselda's yellow hair fell down to her waist in glossy,
rippling curls, that shone like molten gold; though Amanda's black eyes
glittered like the stars in a midnight sky; though the dashing Georgina
was more graceful than Diana, the gentle Lavinia more beautiful than
Venus,—Mr. Dunbar went among them without pleasure, and left them
without regret.

The charms of all these ladies concentrated in the person of one
perfect woman would have had no witchery for the banker. His heart
was dead. He had given all the truth, all the passion of which his nature
was capable, to the one woman who had possessed the power to charm

him.

To seek to win love from him was about as hopeless as it would have been to ask alms of a man whose purse was empty. The bright young English beauties found this out by and by, and devoted themselves to other speculations in the matrimonial market.

Henry Dunbar sent his little girl, his only child, to England. He parted with her, not because of his indifference, but rather by reason of his idolatry. It was the only unselfish act of his life, this parting with his child; and yet even in this there was selfishness.

"It would be sweet to me to keep her here," he thought; "but then, if the climate should kill her; if I should lose her, as I lost her mother? I will send her away from me now, that she may be my blessing by-and-by, when I return to England after my father's death."

Henry Dunbar had sworn when he left the office in St. Gundolph Lane, after the discovery of the forgery, that he would never look upon his father's face again,—and he kept his oath.

This was the father to whose coming Laura Dunbar looked forward with eager anxiety, with a heart overflowing with tender womanly love.

She was a very beautiful girl; so beautiful that her presence was like the sunlight, and made the meanest place splendid. There was a queenliness in her beauty, which she inherited from her mother's high-born race. But though her beauty was queenlike, it was not imperious. There was no conscious pride in her aspect, no cold hauteur in her ever-changing face. She was such a woman as might have sat by the side of an English king to plead for all trembling petitioners kneeling on the steps of the throne. She would have been only in her fitting place beneath the shadow of a regal canopy; for in soul, as well as in aspect, she was worthy to be a queen. She was like some tall white lily, unconsciously beautiful, unconsciously grand; and the meanest natures kindled with a faint glow of poetry when they came in contact with her.

She had been spoiled by an adoring nurse, a devoted governess, masters who had fallen madly in love with their pupil, and servants who were ready to worship their young mistress. Yes, according to the common acceptation of the term, she had been spoiled; she had been allowed to have her own way in everything; to go hither and thither, free as the butterflies in her carefully tended garden; to scatter her money right and left; to be imposed upon and cheated by every wandering vagabond who found his way to her gates; to ride, and hunt, and drive— to do as she liked, in short. And I am fain to say that the consequence of all this foolish and reprehensible indulgence had been to make the young heiress of Maudesley Abbey the most fascinating woman in all Warwickshire.

She was a little capricious, just a trifle wayward, I will confess. But then that trifling waywardness gave just the spice that was wanting to this grand young lily. The white lilies are never more beautiful than when they wave capriciously in the summer wind; and if Laura Dunbar was a little passionate when you tried to thwart her; and if her great blue eyes at such times had a trick of lighting up with sudden fire in them, like a burst of lurid sunlight through a summer storm-cloud, there were plenty of gentlemen in Warwickshire ready to swear that the sight of those lightning-flashes of womanly anger was well worth the penalty of incurring Miss Dunbar's displeasure.

She was only eighteen, and had not yet "come out."[33] But she had seen a great deal of society, for it had been the delight of her grandfather to have her perpetually with him.

She travelled from Maudesley Abbey to Portland Place in the company of her nurse,—a certain Elizabeth Madden, who had been Lady Louisa's own maid before her marriage with Captain Macmahon, and who was devotedly attached to the motherless girl.

But Mrs. Madden was not Laura Dunbar's only companion upon this occasion. She was accompanied by her half-sister, Dora Macmahon, who of late years had almost lived at the Abbey, much to the delight of Laura.

Nor was the little party without an escort; for Arthur Lovell, the son of the principal solicitor in the town of Shorncliffe, near Maudesley Abbey, attended Miss Dunbar to London.

This young man had been a very great favourite with Percival Dunbar and had been a constant visitor at the Abbey. Before the old man died, he told Arthur Lovell to act in everything as Laura's friend and legal adviser; and the young lawyer was very enthusiastic in behalf of his beautiful client. Why should I seek to make a mystery of this gentleman's feelings? He loved her. He loved this girl, who, by reason of her father's wealth, was as far removed from him as if she had been a duchess. He paid a terrible penalty for every happy hour, every delicious day of simple and innocent enjoyment, that he had spent at Maudesley Abbey; for he loved Laura Dunbar, and he feared that his love was hopeless.

It was hopeless in the present, at any rate; for although he was hand-some, clever, high-spirited, and honourable, a gentleman in the noblest sense of that noble word, he was no fit husband for the daughter of Henry Dunbar. He was an only son, and he was heir to a very comfort-

---

[33] To "come out" was to be presented to upper-class British society. Debutantes would traditionally be presented at Court during their first London season. The "season" served to facilitate the introduction and courtship of marriageable age children of the nobility and gentry.

able little fortune: but he knew that the millionaire would have laughed him to scorn had he dared to make proposals for Laura's hand.

But was his love hopeless in the future? That was the question which he perpetually asked himself.

He was proud and ambitious. He knew that he was clever; he could not help knowing this, though he was entirely without conceit. A government appointment in India had been offered to him through the intervention of a nobleman, a friend of his father's. This appointment would afford the chance of a noble career to a man who knew how to seize the golden opportunity, which mediocrity neglects, but which genius makes the stepping-stone to greatness.

The nobleman who made the offer to Arthur Lovell had written to say that there was no necessity for an immediate decision. If Arthur accepted the appointment, he would not be obliged to leave England until the end of a twelvemonth, as the vacancy would not occur before that time.

"In the meanwhile," Lord Herriston wrote to the solicitor, "your son can think the matter over, my dear Lovell, and make his decision with all due deliberation."

Arthur Lovell had already made that decision.

"I will go to India," he said; "for if ever I am to win Laura Dunbar, I must succeed in life. But before I go I will tell her that I love her. If she returns my love, my struggles will be sweet to me, for they will be made for her sake. If she does not——"

He did not finish the sentence even in his own mind. He could not bear to think that it was possible he might hear his death-knell from the lips he worshipped. He had gladly seized upon the opportunity afforded by this visit to the town house.

"I will speak to her before her father returns," he thought; "she will speak the truth to me now fearlessly; for it is her nature to be fearless and candid as a child. But his coming may change her. She is fond of him, and will be ruled by him. Heaven grant he may rule her wisely and gently!"

On the 17th of August, Laura and Mrs. Madden arrived in Portland Place.

Arthur Lovell parted with his beautiful client at the railway station, and drove off to the hotel at which he was in the habit of staying. He called upon Miss Dunbar on the 18th; but found that she was out shopping with Mrs. Madden. He called again, on the morning of the 19th; that bright sunny August morning on which the body of the murdered man lay in the darkened chamber at Winchester.

It was only ten o'clock when the young lawyer made his appearance in the pleasant morning-room occupied by Laura Dunbar whenever she stayed in Portland Place. The breakfast equipage was still upon the table in the centre of the room. Mrs. Madden, who was companion, house-keeper, and confidential maid to her charming young mistress, was officiating at the breakfast-table; Dora Macmahon was sitting near her, with an open book by the side of her breakfast-cup; and Miss Laura Dunbar was lounging in a low easy-chair, near a broad window that opened into a conservatory filled with exotics, that made the air heavy with their almost overpowering perfume.

She rose as Arthur Lovell came into the room, and she looked more like a lily than ever in her long loose morning-dress of soft semi-diaphanous muslin. Her thick auburn hair was twisted into a diadem that crowned her broad white forehead, and added a couple of inches to her height. She held out her little ringed hand, and the jewels on the white fingers scintillated in the sunlight.

"I am so glad to see you, Mr. Lovell," she said. "Dora and I have been miserable, haven't we, Dora? London is as dull as a desert. I went for a drive yesterday, and the Lady's Mile is as lonely as the Great Sahara.[34] There are plenty of theatres open, and there was a concert at one of the opera-houses last night; but that disagreeable Elizabeth wouldn't allow me to go to any one of those entertainments. Grandpapa would have taken me. Dear grandpapa went everywhere with me."

Mrs. Madden shook her head solemnly.

"Your gran'pa would have gone after you to the remotest end of this world, Miss Laura, if you'd so much as held your finger up to beckon of him. Your gran'pa spiled you, Miss Laura. A pretty thing it would have been if your pa had come all the way from India to find his only daughter gallivanting at a theaytre."

Miss Dunbar looked at her old nurse with an arch smile. She was very lovely when she smiled; she was very lovely when she frowned. She was most beautiful always, Arthur Lovell thought.

"But I shouldn't have been gallivanting, you dear old Madden," she cried, with a joyous silver laugh, that was like the ripple of a cascade under a sunny sky. "I should only have been sitting quietly in a private box, with my rapid, precious, aggravating, darling old nurse to keep watch and ward over me. Besides, how could papa be angry with me upon the first day of his coming home?"

Mrs. Madden shook her head again even more solemnly than before.

"I don't know about that, Miss Laura. You mustn't expect to find Mr.

34 The Lady's Mile was a carriage-drive in Hyde Park, along the northern bank of the Serpentine River. Braddon used it for the title of a novel in 1866.

76

Dunbar like your gran'pa."

A sudden cloud fell upon the girl's lovely face.

"Why, Elizabeth," she said, "you don't mean that papa will be unkind to me?"

"I don't know your pa, Miss Laura. I never set eyes upon Mr. Dunbar in my life. But the Indian servant that brought you over, when you was but a bit of a baby, said that your pa was proud and passionate; and that even your poor mar, which he loved her better than any livin' creature upon this earth, was almost afraid of him."

The smile had quite vanished from Laura Dunbar's face by this time, and the blue eyes filled suddenly with tears.

"Oh, what shall I do if my father is unkind to me?" she said, piteously. "I have so looked forward to his coming home. I have counted the very days; and if he is unkind to me—if he does not love me——"

She covered her face with her hands, and turned away her head.

"Laura," exclaimed Arthur Lovell, addressing her for the first time by her Christian name, "how could any one help loving you? How——"

He stopped, half ashamed of his passionate enthusiasm. In those few words he had revealed the secret of his heart: but Laura Dunbar was too innocent to understand the meaning of those eager words.

Mrs. Madden understood them perfectly; and she smiled approvingly at the young man.

Arthur Lovell was a great favourite with Laura Dunbar's nurse. She knew that he adored her young mistress; and she looked upon him as a model of all that is noble and chivalrous.

She began to fidget with the silver tea-canisters; and then looked significantly at Dora Macmahon. But Miss Macmahon did not understand that significant glance. Her dark eyes—and she had very beautiful eyes, with a grave, half-pensive softness in their sombre depths—were fixed upon the two young faces in the sunny window; the girl's face clouded with a look of sorrowful perplexity, the young man's face eloquent with tender meaning. Dora Macmahon's colour went and came as she looked at that earnest countenance, and the fingers which were absently turning the leaves of her book were faintly tremulous.

"Your new bonnet's come home this morning, Miss Dora," Elizabeth Madden said, rather sharply. "Perhaps you'd like to come up-stairs and have a look at it."

"My new bonnet!" murmured Dora, vaguely.

"La, yes, miss; the new bonnet you bought in Regent Street only yesterday afternoon. I never did see such a forgetful wool-gathering young lady in all my life as you are this blessed morning, Miss Dora."

The absent-minded young lady rose suddenly, bewildered by Mrs.

Madden's animated desire for an inspection of the bonnet. But she very willingly left the room with Laura's old nurse, who was accustomed to have her mandates obeyed even by the wayward heiress of Maudesley Abbey; and Laura was left alone with the young lawyer.

Miss Dunbar had seated herself once more in the low easy-chair by the window. She sat with her elbow resting on the cushioned arm of the chair, and her head supported by her hand. Her eyes were fixed, and looked straight before her, with a thoughtful gaze that was strange to her: for her nature was as joyous as that of a bird, whose music fills all the wide heaven with one rejoicing psalm.

Arthur Lovell drew his chair nearer to the thoughtful girl.

"Laura," he said, "why are you so silent? I never saw you so serious before, except after your grandfather's death."

"I am thinking of my father," she answered, in a low, tremulous voice, that was broken by her tears: "I am thinking that, perhaps, he will not love me."

"Not love you, Laura! who could help loving you? Oh, if I dared—if I could venture—I must speak, Laura Dunbar. My whole life hangs upon the issue, and I will speak. I am not a poor man, Laura; but you are so divided from the rest of the world by your father's wealth, that I have feared to speak. I have feared to tell you that which you might have discovered for yourself, had you not been as innocent as your own pet doves in the dovecote at Maudesley."

The girl looked at him with wondering eyes that were still wet with unshed tears.

"I love you, Laura; I love you. The world would call me beneath you in station, now; but I am a man, and I have a man's ambition—a strong man's iron will. Everything is possible to him who has sworn to conquer; and for your sake, Laura, for your love I should overcome obstacles that to another man might be invincible. I am going to India, Laura: I am going to carve my way to fame and fortune, for fame and fortune are *slaves* that come at the brave man's bidding; they are only *masters* when the coward calls them. Remember, my beloved one, this wealth that now stands between you and me may not always be yours. Your father is not an old man; he may marry again, and have a son to inherit his wealth. Would to Heaven, Laura, that it might be so! But be that as it may, I despair of nothing if I dare hope for your love. Oh, Laura, dearest, one word to tell me that I *may* hope! Remember how happy we have been together; little children playing with flowers and butterflies in the gardens at Maudesley; boy and girl, rambling hand-in-hand beside the wandering Avon; man and woman standing in mournful silence by your grandfather's deathbed. The past is a bond of union betwixt us, Laura.

Look back at all those happy days and give me one word, my darling—one word to tell me that you love me."

Laura Dunbar looked up at him with a sweet smile, and laid her soft white hand in his.

"I do love you, Arthur," she said, "as dearly as I should have loved my brother had I ever known a brother's love."

The young man bowed his head in silence. When he looked up, Laura Dunbar saw that he was very pale.

"You only love me as a brother, Laura?"

"How else should I love you?" she asked, innocently.

Arthur Lovell looked at her with a mournful smile; a tender smile that was exquisitely beautiful, for it was the look of a man who is prepared to resign his own happiness for the sake of her he loves.

"Enough, Laura," he said, quietly; "I have received my sentence. You do not love me, dearest; you have yet to suffer life's great fever."

She clasped her hands, and looked at him beseechingly.

"You are not angry with me, Arthur?" she said.

"Angry with you, my sweet one!"

"And you will still love me?"

"Yes, Laura, with all a brother's devotion. And if ever you have need of my services, you shall find what it is to have a faithful friend, who holds his life at small value beside your happiness."

He said no more, for there was the sound of carriage-wheels below the window, and then a loud double-knock at the hall-door.

Laura started to her feet, and her bright face grew pale.

"My father has come!" she exclaimed.

But it was not her father. It was Mr. Balderby, who had just come from St. Gundolph Lane, where he had received Henry Dunbar's telegraphic despatch.

Every vestige of colour faded out of Laura's face as she recognized the junior partner of the banking-house.

"Something has happened to my father!" she cried.

"No, no, Miss Dunbar!" exclaimed Mr. Balderby, anxious to reassure her.

"Your father has arrived in England safely, and is well, as I believe. He is staying at Winchester; and he has telegraphed to me to go to him there immediately."

"Something has happened, then?"

"Yes, but not to Mr. Dunbar individually; so far as I can make out by the telegraphic message. I was to come to you here, Miss Dunbar, to tell you not to expect your papa for some few days; and then I am to go on to Winchester, taking a lawyer with me."

"A lawyer!" exclaimed Laura.

"Yes, I am going to Lincoln's Inn immediately to Messrs. Walford and Walford, our own solicitors."

"Let Mr. Lovell go with you," cried Miss Dunbar; "he always acted as poor grandpapa's solicitor. Let him go with you."

"Yes, Mr. Balderby," exclaimed the young man, "I beg you to allow me to accompany you. I shall be very glad to be of service to Mr. Dunbar."

Mr. Balderby hesitated for a few moments.

"Well, I really don't see why you shouldn't go, if you wish to do so," he said, presently. "Mr. Dunbar says he wants a lawyer; he doesn't name any particular lawyer. We shall save time by your going; for we shall be able to catch the eleven o'clock express."

He looked at his watch.

"There's not a moment to lose. Good morning, Miss Dunbar. We'll take care of your papa, and bring him to you in triumph. Come, Lovell."

Arthur Lovell shook hands with Laura, murmured a few words in her ear, and hurried away with Mr. Balderby.

She had spoken the death-knell of his dearest hopes. He had seen his sentence in her innocent face; but he loved her still.

There was something in her virginal candour, her bright young loveliness, that touched the noblest chords of his heart. He loved her with a chivalrous devotion, which, after all, is as natural to the breast of a young Englishman in these modern days, miscalled degenerate, as when the spotless knight King Arthur loved and wooed his queen.[35]

---

[35] A reference to King Arthur and his queen, Guinevere. Braddon was greatly interested in Arthurian legend and Cornish history generally. This interest is most evident in her novel *Mount Royal* (1882), which bases a love story around the tragic legend of Tristan and Iseult.

- CHAPTER 11 -

THE INQUEST

The coroner's inquest, which had been appointed to take place at noon that day, was postponed until three o'clock in the afternoon, in compliance with the earnest request of Henry Dunbar.

When ever was the earnest request of a millionaire refused?

The coroner, who was a fussy little man, very readily acceded to Mr. Dunbar's entreaties.

"I am a stranger in England," the Anglo-Indian said; "I was never in my life present at an inquest. The murdered man was connected with me. He was last seen in my company. It is vitally necessary that I should have a legal adviser to watch the proceedings on my behalf. Who knows what dark suspicions may arise, affecting my name and honour?"

The banker made this remark in the presence of four or five of the jurymen, the coroner, and Mr. Cricklewood, the surgeon who had been called in to examine the body of the man supposed to have been murdered. Every one of those gentlemen protested loudly and indignantly against the idea of the bare possibility that any suspicion, or the shadow of a suspicion, could attach to such a man as Mr. Dunbar.

They knew nothing of him, of course, except that he was Henry Dunbar, chief of the rich banking-house of Dunbar, Dunbar, and Balderby, and that he was a millionaire.

Was it likely that a millionaire would commit a murder?

When had a millionaire ever been known to commit a murder? Never, of course!

The Anglo-Indian sat in his private sitting-room at the George Hotel, writing, and examining his papers—perpetually writing, perpetually sorting and re-sorting those packets of letters in the despatch-box—while he waited for the coming of Mr. Balderby.

The postponement of the coroner's inquest was a very good thing for the landlord of the Foresters' Arms. People went in and out, and loitered about the premises, and lounged in the bar, drinking and talking all the morning, and the theme of every conversation was the murder that had been done in the grove on the way to St. Cross.

Mr. Balderby and Arthur Lovell arrived at the George a few minutes before two o'clock. They were shown at once into the apartment in which Henry Dunbar sat waiting for them.

Arthur Lovell had been thinking of Laura and Laura's father throughout the journey from London. He had wondered, as he got nearer and nearer to Winchester, what would be his first impression respecting Mr. Dunbar.

That first impression was not a good one—no, it was not a good one. Mr. Dunbar was a handsome man—a very handsome man—tall and aristocratic-looking, with a certain haughty pace in his manner that harmonized well with his good looks. But, in spite of all this, the impression which he made upon the mind of Arthur Lovell was not an agreeable one.

The young lawyer had heard the story of the forgery vaguely hinted at by those who were familiar with the history of the Dunbar family; and he had heard that the early life of Henry Dunbar had been that of a selfish spendthrift.

Perhaps this may have had some influence upon his feelings in this his first meeting with the father of the woman he loved.

Henry Dunbar told the story of the murder. The two men were inexpressibly shocked by this story.

"But where is Sampson Wilmot?" exclaimed Mr. Balderby. "It was he whom I sent to meet you, knowing that he was the only person in the office who remembered you, or whom you remembered."

"Sampson was taken ill upon the way, according to his brother's story,"

Mr. Dunbar answered. "Joseph left the poor old man somewhere upon the road."

"He did not say where?"

"No; and, strange to say, I forgot to ask him the question. The poor fellow amused me by old memories of the past on the road between Southampton and this place, and we therefore talked very little of the present."

"Sampson must be very ill," exclaimed Mr. Balderby, "or he would certainly have returned to St. Gundolph Lane to tell me what had taken place."

Mr. Dunbar smiled.

"If he was too ill to go on to Southampton, he would, of course, be too ill to return to London," he said, with supreme indifference.

Mr. Balderby, who was a good-hearted man, was distressed at the idea of Sampson Wilmot's desolation; an old man, stricken with sudden illness, and abandoned to strangers.

Arthur Lovell was silent: he sat a little way apart from the two others, watching Henry Dunbar.

At three o'clock the inquest commenced. The witnesses summoned were the two Irishmen, Patrick Hennessy and Philip Murtock, who had found the body in the stream near St. Cross; Mr. Cricklewood, the surgeon; the verger, who had seen and spoken to the two men, and who had afterwards shown the cathedral to Mr. Dunbar; the landlord of the George, and the waiter who had received the travellers and had taken Mr. Dunbar's orders for the dinner; and Henry Dunbar himself.

There were a great many people in the room, for by this time the tidings of the murder had spread far and wide. There were influential people present, amongst others, Sir Arden Westhorpe, one of the county magistrates resident at Winchester. Arthur Lovell, Mr. Balderby, and the Anglo-Indian sat in a little group apart from the rest.

The jurymen were ranged upon either side of a long mahogany table. The coroner sat at the top.

But before the examination of the witnesses was commenced, the jurymen were conducted into that dismal chamber where the dead man lay upon one of the long tap-room tables. Arthur Lovell went with them; and Mr. Cricklewood, the surgeon, proceeded to examine the corpse, so as to enable him to give evidence respecting the cause of death.

The face of the dead man was distorted and blackened by the agony of strangulation. The coroner and the jurymen looked at that dead face with wondering, awe-stricken glances. Sometimes a cruel stab, that goes straight home to the heart, will leave the face of the murdered as calm, as the face of a sleeping child.

But in this case it was not so. The horrible stamp of assassination was branded upon that rigid brow. Horror, surprise, and the dread agony of sudden death were all blended in the expression of the face.

The jurymen talked a little to one another in scarcely audible whispers, asked a few questions of the surgeon, and then walked softly from the darkened room.

The facts of the case were very simple, and speedily elicited. But whatever the truth of that awful story might be, there was nothing that threw any light upon the mystery.

Arthur Lovell, watching the case in the interests of Mr. Dunbar, asked several questions of the witnesses. Henry Dunbar was himself the first person examined. He gave a very simple and intelligible account of all that had taken place from the moment of his landing at Southampton.

"I found the deceased waiting to receive me when I landed," he said. "He told me that he came as a substitute for another person. I did not know him at first—that is to say, I did not recognize him as the valet who had been in my service prior to my leaving England five-and-thirty years ago. But he made himself known to me afterwards, and he told me that he had met his brother in London on the sixteenth of this month, and had travelled with him part of the way to Southampton. He also told me that, on the way to Southampton, his brother, Sampson Wilmot, a much older man than the deceased, was taken ill, and that the two men then parted company."

Mr. Dunbar had said all this with perfect self-possession, and with great deliberation. He was so very self-possessed, so very deliberate, that it seemed almost as if he had been reciting something which he had learned by heart.

Arthur Lovell, watching him very intently, saw this, and wondered at it. It is very usual for a witness, even the most indifferent witness, giving evidence about some trifling matter, to be confused, to falter, and hesitate, and contradict himself, embarrassed by the strangeness of his position. But Henry Dunbar was in nowise discomposed by the awful nature of the event which had happened. He was pale; but his firmly-set lips, his erect carriage, the determined glance of his eyes, bore witness to the strength of his nerves and the power of his intellect.

"The man must be made of iron," Arthur Lovell thought to himself. "He is either a very great man, or a very wicked one. I almost fear to ask myself which."

"Where did the deceased Joseph Wilmot say he left his brother Sampson, Mr. Dunbar?" asked the coroner.

"I do not remember."

The coroner scratched his chin, thoughtfully.

"That is rather awkward," he said; "the evidence of this man Sampson might throw some light upon this most mysterious event."

Mr. Dunbar then told the rest of his story.

He spoke of the luncheon at Southampton, the journey from Southampton to Winchester, the afternoon stroll down to the meadows near St. Cross.

"Can you tell us the exact spot at which you parted with the deceased?" asked the coroner.

"No," Mr. Dunbar answered; "you must bear in mind that I am a stranger in England. I have not been in this neighbourhood since I was a boy. My old schoolfellow, Michael Marston, married and settled at the Ferns during my absence in India. I found at Southampton that I should have a few hours on my hands before I could travel express for London, and I came to this place on purpose to see my old friend. I was very much disappointed to find that he was dead. But I thought that I would call upon his widow, from whom I should no doubt hear the history of my poor friend's last moments. I went with Joseph Wilmot through the cathedral yard, and down towards St. Cross. The verger saw us, and spoke to us as we went by."

The verger, who was standing amongst the other witnesses, waiting to be examined, here exclaimed,—

"Ay, that I did, sir; I remember it well."

"At what time did you leave the George?"

"At a little after four o'clock."

"Where did you go then?"

"I went," answered Mr. Dunbar, boldly, "into the grove with the deceased, arm-in-arm. We walked together about a quarter of a mile under the trees, and I had intended to go on to the Ferns, to call upon Michael Marston's widow; but my habits of late years have been sedentary; the heat of the day and the walk together were too much for me. I sent Joseph Wilmot on to the Ferns with a message for Mrs. Marston, asking at what hour she could conveniently receive me to-day; and I returned to the cathedral. Joseph Wilmot was to deliver his message at the Ferns, and rejoin me in the cathedral."

"He was to return to the cathedral?"

"Yes."

"But why should he not have returned to the George Hotel? Why should you wait for him at the cathedral?"

Arthur Lovell listened, with a strange expression upon his face. If Henry Dunbar was pale, Henry Dunbar's legal adviser was still more so. The jurymen stared aghast at the coroner, as if they had been awe-stricken by his impertinence towards the chief partner of the great banking-house of Dunbar, Dunbar, and Balderby. How dared he—a man with an income of five hundred a year at the most—how dared he discredit or question any assertion made by Henry Dunbar?

The Anglo-Indian smiled, a little contemptuously. He stood in a careless attitude, playing with the golden trinkets at his watch-chain, with the hot August sunshine streaming upon his face from a bare unshaded window opposite him. But he did not attempt to escape that almost blinding glare. He stood facing the sunlight; facing the gaze of the coroner and the jurymen; the scrutinizing glance of Arthur Lovell. Unabashed and *nonchalant* as if he had been standing in a ball-room, the hero of the hour, the admired of all who looked upon him, Mr. Dunbar stood before the coroner and jury, and told the broken history of his old servant's death.

"Yes," Mr. Lovell thought again, as he watched the rich man's face, "his nerves must be made of iron."

- CHAPTER 12 -

ARRESTED

The coroner repeated his question:

"Why did you tell the deceased to join you at the cathedral, Mr. Dunbar?"

"Merely because it suited my humour at the time to do so," answered the Anglo-Indian, coolly. "We had been very friendly together, and I had a fancy for going over the cathedral. I thought that Wilmot might return from the Ferns in time to go over some portion of the edifice with me. He was a very intelligent fellow, and I liked his society."

"But the journey to the Ferns and back would have occupied some time."

"Perhaps so," answered Mr. Dunbar; "I did not know the distance to the Ferns, and I did not make any calculation as to time. I merely said to the deceased, 'I shall go back and look at the cathedral; and I will wait for you there.' I said this, and I told him to be as quick as he could."

"That was all that passed between you?"

"It was. I then returned to the cathedral."

"And you waited there for the deceased?"

"I did. I waited until close upon the hour at which I had ordered dinner at the George."

There was a pause, during which the coroner looked very thoughtful.

"I am compelled to ask you one more question, Mr. Dunbar," he said, presently, hesitating a little as he spoke.

"I am ready to answer any questions you may wish to ask," Mr. Dunbar replied, very quietly.

"Were you upon friendly terms with the deceased?"

"I have just told you so. We were on excellent terms. I found him an agreeable companion. His manners were those of a gentleman. I don't know how he had picked up his education, but he certainly had contrived to educate himself some how or other."

"I understand you were friendly together at the time of his death; but prior to that time——"

Mr. Dunbar smiled.

"I have been in India five-and-thirty years," he said.

"Precisely. But before your departure for India, had you any misunderstanding, any serious quarrel with the deceased?"

Mr. Dunbar's face flushed suddenly, and his brows contracted as if even his self-possession were not proof against the unpleasant memories of the past.

"No," he said, with determination; "I never quarrelled with him."

"There had been no cause of quarrel between you?"

"I don't understand your question. I have told you that I never quarrelled with him."

"Perhaps not; but there might have been some hidden animosity, some smothered feeling, stronger than any openly-expressed anger, hidden in your breast. Was there any such feeling?"

"Not on my part."

"Was there any such feeling on the part of the deceased?"

Mr. Dunbar looked furtively at William Balderby. The junior partner's eyelids dropped under that stolen glance.

It was clear that he knew the story of the forged bills.

Had the coroner for Winchester been a clever man, he would have followed that glance of Mr. Dunbar's, and would have understood that the junior partner knew something about the antecedents of the dead man. But the coroner was not a very close observer, and Mr. Dunbar's eager glance escaped him altogether.

"Yes," answered the Anglo-Indian, "Joseph Wilmot had a grudge against me before I sailed for Calcutta, but we settled all that at Southampton, and I promised to allow him an annuity."

"You promised him an annuity?"

"Yes—not a very large one—only fifty pounds a year; but he was quite satisfied with that promise."

"He had some claim upon you, then?"

"No, he had no claim whatever upon me," replied Mr. Dunbar, haughtily.

Of course, it could be scarcely pleasant for a millionaire to be cross-questioned in this manner by an impertinent Hampshire coroner.

The jurymen sympathized with the banker.

The coroner looked rather puzzled.

"If the deceased had no claim upon you, why did you promise him an annuity?" he asked, after a pause.

"I made that promise for the sake of 'auld lang syne,'" answered Mr. Dunbar.[36] "Joseph Wilmot was a favourite servant of mine five-and-thirty years ago. We were young men together. I believe that he had, at one time, a very sincere affection for me. I know that I always liked him."

---

[36] Loosely translates as "days gone by" or "old times". Most famous as the title of Robert Burns' poem "Auld Lang Syne" (1788).

"How long were you in the grove with the deceased?"

"Not more than ten minutes."

"And you cannot describe the spot where you left him?"

"Not very easily; I could point it out, perhaps, if I were taken there."

"What time elapsed between your leaving the cathedral yard with the deceased and your returning to it without him?"

"Perhaps half an hour."

"Not longer?"

"No; I do not imagine that it can have been longer."

"Thank you, Mr. Dunbar; that will do for the present," said the coroner.

The banker returned to his seat.

Arthur Lovell, still watching him, saw that his strong white hand trembled a little as his fingers trifled with those glittering toys hanging to his watch-chain.

The verger was the next person examined.

He described how he had been loitering in the yard of the cathedral as the two men passed across it. He told how they had gone by arm-in-arm, laughing and talking together.

"Which of them was talking as they passed you?" asked the coroner.

"Mr. Dunbar."

"Could you hear what he was saying?"

"No, sir. I could hear his voice, but I couldn't hear the words."

"What time elapsed between Mr. Dunbar and the deceased leaving the cathedral yard, and Mr. Dunbar returning alone?"

The verger scratched his head, and looked doubtfully at Henry Dunbar.

That gentleman was looking straight before him, and seemed quite unconscious of the verger's glance.

"I can't quite exactly say how long it was, sir," the old man answered, after a pause.

"Why can't you say exactly?"

"Because, you see, sir, I didn't keep no particular 'count of the time, and I shouldn't like to tell a falsehood."

"You must not tell a falsehood. We want the truth, and nothing but the truth."

"I know, sir; but you see I am an old man, and my memory is not as good as it used to be. I *think* Mr. Dunbar was away an hour."

Arthur Lovell gave an involuntary start. Every one of the jurymen looked suddenly at Mr. Dunbar.

But the Anglo-Indian did not flinch. He was looking at the verger now with a quiet steady gaze, which seemed that of a man who had nothing to fear, and who was serene and undisturbed by reason of his innocence.

"We don't want to know what you *think*," the coroner said; "you must tell us only what you are certain of."

"Then I'm not certain, sir."

"You are not certain that Mr. Dunbar was absent for an hour?"

"Not quite certain, sir."

"But very nearly certain. Is that so?"

"Yes, sir, I'm very nearly certain. You see, sir, when the two gentlemen went through the yard, the cathedral clock was chiming the quarter after four; I remember that. And when Mr. Dunbar came back, I was just going away to my tea, and I seldom go to my tea until it's gone five."

"But supposing it to have struck five when Mr. Dunbar returned, that would only make it three quarters of an hour after the time at which he went through the yard, supposing him to have gone through, as you say, at the quarter past four."

The verger scratched his head again.

"I'd been loiterin' about yesterday afternoon, sir," he said; "and I was a bit late thinkin' of my tea."

"And you believe, therefore, that Mr. Dunbar was absent for an hour?"

"Yes, sir; an hour—or more."

"An hour, or more?"

"Yes, sir."

"He was absent more than an hour; do you mean to say that?"

"It might have been more, sir. I didn't keep no particular 'count of the time."

Arthur Lovell had taken out his pocket-book, and was making notes of the verger's evidence.

The old man went on to describe his having shown Mr. Dunbar all over the cathedral. He made no mention of that sudden faintness which had seized upon the Anglo-Indian at the door of one of the chapels; but he described the rich man's manner as having been affable in the extreme.

He told how Henry Dunbar had loitered at the door of the cathedral, and afterwards lingered in the quadrangle, waiting for the coming of his servant. He told all this with many encomiums upon the rich man's pleasant manner.

The next, and perhaps the most important, witnesses were the two labourers, Philip Murtock and Patrick Hennessy, who had found the body of the murdered man.

Patrick Hennessy was sent out of the room while Murtock gave his evidence; but the evidence of the two men tallied in every particular.

They were Irishmen, reapers, and were returning from a harvest supper at a farm five miles from St. Cross, upon the previous evening. One of them had knelt down upon the edge of the stream to get a drink of water in the crown of his felt hat, and had been horrified by seeing the face of the dead man looking up at him in the moonlight, through the shallow water that barely covered it. The two men had dragged the body out of the streamlet, and Philip Murtock had watched beside it while Patrick Hennessy had gone to seek assistance.

The dead man's clothes had been stripped from him, with the exception of his trousers and boots, and the other part of his body was bare. There was a revolting brutality in this fact. It seemed that the murderer had stripped his victim for the sake of the clothes which he had worn. There could be little doubt, therefore, that the murder had been committed for the greed of gain, and not from any motive of revenge.

Arthur Lovell breathed more freely; until this moment his mind had been racked in agonizing doubts. Dark suspicions had been working in his breast. He had been tortured by the idea that the Anglo-Indian had murdered his old servant, in order to remove out of his way the chief witness of the crime of his youth.

But if this had been so, the murderer would never have lingered upon the scene of his crime in order to strip the clothes from his victim's body.

No! the deed had doubtless been done by some savage wretch, some lost and ignorant creature, hardened by a long life of crime, and preying like a wild beast upon his fellow-men.

Such murders are done in the world. Blood has been shed for the sake of some prize so small, so paltry, that it has been difficult for men to believe that one human being could destroy another for such an object.

Heaven have pity upon the wretch so lost as to be separated from his fellow-creatures by reason of the vileness of his nature! Heaven strengthen the hands of those who seek to spread Christian enlightenment and education through the land! for it is only those blessings that will thin the crowded prison wards, and rob the gallows of its victims.

The robbery of the dead man's clothes, and such property as he might have had about him at the time of his death, gave a new aspect to the murder in the eyes of Arthur Lovell. The case was clear and plain now, and the young man's duty was no longer loathsome to him; for he no longer suspected Henry Dunbar.

The constabulary had already been busy; the spot upon which the murder had been committed, and the neighbourhood of that spot, had been diligently searched. But no vestige of the dead man's garments had been found.

The medical man's evidence was very brief. He stated, that when he arrived at the Foresters' Arms he found the deceased quite dead, and that he appeared to have been dead some hours; that from the bruises and marks on the throat and neck, some contusions on the back of the head, and other appearances on the body, which witness minutely described, he said there were indications of a struggle having taken place between deceased and some other person or persons; that the man had been thrown, or had fallen down violently; and that death had ultimately been caused by strangling and suffocation.

The coroner questioned the surgeon very closely as to how long he thought the murdered man had been dead. The medical man declined to give any positive statement on this point; he could only say that when he was called in, the body was cold, and that the deceased might have been dead three hours—or he might have been dead five hours. It was impossible to form an opinion with regard to the exact time at which death had taken place.

The evidence of the waiter and the landlord of the George only went to show that the two men had arrived at the hotel together; that they had appeared in very high spirits, and on excellent terms with each other; that Mr. Dunbar had shown very great concern and anxiety about the absence of his companion, and had declined to eat his dinner until nine o'clock.

This closed the evidence; and the jury retired.

They were absent about a quarter of an hour, and then returned a verdict of wilful murder against some person or persons unknown.

Henry Dunbar, Arthur Lovell, and Mr. Balderby went back to the hotel. It was past six o'clock when the coroner's inquest was concluded, and the three men sat down to dinner together at seven.

That dinner-party was not a pleasant one; there was a feeling of oppression upon the minds of the three men. The awful event of the previous day cast its dreadful shadow upon them. They could not talk freely of this subject—for it was too ghastly a theme for discussion—and to talk of any other seemed almost impossible.

Arthur Lovell had observed with surprise that Henry Dunbar had not once spoken of his daughter. And yet this was scarcely strange; the utterance of that name might have jarred upon the father's feelings at such a time as this.

"You will write to Miss Dunbar to-night, will you not, sir?" the young man said at last. "I fear that she will have been very anxious about you all this day. She was alarmed by your message to Mr. Balderby."

"I shall not write," said the banker; "for I hope to see my daughter to-night."

"You will leave Winchester this evening, then?"

"Yes, by the 10.15 express. I should have travelled by that train yesterday evening, but for this terrible event."

Arthur Lovell looked rather astonished at this.

"You are surprised," said Mr. Dunbar.

"I thought perhaps that you might stay—until——"

"Until what?" asked the Anglo-Indian; "everything is finished, is it not? The inquest was concluded to-day. I shall leave full directions for the burial of this poor fellow, and an ample sum for his funeral expenses. I spoke to the coroner upon that subject this afternoon. What more can I do?"

"Nothing, certainly," answered Arthur Lovell, with rather a hesitating manner; "but I thought, under the peculiar circumstances, it might be better that you should remain upon the spot, if possible, until some steps shall have been taken for the finding of the murderer."

He did not like to give utterance to the thought that was in his mind; for he was thinking that some people would perhaps suspect Mr. Dunbar himself, and that it might be well for him to remain upon the scene of the murder until that suspicion should be done away with by the arrest of the real murderer.

The banker shook his head.

"I very much doubt the discovery of the guilty man," he said; "what is there to hinder his escape?"

"Everything," answered Arthur Lovell, warmly. "First, the stupidity of guilt, the blind besotted folly which so often betrays the murderer. It is not the commission of a crime only that is horrible; think of the hideous state of the criminal's mind *after* the deed is done. And it is at that time, immediately after the crime has been perpetrated, when the breast of the murderer is like a raging hell; it is at that time that he is called upon to be most circumspect—to keep guard upon his every look, his smallest word, his most trivial action,—for he knows that every look and action is watched; that every word is greedily listened to by men who are eager to bring his guilt home to him; by hungry men, wrestling for his conviction as a result that will bring them a golden reward; by practised men, who have studied the philosophy of crime, and who, by reason of their peculiar skill, are able to read dark meanings in words and looks that to other people are like a strange language. He knows that the scent of blood is in the air, and that the bloodhounds are at their loathsome work. He knows this; and at such a time he is called upon to face the world with a bold front, and so to fashion his words and looks that he shall deceive the secret watchers. He is never alone. The servant who waits upon him, or the railway guard who shows him to his seat in the first-class carriage, the porter who carries his luggage, or the sailor who looks at him scrutinizingly as he breathes the fresh sea-air upon the deck of that ship which is to carry him to a secure hiding-place—any one of these may be a disguised detective, and at any moment the bolt may fall; he may feel the light hand upon his shoulder, and know that he is a doomed man. Who can wonder, then, that a criminal is generally a coward, and that he betrays himself by some blind folly of his own?"

The young man had been carried away by his subject, and had spoken with a strange energy.

Mr. Dunbar laughed aloud at the lawyer's enthusiasm.

"You should have been a barrister, Mr. Lovell," he said; "that would have been a capital opening for your speech as counsel for the crown. I can see the wretched criminal shivering in the dock, cowering under that burst of forensic eloquence."

Henry Dunbar laughed heartily as he finished speaking, and then threw himself back in his easy-chair, and passed his handkerchief across his handsome forehead, as it was his habit to do occasionally.

"In this case I think the criminal will be most likely arrested," Arthur Lovell continued, still dwelling upon the subject of the murder; "he will be traced by those clothes. He will endeavour to sell them, of course; and as he is most likely some wretchedly ignorant boor, he will very probably try to sell them within a few miles of the scene of the crime."

"I hope he will be found," said Mr. Balderby, filling his glass with claret as he spoke; "I never heard any good of this man Wilmot, and, indeed, I believe he went to the bad altogether after you left England, Mr. Dunbar."

"Indeed!"

"Yes," answered the junior partner, looking rather nervously at his chief; "he committed forgery, I believe; fabricated forged bank notes, or something of that kind, and was transported for life, I heard; but I suppose he got a remission of his sentence, or something of that kind, and returned to England."

"I had no idea of this," said Mr. Dunbar.

"He did not tell you, then?"

"Oh, no; it was scarcely likely that he should tell me."

Very little more was said upon the subject just then. At nine o'clock Mr. Dunbar left the room to see to the packing of his things, at a little before ten the three gentlemen drove away from the George Hotel, on their way to the station.

They reached the station at five minutes past ten; the train was not due until a quarter past.

Mr. Balderby went to the office to procure the three tickets. Henry Dunbar and Arthur Lovell walked arm-in-arm up and down the platform.

As the bell for the up-train was ringing, a man came suddenly upon the platform and looked about him.

He recognized the banker, walked straight up to him, and, taking off his hat, addressed Mr. Dunbar respectfully.

"I am sorry to detain you, sir," he said; "but I have a warrant to prevent you leaving Winchester."

"What do you mean?"

"I hold a warrant for your apprehension, sir."

"From whom?"

"From Sir Arden Westhorpe, our chief county magistrate; and I am to take you before him immediately, sir."

"Upon what charge?" cried Arthur Lovell.

"Upon suspicion of having been concerned in the murder of Joseph Wilmot."

The millionaire drew himself up haughtily, and looked at the constable with a proud smile.

"This is too absurd," he said; "but I am quite ready to go with you. Be good enough to telegraph to my daughter, Mr. Lovell," he added, turning to the young man; "tell her that circumstances over which I have no control will detain me in Winchester for a week. Take care not to alarm her."

Everybody about the station had collected on the platform, and made a circle about Mr. Dunbar. They stood a little aloof from him, looking at him with respectful interest: altogether different from the eager clamorous curiosity with which they would have regarded any ordinary man suspected of the same crime.

He was suspected; but he could not be guilty. Why should a millionaire commit a murder? The motives that might influence other men could have had no weight with him.

The bystanders repeated this to one another, as they followed Mr. Dunbar and his custodian from the station, loudly indignant against the minions of the law.

Mr. Dunbar, the constable, and Mr. Balderby drove straight to the magistrate's house.

The junior partner offered any amount of bail for his chief; but the Anglo-Indian motioned him to silence, with a haughty gesture.

"I thank you, Mr. Balderby," he said, proudly; "but I will not accept my liberty on sufferance. Sir Arden Westhorpe has chosen to arrest me, and I shall abide the issue of that arrest."

It was in vain that the junior partner protested against this. Henry Dunbar was inflexible.

"I hope, and I venture to believe, that you are as innocent as I am myself of this horrible crime, Mr. Dunbar," the baronet said, kindly; "and I sympathize with you in this very terrible position. But upon the information laid before me, I consider it my duty to detain you until the matter shall have been further investigated. You were the last person seen with the deceased."

"And for that reason it is supposed that I strangled my old servant for the sake of his clothes," cried Mr. Dunbar, bitterly. "I am a stranger in England; but if that is your English law, I am not sorry that the best part of my life has been passed in India. However, I am perfectly willing to submit to any examination that may be considered necessary to the furtherance of justice."

So, upon the second night of his arrival in England, Henry Dunbar, chief of the wealthy house of Dunbar, Dunbar, and Balderby, slept in Winchester gaol.

- CHAPTER 13 -

THE PRISONER IS REMANDED

Mr. Dunbar was brought before Sir Arden Westhorpe, at ten o'clock, on the morning after his arrest. The witnesses who had given evidence at the inquest were again summoned, and—with the exception of the verger, and Mr. Dunbar, who was now a prisoner—gave the same evidence, or evidence to the same effect.

Arthur Lovell again watched the proceedings in the interest of Laura's father, and cross-examined some of the witnesses.

But very little new evidence was elicited. The empty pocket-book, which had been found a few paces from the body, was produced. The rope by which the murdered man had been strangled was also produced and examined.

It was a common rope, rather slender, and about a yard and a half in length. It was made into a running noose that had been drawn tightly round the neck of the victim.

Had the victim been a strong man he might perhaps have resisted the attack, and might have prevented his assailant tightening the fatal knot; but the surgeon bore witness that the dead man, though tall and stalwart-looking, had not been strong.

It was a strange murder, a bloodless murder; a deed that must have been done by a man of unfaltering resolution and iron nerve: for it must have been the work of a moment, in which the victim's first cry of surprise was stifled ere it was half uttered.

The chief witness upon this day was the verger; and it was in consequence of certain remarks dropped by him that Henry Dunbar had been arrested.

Upon the afternoon of the inquest this official had found himself a person of considerable importance. He was surrounded by eager gossips, greedy to hear anything he might have to tell upon the subject of the murder; and amongst those who listened to his talk was one of the constables—a sharp, clear-headed fellow—who was on the watch for any hint that might point to the secret of Joseph Wilmot's death. The verger, in describing the events of the previous afternoon, spoke of that one fact which he had omitted to refer to before the coroner. He spoke of the sudden faintness which had come over Mr. Dunbar.

"Poor gentleman!" he said, "I don't think I ever see the like of anything as come over him so sudden. He walked along the aisle with his head up, dashing and millingtary-like; but, all in a minute, he reeled as if he'd been dead drunk, and he would have fell if there hadn't been a bench handy. Down he dropped upon that bench like a stone; and when I turned round to look at him the drops of perspiration was rollin' down his forehead like beads. I never see such a face in my life, as ghastly-like as if he'd seen a ghost. But he was laughin' and smilin' the next minute; and it was only the heat of the weather, he says."

"It's odd as a gentleman that's just come home from India should complain of the heat on such a day as yesterday," said one of the bystanders.

This was the substance of the evidence that the verger gave before Sir Arden Westhorpe. This, with the evidence of a boy who had met the deceased and Henry Dunbar close to the spot where the body was found, was the only evidence against the rich man.

To the mind of Sir Arden Westhorpe the agitation displayed by Henry Dunbar in the cathedral was a very strong point; yet, what more possible than that the Anglo-Indian should have been seized with a momentary giddiness? He was not a young man; and though his broad chest, square shoulders, and long, muscular arms betokened strength, that natural vigour might have been impaired by the effects of a warm climate.

There were new witnesses upon this day, people who testified to having been in the neighbourhood of the grove, and in the grove itself, upon that fatal afternoon and evening.

Other labourers, besides the two Irishmen, had passed beneath the shadow of the trees in the moonlight. Idle pedestrians had strolled through the grove in the still twilight; not one of these had seen Joseph Wilmot, nor had there been heard any cry of anguish, or wild shrieks of terror.

One man deposed to having met a rough-looking fellow, half-gipsy, half-hawker, in the grove between seven and eight o'clock.

Arthur Lovell questioned this person as to the appearance and manner of the man he had met.

But the witness declared that there was nothing peculiar in the man's manner. He had not seemed confused, or excited, or hurried, or frightened. He was a coarse-featured, sunburnt ruffianly-looking fellow; and that was all.

Mr. Balderby was examined, and swore to the splendid position which Henry Dunbar occupied as chief of the house in St. Gundolph Lane; and then the examination was adjourned, and the prisoner remanded, although Arthur Lovell contended that there was no evidence to justify his detention.

Mr. Dunbar still protested against any offer of bail; he again declared that he would rather remain in prison than accept his liberty on sufferance, and go out into the world a suspected man.

"I will never leave Winchester Gaol," he said, "until I leave it with my character cleared in the eyes of every living creature."

He had been treated with the greatest respect by the prison officials, and had been provided with comfortable apartments. Arthur Lovell and Mr. Balderby were admitted to him whenever he chose to receive them.

Meanwhile every voice in Winchester was loud in indignation against those who had caused the detention of the millionaire.

Here was an English gentleman, a man whose wealth was something fabulous, newly returned from India, eager to embrace his only child; and before he had done more than set his foot upon his native soil, he was seized upon by obstinate and pig-headed officials, and thrown into a prison.

Arthur Lovell worked nobly in the service of Laura's father. He did not particularly like the man, though he wished to like him; but he believed him to be innocent of the dreadful crime imputed to him, and he was determined to make that innocence clear to the eyes of other people.

For this purpose he urged on the police upon the track of the strange man, the rough-looking hawker, who had been seen in the grove on the day of the murder.

He himself left Winchester upon another errand. He went away with the determination of discovering the sick man, Sampson Wilmot. The old clerk's evidence might be most important in such a case as this; as he would perhaps be able to throw much light upon the antecedents and associations of the dead man.

The young lawyer travelled along the line, stopping at every station. At Basingstoke he was informed that an old man, travelling with his brother, had been taken ill; and that he had since died. An inquest had been held upon his remains some days before, and he had been buried by the parish.

It was upon the 21st of August that Arthur Lovell visited Basingstoke. The people at the village inn told him that the old man had died at two o'clock upon the morning of the 17th, only a few hours after his brother's desertion of him. He had never spoken after the final stroke of paralysis.

There was nothing to be learned here, therefore. Death had closed the lips of this witness.

But even if Sampson Wilmot had lived to speak, what could he have told? The dead man's antecedents could have thrown little light upon the way in which he had met his death. It was a common murder, after all; a murder that had been done for the sake of the victim's little property; a silver watch, perhaps; a few sovereigns; a coat, waistcoat, and shirt.

The only evidence that tended in the least to implicate Henry Dunbar was the fact that he had been the last person seen in company with the dead man, and the discrepancy between his assertion and that of the verger respecting the time during which he had been absent from the cathedral yard.

No magistrate in his senses would commit the Anglo-Indian for trial upon such evidence as this.

- CHAPTER 14 -

MARGARET'S JOURNEY

While these things were taking place at Winchester, Margaret waited for the coming of her father. She waited until her heart grew sick, but still she did not despair of his return. He had promised to come back to her by ten o'clock upon the evening of the 16th; but he was not a man who always kept his promises. He had often left her in the same manner, and had stayed away for days and weeks together.

There was nothing extraordinary, therefore, in his absence; and if the girl's heart grew sick, it was not with the fear that her father would not return to her; but with the thought of what dishonest work he might be engaged in during his absence.

She knew now that he led a dishonest life. His own lips had told her the cruel truth. She would no longer be able to defend him when people spoke against him. Henceforth she must only plead for him.

The poor girl had been proud of her father, reprobate though he was; she had been proud of his gentlemanly bearing, his cleverness, his air of superiority over other men of his station; and the thought of his acknowledged guilt stung her to the heart. She pitied him, and she tried to make excuses for him in her own mind: and with every thought of the penniless reprobate there was intermingled the memory of the wrong that had been done him by Henry Dunbar.

"If my father has been guilty, that man is answerable for his guilt," she thought perpetually.

Meanwhile she waited, Heaven only knows how anxiously, for her father's coming. A week passed, and another week began, and still he did not come; but she was not alarmed for his personal safety, she was only anxious about him; and she expected his return every day, every hour. But he did not come.

And all this time, with her mind racked by anxious thoughts, the girl went about the weary duties of her daily life. Her thoughts might wander away into vague speculations about her father's absence while she sat by her pupil's side; but her eyes never wandered from the fingers it was her duty to watch. Her life had been a hard one, and she was better able to hide her sorrows and anxieties than any one to whom such a burden had been a novelty. So, very few people suspected that there was anything amiss with the grave young music-mistress.

One person did see the vague change in her manner; but that person was Clement Austin, who had already grown skilled in reading the varying expressions of her face, and who saw now that she was changed. She listened to him when he talked to her of the books or the music she loved; but her face never lighted up now with a bright look of pleasure; and he heard her sigh now and then as she gave her lesson.

He asked her once if there was anything in which his services, or his mother's, could be of any assistance to her; but she thanked him for the kindness of his offer, and told him, "No, there was nothing in which he could help her."

"But I am sure there is something on your mind. Pray do not think me intrusive or impertinent for saying so; but I am sure of it."

Margaret only shook her head.

"I am mistaken, then?" said Clement, interrogatively.

"You are indeed. I have no special trouble. I am only a little uneasy about my father, who has been away from home for the last week or two. But there is nothing strange in that; he is often away. Only I am apt to be foolishly anxious about him. He will scold me when he comes home and hears that I have been so."

Upon the evening of the 27th August, Margaret gave her accustomed lesson, and lingered a little as usual after the lesson, talking to Mrs. Austin, who had taken a wonderful fancy to her granddaughter's music-mistress; and to Clement, who somehow or other had discontinued his summer evening walks of late, more especially on those occasions on which his niece took her music-lesson. They talked of all manner of things, and it was scarcely strange that amongst other topics they should come by and-by to the Winchester murder.

"By the bye, Miss Wentworth," exclaimed Mrs. Austin, breaking in upon Clement's disquisition on his favourite Carlyle's "Hero-Worship," "I suppose you've heard about this dreadful murder that is making such a sensation?"

"A dreadful murder—no, Mrs. Austin; I rarely hear anything of that kind; for the person with whom I lodge is old and deaf. She troubles herself very little about what is going on in the world, and I never read the newspapers myself."

"Indeed," said Mrs. Austin; "well, my dear, you really surprise me. I thought this dreadful business had made such a sensation, on account of the great Mr. Dunbar being mixed up in it."

"Mr. Dunbar!" cried Margaret, looking at the speaker with dilated eyes.

"Yes, my dear, Mr. Dunbar, the rich banker. I have been very much interested in the matter, because my son is employed in Mr. Dunbar's bank. It seems that an old servant, a confidential valet of Mr. Dunbar's, has been murdered at Winchester; and at first Mr. Dunbar himself was suspected of the crime,—though, of course, that was utterly ridiculous; for what motive could he possibly have had for murdering his old servant? However, he has been suspected, and some stupid country magistrate actually had him arrested. There was an examination about a week ago, which was adjourned until to-day. We shan't know the result of it till to-morrow."

Margaret sat listening to these words with a face that was as white as the face of the dead.

Clement Austin saw the sudden change that had come over her countenance.

"Mother," he said, "you should not talk of these things before Miss

Wentworth; you have made her look quite ill. Remember, she may not be so strong-minded as you are."

"No, no!" gasped Margaret, in a choking voice. "I—I—wish to hear of this. Tell me, Mrs. Austin, what was the name of the murdered man?"

"Joseph Wilmot."

"Joseph Wilmot!" repeated Margaret, slowly. She had always known her father by the name of James Wentworth; but what more likely than that Wilmot was his real name! She had good reason to suspect that Wentworth was a false one.

"I'll lend you a newspaper," Mrs. Austin said, good-naturedly, "if you really want to learn the particulars of this murder."

"I do, if you please."

Mrs. Austin took a weekly paper from amongst some others that were scattered upon a side-table. She folded up this paper and handed it to Margaret.

"Give Miss Wentworth a glass of wine, mother," exclaimed Clement Austin; "I'm sure all this talk about the murder has upset her."

"No, no, indeed!" Margaret answered, "I would rather not take anything. I want to get home quickly. Good evening, Mrs. Austin."

She tried to say something more, but her voice failed her. She had been in the habit of shaking hands with Mrs. Austin and Clement when she left them; and the cashier had always accompanied her to the gate, and had sometimes lingered with her there in the dusk, prolonging some conversation that had been begun in the drawing-room; but to-night she hurried from the room before the widow could remonstrate with her. Clement followed her into the hall.

"Miss Wentworth," he said, "I know that something has agitated you. Pray return to the drawing-room, and stop with us until you are more composed."

"No—no—no!"

"Let me see you home, then?"

"Oh! no! no!" she cried, as the young man barred her passage, to the door; "for pity's sake don't detain me, Mr. Austin; don't detain me, or follow me!"

She passed by him, and hurried out of the house. He followed her to the gate, and watched her disappear in the twilight; and then went back to the drawing-room, sighing heavily as he went.

"I have no right to follow her against her own wish," he said to himself. "She has given me no right to interfere with her; or to think of her, for the matter of that."

He threw himself into a chair, and took up a newspaper; but he did not read half-a-dozen lines. He sat with his eyes fixed upon the page before him, thinking of Margaret Wentworth.

"Poor girl!" he said to himself, presently; "poor lonely girl! She is too pure and beautiful for the hard struggles of this world."

$$* \quad * \quad * \quad * \quad *$$

Margaret Wentworth walked rapidly along the road that led her back to Wandsworth. She held the folded newspaper clutched tightly against her breast. It was her death-warrant, perhaps. She never paused or slackened her pace until she reached the lane leading down to the water.

She, opened the gate of the simple cottage-garden—there was no need of bolts or locks for the fortification of Godolphin Cottages—and went up to her own little sitting-room,—the room in which her father had told her the secret of his life,—the room in which she had sworn to remember the name of Henry Dunbar. All was dark and quiet in the house, for the mistress of it was elderly-and old-fashioned in her ways; and Margaret was accustomed to wait upon herself when she came home after nightfall.

She struck a lucifer,[37] lighted her candle, and sat down with the newspaper in her hand. She unfolded it, and examined the pages. She was not long finding what she wanted.

"The Winchester Murder. Latest Particulars."

Margaret Wentworth read that horrible story. She read the newspaper record of the cruel deed that had been done—twice—slowly and deliberately. Her eyes were tearless, and there was a desperate courage at her heart; that miserable, agonized heart, which seemed like a block of ice in her breast.

"I swore to remember the name of Henry Dunbar," she said in, a low, sombre voice; "I have good reason to remember it now."

From the first she had no doubt in her mind—from the very first she had but one idea: and that idea was a conviction. Her father had been murdered by his old master. The man Joseph Wilmot was her father: the murderer was Henry Dunbar. The newspaper record told how the murdered man had, according to his own account, met his brother at the Waterloo station upon the afternoon of the 16th of August. That was the very afternoon upon which James Wentworth had left his daughter to go to London by rail.

He had met his old master, the man who had so bitterly injured him;

---

[37] Lucifers: popular brand of friction matches, manufactured by Samuel Jones.

the cold-hearted scoundrel who had so cruelly betrayed him. He had been violent, perhaps, and had threatened Henry Dunbar: and then—then the rich man, treacherous and cold-hearted in his age as in his youth, had beguiled his old valet by a pretended friendship, had lured him into a lonely place, and had there murdered him; in order that all the wicked secrets of the past might be buried with his victim.

As to the robbery of the clothes—the rifling of the pocketbook—that, of course, was only a part of Henry Dunbar's deep laid scheme.

The girl folded the paper and put it in her breast. It was a strange document to lie against that virginal bosom: and the breast beneath it ached with a sick, cold pain, that was like the pain of death.

Margaret took up her candle, and went into a neatly-kept little room at the back of the house,—the room in which her father had always slept when he stayed in that house.

There was an old box, a battered and dilapidated hair-trunk,[38] with a worn rope knotted about it. The girl knelt down before the box, and put her candle on a chair beside it. Then with her slender fingers she tried to unfasten the knots that secured the cord. This task was not an easy one, and her fingers ached before she had done. But she succeeded at last, and lifted the lid of the trunk.

There were worn and shabby garments, tumbled and dusty, that had been thrown pell-mell into the box: there were broken meerschaum-pipes; old newspapers, pale with age, and with passages here and there marked by thick strokes in faded ink. A faint effluvium that arose from the mass of dilapidated rubbish—the weeds which the great ocean Time casts up upon the shore of the present—testified to the neighbourhood of mice: and scattered about the bottom of the box, amongst loose shreds of tobacco—broken lumps of petrified cavendish[39]—and scraps of paper, there were a few letters.

Margaret gathered together these letters, and examined them. Three of them—very old, faded, and flabby—were directed to "Joseph Wilmot, care of the Governor of Norfolk Island," in a prim, clerk-like hand.

It was an ominous address. Margaret Wentworth bowed her head upon her knees and sobbed aloud.

"He had been very wicked, and had need of a long life of penitence," she thought; "but he has been murdered by Henry Dunbar."

There was no shadow of doubt now in her mind. She had in her own hand the conclusive proof of the identity between Joseph Wilmot and her father; and to her this seemed quite enough to prove that Henry

---

[38] A trunk covered with animal skin, which still retained the hair.
[39] Tobacco that has been softened and pressed into solid cakes.

Dunbar was the murderer of his old servant. He had injured the man, and it was in the man's power to do him injury. He had resolved, therefore, to get rid of this old accomplice, this dangerous witness of the past.

This was how Margaret reasoned. That the crime committed in the quiet grove, near St. Cross, was an every-day deed, done for the most pitiful and sordid motives that can tempt a man to shed his brother's blood, never for a moment entered into her thoughts. Other people might think this in their ignorance of the story of the past.

At daybreak the next morning she left the house, after giving a very brief explanation of her departure to the old woman with whom she lodged. She took the first train to Winchester, and reached the station two hours before noon. She had her whole stock of money with her, but nothing else. Her own wants, her own necessities, had no place in her thoughts. Her errand was a fearful one, for she went to tell so much as she knew of the story of the past, and to bear witness against Henry Dunbar.

The railway official to whom she addressed herself at the Winchester station treated her with civility and good-nature. The pale beauty of her pensive face won her friends wherever she went. It is very hard upon pug-nosed merit and red-haired virtue, that a Grecian profile, or raven tresses, should be such an excellent letter of introduction; but, unhappily, human nature is weak; and while beauty appeals straight to the eye of the frivolous, merit requires to be appreciated by the wise.

"If there is anything I can do for you, miss," the railway official said, politely, "I shall be very happy, I'm sure."

"I want to know about the murder," the girl answered, in a low, tremulous voice, "the murder that was committed——"

"Yes, miss, to be sure. Everybody in Winchester is talking about it; a most mysterious event! But," cried the official, brightening suddenly, "you ain't a witness, miss, are you? You don't know anything about—— eh?"

He was quite excited at the bare idea that this pretty girl had something to say about the murder, and that he might have the privilege of introducing her to his fellow-citizens. To know anybody who knew anything about Joseph Wilmot's murder was to occupy a post of some distinction in Winchester just now.

"Yes," Margaret said; "I want to give evidence against Henry Dunbar."

The railway official started, and stared aghast.

"Evidence against Mr. Dunbar, miss?" he said; "why, Mr. Henry Dunbar was dismissed from custody only yesterday afternoon, and is going up to town by the express this night, and everybody in Winchester is full of the shameful way in which he has been treated. Why, as far as that goes, there was no more ground for suspecting Mr. Dunbar—not that has come out yet, at any rate—than there is for suspecting me!" And the porter snapped his fingers contemptuously. "But if you know anything against Mr. Dunbar, why, of course, that alters the case; and it's yer bounden dooty, miss, to go before the magistrate directly-minute and make yer statement."

The porter could hardly refrain, from smacking his lips with an air of relish as he said this. Distinction had come to him unsought.

"Wait a minute, miss," he said; "I'll go and ask lief to take you round to the magistrate's. You'll never find your way by yourself. The next up isn't till 12.07[40]—I can be spared."

The porter ran away, presented himself to a higher official, told his story, and obtained a brief leave of absence. Then he returned to Margaret.

"Now, miss," he said, "if you'll come along with me I'll take you to Sir Arden Westhorpe's house. Sir Arden is the gentleman that has taken so much trouble with this case."

On the way through the back-streets of the quiet city the porter would fain have extracted from Margaret all that she had to tell. But the girl would reveal nothing; she only said that she wanted to bear witness against Henry Dunbar.

The porter, upon the other hand, was very communicative. He told his companion what had happened at the adjourned examination.

"There was a deal of applause in the court when Mr. Dunbar was told he might consider himself free," said the porter; "but Sir Arden checked it; there was no need for clapping of hands, he says, or for anything but sorrow that such a wicked deed had been done, and that the cruel wretch as did it should escape. A young man as was in the court told me that them was Sir Arden's exack words."

They had reached Sir Arden's house by this time. It was a very handsome house, though it stood in a back street; and a grave man-servant, in a linen jacket, admitted Margaret into the oak-panelled hall.

She might have had some difficulty perhaps in seeing Sir Arden, had not the railway porter immediately declared her business. But the name of the murdered man was a passport, and she was ushered at once into a low room, which was lined with book-shelves, and opened into an old-fashioned garden.

---

[40] Original text has 12.7.

Here Sir Arden Westhorpe, the magistrate, sat at a table writing. He was an elderly man, with grey hair and whiskers, and with rather a stern expression of countenance. But he was a good and a just man; and though Henry Dunbar had been the emperor of half Europe instead of an Anglo-Indian banker, Sir Arden would have committed him for trial had he seen just cause for so doing.

Margaret was in nowise abashed by the presence of the magistrate. She had but one thought in her mind, the thought of her father's wrongs; and she could have spoken freely in the presence of a king.

"I hope I am not too late, sir," she said; "I hear that Mr. Dunbar has been discharged from custody. I hope I am not too late to bear witness against him."

The magistrate looked up with an expression of surprise. "That will depend upon circumstances," he said; "that is to say, upon the nature of the statement which you may have to make."

The magistrate summoned his clerk from an adjoining room, and then took down the girl's information.

But he shook his head doubtfully when Margaret had told him all she had to tell. That which to the impulsive girl seemed proof positive of Henry Dunbar's guilt was very little when written down in a business-like manner by Sir Arden Westhorpe's clerk.

"You know your unhappy father to have been injured by Mr. Dunbar, and you think he may have been in the possession of secrets of a damaging nature to that gentleman; but you do not know what those secrets were. My poor girl, I cannot possibly move in this business upon such evidence as this. The police are at work. This matter will not be allowed to pass off without the closest investigation, believe me. I shall take care to have your statement placed in the hands of the detective officer who is entrusted with the conduct of this affair. We must wait— we must wait. I cannot bring myself to believe that Henry Dunbar has been guilty of this fearful crime. He is rich enough to have bribed your father to keep silence, if he had any reason to fear what he might say. Money is a very powerful agent, and can buy almost anything. It is rarely that a man, with almost unlimited wealth at his command, finds himself compelled to commit an act of violence."

The magistrate read aloud Margaret Wilmot's deposition, and the girl signed it in the presence of the clerk; she signed it with her father's real name: the name that she had never written before that day.

Then, having given the magistrate the address of her Wandsworth lodging, she bade him good morning, and went out into the unfamiliar street.

Nothing that Sir Arden Westhorpe had said had in any way weakened her rooted conviction of Henry Dunbar's guilt. She still believed that he was the murderer of her father.

She walked for some distance without knowing where she went, then suddenly she stopped; her face flushed, her eyes grew bright, and an ominous smile lit up her countenance.

"I will go to Henry Dunbar," she said to herself, "since the law will not help me; I will go to my father's murderer. Surely he will tremble when he knows that his victim left a daughter who will rest neither night nor day until she sees justice done."

Sir Arden had mentioned the hotel at which Henry Dunbar was staying; so Margaret asked the first passer-by to direct her to the George.

She found a waiter lounging in the doorway of the hotel.

"I want to see Mr. Dunbar," she said.

The man looked at her with considerable surprise.

"I don't think it's likely Mr. Dunbar will see you, miss," he said; "but I'll take your name up if you wish it."

"I shall be much obliged if you will do so."

"Certainly, miss. If you'll please to sit down in the hall I'll go to Mr. Dunbar immediately. Your name is———"

"My name is Margaret Wilmot."

The waiter started as if he had been shot.

"Wilmot!" he exclaimed; "any relation to———"

"I am the daughter of Joseph Wilmot," answered Margaret, quietly. "You can tell Mr. Dunbar so if you please."

"Yes, miss; I will, miss. Bless my soul! you really might knock me down with a feather, miss. Mr. Dunbar can't possibly refuse to see *you*, I should think, miss."

The waiter went up-stairs, looking back at Margaret as he went. He seemed to think that the daughter of the murdered man ought to be, in some way or other, different from other young women.

- CHAPTER 15 -

BAFFLED

M r. Dunbar was sitting in a luxurious easy-chair, with a newspaper lying across his knee. Mr. Balderby had returned to London upon the previous evening, but Arthur Lovell still remained with the Anglo-Indian.

Henry Dunbar was a good deal the worse for the close confinement which he had suffered since his arrival in the cathedral city. Everybody who looked at him saw the change which the last ten days had made in his appearance. He was very pale; there were dark purple rings about his eyes; the eyes themselves were unnaturally bright: and the mouth—that tell-tale feature, over whose expression no man has perfect control—betrayed that the banker had suffered.

Arthur Lovell had been indefatigable in the service of his client: not from any love towards the man, but always influenced more or less by the reflection that Henry Dunbar was Laura's father; and that to serve Henry Dunbar was in some manner to serve the woman he loved.

Mr. Dunbar had only been discharged from custody upon the previous evening, after a long and wearisome examination and cross-examination of the witnesses who had given evidence at the coroner's inquest, and that additional testimony upon which the magistrate had issued his warrant. He had slept till late, and had only just finished breakfast, when the waiter entered with Margaret's message.

"A young person wishes to see you, sir," he said, respectfully.

"A young person!" exclaimed Mr. Dunbar, impatiently; "I can't see any one. What should any young person want with me?"

"She wants to see you particularly, sir; she says her name is Wilmot—Margaret Wilmot; and that she is the daughter of——"

The sickly pallor of Mr. Dunbar's face changed to an awful livid hue: and Arthur Lovell, looking at his client at this moment, saw the change.

It was the first time he had seen any evidence of fear either in the face or manner of Henry Dunbar.

"I will not see her," exclaimed Mr. Dunbar; "I never heard Wilmot speak of any daughter. This woman is some impudent impostor, who wants to extort money out of me. I will not see her: let her be sent about her business."

The waiter hesitated.

"She is a very respectable-looking person, sir," he said; "she doesn't look anything like an impostor."

"Perhaps not!" answered Mr. Dunbar, haughtily; "but she *is* an impostor, for all that. Joseph Wilmot had no daughter, to my knowledge. Pray do not let me be disturbed about this business. I have suffered quite enough already on account of this man's death."

He sank back in his chair, and took up his newspaper as he finished speaking. His face was completely hidden behind the newspaper.

"Shall I go and speak to this girl?" asked Arthur Lovell.

"On no account! The girl is an impostor. Let her be sent about her business!"

The waiter left the room.

"Pardon me, Mr. Dunbar," said the young lawyer; "but if you will allow me to make a suggestion, as your legal adviser in this business, I would really recommend you to see this girl."

"Why?"

"Because the people in a place like this are notorious gossips and scandal-mongers. If you refuse to see this person, who, at any rate, calls herself Joseph Wilmot's daughter, they may say——"

"They may say what?" asked Henry Dunbar.

"They may say that it is because you have some special reason for not seeing her."

"Indeed, Mr. Lovell. Then I am to put myself out of the way—after being fagged and harassed to death already about this business—and am to see every adventuress who chooses to trade upon the name of the murdered man, in order to stop the mouths of the good people of Winchester. I beg to tell you, my dear sir, that I am utterly indifferent to anything that may be said of me: and that I shall only study my own ease and comfort. If people choose to think that Henry Dunbar is the murderer of his old servant, they are welcome to their opinion: I shall not trouble myself to set them right."

The waiter re-entered the room as Mr. Dunbar finished speaking.

"The young person says that she must see you, sir," the man said. "She says that if you refuse to see her, she will wait at the door of this house until you leave it. My master has spoken to her, sir; but it's no use: she's the most determined young woman I ever saw."

Mr. Dunbar's face was still hidden by the newspaper. There was a little pause before he replied.

"Lovell," he said at last, "perhaps you had better go and see this person. You can find out if she is really related to that unhappy man. Here is my purse. You can let her have any money you think proper. If she is the daughter of that wretched man, I should, of course, wish her to be well provided for. I will thank you to tell her that, Lovell. Tell her that I am willing to settle an annuity upon her; always on condition that she does not intrude herself upon me. But remember, whatever I give is contingent upon her own good conduct, and must not in any way be taken as a bribe. If she chooses to think and speak ill of me, she is free to do so. I have no fear of her; nor of any one else."

Arthur Lovell took the millionaire's purse and went down stairs with the waiter. He found Margaret sitting in the hall. There was no impatience, no violence in her manner: but there was a steady, fixed, resolute look in her white face. The young lawyer felt that this girl would not be easily put off by any denial of Mr. Dunbar.

He ushered Margaret into a private sitting-room leading out of the hall, and then closed the door behind him. The disappointed waiter lingered upon the door-mat: but the George is a well-built house, and that waiter lingered in vain.

"You want to see Mr. Dunbar?" he said.

"Yes, sir!"

"He is very much fatigued by yesterday's business, and he declines to see you. What is your motive for being so eager to see him?"

"I will tell that to Mr. Dunbar himself."

"You are *really* the daughter of Joseph Wilmot? Mr. Dunbar seems to doubt the fact of his having had a daughter."

"Perhaps so. Mr. Dunbar may have been unaware of my existence until this moment. I did not know until last night what had happened."

She stopped for a moment, half-stifled by a hysterical sob, which she could not repress: but she very quickly regained her self-control, and continued, slowly and deliberately, looking earnestly in the young man's face with her clear brown eyes, "I did not know until last night that my father's name was Wilmot; he had called himself by a false name—but last night, after hearing of the—the—murder"—the horrible word seemed to suffocate her, but she still went bravely on—"I searched a box of my father's and found this."

She took from her pocket the letter directed to Norfolk Island, and handed it to the lawyer.

"Read it," she said; "you will see then how my father had been wronged by Henry Dunbar."

Arthur Lovell unfolded the worn and faded letter. It had been written five-and-twenty years before by Sampson Wilmot. Margaret pointed to one passage on the second page.

"Your bitterness against Henry Dunbar is very painful to me, my dear Joseph; yet I cannot but feel that your hatred against my employer's son is only natural. I know that he was the first cause of your ruin; and that, but for him, your lot in life might have been very different. Try to forgive him; try to forget him, even if you cannot forgive. Do not talk of revenge. The revelation of that secret which you hold respecting the forged bills would bring disgrace not only upon him, but upon his father and his uncle. They are both good and honourable men, and I think that shame would kill them. Remember this, and keep the secret of that painful story."

Arthur Lovell's face grew terribly grave as he read these lines. He had heard the story of the forgery hinted at, but he had never heard its details. He had looked upon it as a cruel scandal, which had perhaps arisen out of some trifling error, some unpaid debt of honour; some foolish gambling transaction in the early youth of Henry Dunbar.

But here, in the handwriting of the dead clerk, here was the evidence of that old story. Those few lines in Sampson Wilmot's letter suggested a *motive*.

The young lawyer dropped into a chair, and sat for some minutes silently poring over the clerk's letter. He did not like Henry Dunbar. His generous young heart, which had yearned towards Laura's father, had sunk in his breast with a dull, chill feeling of disappointment, at his first meeting with the rich man.

Still, after carefully sifting the evidence of the coroner's inquest, he had come to the conclusion that Henry Dunbar was innocent of Joseph Wilmot's death. He had carefully weighed every scrap of evidence against the Anglo-Indian; and had deliberately arrived at this conclusion.

But now he looked at everything in a new light. The clerk's letter suggested a motive, perhaps an adequate motive. The two men had gone down together into that silent grove, the servant had threatened his patron, they had quarrelled, and—

No! the murder could scarcely have happened in this way. The assassin had been armed with the cruel rope, and had crept stealthily behind his victim. It was not a common murder; the rope and the slip-knot, the treacherous running noose, hinted darkly at Oriental experiences: somewhat in this fashion might a murderous Thug have assailed his unconscious victim.[41]

But then, on the other hand, there was one circumstance that always remained in Henry Dunbar's favour—that circumstance was the robbery of the dead man's clothes. The Anglo-Indian might very well have rifled the pocket-book, and left it empty upon the scene of the murder, in order to throw the officers of justice upon a wrong scent. That would have been only the work of a few moments.

But was it probable—was it even possible—that the murderer would have lingered in broad daylight, with every chance against him, long enough to strip off the garments of his victim, in order still more effectually to hoodwink suspicion? Was it not a great deal more likely that Joseph Wilmot had spent the afternoon drinking in the tap-room of some roadside public-house, and had rambled back into the grove after dark, to meet his death at the hands of some every-day assassin, bent only upon plunder?

All these thoughts passed through Arthur Lovell's mind as he sat with Sampson's faded letter in his hands. Margaret Wilmot watched him with eager, scrutinizing eyes. She saw doubt, perplexity, horror, indecision, all struggling in his handsome face.

---

[41] Thugs were professional robbers and murderers in India, believed to practice strangling or garrotting as their preferred method of assassination. From the Hindi word "thag" meaning a cheat or swindler. Thuggee was practised extensively in India until the late 19th century, despite British colonial attempts to suppress the associations.

But the lawyer felt that it was his duty to act, and to act in the interests of his client, whatever vaguely-hideous doubts might arise in his own breast. Nothing but his *conviction* of Henry Dunbar's guilt could justify him in deserting his client. He was not convinced; he was only horror-stricken by the first whisper of doubt.

"Mr. Dunbar declines to see you," he said to Margaret; "and I do not really see what good could possibly arise out of an interview between you. In the meantime, if you are in any way distressed—and you must most likely need assistance at such a time as this—he is quite ready to help you: and he is also ready to give you permanent help if you require it."

He opened Henry Dunbar's purse as he spoke, but the girl rose and looked at him with icy disdain in her fixed white face.

"I would sooner crawl from door to door, begging my bread of the hardest strangers in this cruel world—I would sooner die from the lingering agonies of starvation—than I would accept help from Henry Dunbar. No power on earth will ever induce me to take a sixpence from that man's hand."

"Why not?"

"*You* know why not. I can see that knowledge in your face. Tell Mr. Dunbar that I will wait at the door of this house till he comes out to speak to me. I will wait until I drop down dead."

Arthur Lovell went back to his client, and told him what the girl said.

Mr. Dunbar was walking up and down the room, with his head bent moodily upon his breast.

"By heavens!" he cried, angrily, "I will have this girl removed by the police, if——"

He stopped abruptly, and his head sank once more upon his breast.

"I would most earnestly advise you to see her," pleaded Arthur Lovell; "if she goes away in her present frame of mind, she may spread a horrible scandal against you. Your refusing to see her will confirm the suspicions which——"

"What!" cried Henry Dunbar; "does she dare to suspect me?"

"I fear so."

"Has she said as much?"

"Not in actual words. But her manner betrayed her suspicions. You must not wonder if this girl is unreasonable. Her father's miserable fate must have been a terrible blow to her."

"Did you offer her money?"

"I did."

"And she——"

"She refused it."

Mr. Dunbar winced, as if the announcement of the girl's refusal had stung him to the quick.

"Since it must be so," he said, "I will see this importunate woman. But not to-day. To-day I must and will have rest. Tell her to come to me to-morrow morning at ten o'clock. I will see her then."

Arthur Lovell carried this message to Margaret.

The girl looked at him with an earnest questioning glance.

"You are not deceiving me?" she said.

"No, indeed!"

"Mr. Dunbar said that?"

"He did."

"Then I will go away. But do not let Henry Dunbar try to deceive me! for I will follow him to the end of the world. I care very little where I go in my search for the man who murdered my father!"

She went slowly away. She went down into the cathedral yard, across which the murdered man had gone arm-in-arm with his companion. Some boys, loitering about at the entrance to the meadows, answered all her questions, and took her to the spot upon which the body had been found.

It was a dull misty day, and there was a low wind wailing amongst the wet branches of the old trees. The rain-drops from the fading leaves fell into the streamlet, from whose shallow waters the dead man's face had looked up to the moonlit sky.

Later in the afternoon, Margaret found her way to a cemetery outside the town, where, under a newly-made mound of turf, the murdered man lay.

A great many people had been to see this grave, and had been very much disappointed at finding it in no way different from other graves.

Already the good citizens of Winchester had begun to hint that the grove near St. Cross was haunted; and there was a vague report to the effect that the dead man had been seen there, walking in the twilight.

Punctual to the very striking of the clock, Margaret Wilmot presented herself at the George at the time appointed by Mr. Dunbar.

She had passed a wretched night at a humble inn a little way out of the town, and had been dreaming all night of her meeting with Mr. Dunbar. In those troubled dreams she had met the rich man perpetually: now in one place, now in another: but always in the most unlikely places: yet she had never seen his face. She had tried to see it; but by some strange devilry or other, peculiar to the incidents of a dream, it had been always hidden from her.

The same waiter was lounging in the same attitude at the door of the hotel. He looked up with an expression of surprise as Margaret approached him.

"You've not gone, then, miss?" he exclaimed.

"Gone! No! I have waited to see Mr. Dunbar!"

"Well, that's queer," said the waiter; "did he tell you he'd see you?"

"Yes, he promised to see me at ten o'clock this morning."

"That's uncommon queer."

"Why so?" asked Margaret, eagerly.

"Because Mr. Dunbar, and that young gent as was with him, went away, bag and baggage, by last night's express."

Margaret Wilmot gave no utterance to either surprise or indignation. She walked quietly away, and went once more to the house of Sir Arden Westhorpe. She told him what had occurred, and her statement was written down and signed, as upon the previous day.

"Mr. Dunbar murdered my father!" she said, after this had been done; "and he's afraid to see me!"

The magistrate shook his head gravely.

"No, no, my dear," he said; "you must not say that. I cannot allow you to make such an assertion as that. Circumstantial evidence often points to an innocent person. If Mr. Dunbar had been in any way concerned in this matter, he would have made a point of seeing you, in order to set your suspicions at rest. His declining to see you is only the act of a selfish man, who has already suffered very great inconvenience from this business, and who dreads the scandal of some tragical scene."

- CHAPTER 16 -

IS IT LOVE OR FEAR?

Henry Dunbar and Arthur Lovell slept at the same hotel upon the night of their journey from Winchester to London; for the banker refused to disturb his daughter by presenting himself at the house in Portland Place after midnight.

In this, at least, he showed himself a considerate father.

Arthur Lovell had made every effort in his power to dissuade the banker from leaving Winchester upon that night, and thus breaking the promise that he had made to Margaret Wilmot. Henry Dunbar was resolute; and the young lawyer had no alternative. If his client chose to do a dishonourable thing, in spite of all that the young man could say against it, of course it was no business of his. For his own part, Arthur Lovell was only too glad to get back to London; for Laura Dunbar was there: and wherever she was, there was Paradise, in the opinion of this foolish young man.

Early upon the morning after their arrival in London, Henry Dunbar and the young lawyer breakfasted together in their sitting-room at the hotel. It was a bright morning, and even London looked pleasant in the sunshine. Henry Dunbar stood in the window, looking out into the street below, while the breakfast was being placed upon the table. The hotel was situated in a new street at the West End.

"You find London very much altered, I dare say, Mr. Dunbar?" said Arthur Lovell, as he unfolded the morning paper.

"How do you mean altered?" asked the banker, absently.

"I mean, that after so long an absence you must find great improvements. This street for instance—it has not been built six years."

"Oh, yes, I remember. There were fields upon this spot when I went to India."

They sat down to breakfast. Henry Dunbar was absent-minded, and ate very little. When he had drunk a cup of tea, he took out the locket containing Laura's miniature, and sat silently contemplating it.

By-and-by he unfastened the locket from the chain, and handed it across the table to Arthur Lovell.

"My daughter is very beautiful, if she is like that," said the banker; "do you consider it a good likeness?"

The young lawyer looked at the portrait with a tender smile. "Yes," he said, thoughtfully, "it is very like her—only——"

"Only what?"

"The picture is not lovely enough."

"Indeed! and yet it is very beautiful. Laura resembles her mother, who was a lovely woman."

"But I have heard your father say, that the lower part of Miss Dunbar's face—the mouth and chin—reminded him of yours. I must own, Mr. Dunbar, that I cannot see the likeness."

"I dare say not," the banker answered, carelessly; "you must allow something for the passage of time, my dear Lovell, and the wear and tear of a life in Calcutta. I dare say my mouth and chin are rather harder and sterner in their character than Laura's."

There was nothing more said upon the subject of the likeness; by and by Mr. Dunbar got up, took his hat, and went towards the door.

"You will come with me, Lovell," he said.

"Oh, no, Mr. Dunbar. I would not wish to intrude upon you at such a time. The first interview between a father and daughter, after a separation of so many years, is almost sacred in its character. I——"

"Pshaw, Mr. Lovell! I did not think a solicitor's son would be weak enough to indulge in any silly sentimentality. I shall be very glad to see

115

my daughter; and I understand from her letters that she will be pleased to see me. That is all! At the same time, as you know Laura much better than I do, you may as well come with me."

Mr. Dunbar's looks belied the carelessness of his words. His face was deadly pale, and there was a singularly rigid expression about his mouth.

Laura had received no notice of her father's coming. She was sitting at the same window by which she had sat when Arthur Lovell asked her to be his wife. She was sitting in the same low luxurious easy-chair, with the hot-house flowers behind her, and a huge Newfoundland dog—a faithful attendant that she had brought from Maudesley Abbey—lying at her feet.

The door of Miss Dunbar's morning-room was open: and upon the broad landing-place outside the apartment the banker stopped suddenly, and laid his hand upon the gilded balustrade. For a moment it seemed almost as if he would have fallen: but he leaned heavily upon the bronze scroll-work of the banister, and bit his lower lip fiercely with his strong white teeth. Arthur Lovell was not displeased to perceive this agitation: for he had been wounded by the careless manner in which Henry Dunbar had spoken of his beautiful daughter. Now it was evident that the banker's indifference had only been assumed as a mask beneath which the strong man had tried to conceal the intensity of his feelings.

The two men lingered upon the landing-place for a few minutes; while Mr. Dunbar looked about him, and endeavoured to control his agitation. Everything here was new to him: for neither the house in Portland Place, nor Maudesley Abbey, had been in the possession of the Dunbar family more than twenty years.

The millionaire contemplated his possessions. Even upon that landing-place there was no lack of evidence of wealth. A Persian carpet covered the centre of the floor, and beyond its fringed margin a tessellated pavement of coloured marbles took new and brighter hues from the slanting rays of sunlight that streamed in through a wide stained-glass window upon the staircase. Great Dresden vases of exotics stood on pedestals of malachite and gold: and a trailing curtain of purple velvet hung half-way across the entrance to a long suite of drawing-rooms—a glistening vista of light and splendour.

Mr. Dunbar pushed open the door, and stood upon the threshold of his daughter's chamber. Laura started to her feet.

"Papa!—papa!" she cried; "I thought that you would come to-day!"

She ran to him and fell upon his breast, half-weeping, half-laughing. The Newfoundland dog crept up to Mr. Dunbar with his head down: he sniffed at the heels of the millionaire, and then looked slowly upward at the man's face with sombre sulky-looking eyes, and began to growl ominously.

"Take your dog away, Laura!" cried Mr. Dunbar, angrily.

It happened thus that the very first words Henry Dunbar said to his daughter were uttered in a tone of anger. The girl drew herself away from him, and looked up almost piteously in her father's face. That face was as pale as death: but cold, stern, and impassible. Laura Dunbar shivered as she looked at it. She had been a spoiled child; a pampered, idolized beauty; and had never heard anything but words of love and tenderness. Her lips quivered, and the tears came into her eyes.

"Come away, Pluto," she said to the dog; "papa does not want us."

She took the great flapping ears of the animal in her two hands, and led him out of the room. The dog went with his young mistress submissively enough: but he looked back at the last moment to growl at Mr. Dunbar.

Laura left the Newfoundland on the landing-place, and went back to her father. She flung herself for the second time into the banker's arms.

"Darling papa," she cried, impetuously; "my dog shall never growl at you again. Dear papa, tell me you are glad to come home to your poor girl. You *would* tell me so, if you knew how dearly I love you."

She lifted up her lips and kissed Henry Dunbar's impassible face. But she recoiled from him for the second time with a shudder and a long-drawn shivering sigh. The lips of the millionaire were as cold as ice.

"Papa," she cried, "how cold you are! I'm afraid that you are ill!"

He was ill. Arthur Lovell, who stood quietly watching the meeting between the father and daughter, saw a change come over his client's face, and wheeled forward an arm-chair just in time for Henry Dunbar to fall into it as heavily as a log of wood. The banker had fainted. For the second time since the murder in the grove near St. Cross he had betrayed violent and sudden emotion. This time the emotion was stronger than his will, and altogether overcame him.

Arthur Lovell laid the insensible man flat upon his back on the carpet. Laura rushed to fetch water and aromatic vinegar from her dressing-room: and in five minutes Mr. Dunbar opened his eyes, and looked about him with a wild half-terrified expression in his face. For a moment he glared fiercely at the anxious countenance of Laura, who knelt beside him: then his whole frame was shaken by a convulsive trembling, and his teeth chattered violently. But this lasted only for a few moments. He overcame it: grinding his teeth, and clenching his strong hands: and then staggered heavily to his feet.

"I am subject to these fainting fits," he said, with a wan, sickly smile upon his white face; "and I dreaded this interview on that account: I knew that it would be too much for me."

He seated himself upon the low sofa which Laura had pushed towards him, resting his elbows on his knees, and hiding his face in his hands. Miss Dunbar placed herself beside her father, and wound her arm about his neck.

"Poor papa," she murmured, softly; "I am so sorry our meeting has agitated you like this: and to think that I should have fancied you cold and unkind to me, at the very time when your silent emotion was an evidence of your love!"

Arthur Lovell had gone through the open window into the conservatory: but he could hear the girl talking to her father. His face was very grave: and the same shadow that had clouded it once during the course of the coroner's inquest rested upon it now.

"An evidence of his love! Heaven grant this may be love," he thought to himself; "but to me it seems a great deal more like fear!"

- CHAPTER 17 –

THE BROKEN PICTURE

A rthur Lovell stopped at Portland Place for the rest of the day, and dined with the banker and his daughter in the evening. The dinner-party was a very cheerful one, as far as Mr. Dunbar and his daughter were concerned: for Laura was in very high spirits on account of her father's return, and Dora Macmahon joined pleasantly in the conversation. The banker had welcomed his dead wife's elder daughter with a speech which, if a little studied in its tone, was at any rate very kind in its meaning.

"I shall always be glad to see you with my poor motherless girl," he said; "and if you can make your home altogether with us, you shall never have cause to remember that you are less nearly allied to me than Laura herself."

When he met Arthur and the two girls at the dinner-table, Henry Dunbar had quite recovered from the agitation of the morning, and talked gaily of the future. He alluded now and then to his Indian reminiscences, but did not dwell long upon this subject. His mind seemed full of plans for his future life. He would do this, that, and the other, at Maudesley Abbey, in Yorkshire, and in Portland Place. He had the air of a man who fully appreciates the power of wealth; and is prepared to enjoy all that wealth can give him. He drank a good deal of wine during the course of the dinner, and his spirits rose with every glass.

But in spite of his host's gaiety, Arthur Lovell was ill at ease. Do what he would, he could not shake off the memory of the meeting between the father and daughter. Henry Dunbar's deadly pallor—that wild, scared look in his eyes, as they slowly reopened and glared upon Laura's anxious face—were ever present to the young lawyer's mind.

Why was this man frightened of his beautiful child?—for that it was fear, and not love, which had blanched Henry Dunbar's face, the lawyer felt positive. Why was this father frightened of his own daughter, unless——?

Unless what?

Only one horrible and ghastly suggestion presented itself to Arthur Lovell's mind. Henry Dunbar was the murderer of his old valet: and the consciousness of guilt had paralyzed him at the first touch of his daughter's innocent lips.

But, oh, how terrible if this were true—how terrible to think that Laura Dunbar was henceforth to live in daily and hourly association with a traitor and an assassin!

"I have promised to love her for ever, though my love is hopeless, and to serve her faithfully if ever she should have need of my devotion," Arthur Lovell thought, as he sat silent at the dinner-table, while Henry Dunbar and his daughter talked together gaily.

The lawyer watched his client now with intense anxiety; and it seemed to him that there was something feverish and unnatural in the banker's gaiety. Laura and her step-sister left the room soon after dinner: and the two men remained alone at the long, ponderous-looking dinner-table, on which the sparkling diamond-cut decanters and Sèvres dessert-dishes looked like tiny vases of light and colour on a dreary waste of polished mahogany.

"I shall go to Maudesley Abbey to-morrow," Henry Dunbar said. "I want rest and solitude after all this trouble and excitement: and Laura tells me that she infinitely prefers Maudesley to London. Do you think of returning to Warwickshire, Mr. Lovell?"

"Oh, yes, immediately. My father expected my return a week ago. I only came up to town to act as Miss Dunbar's escort."

"Indeed, that was very kind of you. You have known my daughter for a long time, I understand by her letters."

"Yes. We were children together. I was a great deal at the Abbey in old Mr. Dunbar's time."

"And you will be still more often there in my time, I hope," Henry Dunbar answered courteously. "I fancy I could venture to make a pretty correct guess at a certain secret of yours, my dear Lovell. Unless I am very much mistaken, you have a more than ordinary regard for my daughter."

Arthur Lovell was silent, his heart beat violently, and he looked the banker unflinchingly in the face: but he did not speak, he only bent his head in answer to the rich man's questions.

"I have guessed rightly, then," said Mr. Dunbar.

"Yes, sir, I love Miss Dunbar as truly as ever a man loved the woman of his choice! but——"

"But what? She is the daughter of a millionaire, and you fear her father's disapproval of your pretensions, eh?"

"No, Mr. Dunbar. If your daughter loved me as truly as I love her, I would marry her in spite of you—in spite of the world; and carve my own way to fortune. But such a blessing as Laura Dunbar's love is not for me. I have spoken to her, and——"

"She has rejected you?"

"She has."

"Pshaw! girls of her age are as changeable as the winds of heaven. Do not despair, Mr. Lovell; and as far as my consent goes, you may have it to-morrow, if you like. You are young, good-looking, clever, agreeable: what more, in the name of feminine frivolity, can a girl want? You will find no stupid prejudices in me, Mr. Lovell. I should like to see you married to my daughter: for I believe you love her very sincerely. You have my good will, I assure you. There is my hand upon it."

He held out his hand as he spoke, and Arthur Lovell took it, a little reluctantly perhaps, but with as good a grace as he could.

"I thank you, sir," he said, "for your good will, and——"

He tried to say something more, but the words died away upon his lips. The horrible fear which had taken possession of his breast after the scene of the morning, weighed upon him like the burden that seems to lie upon the sleeper's breast throughout the strange agony of nightmare. Do what he would, he could not free himself from the weight of this dreadful doubt. Mr. Dunbar's words *seemed* to emanate from the kind and generous breast of a good man: but, on the other hand, might it not be possible that the banker wished to *get rid* of his daughter?

He had betrayed fear in her presence, that morning: and now he was eager to give her hand to the first suitor who presented himself: ineligible as that suitor was in a worldly point of view. Might it not be that the girl's innocent society was oppressive to her father, and that he wished therefore to shuffle her off upon a new protector?

"I shall be very busy this evening, Mr. Lovell," said Henry Dunbar, presently; "for I must look over some papers I have amongst the luggage that was sent on here from Southampton. When you are tired of the dining-room, you will be able to find the two girls, and amuse yourself in their society, I have no doubt."

Mr. Dunbar rang the bell. It was answered by an elderly man-servant out of livery.

"What have you done with the luggage that was sent from South-ampton?" asked the banker.

"It has all been placed in old Mr. Dunbar's bed-room, sir," the man answered.

"Very well; let lights be carried there, and let the portmanteaus and packing-cases be unstrapped and opened."

He handed a bunch of keys to the servant, and followed the man out of the room. In the hall he stopped suddenly, arrested by the sound of a woman's voice.

The entrance-hall of the house in Portland Place was divided into two compartments, separated from each other by folding-doors, the upper panels of which were of ground glass. There was a porter's chair in the outer division of the hall, and a bronzed lamp hung from the domed ceiling.

The doors between the inner and outer hall were ajar, and the voice which Henry Dunbar heard was that of a woman speaking to the porter.

"I am Joseph Wilmot's daughter," the woman said. "Mr. Dunbar promised that he would see me at Winchester: he broke his word, and left Winchester without seeing me: but he *shall* see me, sooner or later: for I will follow him wherever he goes, until I look into his face, and say that which I have to say to him."

The girl did not speak loudly or violently. There was a quiet earnest-ness in her voice; an earnestness and steadiness of tone which expressed more determination than any noisy or passionate utterance could have done.

"Good gracious me, young woman!" exclaimed the porter, "do you think as I'm goin' to send such a rampagin' kind of a message as that to Mr. Dunbar? Why, it would be as much as my place is worth to do it. Go along about your business, miss; and don't you preshume to come to such a house as this durin' gentlefolks' dinner-hours another time. Why, I'd sooner take a message to one of the tigers in the Joological-gardings[42] at feedin' time than I'd intrude upon such a gentleman as Mr. Dunbar when he's sittin' over his claret."

Mr. Dunbar stopped to listen to this conversation; then he went back into the dining-room, and beckoned to the servant who was waiting to precede him up-stairs.

---

[42] The Zoological Gardens in London were established in 1828, open to fellows of the Zoological Society of London (est. 1826), and opened fully to the public in 1847.

"Bring me pen, ink, and paper," he said.

The man wheeled a writing-table towards the banker. Henry Dunbar sat down and wrote the following lines; in the firm aristocratic handwriting that was so familiar to the chief clerks in the banking-house.

"The young person who calls herself Joseph Wilmot's daughter is informed that Mr. Dunbar declines to see her now, or at any future time. He is perfectly inflexible upon this point; and the young person will do well to abandon the system of annoyance which she is at present pursuing. Should she fail to do so, a statement of her conduct will be submitted to the police, and prompt measures taken to secure Mr. Dunbar's freedom from persecution. Herewith Mr. Dunbar forwards the young person a sum of money which will enable her to live for some time with ease and independence. Further remittances will be sent to her at short intervals; if she conducts herself with propriety, and refrains from attempting any annoyance against Mr. Dunbar.

"Portland Place, August 30, 1850."

The banker took out his cheque-book, wrote a cheque for fifty pounds, and folded it in the note which he had just written: then he rang the bell, and gave the note to the elderly manservant who waited upon him.

"Let that be taken to the young person in the hall," he said.

Mr. Dunbar followed the servant to the dining-room door and stood upon the threshold, listening. He heard the man speak to Margaret Wilmot as he delivered the letter; and then he heard the crackling of the envelope, as the girl tore it open.

There was a pause, during which the listener waited, with an anxious expression on his face.

He had not to wait long. Margaret spoke presently, in a clear, ringing voice, that vibrated through the hall.

"Tell your master," she said, "that I will die of starvation sooner than I would accept bread from his hand. You can tell him what I did with his generous gift."

There was another brief pause; and then, in the hushed stillness of the house, Henry Dunbar heard a light shower of torn paper flutter down upon the polished marble floor. Then he heard the great door of the house close upon Joseph Wilmot's daughter.

The millionaire covered his face with his hands, and gave a long sigh: but he lifted his head presently, shrugged his shoulders with an impatient gesture, and went slowly up the lighted staircase.

The suite of apartments that had been occupied by Percival Dunbar comprised the greater part of the second floor of the house in Portland Place. There was a spacious bed-chamber, a comfortable study, a dressing-room, bath-room, and antechamber. The furniture was handsome, but of a ponderous style: and, in spite of their splendour, the rooms had a gloomy look. Everything about them was dark and heavy. The house was an old one, and the five windows fronting the street were long and narrow, with deep oaken seats in the recesses between the heavy shutters. The walls were covered with a dark-green paper that looked like cloth. The footsteps of the occupant were muffled by the rich thickness of the sombre Turkey carpet. The voluminous curtains that sheltered the windows, and shrouded the carved rosewood four-post bed, were of a dark green, which looked black in the dim light.

The massive chairs and tables were of black oak, with cushions of green velvet. A few valuable cabinet pictures, by the old masters, set in deep frames of ebony and gold, hung at wide distances upon the wall. There was the head of an ecclesiastic, cut from a large picture by Spagnoletti; a Venetian senator by Tintoretto; the Adoration of the Magi by Caravaggio.[43] An ivory crucifix was the only object upon the high, old-fashioned chimney-piece.

A pair of wax-candles, in antique silver candlesticks, burned upon a writing-table near the fireplace, and made a spot of light in the gloomy bed-chamber. All Henry Dunbar's luggage had been placed in this room. There were packing-cases and portmanteaus of almost every size and shape, and they had all been opened by a man-servant, who was kneeling by the last when the banker entered the room.

"You will sleep here to-night, sir, I presume?" the servant said, interrogatively, as he prepared to quit the apartment. "Mrs. Parkyn thought it best to prepare these rooms for your occupation."

Henry Dunbar looked thoughtfully round the spacious chamber.

"Is there no other place in which I can sleep?" he asked. "These rooms are horribly gloomy."

"There is a spare room upon the floor above this, sir."

"Very well; let the spare room be got ready for me. I have a good many arrangements to make, and shall be late."

"Will you require assistance, sir?"

"No. Let the room up-stairs be prepared. Is it immediately above this?"

"Yes, sir."

"Good; I shall know how to find it, then. No one need sit up for me. Let Miss Dunbar be told that I shall not see her again to-night, and that I

[43] Spagnoletti (meaning "little Spaniard") was the nickname of Jose (sometimes Juseppe) de Ribera (1590-1652), Spanish painter; Tintoretto, real name Jacopo Comin (1518-1594), Italian painter; Michelangelo Merisi da Caravaggio (1571-1610), Italian painter. Braddon implies that the art works in the room are dark and sombre.

shall start for Maudesley in the course of to-morrow. She can make her arrangements accordingly. You understand?"

"Yes, sir."

"Then you can go. Remember, I do not wish to be disturbed again to-night."

"You will want nothing more, sir?"

"Nothing."

The man retired. Henry Dunbar followed him to the door, listened to his receding footsteps in the corridor and upon the staircase, and then turned the key in the lock. He went back to the centre of the room, and kneeling down before one of the open portmanteaus, took out every article which it contained, slowly; removing the things one by one, and throwing most of them into a heap upon the floor. He went through this operation with the contents of all the boxes, throwing the clothes upon the floor, and carrying the papers to the writing-table, where he piled them up in a great mass. This business occupied a very long time, and the hands of an antique clock, upon a bracket in a corner of the room, pointed to midnight when the banker seated himself at the table, and began to arrange and sort his papers.

This operation lasted for several hours. The candles were burnt down, and the flames flickered slowly out in the silver sockets. Mr. Dunbar went to one of the windows, drew back the green-cloth curtain, unbarred the heavy shutters, and let the gray morning light into the room. But he still went on with his work: reading faded documents, tying up old papers, making notes upon the backs of letters, and other notes in his own memorandum-book: very much as he had done at the Winchester Hotel. The broad sunlight streamed in upon the sombre colours of the Turkey carpet, the sound of wheels was in the street below, when the banker's work was finished. By that time he had arranged all the papers with unusual precision, and replaced them in one of the portmanteaus: but he left the clothes in a careless heap upon the floor, just as they had fallen when he first threw them out of the boxes.

Mr. Dunbar did one thing more before he left the room. Amongst the papers which he had arranged upon the writing-table, there was a small square morocco case, containing a photograph done upon glass. He took this picture out of the case, dropped it upon the polished oaken floor beyond the margin of the carpet, and ground the glass into atoms with the heavy heel of his boot. But even then he was not content with his work of destruction: for he stamped upon the tiny fragments until there was nothing left of the picture but a handful of sparkling dust. He scattered this about with his foot, dropped the empty morocco case into his pocket, and went up-stairs in the morning sunlight.

It was past six o'clock, and Mr. Dunbar heard the voices of the women-servants upon the back staircase as he went to his room. He threw himself, dressed as he was, upon the bed, and fell into a heavy slumber.

At three o'clock the same [44] day Mr. Dunbar left London for Maudesley Abbey, accompanied by his daughter, Dora Macmahon, and Arthur Lovell.[45]

- CHAPTER 18 -

THREE WHO SUSPECT[46]

No further discovery was made respecting the murder that had been committed in the grove between Winchester and St. Cross. The police made every effort to find the murderer, but without result. A large reward was offered by the government for the apprehension of the guilty man; and a still larger reward was offered by Mr. Dunbar, who declared that his own honour and good name were in a manner involved in the discovery of the real murderer.

The one clue by which the police hoped to trace the footsteps of the assassin was the booty which his crime had secured to him: the contents of the pocket-book that had been rifled, and the clothes which had been stripped from the corpse of the victim. By means of the clue which these things might afford, the detective police hoped to reach the guilty man. But they hoped in vain. Every pawnbroker's shop in Winchester, and in every town within a certain radius of Winchester, was searched: but without effect. No clothes at all resembling those that had been seen upon the person of the dead man had been pledged within forty miles of the cathedral city. The police grew hopeless at last. The reward was a large one: but the darkness of the mystery seemed impenetrable, and little by little people left off talking of the murder. By slow degrees the gossips resigned themselves to the idea that the secret of Joseph Wilmot's death was to remain a secret for ever. Two or three "sensation" leaders appeared in some of the morning papers, urging the blood-hounds of the law to do their work, and taunting the members of the detective force with supineness and stupidity. I dare say the social leader-

---

[44] The original version has "next day". The revised fifth edition, published by Maxwell, has "same day", which has been used here since the original was obviously an error, which Braddon later corrected.

[45] In the original three-volume edition of *Henry Dunbar*, the first volume ends here.

[46] Chapter I of volume II in the original three-volume publication.

writers were rather hard-up for subjects at this stagnant autumnal period, and were scarcely sorry for the mysterious death of the man in the grove. The public grumbled a little when there was no new paragraph in the papers about "that dreadful Winchester murder;" but the nine-days' period during which the English public cares to wonder elapsed; and nothing had been done. Other murders were committed as brutal in their nature as the murder in the grove: and the world, which rarely stops long to lament for the dead, began to think of other things. Joseph Wilmot was forgotten.

A month passed very quietly at Maudesley Abbey. Henry Dunbar took his place in the county as a person of importance; lights blazed in the splendid rooms; carriages drove in and out of the great gates in the park, and all the landed gentry within twenty miles of the abbey came to pay their respects to the millionaire who had newly returned from India. He did not particularly encourage people's visits; but he submitted him-self to such festivities as his daughter declared to be necessary; and did the honours of his house with a certain haughty grandeur, which was a little stiff and formal as compared to the easy friendly grace of his high-bred visitors. People shrugged their shoulders, and hinted that there was something of the "roturier" in Mr. Dunbar;[47] but they freely acknow-ledged that he was a fine handsome-looking fellow, and that his daughter was an angel, rendered still more angelic by the earthly advantage of half a million or so for her marriage-portion.

Meanwhile Margaret Wilmot lived alone in her simple countrified lodging, and thought sadly enough of the father whom she had lost.

He had not been a good father: but she had loved him nevertheless. She had pitied him for his sorrows, and the wrongs that had been done him. She had loved him for those feeble traces of a better nature that had been dimly visible in his character.

"He had not been *always* a cheat and reprobate," the girl thought as she sat pondering upon her father's fate. "He never would have been dishonest but for Henry Dunbar."

She remembered with bitter feelings the aspect of the rich man's house in Portland Place. She had caught a glimpse of its splendour upon the night after her return from Winchester. Through the narrow opening between the folding-doors she had seen the pictures and the statues glimmering in the lamplight of the inner hall. She had seen in that brief

---

[47] Roturier: A commoner or person of low rank. In this context, because of Dunbar's wealth, the term implies well-bred contempt for the nouveau riche; Dunbar is seen as a parvenu.

moment a bright confusion of hothouse flowers, and trailing satin curtains, gilded mouldings, and frescoed panels, the first few shallow steps of a marble staircase, the filigree-work of the bronze balustrade.

Only for one moment had she peeped wonderingly into the splendid interior of Henry Dunbar's mansion; but the objects seen in that one brief glance had stamped themselves upon the girl's memory.

"He is rich," she thought, "and they say that wealth can buy all the best things upon this earth. But, after all, there are few *real* things that it can purchase. It can buy flattery, and simulated love, and sham devotion: but it cannot buy one genuine heart-throb, one thrill of true feeling. All the wealth of this world cannot buy *peace* for Henry Dunbar, or forget-fulness. So long as I live he shall be made to remember. If his own guilty conscience can suffer him to forget, it shall be my task to recall the past. I promised my dead father that I would remember the name of Henry Dunbar: I have had good reason to remember it."

Margaret Wilmot was not quite alone in her sorrow. There was one person who sympathized with her, with an earnest and pure desire to help her in her sorrow. This person was Clement Austin, the cashier in St. Gundolph's Lane; the man who had fallen head-over-heels in love with the pretty music-mistress, but who felt half ashamed of his sudden and unreasoning affection.

"I have always ridiculed what people call 'love at sight,'" he thought; "surely I am not so silly as to have been bewitched by hazel eyes and a straight nose. Perhaps, after all, I only take an interest in this girl because she is so beautiful and so lonely, and because of the kind of mystery there seems to be about her life."

Never for one moment had Clement Austin suspected that this mystery involved anything discreditable to Margaret herself. The girl's sad face seemed softly luminous with the tender light of pure and holy thoughts. The veriest churl could scarcely have associated vice or false-hood with such a lovely and harmonious image.

Since her return from Winchester, since the failure of her second attempt to see Henry Dunbar, her life had pursued its wonted course; and she went so quietly about her daily duties, that it was only by the settled sadness of her face, the subdued gravity of her manner, that people became aware of some heavy grief that had newly fallen upon her.

Clement Austin had watched her far too closely not to understand her better than other people. He had noticed the change in her costume, when she put on simple inexpensive mourning for her dead father; and he ventured to express his regret for the loss which she had experienced. She told him, with a gentle sorrowful accent in her voice, that she had lately lost some one who was very dear to her; and that the loss had been unexpected, and was very bitter to bear. But she told him no more; and he was too well bred to intrude upon her grief by any further question.

But though he refrained from saying more upon this occasion, the cashier brooded long and deeply upon the conduct of his niece's music-mistress: and one chilly September evening, when Miss Wentworth was *not* expected at Clapham, he walked across Wandsworth Common, and went straight to the lane in which Godolphin Cottages sheltered themselves under the shadow of the sycamores.

Margaret had very few intervals of idleness, and there was a kind of melancholy relief to her in such an evening as this, on which she was free to think of her dead father, and the strange story of his death. She was standing at the low wooden gate opening into the little garden below the window of her room, in the deepening twilight of this September evening. It was late in the month: the leaves were falling from the trees, and drifting with a rustling sound along the dusty roadway.

The girl stood with her elbow resting upon the top of the gate, and a dark shawl covering her head and shoulders. She was tired and unhappy, and she stood in a melancholy attitude, looking with sad eyes towards the glimpse of the river at the bottom of the lane. So entirely was she absorbed by her own gloomy thoughts, that she did not hear a footstep approaching from the other end of the lane; she did not look up until a man's voice said, in subdued tones—

"Good evening, Miss Wentworth; are you not afraid of catching cold? I hope your shawl is thick, for the dews are falling, and here, near the river, there is a damp mist on these autumn nights."

The speaker was Clement Austin.

Margaret Wilmot looked up at him, and a pensive smile stole over her face. Yes, it was something to be spoken to so kindly in that deep manly voice. The world had seemed so blank since her father's death: such utter desolation had descended upon her since her miserable journey to Winchester, and her useless visit to Portland Place: for since that time she had shrunk away from people, wrapped in her own sorrow, separated from the commonplace world by the exceptional nature of her misery. It was something to this poor girl to hear thoughtful and considerate words; and the unbidden tears clouded her eyes.

As yet she had spoken openly of her trouble to no living creature, since that night upon which she had attempted to gain admission to Mr. Dunbar's house. She was still known in the neighbourhood as Margaret Wentworth. She had put on mourning: and she had told the few people about the place where she lived, of her father's death: but she had told no one the manner of that death. She had shared her gloomy secret with neither friends nor counsellors, and had borne her dismal burden alone.

It was for this reason that Clement Austin's friendly voice raised an unwonted emotion in her breast. The desolate girl remembered that night upon which she had first heard of the murder, and she remembered the sympathy that Mr. Austin had evinced on that occasion.

"My mother has been quite anxious about you, Miss Wentworth," said Clement Austin. "She has noticed such a change in your manner for the last month or five weeks; though you are as kind as ever to my little niece, who makes wonderful progress under your care. But my mother cannot be indifferent to your own feelings, and she and I have both perceived the change. I fear there is some great trouble on your mind; and I would give much—ah, Miss Wentworth, you cannot guess how much!—if I could be of help to you in any time of grief or trouble. You seemed very much agitated by the news of that shocking murder at Winchester. I have been thinking it all over since, and I cannot help fancying that the change in your manner dated from the evening on which my mother told you that dreadful story. It struck me, that you must, therefore, in some way or other, be interested in the fate of the murdered man. Even beyond this, it might be possible that, if you knew this Joseph Wilmot, you might be able to throw some light upon his antecedents, and thus give a clue to the assassin. Little by little this idea has crept into my mind, and to-night I resolved to come to you, and ask you the direct question, as to whether you were in any way related to this unhappy man."

At first Margaret Wilmot's only answer was a choking sob; but she grew calmer presently, and said, in a low voice—

"Yes, you have guessed rightly, Mr. Austin; I was related to that most unhappy man. I will tell you everything, but not here," she added, looking back at the cottage windows, in which lights were glimmering; "the people about me are inquisitive, and I don't want to be overheard."

She wrapped her shawl more closely round her, and went out of the little garden. She walked by Clement's side down to the pathway by the river, which was lonely enough at this time of the night.

Here she told him her story. She carefully suppressed all vehement emotion; and in few and simple words related the story of her life.

"Joseph Wilmot was my father," she said. "Perhaps he may not have been what the world calls a good father; but I know that he loved me, and he was very dear to me. My mother was the daughter of a gentleman, a post-captain in the Royal Navy, whose name was Talbot. She met my father at the house of a lady from whom she used to receive music-lessons. She did not know who he was, or what he was. She only knew that he called himself James Wentworth; but he loved her, and she returned his affection. She was very young—a mere child, who had not long emerged from a boarding-school—and she married my poor father in defiance of the advice of her friends. She ran away from her home one morning, was married by stealth in an obscure little church in the City, and then went home with my father to confess what she had done. Her father never forgave her for that secret marriage. He swore that he would never look upon her face after that day: and he never did, until he saw it in her coffin. At my mother's death Captain Talbot's heart was touched: he came for the first time to my father's house, and offered to take me away with him, and to have me brought up amongst his younger children. But my father refused to allow this. He grieved passionately for my poor mother: though I have heard him say that he had much to regret in his conduct towards her. But I can scarcely remember that sad time. From that period our life became a wandering and wretched one. Sometimes, for a little while, we seemed better off. My father got some employment; he worked steadily; and we lived amongst respectable people. But soon—ah, cruelly soon!—the new chance of an honest life was taken away from him.

His employers heard something: a breath, a whisper, perhaps: but it was enough. He was not a man to be trusted. He promised well: so far he had kept his promise: but there was a risk in employing him. My father never met any good Christian who was willing to run that risk, in the hope of saving a human soul. My father never met any one noble enough to stretch out his hand to the outcast and say, 'I know that you have done wrong; I know that you are without a character: but I will forget the blot upon the past, and help you to achieve redemption in the future.' If my father had met such a friend, such a benefactor, all might have been different."

Then Margaret Wilmot related the substance of the last conversation between herself and her father. She told Clement Austin what her father had said about Henry Dunbar; and she showed him the letter which was directed to Norfolk Island—that letter in which the old clerk alluded to the power that his brother possessed over his late master. She also told Mr. Austin how Henry Dunbar had avoided her at Winchester and in Portland Place, and of the letter which he had written to her,—a letter in which he had tried to bribe her to silence.

"Since that night," she added, "I have received two anonymous enclosures—two envelopes containing notes to the amount of a hundred pounds, with the words 'From a True Friend' written across the flap of the envelope. I returned both the enclosures; for I knew whence they had come. I returned them in two envelopes directed to Henry Dunbar, at the office in St. Gundolph's Lane."

Clement Austin listened with a grave face. All this certainly seemed to hint at the guilt of Mr. Dunbar. No clue pointing to any other person had been as yet discovered, though the police had been indefatigable in their search.

Mr. Austin was silent for some minutes; then he said, quietly—

"I am very glad you have confided in me, Miss Wilmot, and, believe me, you shall not find me slow to help you whenever my services can be of any avail. If you will come and drink tea with my mother at eight o'clock to-morrow evening, I will be at home; and we can talk this matter over seriously. My mother is a clever woman, and I know that she has a most sincere regard for you. You will trust her, will you not?"

"Willingly, with my whole heart."

"You will find her a true friend."

They had returned to the little garden-gate by this time. Clement Austin stretched out his hand.

"Good night, Miss Wilmot."

"Good night."

Margaret opened the gate and went into the garden. Mr. Austin walked slowly homewards, past pleasant cottages nestling in suburban gardens, and pretentious villas, with campanello towers and gothic porches.[48] The lighted windows shone out upon the darkness. Here and there he heard the sound of a piano, or a girlish voice stealing softly out upon the cool night air.

The sight of pleasant homes made the cashier think very mournfully of the girl he had just left.

"Poor, desolate girl," he thought, "poor, lonely, orphan girl!" But he thought still more about that which he had heard of Henry Dunbar; and the evidence against the rich man seemed to grow in importance as he reflected upon it. It was not one thing, but many things, that hinted at the guilt of the millionaire.

---

[48] Braddon appears to have held certain trends in modern architecture in contempt. The development of suburbs in the early part of the nineteenth century witnessed a popularity, particularly after the 1840s, for picturesque villas in the gothic or Italianate Renaissance style, often favouring an irregular composition with towers, which Braddon clearly found pretentious. The campanello tower, an elaborate rooftop construction of stucco, seems to have been a particular bugbear, and it is derogatively referred to in several other novels, including *Only a Clod*, *To the Bitter End*, and *Rupert Godwin*. "Woolcote Villas, St. John's Wood, were very pretentious little dwelling-places, ... [they] were of the Elizabethan order of architecture, and went off abruptly into peaks and angles wherever a peak or an angle was possible. [....] why Woolcote Villas should each be finished off with a stuccoed mustard pot, popularly known as a Campanello tower, which was not Elizabethan, and not practicable for habitation, being open to the four winds of heaven, was another problem" (Braddon, *Only a Clod*, London: John and Robert Maxwell, 1865: 180).

The secret possessed, and no doubt traded upon, by Joseph Wilmot; Mr. Dunbar's agitation in the cathedral; his determined refusal to see the murdered man's daughter; his attempt to bribe her—these were strong points: and by the time Clement Austin reached home, he—like Margaret Wilmot, and like Arthur Lovell—suspected the millionaire. So now there were three people who believed Mr. Dunbar to be the murderer of his old servant.

- CHAPTER 19 –

LAURA DUNBAR'S DISAPPOINTMENT

Arthur Lovell went often to Maudesley Abbey. Henry Dunbar welcomed him freely, and the young man had not the power to resist temptation. He went to his doom as the foolish moth flies to the candle. He went, he saw Laura Dunbar, and spent hour after hour in her society: for his presence was always agreeable to the impetuous girl. To her he seemed, indeed, that which he had promised to be, a brother—kind, devoted, affectionate: but no more. He was endeared to Laura by the memory of a happy childhood. She was grateful to him, and she loved him: but only as she would have loved him had he been indeed her brother. Whatever deeper feeling lay beneath the playful gaiety of her manner had yet to be awakened.

So, day after day, the young man bowed down before the goddess of his life, and was happy—ah, fatally happy!—in her society. He forgot everything except the beautiful face that smiled on him. He forgot even those dark doubts which he had felt as to the secret of the Winchester murder.

Perhaps he would scarcely have forgotten the suspicions that had entered his mind after the first interview between the banker and his daughter, had he seen much of Henry Dunbar. But he saw very little of the master of Maudesley Abbey. The rich man took possession of the suite of apartments that had been prepared for him, and rarely left his own rooms: except to wander alone amongst the shady avenues of the park: or to ride out upon the powerful horse he had chosen from the stud purchased by Percival Dunbar.

This horse was a magnificent creature; the colt of a thorough-bred sire, but of a stronger and larger build than a purely thorough-bred animal. He was a chestnut horse, with a coat that shone like satin, and not a white hair about him. His nose was small, his eyes large, his ears

132

and neck long. He had all the points which an Arab prizes in his favourite barb.[49]

To this horse Henry Dunbar became singularly attached. He had a loose box built on purpose for the animal in a private garden adjoining his own dressing-room, which, like the rest of his apartments, was situated upon the ground-floor of the abbey. Mr. Dunbar's groom slept in a part of the house near this loose box; and horse and man were at the service of the banker at any hour of the day or night.

Henry Dunbar generally rode either early in the morning, or in the gray twilight after his dinner-hour. He was a proud man, and he was not a sociable man. When the county gentry came to welcome him to England, he received them, and thanked them for their courtesy. But there was something in his manner that repelled rather than invited friendship. He gave one great dinner-party soon after his arrival at Maudesley, a ball, at which Laura floated about in a cloud of white gauze, and with diamonds in her hair; and a breakfast and morning concert on the lawn, in compliance with the urgent entreaties of the same young lady. But when invitations came flooding in upon Mr. Dunbar, he declined them one after another, on the ground of his weak health. Laura might go where she liked, always provided that she went under the care of a suitable chaperone; but the banker declared that the state of his health altogether unfitted him for society. His constitution had been much impaired, he said, by his long residence in Calcutta. And yet he looked a strong man. Tall, broad-chested, and powerful, it was very difficult to perceive in Henry Dunbar's appearance any one of the usual evidences of ill-health. He was very pale: but that unchanging pallor was the only sign of the malady from which he suffered.

He rose early, rode for a couple of hours upon his chestnut horse Dragon, and then breakfasted. After breakfast he sat in his luxurious sitting-room, sometimes reading, sometimes writing, sometimes sitting for hours together brooding silently over the low embers in the roomy fireplace. At six o'clock he dined, still keeping to his own room—for he was not well enough to dine with his daughter, he said—and he sat alone late into the night, drinking heavily, according to the report current in the servants' hall.

He was respected and he was feared in his household: but he was not liked. His silent and reserved manner had a gloomy influence upon the servants who came in contact with him: and they compared him very disadvantageously with his predecessor, Percival Dunbar: the genial, kind,

---

[49] Barb: a desert horse, possessing immense strength and stamina. The breed was originally developed on the Barbary Coast, North Africa.

old master, who had always had a cheerful, friendly word for every one
of his dependants: from the stately housekeeper in rustling silken robes,
to the smallest boy employed in the stables.

No, the new master of the abbey was not liked. Day after day he lived
secluded and alone. At first, his daughter had broken in upon his solitude,
and, with bright, caressing ways, had tried to win him from his
loneliness: but she found that all her efforts to do this were worse than
useless: they were even disagreeable to her father: and, by degrees, her
light footstep was heard less and less often in that lonely wing of the
house where Henry Dunbar had taken up his abode.

Maudesley Abbey was a large and rambling old mansion, which had
been built in half-a-dozen different reigns. The most ancient part of the
building was that very northern wing which Mr. Dunbar had chosen for
himself. Here the architecture belonged to the early Plantagenet era;[50] the
stone walls were thick and massive, the lancet-headed windows were
long and narrow, and the arms of the early benefactors of the monastery
were emblazoned here and there upon the richly stained glass. The walls
were covered with faded tapestry, from which grim faces scowled upon
the lonely inhabitant of the chambers. The groined ceiling was of oak,
that had grown black with age.[51] The windows of Mr. Dunbar's bedroom
and dressing-room opened into a cloistered court, beneath whose
solemn shadow the hooded monks had slowly paced, in days that were
long gone. The centre of this quadrangular court had been made into a
garden, where tall hollyhocks and prim dahlias flaunted in the autumn
sunshine. And within this cloistered courtway Mr. Dunbar had erected
the loose box for his favourite horse.

The southern wing of Maudesley Abbey owed its origin to a much
later period. The windows and fireplaces at this end of the house were in
the Tudor style; the polished oak wainscoting was very beautiful; the
rooms were smaller and snugger than the tapestried chambers occupied
by the banker; Venetian glasses and old crystal chandeliers glimmered
and glittered against the sombre woodwork: and elegant modern
furniture contrasted pleasantly with the Elizabethan casements and
carved oaken chimney-pieces. Everything that unlimited wealth can do
to make a house beautiful had been done for this part of the mansion by
Percival Dunbar; and had been done with considerable success. The
doting grandfather had taken a delight in beautifying the apartments
occupied by his girlish companion: and Miss Dunbar had walked upon
velvet pile, and slept beneath the shadow of satin curtains, from a very

---

[50] The House of Plantagenet reigned between 1216 -1485, from Henry III to Richard III.
[51] A groin vault ceiling has arches which are divided or intersected.

early period of her existence.

She was used to luxury and elegance: she was accustomed to be surrounded by all that is refined and beautiful: but she had that inexhaustible power of enjoyment which is perhaps one of the brightest gifts of a fresh young nature: and she did not grow tired of the pleasant home that had been made for her. Laura Dunbar was a pampered child of fortune: but there are some natures that it seems very difficult to spoil: and I think hers must have been one of these.

She knew no weariness of the "rolling hours." To her the world seemed a paradise of beauty. Remember, she had never seen real misery: she had never endured that sick feeling of despair, which creeps over the most callous of us when we discover the amount of hopeless misery that is, and has been, and is to be, for ever and ever upon this weary earth. She had seen sick cottagers, and orphan children, and desolate widows, in her pilgrimages amongst the dwellings of the poor: but she had always been able to relieve these afflicted ones, and to comfort them more or less.

It is the sight of sorrows which we cannot alleviate that sends a palpable stab home to our hearts, and for a time almost sickens us with a universe which cannot go upon its course *without* such miseries as these.

To Laura Dunbar the world was still entirely beautiful, for the darker secrets of life had not been revealed to her.

Only once had affliction come near her; and then it had come in a calm and solemn shape, in the death of an old man, who ended a good and prosperous life peacefully upon the breast of his beloved granddaughter.

Perhaps her first real trouble came to her now in the bitter disappointment which had succeeded her father's return to England. Heaven only knows with what a tender yearning the girl had looked forward to Henry Dunbar's return. They had been separated for the best part of her brief lifetime; but what of that? He would love her all the more tenderly because of those long years during which they had been divided. She meant to be the same to her father that she had been to her grandfather—a loving companion, a ministering angel.

But it was never to be. Her father, by a hundred tacit signs, rejected her affection. He had shunned her presence from the first: and she had grown now to shun him. She told Arthur Lovell of this unlooked-for sorrow.

"Of all the things I ever thought of, Arthur, this never entered my head," she said, in a low, pensive voice, as she stood one evening in the deep embrasure of the Tudor window, looking thoughtfully out at the wide-spreading lawn, where the shadows of the low cedar branches made

135

patches of darkness on the moonlit surface of the grass: "I thought that papa might fall ill on the voyage home, and die, and that the ship for whose safe course I prayed night and day, might bring me nothing but the sacred remains of the dead. I have thought this, Arthur, and I have lain awake at night, torturing myself with the thought: till my mind has grown so full of the dark picture, that I have seen the little cabin in the cruel, restless ship, and my father lying helpless on a narrow bed, with only strangers to watch his death-hour. I cannot tell you how many different things I have feared: but I never, never thought that he would not love me. I have even thought that it was just possible he might be unlike my grandfather, and a little unkind to me sometimes when I vexed or troubled him: but I thought his heart would be true to me through all, and that even in his harshest moments he would love me dearly, for the sake of my dead mother."

Her voice broke, and she sobbed aloud: but the man who stood by her side had no word of comfort to say to her. Her complaint awoke that old suspicion which had lately slumbered in his breast—the horrible fear that Mr. Dunbar was guilty of the murder of his old servant.

The young lawyer was bound to say something, however. It was too cruel to stand by and utter no word of comfort to this sobbing girl.

"Laura, dear Laura," he said, "this is foolish, believe me. You must have patience, and still hope for the best. How *can* your father do otherwise than love you, when he grows to know you well? You may have expected too much of him. Remember, that people who have lived long in the East Indies are apt to become cold and languid in their manners. When Mr. Dunbar has seen more of you, when he has become better accustomed to your society——"

"That he will never be," Laura answered, impetuously. "How can he ever know me better when he scrupulously avoids me? Sometimes whole days pass during which I do not see him. Then I summon up courage and go to his dreary rooms. He receives me graciously enough, and treats me with politeness. With politeness! when I am yearning for his affection: and I linger a little, perhaps, asking him about his health, and trying to get more at home in his presence. But there is always a nervous restlessness in his manner: which tells me,—oh, too plainly!—that my presence is unwelcome to him. So I go away at last, half heart-broken. I remember, now, how cold and brief his letters from India always seemed: but then he used to excuse himself to me on account of the hurry of business: and he seldom finished his letter without saying that he looked joyfully forward to our meeting. It was very cruel of him to deceive me!"

Arthur Lovell was a sorry comforter. From the first he had tried in vain to like Henry Dunbar. Since that strange scene in Portland Place, he had suspected the banker of a foul and treacherous murder,—that worst and darkest crime, which for ever separates a man from the sympathy of his fellow-men, and brands him as an accursed and abhorred creature, beyond the pale of human compassion. Ah, how blessed is that Divine and illimitable compassion which can find pity for those whom sinful man rejects!

- CHAPTER 20 -

NEW HOPES MAY BLOOM

Jocelyn's Rock was ten miles from Maudesley Abbey, and only one mile from the town of Shorncliffe. It was a noble place, and had been in the possession of the same family ever since the days of the Plantagenets.[52]

The house stood upon a rocky cliff, beneath which rushed a cascade that leapt from crag to crag, and fell into the bosom of a deep stream, that formed an arm of the river Avon. This cascade was forty feet below the edge of the cliff upon which the mansion stood.

It was not a very large house, for most of the older part of it had fallen into ruin long ago, and the ruined towers and shattered walls had been cleared away; but it was a noble mansion notwithstanding.

One octagonal tower, with a battlemented roof, still stood almost as firmly as it had stood in the days of the early Plantagenets, when rebel soldiers had tried the strength of their battering-rams against the grim stone walls. The house was built entirely of stone; the Gothic porch was ponderous as the porch of a church. Within all was splendour; but splendour that was very different from the modern elegance that was to be seen in the rooms of Maudesley Abbey.

At Jocelyn's Rock the stamp of age was upon every decoration, on every ornament. Square-topped helmets that had been hacked by the scimitars of Saracen kings, spiked chamfronts that had been worn by the fiery barbs of haughty English crusaders, fluted armour from Milan, hung against the blackened wainscoting in the shadowy hall; Scottish hackbuts, primitive arquebuses that had done service on Bosworth field, Homeric bucklers and brazen greaves, javelins, crossbows, steel-pointed lances, and two-handed swords, were in symmetrical design upon the

---

[52] See note 50, p.134 above.

dark and polished panels; while here and there hung the antlers of a giant red-deer, or the skin of a fox, in testimony to the triumphs of long-departed sportsmen of the house of Jocelyn.[53]

It was a noble old house. Princes of the blood royal had sat in the ponderous carved oak-chairs. A queen had slept in the state-bed, in the blue-satin chamber. Loyal Jocelyns, fighting for their king against low-born Roundhead soldiers, had hidden themselves in the spacious chimneys, or had fled for their lives along the secret passages behind the tapestry. There were old pictures and jewelled drinking-cups that dead-and-gone Jocelyns had collected in the sunny land of the Medicis.[54]

There were costly toys of fragile Sèvres china that had been received by one of the earls from the hand of the lovely Pompadour herself in the days when the manufacturers of Sèvres only worked for their king, and were liable to fall a sacrifice to their art and their loyalty by the inhalation of arsenicated vapours.[55] There was golden plate that a king had given to his proud young favourite in those feudal days when favourites were powerful in England. There was scarcely any object of value in the mansion that had not a special history attached to it, redounding to the honour and glory of the ancient house of Jocelyn.

And this splendid dwelling-place, rendered almost sacred by legendary associations and historical recollections, was now the property of a certain Sir Philip Jocelyn—a dashing young baronet, who had been endowed by nature with a handsome face, frank, fearless eyes that generally had a smile in them, and the kind of manly figure which the late Mr. G.P.R. James was wont to designate stalwart;[56] and who was more-over a crack shot, a reckless cross-country-going rider, and a very tolerable amateur artist.

Sir Philip Jocelyn was not what is usually called an intellectual man. He was more warmly interested in a steeplechase on Shorncliffe Com-

---

[53] Archaic weaponry. Chamfronts were horse armour, a front plate worn to protect the horse's head in battle. Hackbuts and arquebuses were early portable firearms. A buckler was a small round shield; greaves were leg-armour, specifically for the shins.

[54] The House of Medici was an Italian political dynasty, powerful from the 14th century to the 18th. There are repeated references to Catherine de Medici (1519-1589) throughout Braddon's fiction.

[55] Sèvres, established in the 18th century, is the foremost porcelain manufacturer in France. As in glass production, workers in ceramic manufacture were in danger from inhaling compounds mixed or treated with arsenic; Madame La Pompadour (Jeanne-Antoinette Poisson) was the mistress of King Louis XV of France between 1745 and 1750.

[56] George Payne Rainsford James (1801-1860): prolific English novelist and historian. He wrote over 100 novels in total, specializing in historical romances such as *Richelieu: A Tale of France* (1829), *The Gypsy* (1835), *Attila* (1837), and *The Mysterious Chevalier* (1843).

mon than in a pamphlet on political economy, even though Mr. Stuart Mill should himself be the author of the *brochure*.[57] He thought John Scott a greater man than Maculloch; and Manton the gunmaker only second to Dr. Jenner as a benefactor of his race.[58] He found the works of the late Mr. Apperly more entertaining than the last new Idyll from the pen of the Laureate; and was rather at a loss for small-talk when he found his feminine neighbour at a dinner-table was "deeply, darkly, beautifully blue."[59] But the young baronet was by no means a fool, notwithstanding these sportsmanlike proclivities. The Jocelyns had been hard riders for half-a-dozen centuries or so, and crack shots ever since the invention of firearms. Sir Philip was a sportsman, but he did not "hunt in dreams," and he was prepared to hold his wife a great deal "higher than his horse," whenever he should win that pleasant addition to his household. As yet he had thought very little of the future Lady Jocelyn.

He had a vague idea that he should marry, as the rest of the Jocelyns had married; and that he should live happily with his wife, as his ancestors had lived with their wives: with the exception of one dreadful man, called Hildebrande Jocelyn, who, at some remote and mediaeval period, had been supposed to throw his liege lady out of an oriel window that overhung the waterfall, upon the strength of an unfounded suspicion; and who afterwards, according to the legend, dug, or rather scooped, for himself a cave out of the cliff-side with no better tools than his own finger-nails, which he never cut after the unfortunate lady's foul murder. The legend went on further to state that the white wraith of the innocent victim might be seen, on a certain night in the year, rising out of the misty spray of the waterfall: but as nobody except one very weak-

[57] John Stuart Mill (1806-1873): British philosopher, economist, moral and political theorist, and supporter of women's equality. His works include *The Principles of Political Economy* (1848), *On Liberty* (1859), and *The Subjection of Women* (1869).
[58] Given the context, it is likely that Braddon is referring to John Scott (1794-1871), the famous racehorse trainer; John Maculloch (1773–1835), surgeon and geologist; Joseph Manton (1766–1835), famous gunmaker; Edward Jenner (1749-1823), English doctor and scientist who pioneered the smallpox vaccine.
[59] Charles James Apperley (1777-1843), sportsman and sporting writer, known as "Nimrod"; Alfred, Lord Tennyson (1809-1892), Poet Laureate 1850-92, published *Idylls of the King* between 1856 and 1885; "darkly, deeply, beautifully blue" is a quotation from Byron's *Don Juan*, Canto 4, stanza 110. However, Byron is quoting too, from Robert Southey: "language cannot paint / Their splendid tints; though in blue ocean seen, / Blue, darkly, deeply, beautifully blue". Southey, *Madoc* (1805), part I, book V, lines 100-102. Braddon has the first two words the wrong way round. It is more likely she is quoting from Byron, rather than Southey, given her predilection for his poetry and her frequent allusions to him throughout her fiction. The reference here seems to signify a woman of intellectual leanings, a "Bluestocking", rather than the original meaning in the poem(s).

witted female Jocelyn had ever seen the vision, the inhabitants of the house upon the crag had taken so little heed of the legend that the date of the anniversary had come at last to be forgotten.

Sir Philip Jocelyn thought that he should marry "some of these days," and in the meantime troubled himself very little about the pretty daughters of country gentlemen whom he met now and again at races, and archery-meetings, and flower-shows, and dinner-parties, and hunting-balls, in the queer old town-hall at Shorncliffe. He was heart-whole; and looking out at life from the oriel window of his dressing-room, whence he saw nothing but his own land, neatly enclosed in a ring-fence, he thought the world, about which some people made such dismal howling, was, upon the whole, an extremely pleasant place, containing very little that "a fellow" need complain of. He built himself a painting-room at Jocelyn's Rock; and-whistled to himself for the hour together, as he stood before the easel, painting scenes in the hunting-field, or Arab horsemen whom he had met on the great flat sandy plains beyond Cairo, or brown-faced boys, or bright Italian peasant-girls; all sorts of pleasant objects, under cloudless skies of ultra-marine, with streaks of orange and vermilion to represent the sunset. He was not a great painter, nor indeed was there any element of greatness in his nature; but he painted as recklessly as he rode; his subjects were bright and cheerful; and his pictures were altogether of the order which unsophisticated people admire and call "pretty."

He was a very cheerful young man, and perhaps that cheerfulness was the greatest charm he possessed. He was a man in whom no force of fashion or companionship would ever engender the peevish *blasé*-ness so much affected by modern youth. Did he dance? Of course he did, and he adored dancing. Did he sing? Well, he did his best, and had a fine volume of rich bass voice, that sounded remarkably well on the water, after a dinner at the Star and Garter, in that dim dewy hour, when the willow shadowed Thames is as a southern lake, and the slow dip of the oars is in itself a kind of melody. Had he been much abroad? Yes, and he gloried in the Continent; the dear old inconvenient inns, and the extortionate landlords, and the insatiable commissionaires—he revelled in the commissionaires;[60] and the dear drowsy slow trains, with an absurd guard, who talks an unintelligible *patois*,[61] and the other man, who always loses one's luggage! Delicious! And the dear little peasant-girls with white caps, who are so divinely pretty when you see them in the

---

[60] Hotel attendants and messengers.
[61] Patois is regional dialect, particularly a spoken dialect which may differ significantly from the written version of the language.

distance under a sunny meridian sky, and are so charming in coloured chalk upon tinted paper, but such miracles of ugliness, comparatively speaking, when you behold them at close quarters. And the dear jingling diligences,[62] with very little harness to speak of, but any quantity of old rope; and the bad wines, and the dust, and the cathedrals, and the beggars, and the trente-et-quarante tables,[63] and in short everything. Sir Philip Jocelyn spoke of the universe as a young husband talks of his wife; and was never tired of her beauty or impatient of her faults.

The poor about Jocelyn's Rock idolized the young lord of the soil. The poor like happy people, if there is nothing insolent in their happiness. Philip was rich, and he distributed his wealth right royally: he was happy, and he shared his happiness as freely as he shared his wealth. He would divide a case of choice Manillas with a bedridden pensioner in the Union, or carry a bottle of the Jocelyn Madeira—the celebrated Madeira with the brown seal—in the pocket of his shooting-coat, to deliver it into the horny hands of some hard-working mother who was burdened with a sick child. He would sit for an hour together telling an agricultural labourer of the queer farming he had seen abroad; and he had stood godfather—by proxy—to half the yellow-headed urchins within ten miles' radius of Jocelyn's Rock. No taint of vice or dissipation had ever sullied the brightness of his pleasant life. No wretched country girl had ever cursed his name before she cast herself into the sullen waters of a lonely mill-stream. People loved him; and he deserved their love, and was worthy of their respect. He had taken no high honours at Oxford; but the sternest officials smiled when they spoke of him, and recalled the boyish follies that were associated with his name; a sickly bedmaker had been pensioned for life by him; and the tradesmen who had served him testified to his merits as a prompt and liberal paymaster. I do not think that in all his life Philip Jocelyn had ever directly or indirectly caused a pang of pain or sorrow to any human being, unless it was, indeed, to a churlish heir-at-law, who may have looked with a somewhat evil eye upon the young man's vigorous and healthful aspect, which gave little hope to his possible successor.

The heir-at-law would have gnashed his teeth in impotent rage had he known the crisis which came to pass in the baronet's life a short time after Mr. Dunbar's return from India; a crisis very common to youth, and very lightly regarded by youth, but a solemn and a fearful crisis

---

[62] Diligences were vehicles used for public conveyance in France; a closed stagecoach drawn by horses.

[63] Trente-et-quarante (French for thirty and forty) is a card game, originating in 17th century France, and played on a purpose-built table.

notwithstanding.

The master of Jocelyn's Rock fell in love. All the poetry of his nature, all the best feelings, the purest attributes of an imperfect character, concentrated themselves into one passion, Sir Philip Jocelyn fell in love. The arch magician waved his wand, and all the universe was transformed into fairyland: a lovely Paradise, a modern Eden, radiant with the reflected light that it received from the face of a woman. I almost hesitate to tell this old, old story over again—this perpetual story of love at first sight.

It is very beautiful, this sudden love, which is born of one glance at the wonderful face that has been created to bewitch us; but I doubt if it is not, after all, the baser form of the great passion. The love that begins with esteem, that slowly grows out of our knowledge of the loved one, is surely the purer and holier type of affection.

This love, whose gradual birth we rarely watch or recognize—this love, that steals on us like the calm dawning of the eastern light, strikes to a deeper root and grows into a grander tree than that fair sudden growth, that marvellous far-shooting butterfly-blossoming orchid, called love at first sight. The glorious exotic flower may be wanting, but the strong root lies deeply hidden in the heart.

The man who loves at first sight generally falls in love with the violet blue of a pair of tender eyes, the delicate outline of a Grecian nose. The man who loves the woman he has known and watched, loves her because he believes her to be the purest and truest of her sex.

To this last, love is faith. He cannot doubt the woman he adores: for he adores her because he believes and has proved her to be above all doubt. We may fairly conjecture that Othello's passion for the simple Venetian damsel was love at first sight. He loved Desdemona because she was pretty, and looked at him with sweet maidenly glances of pity when he told those prosy stories of his—with full traveller's license, no doubt—over Brabantio's mahogany.

The tawny-visaged general loved the old man's daughter because he admired her, and not because he knew her; and so, by and bye, on the strength of a few foul hints from a scoundrel, he is ready to believe this gentle, pitiful girl the basest and most abandoned of women.[64]

Hamlet would not so have acted had it been his fate to marry the woman he loved. Depend upon it, the Danish prince had watched Ophelia closely, and knew all the ins and outs of that young lady's

---

[64] William Shakespeare, *Othello: The Moor of Venice* (first performed 1604-05; printed 1622). Othello marries Brabantio's daughter, Desdemona, but ends in murdering her through misplaced jealousy.

temper, and had laid conversational traps for her occasionally, I dare say, trying to entice her into some bit of toadyism that should betray any latent taint of falsehood inherited from poor time-serving Polonius. The Prince of Denmark would have been rather a fidgety husband, perhaps, but he would never have had recourse to a murderous bolster at the instigation of a low-born knave.[65]

Unhappily, some women are apt to prefer passionate, blustering Othello to sentimental and metaphysical Hamlet. The foolish creatures are carried away by noise and clamour, and most believe him who protests the loudest.

Philip Jocelyn and Laura Dunbar met at that dinner-party which the millionaire gave to his friends in celebration of his return. They met again at the ball, where Laura waltzed with Philip; the young man had learned to waltz upon the other side of the Alps, and Miss Dunbar preferred him to any other of her partners. At the *fête champêtre* [66] they met again; and had their future lives revealed to them by a theatrical-looking gipsy imported from London for the occasion, whose arch prophecies brought lovely blushes into Laura's cheeks, and afforded Philip an excellent opportunity for admiring the effect of dark-brown eyelashes drooping over dark-blue eyes. They met again and again; now at a steeple-chase, now at a dinner-party, where Laura appeared with some friendly *chaperon*; and the baronet fell in love with the banker's beautiful daughter.

He loved her truly and devotedly, after his own mad-headed fashion. He was a true Jocelyn—impetuous, mad-headed daring; and from the time of those festivities at Maudesley Abbey he only dreamed and thought of Laura Dunbar. From that hour he haunted the neighbour-hood of Maudesley Abbey. There was a bridle-path through the park to a little village called Lisford; and if that primitive Warwickshire village had been the most attractive place upon this earth, Sir Philip could scarcely have visited it oftener than he did.

Heaven knows what charm he found in the shady slumberous old street, the low stone market-place, with rusty iron gates surmounted by the Jocelyn escutcheon.[67] The grass grew in the quiet quadrangle; the square church-tower was half hidden by the sheltering ivy; the gabled cottage-roofs were lop-sided with age. It was scarcely a place to offer any very great attraction to the lord of Jocelyn Rock in all the glory of his

---

[65] William Shakespeare, *The Tragedy of Hamlet: Prince of Denmark* (first performed 1600-01; printed 1603).

[66] Literally "country" or "rural" party. An entertainment held out of doors; a garden party.

[67] In heraldry, the shield in a coat of arms.

early man-hood; and yet Philip Jocelyn went there three times a week upon an average, during the period that succeeded the ball and morning concert at Maudesley Abbey.

The shortest way from Jocelyn's Rock to Lisford was by the high road, but Philip Jocelyn did not care to go by the shortest way. He preferred to take that pleasant bridle-path through Maudesley Park, that delicious grassy arcade where the overarching branches of the old elms made a shadowy twilight, only broken now and then by sudden patches of yellow sunshine; where the feathery ferns trembled with every low whisper of the autumn breeze: where there was a faint perfume of pine wood; where every here and there, between the lower branches of the trees, there was a blue glimmer of still water-pools, half-hidden under flat green leaves of wild aquatic plants, where there was a solemn stillness that reminded one of the holy quiet of a church, and where Sir Philip Jocelyn had every chance of meeting with Laura Dunbar.

He met her there very often. Not alone, for Dora Macmahon was sometimes with her, and the faithful Elizabeth Madden was always at hand to play propriety, and to keep a sharp eye upon the interests of her young mistress. But then it happened unfortunately that the faithful Elizabeth was very stout, and rather asthmatic; and though Miss Dunbar could not have had a more devoted duenna, she might certainly have had a more active one. And it also happened that Miss Macmahon, having received several practical illustrations of the old adage with regard to the disadvantage of a party of three persons as compared to a party of two persons, fell into the habit of carrying her books with her, and would sit and read in some shady nook near the abbey, while Laura wandered into the wilder regions of the park.

Beneath the shelter of the overarching elms, amidst the rustling of the trembling ferns, Laura Dunbar and Philip Jocelyn met very often during that bright autumnal weather. Their meetings were purely accidental of course, as such meetings always are, but they were not the less pleasant because of their uncertainty.

They were all the more pleasant, perhaps. There was that delicious fever of suspense which kept both young eager hearts in a constant glow. There were Laura's sudden blushes, which made her wonderful beauty doubly wonderful. There was Philip Jocelyn's start of glad astonishment, and the bright sparkle in his dark-brown eyes as he saw the slender, queenly figure approaching him under the shadow of the trees. How beautiful she looked, with the folds of her dress trailing over the dewy grass, and a flickering halo of sunlight tremulous upon her diadem of golden hair! Sometimes she wore a coquettish little hat, with a turned-up brim and a peacock's plume; sometimes a broad-leaved hat of yellow straw, with floating ribbon and a bunch of feathery grasses perched bewitchingly upon the brim. She had the dog Pluto with her always, and generally a volume of some new novel under her arm. I am ashamed to be obliged to confess that this young heiress was very frivolous, and liked reading novels better than improving her mind by the perusal of grave histories, or by the study of the natural sciences. She spent day after day in happy idleness—reading, sketching, playing, singing, talking, sometimes gaily sometimes seriously, to her faithful old nurse, or to Dora, or to Arthur Lovell, as the case might be. She had a thorough-bred horse that had been given to her by her grandfather, but she very rarely rode him beyond the grounds, for Dora Macmahon was no horsewoman, having been brought up by a prim aunt of her dead mother's, who looked upon riding as an unfeminine accomplishment; and Miss Dunbar had therefore no better companion for her rides than a grey-haired old groom, who had ridden behind Percival Dunbar for forty years or so.

Philip Jocelyn generally went to Lisford upon horseback; but when, as so often happened, he met Miss Dunbar and her companion strolling amongst the old elms, it was his habit to get off his horse, and to walk by Laura's side, leading the animal by the bridle. Sometimes he found the two young ladies sitting on camp-stools at the foot of one of the trees, sketching effects of light and shadow in the deep glades around them. On such occasions the baronet used to tie his horse to the lower branch of an old elm, and taking his stand behind Miss Dunbar, would amuse himself by giving her a lesson in perspective, with occasional hints to Miss Macmahon, who, as the young man remarked, drew so much better than her sister, that she really required very little assistance.

By-and-by this began to be an acknowledged thing. Special hours were appointed for these artistic studies: and Philip Jocelyn ceased to go to Lisford at all, contenting himself with passing almost every fine morning under the elms at Maudesley. He found that he had a very intelligent pupil in the banker's daughter; but I think, if Miss Dunbar had been less intelligent, her instructor would have had patience with her, and would have still found his best delight beneath the shadow of those dear old elms.

What words can paint the equal pleasure of giving and receiving those lessons, in the art which was loved alike by pupil and master; but which was so small an element in the happiness of those woodland meetings? What words can describe Laura's pleading face when she found that the shadow of a ruined castle wouldn't agree with the castle itself, or that a row of poplars in the distance insisted on taking that direction which our transatlantic brothers call "slantindicular?"[68] And then the cutting of pencils, and crumbling of bread, and searching for mislaid scraps of India-rubber, and mixing of water-colours, and adjusting of palettes on the prettiest thumb in Christendom, or the planting a sheaf of brushes in the dearest little hand that ever trembled when it met the tenderly timid touch of an amateur drawing-master's fingers;—all these little offices, so commonplace and wearisome when a hard-worked and poorly-paid professor performs them for thirty or forty clamorous girls, on a burning summer afternoon, in a great dust-flavoured schoolroom with bare curtainless windows, were in this case more delicious than any words of mine can tell.

But September and October are autumnal months; and their brightest sunshine is, after all, only a deceptive radiance when compared to the full glory of July. The weather grew too cold for the drawing-lessons under the elms, and there could be no more appointments made between Miss Dunbar and her enthusiastic instructor.

"I can't have my young lady ketch cold, Sir Philip, for all the perspectives in the world," said the faithful Elizabeth. "I spoke to her par about it only the other day; but, lor'! you may just as well speak to a post as to Mr. Dunbar. If Miss Laura comes out in the park now, she must wrap herself up warm, and walk fast, and not go getting the cold shivers for the sake of drawing a parcel of stumps of trees and such-like tomfoolery."

Mrs. Madden made this observation in rather an unpleasant tone of voice one morning when the baronet pleaded for another drawing-lesson. The truth of the matter was that Elizabeth Madden felt some slight pangs of conscience with regard to her own part in this sudden friendship which had arisen between Laura Dunbar and Philip Jocelyn. She felt that she had been rather remiss in her duties as duenna,[69] and was angry with herself. But stronger than this feeling of self-reproach was her indignation against Sir Philip.

Why did he not immediately make an offer of his hand to Laura Dunbar?

Mrs. Madden had expected the young man's proposal every day for the last few weeks: every day she had been doomed to disappointment. And yet she was perfectly convinced that Philip Jocelyn loved her young mistress. The sharp eyes of the matron had fathomed the young man's sentiments long before Laura Dunbar dared to whisper to herself that she was beloved. Why, then, did he not propose? Who could be a more

---

[68] Slanting; oblique.

[69] A chaperone to young girls. Derived from the old Spanish word *dueña*.

fitting bride for the lord of Jocelyn's Rock than queenly Laura Dunbar, with her splendid dower of wealth and beauty?

Full of these ambitious hopes, Elizabeth Madden had played her part of duenna with such discretion as to give the young people plenty of opportunity for sweet, half-whispered converse, for murmured confidences, soft and low as the cooing of turtle-doves. But in all these conversations no word hinting at an offer of marriage had dropped from the lips of Philip Jocelyn.

He was so happy with Laura; so happy in those pleasant meetings under the Maudesley elms, that no thought of anything so commonplace as a stereotyped proposal of marriage had a place in his mind.

Did he love her? Of course he did: more dearly than he had ever before loved any human creature; except that tender and gentle being, whose image, vaguely beautiful, was so intermingled with the dreams and realities of his childhood in that dim period in which it is difficult to distinguish the shadows of the night from the events of the day,—that pale and lovely creature whom he had but just learned to call "mother," when she faded out of his life for ever.

It was only when the weather grew too cold for out-of-door drawing lessons that Sir Philip began to think that it was time to contemplate the very serious business of a proposal. He would have to speak to the banker, and all that sort of thing, of course, the baronet thought, as he sat by the fire in the oak-panelled breakfast-room at the Rock, pulling his thick moustaches reflectively, and staring at the red embers on the open hearth. The young man idolized Laura; but he did *not* particularly affect the society of Henry Dunbar. The millionaire was very courteous, very conciliating: but there was something in his stiff politeness, his studied smile, his deliberate speech, something entirely vague and indefinable, which had the same chilly effect upon Sir Philip's friendliness, as a cold cellar has on delicate-flavoured port. The subtle aroma vanished under that dismal influence.

"He's *her* father, and I'd kneel down, like the little boys in the streets, and clean his boots, if he wanted them cleaned, because he is her father," thought the young man; "and yet, somehow or other, I can't get on with him."

No! between the Anglo-Indian banker and Sir Philip Jocelyn there was no sympathy. They had no tastes in common: or let me rather say, Henry Dunbar revealed no taste in common with those of the young man whose highest hope in life was to be his son-in-law. The frank-hearted young country gentleman tried in vain to conciliate him, or to advance from the cold out-work of ceremonious acquaintanceship into the inner stronghold of friendly intercourse.

But when Sir Philip, after much hesitation and deliberation, presented himself one morning in the banker's tapestried sitting-room, and unburdened his heart to that gentleman—stopping every now and then to stare at the maker's name imprinted upon the lining of his hat, as if that name had been a magical symbol whence he drew certain auguries by which he governed his speech—Mr. Dunbar was especially gracious. "Would he honour Sir Philip by entrusting his daughter's happiness to his keeping? would he bestow upon Sir Philip the inestimable blessing of that dear hand? Why, of course he would, provided always that Laura wished it. In such a matter as this Laura's decision should be supreme. He never had contemplated interfering in his daughter's bestowal of her affections: so long as they were not wasted upon an unworthy object. He wished her to marry whom she pleased; provided that she married an honest man."

Mr. Dunbar gave a weary kind of sigh as he said this; but the sigh was habitual to him, and he apologized for and explained it sometimes by reference to his liver, which was disordered by five-and-thirty years in an Indian climate.

"I wish Laura to marry," he said; "I shall be glad when she has secured the protection of a good husband."

Sir Phillip Jocelyn sprang up with his face all a-glow with rapture, and would fain have seized the banker's hand in token of his gratitude; but Henry Dunbar waved him off with an authoritative gesture.

"Good morning, Sir Philip," he said; "I am very poor company, and I shall be glad to be alone with the *Times*. You young men don't appreciate the *Times*. You want your newspapers filled with prize-fighting and boat-racing, and the last gossip from 'the Corner.'[70] You'll find Miss Dunbar in the blue drawing-room. Speak to her as soon as you please; and let me know the result of the interview."

It is not often that the heiress of a million or thereabouts is quite so readily disposed of. Sir Philip Jocelyn walked on air as he quitted the banker's apartments.

"Who ever would have thought that he was such a delicious old brick?" he thought. "I expected any quantity of cold water; and instead of that, he sends me straight to my darling with *carte blanche* to go in and win, if I can. If I can! Suppose Laura doesn't love me, after all. Suppose she's only a beautiful coquette, who likes to see men go mad for love of her. And yet I won't think that; I won't be down-hearted; I won't believe she's anything but what she seems—an angel of purity and truth."

---

[70] "The Corner" probably refers to Hyde Park Corner, where Tattersall's, the racehorse auctioneers, were located until they moved to Knightsbridge in 1865. This area was a popular rendezvous for sporting and gambling men of all classes.

But, in spite of his belief in Laura's truth, the young baronet's courage was very low when he went into the blue drawing-room, and found Miss Dunbar seated in a deep embayed window, with the sunshine lighting up her hair and gleaming amongst the folds of her violet silk dress. She had been drawing; but her sketching apparatus lay idle on the little table by her side, and one listless hand hung down upon her dress, with a pencil held loosely between the slender fingers. She was looking straight before her, out upon the sunlit lawn, all gorgeous with flaunting autumn flowers; and there was something dreamy, not to say pensive, in the attitude of her drooping head.

But she started presently at the sound of that manly footstep; the pencil dropped from between her idle fingers, and she rose and turned towards the intruder. The beautiful face was in shadow as she turned away from the window; but no shadow could hide its sudden brightness, the happy radiance which lit up that candid countenance, as Miss Dunbar recognized her visitor.

The lover thought that one look more precious than Jocelyn's Rock, and a baronetcy that dated from the days of England's first Stuarts—that one glorious smile, which melted away in a moment, and gave place to bright maidenly blushes, fresh and beautiful as the dewy heart of an old-fashioned cabbage-rose gathered at sunrise.

That one smile was enough. Philip Jocelyn was no cox-comb,[71] but he knew all at once that he was beloved, and that very few words were needed. A great many were said, nevertheless; and I do not think two happier people ever sat side by side in the late autumn sunshine than those two, who lingered in the deep embayed window till the sun was low in the rosy western sky, and told Philip Jocelyn that his visit to Maudesley Abbey had very much exceeded the limits of a morning call.

So Philip Jocelyn was accepted. Early the next morning he called again upon Mr. Dunbar, and begged that an early date might be chosen for the wedding. The banker assented willingly enough to the proposition.

"Let the marriage take place in the first week in November," he said. "I am tired of living at Maudesley, and I want to get away to the Continent. Of course I must remain here to be present at my daughter's wedding."

Philip Jocelyn was only too glad to receive this permission to hurry the day of the ceremonial. He went at once to Laura, and told her what Mr. Dunbar had said. Mrs. Madden was indignant at this unceremonious manner of arranging matters.

[71] Usually as one word – coxcomb – meaning a foppish, vain, or conceited person.

"Where's my young lady's *trussaw* [72] to be got at a moment's notice, I should like to know? A deal you gentlemen know about such things. It's no use talking, my lord, there ain't a dressmaker livin' as would undertake the wedding-clothes for a baronet's lady in little better than a month."

But Mrs. Madden's objections were speedily overruled. To tell the truth, the honest-hearted creature was very much pleased to find that her young lady was going to be a baronet's wife, after all. She forgot all about her old favourite, Arthur Lovell, and set herself to work to expedite that most important matter of the wedding-garments. A man came down express from Howell and James's to Maudesley Abbey, with a bundle of patterns; and silks and velvets, gauzes and laces, and almost every costly fabric that was made, were ordered for Miss Dunbar's equipment. West-end dressmakers were communicated with. A French milliner, who looked like a lady of fashion, arrived one morning at Maudesley Abbey, and for a couple of hours poor Laura had to endure the slow agony of "trying on," while Mrs. Madden and Dora Macmahon discussed all the colours in the rainbow, and a great many new shades and combinations of colour, invented by aspiring French chemists.

- CHAPTER 21 -

A NEW LIFE

For the first time in her life, Margaret Wilmot knew what it was to have friends, real and earnest friends, who interested themselves in her welfare, and were bent upon securing her happiness; and I must admit that in this particular case there was something more than friendship—something holier and higher in its character—the pure and unselfish love of an honourable man.

Clement Austin, the cashier at Dunbar, Dunbar, and Balderby's Anglo-Indian banking-house, had fallen in love with the modest hazel-eyed music-mistress, and had set himself to work to watch her, and to find out all about her, long before he was conscious of the real nature of his feelings.

He had begun by pitying her. He had pitied her because of her hard life, her loneliness, her beauty, which doubtless exposed her to many dangers that would have been spared to a plain woman.

Now, when a man allows himself to pity a very pretty girl, he places

---

[72] *Trousseau.* from the French, meaning a bride's wedding gown, clothes, and linen, etc.

himself on a moral tight-rope; and he must be a moral Blondin if he expects to walk with any safety upon the narrow line which alone divides him from the great abyss called love.[73]

There are not many Blondins, either physical or intellectual; and the consequence is, that nine out of ten of the gentlemen who place themselves in this perilous position find the narrow line very slippery, and, before they have gone twenty paces, plunge overboard plump to the very bottom of the abyss, and are over head and ears in love before they know where they are.

Clement Austin fell in love with Margaret Wilmot; and his tender regard, his respectful devotion, were very new and sweet to the lonely girl. It would have been strange, then, under such circumstances, if his love had been hopeless.

He was in no very great hurry to declare himself; for he had a powerful ally in his mother, who adored her son, and would have allowed him to bring home a young negress, or a North American squaw, to the maternal hearth, if such a bride had been necessary to his happiness.

Mrs. Austin very speedily discovered her son's secret; for he had taken little pains to conceal his feelings from the indulgent mother who had been his confidante ever since his first boyish loves at a Clapham seminary, within whose sacred walls he had been admitted on Tuesdays and Fridays to learn dancing in the delightful society of five-and-thirty young ladies.

Mrs. Austin confessed that she would rather her son had chosen some damsel who could lay claim to greater worldly advantages than those possessed by the young music-mistress; but when Clement looked disappointed, the good soul's heart melted all in a moment, and she declared, that if Margaret was only as good as she was pretty, and truly attached to her dear noble-hearted boy, she (Mrs. Austin) would ask no more.

It happened fortunately that she knew nothing of Joseph Wilmot's antecedents, or of the letter addressed to Norfolk Island; or perhaps she might have made very strong objections to a match between her son and a young lady whose father had spent a considerable part of his life in a penal settlement.

"We will tell my mother nothing of the past, Miss Wilmot," Clement Austin said, "except that which concerns yourself alone. Let the history of your unhappy father's life remain a secret between you and me. My

---

[73] Jean François Gravelet-Blondin (1824-1897). French tight-rope walker and acrobat, who caused a popular sensation when he performed his daring feats in London during the early 1860s.

mother is very fond of you; I should be sorry, therefore, if she heard anything to shock her prejudices. I wish her to love you better every day."

Clement Austin had his wish; for the kind-hearted widow grew every day more and more attached to Margaret Wilmot. She discovered that the girl had more than an ordinary talent for music; and she proposed that Margaret should take a prettily furnished first-floor in a pleasant-looking detached house, half cottage, half villa, at Clapham, and at once set to work as a teacher of the piano.

"I can get you plenty of pupils, my dear," Mrs. Austin said; "for I have lived here more than thirty years—ever since Clement's birth, in fact—and I know almost everybody in the neighbourhood. You have only to teach upon moderate terms, and the people will be glad to send their children to you. I shall give a little evening party, on purpose that my friends may hear you play."

So Mrs. Austin gave her evening party, and Margaret appeared in a simple black-silk dress that had been in her wardrobe for a long time, and which would have seemed very shabby in the glaring light of day. The wearer of it looked very pretty and elegant, however, by the light of Mrs. Austin's wax-candles; and the aristocracy of Clapham remarked that the "young person" whom Mrs. Austin and her son had "taken up" was really rather nice-looking.

But when Margaret played and sang, people were charmed in spite of themselves. She had a superb contralto voice, rich, deep, and melodious; and she played with brilliancy, and, what is much rarer, with expression.

Mrs. Austin, going backwards and forwards amongst her guests to ascertain the current of opinions, found that her protégée's success was an accomplished fact before the evening was over.

Margaret took the new apartments in the course of the week; and before a fortnight had passed, she had secured more than a dozen pupils, who gave her ample employment for her time; and who enabled her to earn more than enough for her simple wants.

Every Sunday she dined with Mrs. Austin. Clement had persuaded his mother to make this arrangement a settled thing; although as yet he had said nothing of his growing love for Margaret.

Those Sundays were pleasant days to Clement and the girl whom he hoped to win for his wife.

The comfortable elegance of Mrs. Austin's drawing-room, the peaceful quiet of the Sabbath-evening, when the curtains were drawn before the bay-window, and the shaded lamp brought into the room; the intellectual conversation; the pleasant talk about new books and music: all were new and delightful to Margaret.

This was her first experience of a home, a real home, in which there was nothing but union and content; no overshadowing fear, no horrible unspoken dread, no half-guessed secrets always gnawing at the heart. But in all this new comfort Margaret Wilmot had not forgotten Henry Dunbar. She had not ceased to believe him guilty of her father's murder. Calm and gentle in her outward demeanour, she kept her secret buried in her breast, and asked for no sympathy.

Clement Austin had given her his best attention, his best advice; but it all amounted to nothing. The different scraps of evidence that hinted at Henry Dunbar's guilt were not strong enough to condemn him. The cashier communicated with the detective police, who had been watching the case; but they only shook their heads gravely, and dismissed him with their thanks for his information. There was nothing in what he had to tell them that could implicate Mr. Dunbar.

"A gentleman with a million of money doesn't put himself in the power of the hangman unless he's very hard pushed," said the detective. "The motive's what you must look to in these cases, sir. Now, where's Mr. Dunbar's motive for murdering this man Wilmot?"

"The secret that Joseph Wilmot possessed——"

"Bah, my dear sir! Henry Dunbar could afford to buy all the secrets that ever were kept. Secrets are like every other sort of article: they're only kept to sell. Good morning."

After this, Clement Austin told Margaret that he could be of no use to her. The dead man must rest in his grave: there was little hope that the mystery of his fate would ever be fathomed by human intelligence.

But Margaret Wilmot did not cease to remember Mr. Dunbar. She only waited.

One resolution was always uppermost in her mind, even when she was happiest with her new friends. She would see Henry Dunbar. In spite of his obstinate determination to avoid an interview with her, she would see him: and then, when she had gained her purpose, and stood face to face with him, she would boldly denounce him as her father's murderer. If then he did not flinch or falter, if she saw innocence in his face, she would cease to doubt him, she would be content to believe that Joseph Wilmot had met his untimely death from a stranger's hand.

- CHAPTER 22 -

THE STEEPLE-CHASE

After considerable discussion, it was settled that Laura Dunbar's wedding should take place upon the 7th of November. It was to be a very quiet wedding. The banker had especially impressed that condition upon his daughter. His health was entirely broken, and he would assist in no splendid ceremonial to which half the county would be invited. If Laura wanted bridesmaids, she might have Dora Macmahon and any particular friend who lived in the neighbourhood. There was to be no fuss, no publicity. Marriage was a very solemn business, Mr. Dunbar said, and it would be as well for his daughter to be undisturbed by any pomp or gaiety on her wedding-day. So the marriage was appointed to take place on the 7th, and the arrangements were to be as simple as the circumstances of the bride would admit. Sir Philip was quite willing that it should be so. He was much too happy to take objection to any such small matters. He only wanted the sacred words to be spoken which made Laura Dunbar his own for ever and for ever. He wanted to take her away to the southern regions, where he had travelled so gaily in his careless bachelor days, where he would be so supremely happy now with his bright young bride by his side. Fortune, who certainly spoils some of her children, had been especially beneficent to this young man. She had given him so many of her best gifts, and had bestowed upon him, over and above, the power to enjoy her favours.

It happened that the 6th of November was a day which, some time since, Philip Jocelyn would have considered the most important, if not the happiest, day of the year. It was the date of the Shorncliffe steeple-chases, and the baronet had engaged himself early in the preceding spring to ride his thorough-bred mare Guinevere, for a certain silver cup, subscribed for by the officers stationed at the Shorncliffe barracks.

Philip Jocelyn looked forward to this race with a peculiar interest, for it was to be the last he would ever ride—the very last: he had given this solemn promise to Laura, who had in vain tried to persuade him against even this race. She was brave enough upon ordinary occasions; but she loved her betrothed husband too dearly to be brave on this.

"I know it's very foolish of me, Philip," she said, "but I can't help being frightened. I can't help thinking of all the accidents I've ever heard of, or read of. I've dreamt of the race ever so many times, Philip. Oh, if you would only give it up for my sake!"

"My darling, my pet, is there anything I would not do for your sake that I could do in honour? But I can't do this, Laura dearest. You see I'm all right myself, and the mare's in splendid condition;—well, you saw her take her trial gallop the other morning, and you must know she's a flyer, so I won't talk about her. My name was entered for this race six months ago, you know, dear; and there are lots of small farmers and country people who have speculated their money on me; and they'd all lose, poor fellows, if I hung back at the last. You don't know what play-or-pay bets are, Laura dear. There's nothing in the world I wouldn't do for your sake; but my backers are poor people, and I can't put them in a hole. I must ride, Laura, and ride to win, too."

Miss Dunbar knew what this last phrase meant, and she conjured up the image of her lover flying across country on that fiery chestnut mare, whose reputation was familiar to almost every man, woman, and child in Warwickshire; but whatever her fears might be, she was obliged to be satisfied with her lover's promise that this should be his last steeple-chase.

The day came at last, a pale November day, mild but not sunny. The sky was all of one equal grey tint, and seemed to hang only a little way above the earth. The caps and jackets of the gentleman riders made spots of colour against that uniform grey sky; and the dresses of the ladies in the humble wooden structure which did duty as a grand stand, brightened the level landscape.

The course formed a long oval, and extended over three or four meadows, and crossed a country lane. It was a tolerably flat course; but the leaps, though roughly constructed, were rather formidable. Laura had been over all the ground with her lover on the previous day, and had looked fearfully at the high ragged hedges, and the broad ditches of muddy water. But Philip only made light of her fears, and told her the leaps were nothing, scarcely worthy of the chestnut mare's powers.

The course was not crowded, but there was a considerable sprinkling of spectators on each side of the rope—soldiers from the Shorncliffe barracks, country people, and loiterers of all kinds. There were a couple of drags, crowded with the officers and their friends, who clustered in all manner of perilous positions on the roof, and consumed unlimited champagne, bitter beer, and lobster-salad, in the pauses between the races. A single line of carriages extended for some little distance opposite the grand stand. The scene was gay and pleasant, as a race-ground always must be, even though it were in the wildest regions of the New World; but it was very quiet as compared to Epsom Downs or the open heath at Ascot.[74]

---

[74] Epsom Downs racecourse in Surrey, England, is the home of the Derby (see note 5,

Conspicuous amongst the vehicles there was a close carriage drawn by a pair of magnificent bays—an equipage which was only splendid in the perfection of its appointments. It was a clarence, with dark subdued-looking panels, only ornamented by a vermilion crest.[75] The liveries of the servants were almost the simplest upon the course; but the powdered heads of the men, and an indescribable something in their style, distinguished them from the country-bred coachmen and hobbledehoy pages in attendance on the other carriages.

Almost every one on the course knew that crest of an armed hand clasping a battle-axe, and knew that it belonged to Henry Dunbar. The banker appeared so very seldom in public that there was always a kind of curiosity about him when he did show himself; and between the races, people who were strolling upon the ground contrived to approach very near the carriage in which the master of Maudesley Abbey sat, wrapped in Cashmere shawls, and half-hidden under a great fur rug, in legitimate Indian fashion.

He had consented to appear upon the racecourse in compliance with his daughter's most urgent entreaties. She wanted him to be near her. She had some vague idea that he might be useful in the event of any accident happening to Philip Jocelyn. He might help her. It would be some consolation, some support to have him with her. He might be able to do something. Her father had yielded to her entreaties with a very tolerable grace, and he was here; but having conceded so much, he seemed to have done all that his frigid nature was capable of doing. He took no interest in the business of the day, but lounged far back in the carriage, and complained very much of the cold.

The vehicle had been drawn close up to the boundary of the course, and Laura sat at the open window, pale and anxious, straining her eyes towards the weighing-house and the paddock, the little bit of enclosed ground where the horses were saddled. She could see the gentleman riders going in and out, and the one rider on whose safety her happiness depended, muffled in his greatcoat, and very busy and animated amongst his grooms and helpers. Everybody knew who Miss Dunbar was, and that she was going to be married to the young baronet; and people looked with interest at that pale face, keeping such anxious watch at the carriage-window. I am speaking now of the simple country people, for

p.9 above). Royal Ascot racecourse in Berkshire, England, was founded in 1711, but only hosted the Royal Meeting (an annual four-day event), until more racing fixtures were introduced after 1945.
[75] Clarence: a closed, four-wheeled carriage with a glass front, named after the Duke of Clarence (later William IV). Also known as a growler.

whom a race meant a day's pleasure. There were people on the other side of the course who cared very little for Miss Dunbar or her anxiety; who would have cared as little if the handsome young baronet had rolled upon the sward, crushed to death under the weight of his chestnut mare, so long as they themselves were winners by the event. In the little enclosure below the grand stand the betting men—that strange fraternity which appears on every racecourse from Berwick-on-Tweed to the Land's-End, from the banks of the Shannon to the smooth meads of pleasant Normandy—were gathered thick, and the talk was loud about Sir Philip and his competitors.

Among the men who were ready to lay against anything, and were most unpleasantly vociferous in the declaration of their readiness, there was one man who was well known to the humbler class of bookmen with whom he associated, who was known to speculate upon very small capital, but who had never been known as a defaulter. The knowing ones declared this man worthy to rank high amongst the best of them; but no one knew where he lived, or what he was. He was rarely known to miss a race; and he was conspicuous amongst the crowd in those mysterious purlieus where the plebeian bookmen, who are unworthy to enter the sacred precincts of Tattersall's, mostly do congregate, in utter defiance of the police.[76] No one had ever heard the name of this man; but in default of any more particular cognomen, they had christened him the Major; because in his curt manners, his closely buttoned-up coat, tightly-strapped trousers, and heavy moustache, there was a certain military flavour, which had given rise to the rumour that the unknown had in some remote period been one of the defenders of his country. Whether he had enlisted as a private, and had been bought-off by his friends; whether he had borne the rank of an officer, and had sold his commission, or had been cashiered, or had deserted, or had been drummed-out of his regiment,—no one pretended to say. People called him the Major; and wherever he appeared, the Major made himself conspicuous by means of a very tall white hat, with a broad black crape band round it.

He was tall himself, and the hat made him seem taller. His clothes were very shabby, with that peculiar shiny shabbiness which makes a man look as if he had been oiled all over, and then rubbed into a high state of polish. He wore a greenish-brown greatcoat with a poodle collar, and was supposed to have worn the same for the last ten years. Round his neck, be the weather ever so sultry, he wore a comforter of rusty worsted that had once been scarlet, and above this comforter appeared

---

[76] Tattersall's: leading race horse auctioneers situated near Hyde Park Corner, London.

his nose, which was a prominent aquiline.[77] Nobody ever saw much more of the Major than his nose and his moustache. His hat came low down over his forehead, which was itself low, and a pair of beetle brows, of a dense purple-black, were faintly visible in the shadow of the brim. He never took off his hat in the presence of his fellow-men; and as he never encountered the fair sex, except in the person of the barmaid at a sporting public, he was not called upon to unbonnet himself in ceremonious obeisance to lovely woman. He was eminently a mysterious man, and seemed to enjoy himself in the midst of the cloud of mystery which surrounded him.

The Major had inspected the starters for the great event of the day, and had sharply scrutinized the gentleman riders as they went in and out of the paddock. He was so well satisfied with the look of Sir Philip Jocelyn, and the chestnut mare Guinevere, that he contented himself with laying the odds against all the other horses, and allowed the baronet and the chestnut to run for him. He asked a few questions presently about Sir Philip, who had taken off his greatcoat by this time, and appeared in all the glory of a scarlet satin jacket and a black velvet cap. A Warwickshire farmer, who had found his way in among the knowing ones, informed the Major that Sir Philip Jocelyn was going to be married to Miss Dunbar, only daughter and sole heiress of the great Mr. Dunbar.

The great Mr. Dunbar! The Major, usually so imperturbable, gave a little start at the mention of the banker's name.

"What Mr. Dunbar?" he asked.

"The banker. Him as come home from the Indies last August."

The Major gave a long low whistle; but he asked no further question of the farmer. He had a memorandum-book in his hand—a greasy and grimy-looking little volume, whose pages he was wont to study profoundly from time to time, and in which he jotted down all manner of queer hieroglyphics with half an inch of fat lead-pencil. He relapsed into the contemplation of this book now; but he muttered to himself ever and anon in undertones, and his mutterings had relation to Henry Dunbar.

"It's him," he muttered; "that's lucky. I read all about that Winchester business in the Sunday papers. I've got it all at my fingers'-ends, and I don't see why I shouldn't make a trifle out of it. I don't see why I shouldn't win a little money upon Henry Dunbar. I'll have a look at my gentleman presently, when the race is over."

The bell rang, and the seven starters went off with a rush; four

---

[77] Comforter: long woollen scarf, often made from worsted, a woollen fabric made from twisted yarn.

abreast, and three behind. Sir Philip was among the four foremost riders, keeping the chestnut well in hand, and biding his time very quietly. This was his last race, and he had set his heart upon winning. Laura leaned out of the carriage-window, pale and breathless, with a powerful race-glass in her hand. She watched the riders as they swept round the curve in the course. Then they disappeared, and the few minutes during which they were out of sight seemed an age to that anxious watcher. The people run away to see them take the double leap in the lane, and then come trooping back again, panting and eager, as three of the riders appear again round another bend of the course.

The scarlet leads this time. The honest country people hurrah for the master of Jocelyn's Rock. Have they not put their money upon him, and are they not proud of him?—proud of his handsome face, which, amid all its easy good-nature, has a certain dash of hauteur that befits one who has a sprinkling of the blood of Saxon kings in his veins; proud of his generous heart, which beats with a thousand kindly impulses towards his fellow-men. They shout aloud as he flies past them, the long stride of the chestnut skimming over the ground, and spattering fragments of torn grass and ploughed-up earth about him as he goes. Laura sees the scarlet jacket rise for a moment against the low grey sky, and then fly onward, and that is about all she sees of the dreaded leap which she had looked at in fear and trembling the day before. Her heart is still beating with a strange vague terror, when her lover rides quietly past the stand, and the people about her cry out that the race has been nobly won. The other riders come in very slowly, and are oppressed by that indescribable air of sheepishness which is peculiar to gentleman jockeys when they do not win.

The girl's eyes fill suddenly with tears, and she leans back in the carriage, glad to hide her happy face from the crowd.

Ten minutes afterwards Sir Philip Jocelyn came across the course with a great silver-gilt cup in his arms, and surrounded by an admiring throng, amongst whom he had just emptied his purse.

"I've brought you the cup, Laura; and I want you to be pleased with my victory. It's the last triumph of my bachelor days, you know, darling."

"Three cheers for Miss Dunbar!" shouted some adventurous spirit among the crowd about the baronet.

In the next moment the cry was taken up, and two or three hundred voices joined in a loud hurrah for the banker's daughter. The poor girl drew back into the carriage, blushing and frightened.

"Don't mind them, Laura dear," Sir Philip said; "they mean well, you know, and they look upon me as public property. Hadn't you better give them a bow, Mr. Dunbar?" he added, in an undertone to the banker.

"It'll please them, I know."

Mr. Dunbar frowned, but he bent forward for a moment, and, leaning his head a little way out of the window, made a stately acknowledgment of the people's enthusiasm. As he did so, his eyes met those of the Major, who had crossed the course with Sir Philip and his admirers, and who was staring straight before him at the banker's carriage. Henry Dunbar drew back immediately after making that very brief salute to the populace.

"Tell them to drive home, Sir Philip," he said. "The people mean well, I dare say; but I hate these popular demonstrations. There's something to be done about the settlements, by-the-bye; you'd better dine at the Abbey this evening. John Lovell will be there to meet you."

The carriage drove away; and though the Major pushed his way through the crowd pretty rapidly, he was too late to witness its departure. He was in a very good temper, however, for he had won what his companions called a hatful of money on the steeple-chase, and he stood to win on other races that were to come off that afternoon. During the interval that elapsed before the next race, he talked to a sociable bystander about Sir Philip Jocelyn, and the young lady he was going to marry. He ascertained that the wedding was to take place the next morning, and at Lisford church.

"In that case," thought the Major, as he went back to the ring, "I shall sleep at Lisford to-night; I shall make Lisford my quarters for the present, and I shall follow up Henry Dunbar."

- CHAPTER 23 -

THE BRIDE THAT THE RAIN RAINS ON

There was no sunshine upon Laura Dunbar's wedding morning. The wintry sky was low and dark, as if the heavens had been coming gradually down to crush this wicked earth. The damp fog, the slow, drizzling rain shut out the fair landscape upon which the banker's daughter had been wont to look from the pleasant cushioned seat in the deep bay-window of her dressing-room.

The broad lawn was soddened by that perpetual rain. The incessant rain-drops dripped from the low branches of the black spreading cedars of Lebanon; the smooth beads of water ran off the shining laurel-leaves; the rhododendrons, the feathery furze, the glistening arbutus— everything was obscured by that cruel rain.

The water gushed out of the quaint dragons' mouths, ranged along the parapet of the Abbey roof; it dripped from every stone coping and abutment; from window-ledge and porch, from gable-end and sheltering ivy. The rain was everywhere, and the incessant pitter-patter of the drops beating against the windows of the Abbey made a dismal sound, scarcely less unpleasant to hear than the perpetual lamentation of the winds, which to-day had the sound of human voices; now moaning drearily, with a long, low, wailing murmur, now shrieking in the shrilly tones of an angry vixen.

Laura Dunbar gave a long discontented sigh as she seated herself at her favourite bay-window, and looked out at the dripping trees upon the lawn below.

She was a petted heiress, remember, and the world had gone so smoothly with her hitherto, that perhaps she scarcely endured calamity or contradiction with so good a grace as she might have done had she been a little nearer perfection. She was hardly better than a child as yet, with all a child's ignorant hopefulness and blind trust in the unknown future. She was a pampered child, and she expected to have life made very smooth for her.

"What a horribly dismal morning!" Miss Dunbar exclaimed. "Did you ever see anything like it, Elizabeth?"

Mrs. Madden was bustling about, arranging her young mistress's breakfast upon a little table near the blazing fire. Laura had just emerged from her bath room, and had put on a loose dressing-gown of wadded blue silk, prior to the grand ceremonial of the wedding toilet, which was not to take place until after breakfast.

I think Miss Dunbar looked lovelier in this _déshabille_[78] than many a bride in her lace and orange-blossoms. The girl's long golden hair, wet from the bath, hung in rippling confusion about her fresh young face. Two little feet, carelessly thrust into blue morocco slippers, peeped out from amongst the folds of Miss Dunbar's dressing-gown, and one coquettish scarlet heel tapped impatiently upon the floor as the young lady watched that provoking rain.

"What a wretched morning!" she said.

"Well, Miss Laura, it is rather wet," replied Mrs. Madden, in a conciliating tone.

"Rather wet!" echoed Laura, with an air of vexation; "I should think it was _rather_ wet, indeed. It's miserably wet; it's horribly wet. To think that the frost should have lasted very nearly three weeks, and then must needs break up on my wedding morning. Did ever anybody know

---

[78] State of undress.

anything so provoking?"

"Lor', Miss Laura," rejoined the sympathetic Madden, "there's all manner of provoking things allus happenin' in this blessed, wicked, rampageous world of ours; only such young ladies as you don't often come across 'em. Talk of being born with a silver spoon in your mouth, Miss Laura; I do think as you must have come into this mortal spear[79] with a whole service of gold plate. And don't you fret your precious heart, my blessed Miss Laura, if the rain *is* contrary. I dare say the clerk of the weather is one of them rampagin' radicals that's allus a goin' on about the bloated aristocracy, and he's done it a purpose to aggeravate you. But what's a little rain more or less to you, Miss Laura, when you've got more carriages to ride in than if you was a princess in a fairy tale, which I think the Princess Baltroubadore,[80] or whatever her hard name was, in the story of Aladdin, must have had no carriage whatever, or she wouldn't have gone walkin' to the baths. Never you mind the rain, Miss Laura."

"But it's a bad omen, isn't it, Elizabeth?" asked Laura Dunbar. "I seem to remember some old rhyme about the bride that the sun shines on, and the bride that the rain rains on."

"Laws, Miss Laura, you don't mean to say as you'd bemean yourself by taking any heed of such low rubbish as that?" exclaimed Mrs. Madden; "why, such stupid rhymes as them are only made for vulgar people that have the banns put up in the parish church. A deal it matters to such as you, Miss Laura, if all the cats and dogs as ever was come down out of the heavens this blessed day."

But though honest-hearted Elizabeth Madden did her best to comfort her young mistress after her own simple fashion, she was not herself altogether satisfied.

The low, brooding sky, the dark and murky atmosphere, and that monotonous rain would have gone far to depress the spirits of the gayest reveller in all the universe.

In spite of ourselves, we are the slaves of atmospheric influences; and we cannot feel very light-hearted or happy upon black wintry days, when the lowering heavens seem to frown upon our hopes; when, in the darkening of the earthly prospect, we fancy that we see a shadowy curtain closing round an unknown future.

Laura felt something of this; for she said, by and by, half impatiently, half mournfully,—

---

[79] Elizabeth Madden means mortal *sphere*. This is one of her many malapropisms.
[80] Princess Badroulbadour, who marries Aladdin. From *One Thousand and One Nights* (usually referred to in English as the *Arabian Nights*).

162

"What is the matter with me, Elizabeth. Has all the world changed since yesterday? When I drove home with papa, after the races yesterday, everything upon earth seemed so bright and beautiful. Such an overpowering sense of joy was in my heart, that I could scarcely believe it was winter, and that it was only the fading November sunshine that lit up the sky. All my future life seemed spread before me, like an endless series of beautiful pictures—pictures in which I could see Philip and myself, always together, always happy. To-day, to-day, oh! *How* different everything is!" exclaimed Laura, with a little shudder.

"The sky that shuts in the lawn yonder seems to shut in my life with it. I can't look forward. If I was going to be parted from Philip to-day, instead of married to him, I don't think I could feel more miserable than I feel now. Why is it, Elizabeth, dear?"

"My goodness gracious me!" cried Mrs. Madden, "how should I tell, my precious pet? You talk just like a poetry-book, and how can I answer you unless I was another poetry-book? Come and have your breakfast, do, that's a dear sweet love, and try a new-laid egg. New-laid eggs is good for the spirits, my poppet."

Laura Dunbar seated herself in the comfortable arm-chair between the fireplace and the little breakfast-table. She made a sort of pretence at eating, just to please her old nurse, who fidgeted about the room; now stopping by Laura's chair, and urging her to take this, that, or the other; now running to the dressing-table to make some new arrangement about the all-important wedding-toilet; now looking out of the window and perjuring her simple soul by declaring that "it"—namely, the winter sky—was going to clear up.

"It's breaking up above the elms yonder, Miss Laura," Elizabeth said; "there's a bit of blue peepin' through the clouds; leastways, if it ain't quite blue, it's a much lighter black than the rest of the sky, and that's something. Eat a bit of Perrigorge[81] pie, or a thin wafer of a slice off that Strasbog 'am, Miss Laura, do now. You'll be ready to drop with feelin' faint when you get to the altar-rails, if you persist on bein' married on a empty stummick, Miss Laura. It's a moriel impossible as you can look your best, my precious love, if you enter the church in a state of starvation, just like one of them respectable beggars wot pins a piece of paper on their weskits[82] with 'I AM HUNGRY' wrote upon it in large

---

[81] Doubtless Madden's mispronunciation of a French brand. Possibly Perrier-Jouët, a fine champagne popular with the upper-classes at this time. Such a Victorian culinary specialty would be in keeping with the opulent luxury of Maudesley Abbey, particularly on Laura's wedding day.

[82] Waistcoats.

hand, and stands at the foot of one of the bridges on the Surrey side of the water. And I shouldn't think as you would wish to look like *that*, Miss Laura, on your wedding-day? *I* shouldn't if *I* was goin' to be own wife to a baronet!"

Laura Dunbar took very little notice of her nurse's rambling discourse; and I am fain to confess that, upon this occasion, Mrs. Madden talked rather more for the sake of talking than from any overflow of animal spirits.

The good creature felt the influence of the cold, wet, cheerless morning quite as keenly as her mistress. Mrs. Madden was superstitious, as most ignorant and simple-minded people generally are, more or less. Superstition is, after all, only a dim, unconscious poetry, which is latent in most natures, except in such very hard practical minds as are incapable of believing in anything—not even in Heaven itself.

Dora Macmahon came in presently, looking very pretty in blue silk and white lace. She looked very happy, in spite of the bad weather, and Miss Dunbar suffered herself to be comforted by her half-sister. The two girls sat at the table by the fire, and breakfasted, or pretended to breakfast, together. Who could really attend to the common business of eating and drinking on such a day as this?

"I've just been to see Lizzie and Ellen," Dora said, presently; "they wouldn't come in here till they were dressed, and they've had their hair screwed up in hair-pins all night to make it wave, and now it's a wet day their hair won't wave after all, and their maid's going to pinch it with the fire-irons—the tongs, I suppose."

Miss Macmahon had brown hair, with a natural ripple in it, and could afford to laugh at beauty that was obliged to adorn itself by means of hair-pins and tongs.

Lizzie and Ellen were the daughters of a Major Melville, and the special friends of Miss Dunbar. They had come to Maudesley to act as her bridesmaids, according to that favourite promise which young ladies so often make to each other, and so very often break.

Laura did not appear to take much interest in the Miss Melvilles' hair. She was very meditative about something; but her meditations must have been of a pleasant nature, for there was a smile upon her face.

"Dora," she said, by-and-by, "do you know I've been thinking about something?"

"About what, dear?"

"Don't you know that old saying about one wedding making many?"

Dora Macmahon blushed.

"What of that, Laura dear?" she asked, very innocently.

"I've been thinking that perhaps another wedding may follow mine.

Oh, Dora, I can't help saying it, I should be so happy if Arthur Lovell and you were to marry."

Miss Macmahon blushed a much deeper red than before.

"Oh, Laura," she said, "that's quite impossible."

But Miss Dunbar shook her head.

"I shall live in the hope of it, notwithstanding," she said. "I love Arthur almost as much—or perhaps quite as much, as if he were my brother—so it isn't strange that I should wish to see him married to my sister."

The two girls might have sat talking for some time longer, but they were interrupted by Miss Dunbar's old nurse, who never for a moment lost sight of the serious business of the day.

"It's all very well for you to sit there jabber, jabber, jabber, Miss Dora," exclaimed the unceremonious Elizabeth; "you're dressed, all but your bonnet. You've only just to pop that on, and there you are. But my young lady isn't half dressed yet. And now, come along, Miss Laura, and have your hair done, if you mean to have any back-hair at all to-day. It's past nine o'clock, and you're to be at the church at eleven."

"And papa is to give me away!" murmured Laura, in a low voice, as she seated herself before the dressing-table. "I wish he loved me better."

"Perhaps, if he loved you too well, he'd keep you, instead of giving you away, Miss Laura," observed Mrs. Madden, with evident enjoyment of her own wit; "and I don't suppose you'd care about that, would you, miss? Hold your head still, that's a precious darling, and don't you trouble yourself about anything except looking your very best this day."

- CHAPTER 24 -

THE UNBIDDEN GUEST WHO CAME TO LAURA DUNBAR'S WEDDING

The wedding was to take place in Lisford church—that pretty, quaint, old church of which I have already spoken.

The wandering Avon flowed through this rustic churchyard, along a winding channel fringed by tall, trembling rushes. There was a wooden bridge across the river, and there were two opposite entrances to the churchyard. Pedestrians who chose the shortest route between Lisford and Shorncliffe went in at one gate and out at another, which opened on to the high-road.

The worthy inhabitants of Lisford were almost as much distressed by the unpromising aspect of the sky as Laura Dunbar and her faithful nurse themselves. New bonnets had been specially prepared for this festive occasion. Chrysanthemums and dahlias, gay-looking China-asters, and all the lingering flowers that light up the early winter landscape, had been collected to strew the pathway beneath the bride's pretty feet. All the brightest evergreens in the Lisford gardens had been gathered as a fitting sacrifice for the "young lady from the Abbey."

Laura Dunbar's frank good-nature and reckless generosity were well remembered upon this occasion; and every creature in Lisford was bent upon doing her honour.

But this aggravating rain balked everybody. What was the use of throwing wet dahlias and flabby chrysanthemums into the puddles through which the bride must tread, heiress though she was? How miserable would be the aspect of two rows of damp charity children, with red noses and no pocket-handkerchiefs! The rector himself had a cold in his head, and would be obliged to omit all the *n*'s and *m*'s in the marriage service.

In short, everybody felt that the Abbey wedding was destined to be more or less a failure. It seemed very hard that the chief partner in the firm of Dunbar, Dunbar, and Balderby could not, with all his wealth, buy a little glimmer of sunshine to light up his daughter's wedding. It grew so dark and foggy towards eleven o'clock, that a dozen or so of wax-candles were hastily stuck about the neighbourhood of the altar, in order that the bride and bridegroom might be able, each of them, to see the person that he or she was taking for better or worse.

Yes, the dismal weather made everything dismal in unison with itself. A wet wedding is like a wet pic-nic. The most heroic nature gives way before its utter desolation; the wit of the party forgets his best anecdote; the funny man breaks down in the climactic verse of his great buffo song; there is no brightness in the eyes of the beauty; there is neither sparkle nor flavour in the champagne, though the grapes thereof have been grown in the vineyards of Widow Cliquot herself.[83]

There are some things that are more powerful than emperors, and the atmosphere is one of them. Alexander[84] might conquer nations in very sport; but I question whether he could have resisted the influence of a wet day.

Of all the people who were to assist at Sir Philip Jocelyn's wedding, perhaps the father of the bride was the person who seemed least affected by that drizzling rain, that hopelessly-black sky.

If Henry Dunbar was grave and silent to-day, why that was nothing new: for he was always grave and silent. If the banker's manner was stern and moody to-day, that stern moodiness was habitual to him: and there was no need to blame the murky heavens for any change in his temper. He sat by the broad fireplace watching the burning coals, and waiting until he should be summoned to take his place by his daughter's side in the carriage that was to convey them both to Lisford church; and he did not utter one word of complaint about that aggravating weather.

He looked very handsome, very aristocratic, with his grey moustache carefully trimmed, and a white camellia in his button-hole. Nevertheless, when he came out into the hall by-and-by, with a set smile upon his face, like a man who is going to act a part in a play, Laura Dunbar recoiled from him with an involuntary shiver, as she had done upon the day of her first meeting with him in Portland Place.

But he offered her his hand, and she laid the tips of her fingers in his broad palm, and went with him to the carriage. "Ask God to bless me upon this day, papa," the girl said, in a low, tender voice, as these two people took their places side by side in the roomy chariot.

Laura Dunbar laid her hand caressingly upon the banker's shoulder as she spoke. It was not a time for reticence; it was not an occasion upon which to be put off by any girlish fear of this stern, silent man.

"Ask God to bless me, father dearest," the soft, tremulous voice

---

[83] Clicquot champagne house, founded in 1772, later became Veuve Clicquot (*Veuve* meaning widow in French). On the death of François Clicquot in 1805, his widow Madame Clicquot (Barbe-Nicole Ponsardin) took control of the company and established it as one of the most respected and successful champagne houses.
[84] Alexander III of Macedon, known as Alexander the Great (356-323 BC).

pleaded, "for the sake of my dead mother."

She tried to see his face: but she could not. His head was turned away, and he was busy making some alteration in the adjustment of the carriage-window. The chariot had cost nearly three hundred pounds, and was very well built: but there was something wrong about the window nevertheless, if one might judge by the difficulty which Mr. Dunbar had, in settling it to his satisfaction.

He spoke presently, in a very earnest voice, but with his head still turned away from Laura.

"I hope God will bless you, my dear," he said; "and that He will have pity upon your enemies."

This last wish was more Christianlike than natural; since fathers do not usually implore compassion for the enemies of their children.

But Laura Dunbar did not trouble herself to think about this. She only knew that her father had called down Heaven's blessing upon her; and that his manner had betrayed such agitation as could, of course, only spring from one cause, namely, his affection for his daughter.

She threw herself into his arms with a radiant smile, and putting up her hands, drew his face round, and pressed her lips to his.

But, as on the day in Portland Place, a chill crept through her veins, as she felt the deadly coldness of her father's hands lifted to push her gently from him.

It is a common thing for Anglo-Indians to be quiet and reserved in their manners, and strongly adverse to all demonstrations of this kind. Laura remembered this, and made excuses to herself for her father's coldness.

The rain was still falling as the carriage stopped at the churchyard. There were only three carriages in this brief bridal train, for Mr. Dunbar had insisted that there should be no grandeur, no display.

The two Miss Melvilles, Dora Macmahon, and Arthur Lovell rode in the same carriage. Major Melville's daughters looked very pale and cold in their white-and-blue dresses, and the north-easter had tweaked their noses, which were rather sharp and pointed in style. They would have looked pretty enough, poor girls, had the wedding taken place in summer-time; but they had not that splendid exceptional beauty which can defy all changes of temperature, and which is alike glorious, whether clad in abject rags or robed in velvet and ermine.

The carriages reached the little gate of Lisford churchyard; Philip Jocelyn came out of the porch, and down the narrow pathway leading to the gate.

The drizzling rain descended on him, though he was a baronet, and though he came bareheaded to receive his bride.

I think the Lisford beadle, who was a sound Tory of the old school, almost wondered that the heavens themselves should be audacious enough to wet the uncovered head of the lord of Jocelyn's Rock.

But it went on raining, nevertheless.

"Times has changed, sir," said the beadle, to an idle-looking stranger who was standing near him. "I have read in a history of Warwickshire, that when Algernon Jocelyn was married to Dame Margery Milward, widow to Sir Stephen Milward, knight, in Charles the First's time, there was a cloth-of-gold canopy from the gate yonder to this porch here, and two moving turrets of basket-work, each of 'em drawn by four horses, and filled with forty poor children, crowned with roses, lookin' out of the turret winders, and scatterin' scented waters on the crowd; and there was a banquet, sir, served up at noon that day at Jocelyn's Rock, with six peacocks brought to table with their tails spread; and a pie, served in a gold dish, with live doves in it, every feather of 'em steeped in the rarest perfume, which they was intended to sprinkle over the company as they flew about here and there. But—would you believe in such a radical spirit pervadin' the animal creation?—every one of them doves flew straight out of the winder, and went and scattered their perfumes on the poor folks outside. There's no such weddin's as that nowadays, sir," said the old beadle, with a groan. "As I often say to my old missus, I don't believe as ever England has held up its head since the day when Charles the Martyr lost his'n."

Laura Dunbar went up the narrow pathway by her father's side; but Philip Jocelyn walked upon her left hand, and the crowd had enough to do to stare at bride and bridegroom.

The baronet's face, which was always a handsome one, looked splendid in the light of his happiness. People disputed as to whether the bride or bridegroom was handsomest; and Laura forgot all about the wet weather as she laid her light hand on Philip Jocelyn's arm.

The churchyard was densely crowded in the neighbourhood of the pathway along which the bride and bridegroom walked. In spite of the miserable weather, in defiance of Mr. Dunbar's desire that the wedding should be a quiet one, people had come from a very long distance in order to see the millionaire's beautiful daughter married to the master of Jocelyn's Rock.

Amongst the spectators who had come to witness Miss Dunbar's wedding was the tall gentleman in the high white hat, who was known in sporting circles as the Major, and who had exhibited so much interest when the name of Henry Dunbar was mentioned on the Shorncliffe racecourse. The Major had been very lucky in his speculations on the Shorncliffe races, and had gone straight away from the course to the village of Lisford, where he took up his abode at the Rose and Crown, a bright-looking hostelry, where a traveller could have his steak or his chop done to a turn in one of the cosiest kitchens in all Warwickshire. The Major was very reserved upon the subject of his sporting operations when he found himself among unprofessional people; and upon such occasions, though he would now and then condescend to lay the odds against anything with some unconscious agriculturalist or village tradesman, his innocence with regard to all turf matters was positively refreshing.

He was a traveller in Birmingham jewellery, he told the land lady of the quiet little inn, and was on his way to that busy commercial centre to procure a fresh supply of glass emeralds, and a score or so of gigantic rubies with crinkled tinsel behind them. The Major, usually somewhat silent and morose, contrived to make himself very agreeable to the jovial frequenters of the comfortable little public parlour of the Rose and Crown.

He took his dinner and his supper in that cosy apartment; and he sat there all the evening, listening to and joining in the conversation of the Lisfordians, and drinking sixpenn'orths of gin-and-water, with the air of a man who could consume a hogshead of the juice of the juniper-berry without experiencing any evil consequences therefrom. He ate and drank like a man of iron; and his glittering black eyes kept perpetual watch upon the faces of the simple country people, and his eager ears drank in every word that was spoken. Of course a great deal was said about the event of the next morning. Everybody had something to say about Miss Dunbar and her wealthy father, who lived so lonely and secluded at the Abbey, and whose ways were altogether so different from those of his father before him.

The Major listened to every syllable, and only edged-in a word or two now and then, when the conversation flagged, or when there was a chance of the subject being changed.

By this means he contrived to keep the Lisfordians constant to one topic all the evening, and that topic was the manners and customs of Henry Dunbar.

Very early on the morning of the wedding the Major made his appearance in the churchyard. As for the incessant rain, that was nothing to *him*; he was used to it; and, moreover, the wet weather gave him a good excuse for buttoning his coat to the chin, and turning the poodle collar over his big red ears.

He found the door of the church ajar, early though it was, and going in softly, he came upon the Tory beadle and some damp charity children.

The Major contrived to engage the Tory beadle in conversation, which was not very difficult, seeing that the aforesaid beadle was always ready to avail himself of any opportunity of hearing his own voice. Of course the loquacious beadle talked chiefly of Sir Philip Jocelyn and the banker's daughter; and again the sporting gentleman from London heard of Henry Dunbar's riches.

"I *have* heerd as Mr. Dunbar is the richest man in Europe, exceptin' the Hemperore of Roosia and Baron Rothschild,"[85] the beadle said; "but I don't know anythink more than that he's got a deal more money than he knows what to do with, seein' that he passes the best part of his days sittin' over the fire in his own room, or ridin' out after dark on horseback, if report speaks correct."

"I tell you what I'll do," said the Major; "as I am in Lisford,—and, to be candid with you, Lisford's about the dullest place it was ever my bad luck to visit,—why, I'll stay and have a look at this wedding. I suppose you can put me into a quiet pew, back yonder in the shadow, where I can see all that's going on, without any of your fine folks seeing me, eh?"

As the Major emphasized this question by dropping half-a-crown into the beadle's hand, that official answered it very promptly,—

"I'll put you into the comfortablest pew you ever sat in," answered the official.

"You might do that easily," muttered the sporting gentleman, below his breath; "for there's not many pews, or churches either, that I've ever sat in."

The Major took his place in a corner of the church whence there was a very good view of the altar, where the feeble flames of the wax-candles made little splashes of yellow light in the fog.

The fog got thicker and thicker in the church as the hour for the marriage ceremony drew nearer and nearer, and the light of the wax-candles grew brighter as the atmosphere became more murky.

The Major sat patiently in his pew, with his arms folded upon the ledge, where the prayer-books in the corner of the seats were wont to rest during divine service. He planted his bristly chin upon his folded arms, and closed his eyes in a kind of dog-sleep.

But in this sleep he could hear everything going on. He heard the

---

[85] The Emperor of Russia and Baron Rothschild: The Rothschild dynasty was spread throughout Europe and in the nineteenth century their private fortune, derived from banking and finance houses, was the largest in the world. There were several members of the Austrian branch of the family who held the title Baron Rothschild. In England, Anthony Nathan de Rothschild was created 1st Baronet de Rothschild in 1847. His nephew Nathan Mayer Rothschild II inherited that title and was subsequently elevated to the House of Lords and created Baron Rothschild in 1885.

hobnailed soles of the charity children pattering upon the floor of the church; he heard the sharp rustling of the evergreens and wet flowers under the children's figures; and he could hear the deep voice of Philip Jocelyn, talking to the clergyman in the porch, as he waited the arrival of the carriages from Maudesley Abbey.

The carriages arrived at last; and presently the wedding-train came up the narrow aisle, and took their places about the altar-rails. Henry Dunbar stood behind his daughter, with his face in shadow.

The marriage-service was commenced. The Major's eyes were wide open now. Those sharp eager black eyes took notice of everything. They rested now upon the bride, now upon the bridegroom, now upon the faces of the rector and his curate.

Sometimes those glittering eyes strove to pierce the gloom, and to see the other faces, the faces that were farther away from the flickering yellow light of the wax-candles; but the gloom was not to be pierced even by the sharpest eyes.

The Major could only see four faces;—the faces of the bride and bridegroom, the rector, and his curate. But by-and-by, when one of the clergymen asked the familiar question—"*Who giveth this woman to be married, to this man?*" Henry Dunbar came forward into the light of the wax-candles, and gave the appointed answer.

The Major's folded arms dropped off the ledge, as if they had been suddenly paralyzed. He sat, breathing hard and quick, and staring at Mr. Dunbar.

"Henry Dunbar?" he muttered to himself, presently—"Henry Dunbar!"

Mr. Dunbar did not again retire into the shadow. He remained during the rest of the ceremony standing where the light shone full upon his handsome face.

When all was over, and the bride and bridegroom had signed their names in the vestry, before admiring witnesses, the sporting gentleman rose and walked softly out of the pew, and along one of the obscure side-aisles.

The wedding-party passed out of the church-porch. The Major followed slowly.

Philip Jocelyn and his bride went straight to the carriage that was to convey them back to the Abbey.

Dora Macmahon and the two pale Bridesmaids, with areophane[86] bonnets that had become hopelessly limp from exposure to that cruel rain, took their places in the second carriage. They were accompanied by

---

[86] A very thin type of crape, a gauzy material used in bonnets and for decorating gowns.

Arthur Lovell, whom they looked upon with no very great favour; for he had been silent and melancholy throughout the drive from Maudesley Abbey to Lisford Church, and had stared at them with vacant indifference, while handing them out of the carriage with a mechanical kind of politeness that was almost insulting.

The two first carriages drove away from the churchyard-gate, and the mud upon the high-road splashed the closed windows of the vehicles as the wheels went round.

The third carriage waited for Henry Dunbar, and the crowd in the churchyard waited to see him get into it.

He had his foot upon the lowest step, and his hand upon the door, when the Major went up to him, and tapped him lightly upon the shoulder.

The spectators recoiled, aghast with indignant astonishment.

How dared this shabby-looking man, with clumsy boots that were queer about the heels, and a mangy fur collar, like the skin of an invalid French poodle, to his threadbare coat—how in the name of all that is audacious, dared such a low person as this lay his dirty fingers upon the sacred shoulder of Henry Dunbar of Dunbar, Dunbar, and Balderby's banking-house, St. Gundolph Lane, City?

The millionaire turned, and grew as ashy pale at sight of the shabby stranger as he could have done if the sheeted dead had risen from one of the graves near at hand. But he uttered no exclamation of horror or surprise. He only shrank haughtily away from the Major's touch, as if there had been some infection to be dreaded from those dirty finger-tips.

"May I be permitted to know your motive for this intrusion, sir?" the banker asked, in a cold, repellent voice, looking the shabby intruder full in the eyes as he spoke.

There was something so resolute, so defiant, in the rich man's gaze, that it is a wonder the poor man did not shrink from encountering it.

But he did not: he gave back look for look.

"Don't say you've forgotten me, Mr. Dunbar," he said; "don't say you've forgotten a very old acquaintance."

This was spoken after a pause, in which the two men had looked at each other as earnestly as if each had been trying to read the inmost secrets of the other's soul.

"Don't say you've forgotten me, Mr. Dunbar," repeated the Major.

Henry Dunbar smiled. It was a forced smile, perhaps; but, at any rate, it was a smile.

"I have a great many acquaintances," he said; "and I fancy you must have gone down in the world since I knew you, if I may judge from appearances."

The bystanders, who had listened to every word, began to murmur among themselves. "Yes, indeed, they should rather think so:—if ever this shabby stranger had known Mr. Dunbar, and if he was not altogether an impostor, he must have been a very different sort of person at the time of his acquaintance with the millionaire."

"When and where did I know you?" asked Henry Dunbar, with his eyes still looking straight into the eyes of the other man.

"Oh, a long time ago—a very long way off!"

"Perhaps it was—somewhere in India—up the country?' said the banker, very slowly.

"Yes, it was in India—up the country," answered the other.

"Then you won't find me slow to befriend you," said Mr. Dunbar. "I am always glad to be of service to any of my Indian acquaintances—even when the world has treated them badly. Get into my carriage, and I'll drive you home. I shall be able to talk to you by-and-by, when all this wedding business is over."

The two men seated themselves side by side upon the spring cushions of the banker's luxurious carriage; and the vehicle drove rapidly away, leaving the spectators in a rapture of admiration at Henry Dunbar's condescension to his shabby Indian acquaintance.

- CHAPTER 25 -

AFTER THE WEDDING

The banker and the man who was called the Major talked to each other earnestly enough throughout the short drive between Lisford churchyard and Maudesley Abbey; but they spoke in low confidential whispers, and their conversation was interlarded by all manner of strange phrases; the queer, outlandish words were Hindo-stanee, no doubt, and were by no means easy to comprehend.

As the carriage drove up to the grand entrance of the Abbey, the stranger looked out through the mud-spattered window.

"A fine place!" he exclaimed; "a splendid place!"

"What am I to call you here?" muttered Mr. Dunbar, as he got out of the carriage.

"You may call me anything; as long as you do not call me when the soup is cold. I've a two-pair back in the neighbourhood of St. Martin's Lane, and I'm known *there* as Mr. Vavasor. But I'm not particular to a shade. Call me anything that begins with a V. It's as well to stick to one initial, on account of one's linen."

From the very small amount of linen exhibited in the Major's toilette, a malicious person might have imagined that such a thing as a shirt was a luxury not included in that gentleman's wardrobe.

"Call me Vernon," he said: "Vernon is a good name. You may as well call me Major Vernon. My friends at the Corner—not the Piccadilly corner, but the corner of the waste ground at the back of Field Lane—have done me the honour to give me the rank of Major, and I don't see why I shouldn't retain the distinction. My proclivities are entirely aristo-cratic: I have no power of assimilation with the *canaille*.[87] This is the sort of thing that suits me. Here I am in my element."

Mr. Dunbar had led his shabby acquaintance into the low, tapestried room in which he usually sat. The Major rubbed his hands with a gesture of enjoyment as he looked at the evidences of wealth that were heed-lessly scattered about the apartment. He gave a long sigh of satisfaction as he dropped with a sudden plump upon the spring cushion of an easy-chair on one side of the fireplace.

"Now, listen to me," said Mr. Dunbar. "I can't afford to talk to you this morning; I have other duties to perform. When they're over, I'll come and talk to you. In the meantime, you may sit here as long as you like, and have what you please to eat or drink."

"Well, I don't mind the wing of a fowl, and a bottle of Burgundy. It's a long time since I've tasted Burgundy. Chambertin, or Clos de Vougeot, at twelve bob[88] a bottle—that's the sort of tipple, I rather flatter my-self—eh?"

Henry Dunbar drew himself up with a slight shudder, as if repelled and disgusted by the man's vulgarity.

"What do you want of me?" he asked. "Remember that I am waited for. I am quite ready to serve you—for the sake of 'auld lang syne!'"

"Yes," answered the Major, with a sneer; "it's so pleasant to remem-ber 'auld lang syne!'"

"Well," asked Mr. Dunbar, impatiently, "what is it you want of me?"

"A bottle of Burgundy—the best you have in your cellar—something to eat, and—that which a poor man generally asks of his rich friends—his fortunate friends—MONEY!"

"You shall not find me illiberal towards you. I'll come back by-and-by,

---

[87] The rabble, riffraff.
[88] A "bob" was a shilling (twelve old pence). A "Twelve bob bottle" of wine would therefore cost roughly the week's wages of a footman, a grocer's assistant, or female shop assistant.

and write you a cheque."

"You'll make it a thumping one?"

"I'll make it as much as you want."

"That's the sort of thing. There always was something princely and magnificent about you, Mr. Dunbar."

"You shall not have any reason to complain," answered the banker, very coldly.

"You'll send me the lunch?"

"Yes. You can hold your tongue, I suppose? You won't talk to the servant who waits upon you?"

"Has your friend the manners of a gentleman, or has he not? Hasn't he had the eminent advantage of a collegiate education—I may say, a prolonged course of collegiate study? But look here, since you're so afraid of my putting my foot in it, suppose I go back to Lisford now, and I can return to you to-night after dark. Our business will keep. I want a long talk, and a quiet talk; but I must suit my convenience to yours. It's the dee-yuty of the poor-r-r dependant to wait upon the per-leasure of his patron," exclaimed Major Vernon, in the studied tones of the villain in a melodrama.

Henry Dunbar gave a sigh of relief.

"Yes, that will be much better," he said. "I can talk to you comfortably after dinner."

"Ta-ta, then, old boy. 'Oh, reservoir!'[89] as we say in the classics."

Major Vernon extended a brawny hand of rather doubtful purity. The millionaire touched the broad palm with the tips of his gloved fingers.

"Good-bye," he said; "I shall expect you at nine o'clock. You know your way out?"

He opened the door as he spoke, and pointed through a vista of two or three adjoining rooms to the hall. It was rather a broad hint. The Major pulled the poodle collar still higher above his ears, and went out with only his nose exposed to the influence of the atmosphere.

Henry Dunbar shut the door, and walked to one of the windows. He leaned his forehead against the glass, and looked out, watching the tall figure of the Major, as he walked rapidly along the broad carriage-drive that skirted the lawn.

The banker watched his shabby acquaintance until Major Vernon was quite out of sight. Then he went back to the fireplace, dropped heavily into his chair, and gave a long groan. It was not a sigh, it was a groan—a groan that seemed to come from a bosom that was rent by all the agony

[89] Humourous corruption of "Au revoir" – French for farewell or goodbye, with the implication of meeting again soon.

of despair.

"This decides it!" he muttered to himself. "Yes, this decides it! I've seen it for a long time coming to a crisis. But *this* settles everything."

He got up, passed his hand across his forehead and over his eyelids, like a man who had just been awakened from a long sleep; and then went to play his part in the grand business of the day.

There is a very wide difference between the feelings of the poor adventurer—who, by some lucky accident, is enabled to pounce upon a rich friend—and the sentiments of the wealthy victim who is pounced upon. Nothing could present a stronger contrast than the manner of Henry Dunbar, the banker, and the gentleman who had elected to be called Major Vernon. Whereas Mr. Dunbar seemed plunged into the uttermost depths of despair by the sudden appearance of his old acquaintance, the worthy Major exhibited a delight that was almost up-roarious in its manifestation.

It was not until he found himself in a very lonely part of the park, where there were no other witnesses than the timid deer, lurking here and there under the poor shelter of a clump of leafless elms,—it was not till Major Vernon felt himself quite alone, that he gave way to the full exuberance of his spirits.

"It's a gold-mine!" he cried, rubbing his hands; "it's a regular California!"

He executed a grim caper in his delight, and the scared deer fled away from the neighbourhood of his path; perhaps they took him for some modern gnome, dancing wild dances in the wet woodland. He laughed aloud, with a hollow, fiendish-sounding laugh, and then clapped his hands together till the noise of his brawny palms echoed in the rustic silence.

"Henry Dunbar," he said to himself; "Henry Dunbar! He'll be a milch cow—nothing but a milch cow. If—" he stopped suddenly, and the triumphant grin upon his face changed to a thoughtful expression. "If he doesn't run away," he said, standing quite still, and rubbing his chin slowly with the palm of his hand. "What if he should give me the slip? He *might* do that!"

But, after a moment's pause, he laughed aloud again, and walked on briskly.

"No, he'll not do that," he said; "it won't serve his turn to run away."

While Major Vernon went back to Lisford, Henry Dunbar took his seat at the breakfast-table, with Laura Lady Jocelyn by his side.

There was very little more gaiety at the wedding-breakfast than there had been at the wedding. Everything was very elegant, very subdued, and aristocratic. Silent footmen glided noiselessly backwards and forwards behind the chairs of the guests; champagne, Moselle, hock, and Burgundy sparkled in shallow glasses that were shaped like the broad leaf of a water-lily. Dresden-china shepherdesses, in the centre of the oval table, held up their chintz-patterned aprons filled with some forced strawberries that had cost about half-a-crown apiece. [90] Smirking shepherds supported open-work baskets, laden with tiny Algerian apples, China oranges, and big purple hothouse grapes.

The bride and bridegroom were very happy; but theirs was a subdued and quiet happiness that had little influence upon those around them. The wedding-breakfast was a very silent meal, for the face of the giver of the feast was as gloomy as the sky above Maudesley Abbey; and every now and then, in awkward pauses of the conversation, the pattering of the incessant raindrops sounded upon the windows.

At last the breakfast was finished. A knife had been cunningly inserted in the outer-wall of the splendid cake, and a few morsels of the rich interior, which looked like a kind of portable Day-and-Martin, had been eaten by one of the bridesmaids.[91] Laura Jocelyn rose and left the table, attended by the three young ladies.

Elizabeth Madden was waiting in the bride's dressing-room with Lady Jocelyn's travelling-dress laid in state upon a big sofa. She kissed her young Miss, and cried over her a little, before she was equal to begin the business of the toilette: and then the voices of the bridesmaids broke loose, and there was a pleasant buzz of congratulation, which beguiled the time while Laura was exchanging her bridal costume for a long rustling dress of dove-coloured silk, a purple-velvet cloak trimmed and lined with sable, and a miraculous fabric of pale-pink areophane, and starry jasmine-blossoms, which the Parisian milliner facetiously entitled "a bonnet."

She went down stairs presently in this rich attire, looking like a Russian empress, in all the glory of her youth and beauty. The travelling-carriage was standing at the door; Arthur Lovell and Mr. Dunbar were in the hall with the two clergymen. Laura went up to her father to bid him good-bye.

"It will be a long time before we see each other again, papa dear," she said, in tones that were only loud enough for Mr. Dunbar to hear; "say

---

[90] Two and a half shillings.

[91] Day and Martin were a well-known manufacturer of boot-blacking, and Braddon seems to be comparing the centre of the cake to their product. The serialized version of the novel is more explicit on this point. "The Outcasts" in *The Golden Era* has: "a few morsels of the rich interior, which looked like a kind of black paste, had been eaten by one of the bridesmaids" (Sunday 3 Jan 1864, Vol. XII, no.5: 1).

'God bless you!' once more before I go."

Her head was on his breast, and her face lifted up towards his own as she said this.

The banker looked straight before him with a forced smile upon his face, that was little more than a nervous contraction of the muscles about the lips.

"I will give you something better than my blessing, Laura," he said aloud; "I have given you no wedding-present yet, but I have not forgotten. The gift I mean to present to you will take some time to prepare. I shall give you the handsomest diamond-necklace that was ever made in England. I shall buy the diamonds myself, and have them set according to my own design."

The bridesmaids gave a little murmur of delight.

Laura pressed the speaker's cold hand.

"I don't want any diamonds, papa," she whispered; "I only want your love."

Mr. Dunbar did not make any response to that entreating whisper. There was no time for any answer, perhaps, for the bride and bridegroom had to catch an appointed train at Shorncliffe station, which was to take them on the first stage of their Continental journey; and in the bustle and confusion of their hurried departure, the banker had no opportunity of saying anything more to his daughter. But he stood in the Gothic porch, watching the departing carriage with a kind of mournful tenderness in his face.

"I hope that she will be happy," he muttered to himself as he went back to the house. "Heaven knows I hope she may be happy."

He did not stop to make any ceremonious adieu to his guests, but walked straight to his own apartments. People were accustomed to his strange manners, and were very indulgent towards his foibles.

Arthur Lovell and the three bridesmaids lingered a little in the blue drawing-room. The Melvilles were to drive home to their father's house in the afternoon, and Dora Macmahon was going with them. She was to stay at their father's house a few weeks, and was then to go back to her aunt in Scotland.

"But I am to pay my darling Laura an early visit at Jocelyn's Rock," she said, when Arthur made some inquiry about her arrangements; "that has been all settled."

The ladies and the young lawyer took an afternoon tea together before they left Maudesley, and were altogether very sociable, not to say merry. It was upon this occasion that Arthur Lovell, for the first time in his life, observed that Dora Macmahon had very beautiful brown eyes, and rippling brown hair, and the sweetest smile he had ever seen—

except in one lovely face, which was like the splendour of the noonday sun, and seemed to extinguish all lesser lights.

The carriage was announced at last; and Mr. Lovell had enough to do in attending to the three young ladies, and the stowing away of all those bonnet-boxes, and shawls, and travelling-bags, and desks, and dressing-cases, and odd volumes of books, and umbrellas, parasols, and sketching-portfolios, which are the peculiar attributes of all female travellers. And then, when all was finished, and he had bowed for the last time in acknowledgment of those friendly becks and wreathed smiles which greeted him from the carriage-window till it disappeared in the curve of the avenue, Arthur Lovell walked slowly home, thinking of the business of the day.

Laura was lost to him for ever. The dreadful grief which had so long brooded darkly over his life had come down upon him at last, and the pang had not been so insupportable as he had expected it to be.

"I never had any hope," he thought to himself, as he walked along the soddened road between the gates of Maudesley and the old town that lay before him. "I never really hoped that Laura Dunbar would be my wife."

John Lovell's house was one of the best in the town of Shorncliffe. It was a queer old house, with a sloping roof, and gable-ends of solid oak, adorned here and there by grim devices, carved by a skilful hand. It was a large house; but low and straggling; and unpretending in its exterior. The red light of a fire was shining in a wainscoted chamber, half sitting-room, half library. The crimson curtains were not yet drawn across the diamond-paned window. Arthur Lovell looked into the room as he passed, and saw his father sitting by the fire, with a newspaper at his feet.

There was no need to bolt doors against thieves and vagabonds in such a quiet town as Shorncliffe. Arthur Lovell turned the handle of the street door and went in. The door of his father's sitting-room was ajar, and the lawyer heard his son's step in the hall.

"Is that you, Arthur?" he asked.

"Yes, father," the young man answered, going into the room.

"I want to speak to you very particularly. I suppose this wedding at Maudesley Abbey has put all serious business out of your head."

"What serious business, father?"

"Have you forgotten Lord Herriston's offer?"

"The offer of the appointment in India? Oh, no, father, I have not forgotten, only——"

"Only what?"

"I have not been able to decide."

As he spoke, Arthur Lovell thought of Laura Dunbar. No; she was

Laura Jocelyn now. It was a hard thing for the young man to think of her by that new name. Would it not be better for him to go away—to put immeasurable distance between himself and the woman he had loved so dearly? Would it not be better and wiser to go away? And yet what if by so doing he turned his back upon another chance of happiness? What if a lesser star than that which had gone down in the darkness might now be rising dim and distant in the pale grey sky?

"There is no reason that I should decide in a hurry," the young man said, presently. "Lord Herriston told you that I might take twelve months to think about his offer."

"He did," answered John Lovell; "but half of the time is gone, and I've had a letter from Lord Herriston by this afternoon's post. He wants your decision immediately; for a connection of his own has applied to him for the appointment. He still holds to his promise, and will give you the preference; but you must make up your mind at once."

"Do you wish me to go to India, father?"

"Do I wish you to go to India! Of course not, my dear boy, unless your own ambition takes you there. Remember, you are an only son. You have no occasion to leave this place. You will inherit a very good practice and a comfortable fortune. I thought you were ambitious, and that Shorncliffe was too narrow a sphere for your ambition, or else I should never have entertained any idea of this Indian appointment."

"And you will not be sorry if I remain in England?"

"Sorry! No, indeed; I shall be very glad. Do you suppose, when a man has only one son, a handsome, clever, high-minded young fellow, whose presence is like sunshine in his father's gloomy old house—do you think the father wants to get rid of the lad? If you do think so, you must have a very small idea of parental affection."

"Then I'll refuse the appointment, father."

"God bless you, my boy!" exclaimed the lawyer.

The letter to Lord Herriston was written that night; and Arthur Lovell resigned himself to a perpetual residence in that quiet town; within a mile of which the towers of Jocelyn's Rock crowned the tall cliff above the rushing waters of the Avon.

Mr. Dunbar had given all necessary directions for the reception of his shabby friend.

The Major was ushered at once to the tapestried room, where the banker was still sitting at the dinner-table. He had that meal laid upon a round table near the fire, and the room looked a very picture of comfort and luxury as Major Vernon went into it, fresh from the black foggy night, and the leafless avenue, where the bare trunks of the elms looked like gigantic shadows looming through the obscurity.

The Major's eyes were almost dazzled by the brightness of that pleasant chamber. This man was a reprobate; but he had begun life as a gentleman. He remembered such a room as this long ago, across a dreary gulf of forty ill-spent years. The sight of this room brought back the memory of a pretty lamplit parlour, with an old man sitting in a high-backed easy-chair: a genial matron bending over her work; two fair-faced girls; a favourite mastiff stretched full length upon the hearth; and, last of all, a young man at home from college, yawning over a sporting newspaper, weary to death of all the simple innocent delights of home, sick of the companionship of gentle sisters, the love of a fond mother, and wishing to be back again at the old uproarious wine-parties, the drunken orgies, the card-playing and prize-fighting, the extravagance and debauchery of the bad set in which he was a chief.

The Major gave a profound sigh as he looked round the room. But the melancholy shadow on his face changed into a grim smile, as he glanced from the tapestried walls and curtained window, with a great Indian jar of hothouse flowers standing upon an inlaid table before it, and filling the room with a faint perfume of jasmine and almond, to the figure of Henry Dunbar.

"It's comfortable," said Major Vernon; "to say the least of it, it's very comfortable. And with a balance of half a million or so at one's banker's, or in one's own bank—which is better still perhaps—one is not so badly off, eh, Mr. Dunbar?"

"Sit down and eat one of those birds," answered the banker. "I'll talk to you by-and-by."

The Major obeyed his friend; he unwound three or four yards of dingy woollen stuff from his scraggy throat, turned down the poodle collar, pulled his chair close to the table, squared his brows, and began business. He made very light of a brace of partridges and a bottle of sparkling Moselle.

When the table had been cleared, and the two men left alone together, Major Vernon stretched his long legs upon the hearth-rug, plunged his hands deep down in his trousers' pockets, and gave a sigh of satisfaction.

"And now," said Mr. Dunbar, filling his glass from the starry crystal claret-jug, "what is it that you want to say to me, Stephen Vallance, or Major Vernon, or whatever ridiculous name you may call yourself—what is it you've got to say?"

"I'll tell you that in a very few words," answered the Major, quietly; "I want to talk to you about the man who was murdered at Winchester some months ago."

The banker's hand lost its steadiness, the neck of the claret-jug knocked against the thin lip of the glass, and shivered it into half-a-dozen pieces.

"You'll spill your wine," said Major Vernon. "I'm very sorry for you if your nerves are no better than that."

*   *   *   *   *

When Major Vernon that night left his friend, he carried away with him half-a-dozen cheques for different amounts, making in all two thousand pounds, upon that private banking-account which Mr. Dunbar kept for himself in the house of Dunbar, Dunbar, and Balderby.

It was after midnight when the banker opened the hall-door, and passed out with the Major upon the broad stone flags under the Gothic porch. There was no rain now; but it was very dark, and the north-easterly winds were blowing amongst the leafless branches of giant oaks and elms.

"Shall you present those cheques yourself?" Henry Dunbar asked, as the two men were about to part.

"Yes, I think so."

"Dress yourself decently, then, before you do so," said the banker; "they'd wonder what dealings you and I could have together, if you were to show yourself in St. Gundolph Lane in your present costume."

"My friend is proud," exclaimed the Major, with a mock tragic accent; "he is proud, and he despises his humble dependant."

"Good night," said Mr. Dunbar, rather abruptly; "it's past twelve o'clock, and I'm tired."

"To be sure. You're tired. Do you—do you—sleep well?" asked Major Vernon, in a whisper. There was no mock solemnity in his tone now.

The banker turned away from him with a muttered oath. The light of a lamp suspended from the groined roof of the porch shone upon the two men's faces. Henry Dunbar's countenance was overclouded by a black frown, and was by no means agreeable to look upon; but the grinning face of the Major, the thin lips wreathed into a malicious smile, the small black eyes glittering with a sinister light, looked like the face of a Mephistopheles.

"Good night," repeated the banker, turning his back upon his friend, and about to re-enter the house.

Major Vernon laid his bony fingers upon Henry Dunbar's shoulder, and stopped him before he could cross the threshold.

"You've given me two thou'," he said; "that's liberal enough to start with; but I'm an old man; I'm tired of the life of a vagabond, and I want to live like a gentleman;—not as you do, of course; *that's* out of the question; it isn't everybody that has the good luck to be a millionaire, like Henry Dunbar; but I want a bottle of claret with my dinner, a good coat upon my back, and a five-pound note in my pocket constantly. You must do as much as that for me; eh, dear boy?"

"I don't refuse to do it, do I?" asked Henry Dunbar, impatiently; "I should think what you've got in your pocket already is a pretty good beginning."

"My dear fellow, it's a stupendous beginning!" exclaimed Major Vernon; "it's a princely beginning; it's a Napoleonic beginning. But that two thou isn't meant for a blind, is it? It's not to be the beginning, middle, and the end? You're not going to do the gentle bolt—eh?"

"What do you mean?"

"You're not going to run away? You're not going to renounce the pomps and vanities of this wicked world, and make an early expedition across the herring-pond[92]—eh, friend of my soul?"

"Why should I run away?" asked Henry Dunbar, sternly.

"That's the very thing I say myself, dear boy. Why should you? A wise man doesn't run away from landed estates, and fine houses, and half a million of money. But when you broke that claret-glass after dinner, it struck me somehow that you were—shall I venture the word?—*rather* nervous! Nervous people do all manner of things. Give me your word that you're not going to bolt, and I'm satisfied."

"I tell you, I have no such idea in my mind," Mr. Dunbar answered, with increasing impatience. "Will that do?"

"It will, dear boy. Your hand upon it! What a cold hand you've got! Take care of yourself; and once more—good night!"

"You're going to London?"

"Yes—to cash the cheques, and make a few business arrangements."

Mr. Dunbar bolted the great door as the footsteps of his friend the Major died away upon the gravelled walk, which had been quickly dried by the frosty wind. The banker had dismissed his servants at ten o'clock that night; so there was nobody to wait upon him, or to watch him, when he went back to the tapestried room.

He sat by the low fire for a little time, thinking, with a settled gloom upon his face, and drinking Burgundy out of a tumbler. Then he went to bed; and the light of the night-lamp shining upon his face as he slept,

---

[92] Slang term for the sea. The "herring pond" could refer variously to the British Channel, the Atlantic Ocean, or the sea between Britain and Australasia (hence, "crossing the herring pond at the King's expense" was a common euphemism for being transported). The Major is most likely suggesting an escape to America.

showed it distorted by strange shadows, that were not altogether the shadows of the draperies above his head.

Major Vernon walked briskly down the long avenue leading to the lodge-gates.

"Two thou' is comfortable," he muttered to himself; "very satisfactory for a first go-in at the gold-diggin's! but I shall expect my California to produce a little more than that before we close the shaft, and retire upon the profits of the speculation. I *think* my friend is safe—I don't think he'll run away. But I shall keep my eye upon him, nevertheless. The human eye is a great institution; and I shall watch my friend."

In spite of a natural eagerness to transform those oblong slips of paper—the cheques signed with the well-known name of Henry Dunbar—into the still more convenient and flimsy paper circulating medium dispensed by the Old Lady in Threadneedle Street,[93] or the yellow coinage of the realm, Major Vernon did not seem in any very great hurry to leave Lisford.

A great many of the Lisfordians had seen the shabby stranger take his seat in Henry Dunbar's carriage, side by side with the great banker.

This fact became universally known throughout the parish of Lisford and two neighbouring parishes, before the shadows of night came down upon the day of Laura Dunbar's wedding, and the Major was respected accordingly.

He was shabby, certainly; queer-about the heels of his boots; and very mangy with regard to the poodle collar. His hat was more shiny than was consistent with the hat-manufacturing interest. His bony hands were red and bare, and only one miserable mockery of a glove dangled between his thumb and finger as he swaggered along the village street.

But he had been seen riding in Henry Dunbar's carriage, and from that moment he had become invested with a romantic interest. He was a reduced gentleman, who had seen better days; or he was a miser, perhaps—an eccentric individual, who wore shabby boots and shiny hats for his own love and pleasure.

People paid respect, therefore, to the stranger at the Rose and Crown, and touched their hats to him as he went in and out, and were glad to answer any questions he chose to put to them as he loitered about the

---

[93] "The old lady of Threadneedle Street" is a nickname for the Bank of England. The term originates in the story of Sarah Whitehead, whose brother, Philip, (an employee of the bank) was executed for forgery in 1811, whereupon Sarah lost her sanity and visited the bank every day for 25 years asking for him. Upon her death, Sarah was buried on land that subsequently became the property of the Bank of England and her ghost is said to haunt the area.

village. He contrived to find out a good deal in this way about things in general, and the habits of Henry Dunbar in particular. The banker had given his shabby acquaintance a handful of sovereigns for present use, as well as the cheques; and the Major was able to live upon the best the Rose and Crown could afford, and pay liberally for all he consumed.

"I find the Warwickshire air agrees with me remarkably well," he said to the landlord, as he sat at breakfast in the bar-parlour, upon the second day after his interview with Henry Dunbar; "and if you know of any snug little box in the neighbourhood that would suit a lonely old bachelor with a comfortable income, and nobody to help him spend it, why, I really should have a very great inclination to take it, and furnish it."

The landlord scratched his head, and reflected for a few minutes. Then he slapped his leg with a sounding and triumphant slap.

"I know the very thing as would suit you, Major Vernon," he said— the Major had assumed the name of Vernon, as agreed upon between himself and Henry Dunbar—"the very thing," repeated the landlord; "you might say it had been made to order like. There's a sale comes off next Thursday. Mr. Grogson, the Shorncliffe auctioneer, will sell, at eleven o'clock precisely, the furniture and lease of the snuggest little box in these parts—Woodbine Cottage it's called—a sweet pretty little place, as was the property of old Admiral Manders. The admiral died in the house, and having been a bachelor, and his money having gone to distant relatives, the lease and furniture of the cottage will be sold. But I should think," added the landlord, gravely, looking rather doubtfully at his guest as he spoke, "I should think the lease and furniture, pictures and plate, will fetch a matter of eight hundred to a thousand pound; and perhaps you mightn't care to go to that?"

The landlord could not refrain from glancing furtively at the white and shining aspect of the cloth that covered the sharp knees of his customer, which were exactly under his eyes as the two men sat opposite to each other beside the snug little round table.

"You mightn't care to go to that price," he repeated, as he helped himself to about three-quarters of a pound of cold ham.

The Major lifted his bristly eyebrows with a contemptuous twitch.

"If the cottage suits me," he said, "I don't mind a thousand for it. To-day's Saturday;—I shall run up to town to-morrow, or Monday morning, to settle a bit of business I've got on hand, and come back here in time to attend the sale."

"My wife and me was thinkin' of goin' sir," the landlord answered, with, unwonted reverence in his voice; and, if it was agreeable, we could drive you over in a four-wheel shay.[94] Woodbine Cottage is about a mile and a half from here, and little better than a mile from Maudesley Abbey. There's a copper coal-scuttle of the old admiral's as my wife has got rather a fancy for. But p'raps if you was to make a hoffer previous to the sale, the property might be disposed of as it stands by private contrack."

"I'll see about that," answered Major Vernon. "I'll stroll over to Shorncliffe, this, morning, and look in upon Mr. Grogson—Grogson, I think you said was the auctioneer's name?"

"Yes, sir; Peter Grogson, and very much looked up to be is, and a warm man, folks do say. His offices is in Shorncliffe High Street, sir; next door but two from Mr. Lovell's, the solicitor's, and not more than half-a-dozen yards from St. Gwendoline's Church."

Major Vernon, as he now chose to call himself, walked from Lisford to Shorncliffe. He was a very good walker, and, indeed, had become pretty well used to pedestrian exercise in the course of long weary trampings from one racecourse to another, when he was so far down on his luck as to be unable to pay his railway fare. The frost had set in for the first time this year; so the roads were dry and hard once more, and the sound of horses' hoofs and rolling wheels, the jingling of bells, the occasional barking of a noisy sheep-dog, and sturdy labourers' voices calling to each other on the high-road, travelled far in the thin frosty air.

The town of Shorncliffe was very quiet to-day, for it was only on market-days that there was much life or bustle in the queer old streets, and Major Vernon found no hindrance to the business that had brought him from Lisford.

He went straight to Mr. Grogson, the auctioneer, and from that gentleman heard all particulars respecting the pending sale at Woodbine Cottage. The Major offered to take the lease at a fair price, and the furniture, as it stood, by valuation.

"All I want is a comfortable little place that I can jump into without any trouble to myself," Major Vernon said, with the air of a man of the world. "I like to take life easily. If you can honestly recommend the place as worth seven or eight hundred pounds, I'm willing to pay that money for it down on the nail. I'll take it at your valuation, if the present owners are agreeable to sell it on those terms, and I'll pay a deposit of a couple of hundred or so on Tuesday afternoon, to show that my proposition is a *bona fide* one."

A little more was said, and then Mr. Grogson pledged himself to act for the best in the interests of Major Vernon, consistently with his allegiance to the present owners of the property.

---

[94] Chaise: a small, light carriage.

The auctioneer had been at first a little doubtful of this tall, shabby stranger in the napless dirty-white beaver and the mangy poodle collar; but the offer of a deposit of two hundred pounds or so gave a different aspect to the case. There are always eccentric people in the world, and appearances are very apt to be deceptive. There was a confident air about the Major which seemed like that of a man with a balance at his banker's.

The Major went back to the Rose and Crown, ate a comfortable little dinner, which he had ordered before setting out for Shorncliffe, paid his bill, and made all arrangements for starting by the first train for London on the following morning. It was nearly ten o'clock by the time he had done this; but late as it was, Major Vernon put on his hat, turned his poodle collar up about his ears, and went out into Lisford High Street.

There was scarcely one glimmer of light in the street as the Major walked along it. He took the road leading to Maudesley Abbey, and walked at a brisk pace, heedless of the snow, which was still falling thick and fast.

He was covered from head to foot with snow when he stopped before the stone porch, and rang a bell, that made a clanging noise in the stillness of the night. He looked like some grim white statue that had descended from its pedestal to stalk hither and thither in the darkness.

The servant who opened the door yawned undisguisedly in the face of his master's friend.

"Tell Mr. Dunbar that I shall be glad to speak to him for a few minutes," the Major said, making as if he would have passed into the hall.

"Mr. Dunbar left the habbey uppards of a hour ago," the footman answered, with supreme hauteur; "but he left a message for you, in case you was to come. The period of his habsence is huncertain, and if you wants to kermoonicate with him, you was to please to wait till he come back."

Major Vernon pushed aside the servant, and strode into the hall. The doors were open, and through two or three intermediate rooms the Major saw the tapestried chamber, dark and empty.

There was no doubt that Henry Dunbar had given him the slip—for the time, at least; but did the banker mean mischief? was there any deep design in this sudden departure?—that was the question.

"I'll write to your master," the Major said, after a pause; "what's his London address?"

"Mr. Dunbar left no address."

"Humph! That's no matter. I can write to him at the bank. Good night."

Major Vernon stalked away through the snow. The footman made no response to his parting civility, but stood watching him for a few moments, and then closed the door with a bang.

"Hif that's a spessermin of your Hinjun acquaintances, I don't think much of Hinjur or Hinjun serciety. But what can you expect of a nation as insults the gentleman who waits behind his employer's chair at table by callin' him a kitten-muncher?"[95]

- CHAPTER 26 -

WHAT HAPPENED IN THE BACK PARLOUR OF THE BANKING-HOUSE

Henry Dunbar arrived in London a couple of hours after Mr. Vernon left the Abbey. He went straight to the Clarendon Hotel. He had no servant with him, and his luggage consisted only of a portmanteau, a dressing-case, and a despatch-box; the same despatch-box whose contents he had so carefully studied at the Winchester hotel, upon the night of the murder in the grove.

The day after his arrival was Sunday, and all that day the banker occupied himself in reading a morocco-bound manuscript volume, which he took from the despatch-box.

There was a black fog upon this November day, and the atmosphere out of doors was cold and bleak. But the room in which Henry Dunbar sat looked the very picture of comfort and elegance.

He had drawn his chair close to the fire, and on a table near his elbow were arranged the open despatch-box, a tall crystal jug of Burgundy, with a goblet-shaped glass, on a salver, and a case of cigars.

Until long after dark that evening, Henry Dunbar sat by the fire, smoking and drinking, and reading the manuscript volume. He only paused now and then to take pencil-notes of its contents in a little memorandum-book, which he carried in the breast-pocket of his coat.

It was not till seven o'clock, when the liveried servant who waited upon him came to inform him that his dinner was served in an adjoining

---

[95] Kitten-muncher: Almost certainly a humorous mispronunciation of Kitmutgar, an Anglo-Indian word for a waiter. "KITMUTGAR (Hind.) *Khidmatgar*, from Ar.—P. *Khidmat*, 'service', therefore 'one rendering service'. The Anglo-Indian use is peculiar to the Bengal Presidency, where the word is habitually applied to a Musulman servant, whose duties are connected with serving meals and waiting at table". *Hobson-Jobson: A Glossary of Colloquial Anglo-Indian words and phrases, and of kindred terms, etymological, historical, geographical and discursive*, Sir Henry Yule, A. C. Burnell, William Crooke. (New Delhi and London: Asian Educational Services, 1995, 2006): 486.

chamber, that Mr. Dunbar rose from his seat and put away the book in the despatch-box. He laid down the volume on the table while he replaced other papers in the box, and it fell open at the first page. On that first page was written, in Henry Dunbar's bold, legible hand—

"Journal of my life in India, from my arrival in 1815 until my departure in 1850."

This was the book the banker had been studying all that winter's day.

At twelve o'clock the next day he ordered a brougham,[96] and was driven to the banking-house in St. Gundolph Lane. This was the first time that Henry Dunbar had visited the house in St. Gundolph Lane since his return from India.

Those who knew the history of the present chief partner of the house of Dunbar, Dunbar, and Balderby, were in nowise astonished by this fact. They knew that, as a young man, Henry Dunbar had contracted the tastes and habits of an aristocrat, and that, if he had afterwards developed into a clever and successful man of business, it was only by reason of the force of circumstances, which had thrust him into a position that he hated.

It was by no means wonderful, then, that, after becoming possessor of the united fortunes of his father and his uncle, Henry Dunbar should keep aloof from a place that had always been obnoxious to him. The business had gone on without him very well during his absence, and it went on without him now, for his place in India had been assumed by a very clever man, who for twenty years had acted as cashier in the Calcutta house.

It may be that the banker had an unpleasant recollection of his last visit to St. Gundolph Lane, upon the day when the existence of the forged bills was discovered by Percival and Hugh Dunbar. All the width of thirty-five years between the present hour and that day might not be wide enough to separate the memory of the past from the thoughts which were busy this morning in the mind of Henry Dunbar.

Be it as it might, Mr. Dunbar's reflections this day were evidently not of a pleasant nature. He was very pale as he rode citywards, in the comfortable brougham, from the Clarendon; and his face had a stern, fixed look, like a man who has nerved himself to meet some crisis, which he knows is near at hand.

There was a stoppage upon Ludgate Hill. Great wooden barricades and mountains of uprooted paving-stones, amidst which sturdy navigators disported themselves with spades and pickaxes, and wheelbarrows full of rubbish, blocked the way; so the brougham turned into

---

[96] A light, four-wheeled horse-drawn carriage.

Farringdon Street, and went up Snow Hill, and under the grim black walls of dreadful Newgate.[97]

The vehicle travelled very slowly, for the traffic was concentrated in this quarter by reason of the stoppage on Ludgate Hill, and Mr. Dunbar was able to contemplate at his leisure the black prison-walls, and the men and women selling dogs'-collars under their dismal shadows.

It may be that the banker's face grew a shade paler after that contemplation. The corners of his mouth twitched nervously as he got out of the carriage before the mahogany doors of the banking-house in St. Gundolph Lane. But he drew a long breath, and held his head proudly erect as he pushed open the doors and went in.

Never since the day of the discovery of the forged bills had that man entered the banking-house. Dark thoughts came back upon his mind, and the shadows deepened on his face as he gave one rapid glance round the familiar office.

He walked straight towards the private parlour in which that well-remembered scene had occurred five-and-thirty years ago. But before he arrived at the door leading from the public offices to the back of the house, he was stopped by a gentlemanly-looking man, who came forward from a desk in some shadowy region, and intercepted the stranger.

This man was Clement Austin, the cashier.

"Do you wish to see Mr. Balderby, sir?" he asked.

"Yes. I have an appointment with him at one o'clock. My name is Dunbar."

The cashier bowed and opened the door. The banker passed across the threshold, which he had not crossed for five-and-thirty years until to-day.

But as Mr. Dunbar went towards the familiar parlour at the back of the banking-house, he stopped for a minute, and looked at the cashier.

Clement Austin was scarcely less pale than Henry Dunbar himself. He had heard of the banker's intended visit to St. Gundolph Lane, and had looked forward with strange anxiety to a meeting with the man whom Margaret Wilmot declared to be the murderer of her father. Now that the meeting had come to pass, he looked at Henry Dunbar with an earnest, scrutinizing gaze, as if he would fain have discovered the secret of the man's guilt or innocence in his countenance.

---

[97] London's main prison. Newgate prison was demolished and rebuilt several times over the course of 700 years, with the original building dating back to the 12th century. By the nineteenth century Newgate was also the location of public executions (previously carried out at Tyburn until the late 18th century). When public hangings were abolished in 1868, the gallows were moved inside the walls of Newgate.

The banker's face was pale, and grave, and stern; but Clement Austin knew that for Henry Dunbar there were very humiliating and unpleasant circumstances connected with the offices in St. Gundolph Lane, and it was scarcely to be expected that a man would come smiling into a place out of which he had gone five-and-thirty years before a disgraced and degraded creature.

For a few moments the two men paused in the passage between the public offices and the private parlour, looking at each other.

The banker's gaze never flinched during that encounter. It is taken as a strong proof of a man's innocence that he should look you full in the face with a steadfast gaze when you look at him with suspicion plainly visible in your eyes; but would he not be the poorest villain if he shirked that encounter of glances when he knows full surely that he is in that moment put to the test? It is rather innocence whose eyelids drop when you peer too closely into its eyes, for innocence is appalled by the stern, accusing glances which it is unprepared to meet. Guilt stares you boldly in the face, for guilt is hardened and defiant, and has this one grand superiority over innocence—that it is *prepared for the worst*.

Clement Austin opened the door of Mr. Balderby's parlour; Mr. Dunbar went in unannounced. The cashier closed the parlour-door and returned to his desk in the public office.

The junior partner was sitting at an office table near the fire writing, but he rose as the banker entered the room, and went forward to meet him.

"You are very punctual, Mr. Dunbar," he said.

"Yes, I am generally punctual."

The two men shook hands, and Mr. Balderby wheeled forward a morocco-covered arm-chair for his senior partner, and then took his seat opposite to him, with only the small office table between them.

"It may seem late in the day to bid you welcome to the bank, Mr. Dunbar," said the junior partner, "but I do so, nevertheless—most heartily!"

There was a flatness in the accent in which these two last words were spoken, which was like the sound of a false coin when it falls dead upon a counter and proclaims itself spurious.

Henry Dunbar did not return his partner's greeting. He was looking round the room, and remembering the day upon which he had last seen it. There was very little alteration in the appearance of the dismal city chamber. There was the same wire-blind before the window, the same solitary tree, leafless, in the narrow courtyard without. The morocco-covered arm-chairs had been re-covered, perhaps, during that five-and-thirty years; but if so, the covering had grown shabby again. Even the

Turkey carpet was in the very stage of dusky dinginess that had distinguished the carpet on which Henry Dunbar had stood five-and-thirty years before.

"I received your letter announcing your journey to London, and your desire for a private interview, on Saturday afternoon," Mr. Balderby said, after a pause. "I have made arrangements to assure our being undisturbed so long as you may remain here. If you wish to make any investigation of the affairs of the house, I——"

Mr. Dunbar waved his hand with a deprecatory air.

"Nothing is farther from my thoughts than any such design," he said.

"No, Mr. Balderby, I have only been a man of business because all chance of another career, which I infinitely preferred, was closed upon me five-and-thirty years ago. I am quite content to be a sleeping-partner in the house of Dunbar, Dunbar, and Balderby. For ten years prior to my father's death he took no active part in the business. The house got on very well without his aid; it will get on equally well without mine. The business that brings me to London is an entirely personal matter. I am a rich man, but I don't exactly know how rich I am, and I want to realize rather a large sum of money."

Mr. Balderby bowed, but his eyebrows went up a little, as if he found it impossible to control some slight evidence of his surprise.

"Previous to my daughter's marriage I settled upon her the house in Portland Place and the Yorkshire property. She will have all my money when I die; and, as Sir Philip Jocelyn is a rich man, she will perhaps be one of the wealthiest women in England. So far so good. Neither Laura nor her husband will have any reason for dissatisfaction. But this is not quite enough, Mr. Balderby. I am not a demonstrative man, and I have never made any great fuss about my love for my daughter; but I do love her, nevertheless."

Mr. Dunbar spoke very slowly here, and stopped once or twice to pass his handkerchief across his forehead, as he had done in the hotel at Winchester.

"We Anglo-Indians have rather a magnificent way of doing things, Mr. Balderby" he continued, "when we take it into our heads to do them at all. I want to give my daughter a diamond-necklace as a wedding present, and I want it to be such as an Eastern prince or a Rothschild might offer to his only child. You understand?"

"Oh, perfectly," answered Mr. Balderby; "I shall be most happy to be of any use to you in the matter."

"All I want is a large sum of money at my command. I may go rather recklessly to work and make a large investment in this necklace; it will be something for Lady Jocelyn to bequeath to her children. You and John

Lovell, of Shorncliffe, were the executors to my father's will. You signed an order for the transfer of my father's money to my account some time in last September."

"I did, in concurrence with Mr. Lovell."

"Precisely; Lovell wrote me a letter to that effect. My father kept two accounts here, I believe—a deposit and a drawing account?"

"He did."

"And those two accounts have gone on since my return in the same manner as during his lifetime?"

"Precisely. The income which Mr. Percival Dunbar set aside for his own use was seven thousand a year. He rarely spent as much as that; sometimes he spent less than half. The balance of this income, and his double share in the profits of the business, went to the credit of his deposit account, and various sums have been withdrawn from time to time, and duly invested under his order."

"Perhaps you can let me see the ledgers containing those two accounts?"

"Most certainly."

Mr. Balderby touched the spring of a handbell upon his table.

"Ask Mr. Austin to bring the daily balance and deposit accounts ledgers," he said to the person who answered his summons.

Clement Austin appeared five minutes afterwards, carrying two ponderous morocco-bound volumes.

Mr. Balderby opened both ledgers, and placed them before his senior partner. Henry Dunbar looked at the deposit account. His eyes ran eagerly down the long row of figures before him until they came to the sum total. Then his chest heaved, and he drew a long breath, like a man who feels almost stifled by some internal oppression.

The last figures in the page were these:

137,926l. 17s. 2d.

One hundred and thirty-seven thousand nine hundred and twenty-six pounds seventeen shillings and twopence. The twopence seemed a ridiculous anti-climax; but business-men are necessarily as exact in figures as calculating-machines.

"How is this money invested?" asked Henry Dunbar, pointing to the page. His fingers trembled a little as he did so, and he dropped his hand suddenly upon the ledger.

"There's fifty thousand in India stock," Mr. Balderby answered, as indifferently as if fifty thousand pounds more or less was scarcely worth speaking of; "and there's five-and-twenty in railway debentures, Great Western. Most of the remainder is floating in Exchequer bills."

"Then you can realize the Exchequer bills?"

Mr. Balderby winced as if some one had trodden upon one of his corns. He was a banker heart and soul, and he did not at all relish the idea of any withdrawal of the bank's resources, however firm that establishment might stand.

"It's rather a large amount of capital to withdraw from the business," he said, rubbing his chin, thoughtfully.

"I suppose the bank can afford it!" Mr. Dunbar exclaimed, with a tone of surprise.

"Oh, yes; the bank can afford it well enough. Our calls are sometimes heavy. Lord Yarsfield—a very old customer—talks of buying an estate in Wales; he may come down upon us at any moment for a very stiff sum of money. However, the capital is yours, Mr. Dunbar; and you've a right to dispose of it as you please. The Exchequer bills shall be realized immediately."

"Good; and if you can dispose of the railway bonds to advantage, you may do so."

"You think of spending——"

"I think of reinvesting the money. I have an offer of an estate north of the metropolis, which I think will realize cent per cent a few years hence: but that is an after consideration. At present we have only to do with the diamond-necklace for my daughter. I shall buy the diamonds myself, direct from the merchant-importers. You will hold yourself ready after Wednesday, we'll say, to cash some very heavy cheques on my account?"

"Certainly, Mr. Dunbar."

"Then I think that is really all I have to say. I shall be happy to see you at the Clarendon, if you will dine with me any evening that you are disengaged."

There was very little heartiness in the tone of this invitation; and Mr. Balderby perfectly understood that it was only a formula which Mr. Dunbar felt himself called upon to go through. The junior partner murmured his acknowledgment of Henry Dunbar's politeness; and then the two men talked together for a few minutes on indifferent subjects.

Five minutes afterwards Mr. Dunbar rose to leave the room. He went into the passage between Mr. Balderby's parlour and the public offices of the bank. This passage was very dark; but the offices were well lighted by lofty plate-glass windows. Between the end of the passage and the outer doors of the bank, Henry Dunbar saw the figure of a woman sitting near one of the desks and talking to Clement Austin.

The banker stopped suddenly, and went back to the parlour.

He looked about him a little absently as he re-entered the room.

"I thought I brought a cane," he said.

"I think not," replied Mr. Balderby, rising from before his desk. "I don't remember seeing one in your hand."

"Ah, then, I suppose I was mistaken."

He still lingered in the parlour, putting on his gloves very slowly, and looking out of the window into the dismal backyard, where there was a dingy little wooden door set deep in the stone wall.

While the banker loitered near the window, Clement Austin came into the room, to show some document to the junior partner. Henry Dunbar turned round as the cashier was about to leave the parlour.

"I saw a woman just now talking to you in the office. That's not very business-like, is it, Mr. Austin? Who is the woman?"

"She is a young lady, sir."

"A young lady?"

"Yes, sir."

"What brings her here?"

The cashier hesitated for a moment before he replied, "She—wishes to see you, Mr. Dunbar," he said, after that brief pause.

"What is her name?—who—who is she?"

"Her name is Wilmot—Margaret Wilmot."

"I know no such person!" answered the banker, haughtily, but looking nervously at the half-opened door as he spoke.

"Shut that door, sir!" he said, impatiently, to the cashier; "the draught from the passage is strong enough to cut a man in two. Who is this Margaret Wilmot?"

"The daughter of that unfortunate man, Joseph Wilmot, who was cruelly murdered at Winchester!" answered the cashier, very gravely.

He looked Henry Dunbar full in the face as he spoke.

The banker returned his look as unflinchingly as he had done before, and spoke in a hard, unfaltering voice as he answered: "Tell this person, Margaret Wilmot, that I refuse to see her to-day, as I refused to see her in Portland Place, and as I refused to see her at Winchester!" he said, deliberately. "Tell her that I shall always refuse to see her, whenever or wherever she makes an attack upon me. I have suffered enough already on account of that hideous business at Winchester, and I shall most resolutely defend myself from any further persecution. This young person can have no possible motive for wishing to see me. If she is poor and wants money of me, I am ready and willing to assist her. I have already offered to do so—I can do no more. But if she is in distress—"

"She is not in distress, Mr. Dunbar," interrupted Clement Austin. "She has friends who love her well enough to shield her from that."

"Indeed; and you are one of those friends, I suppose, Mr. Austin?"

"I am."

"Prove your friendship, then, by teaching Margaret Wilmot that she has a friend and not an enemy in me. If you are—as I suspect from your manner—something more than a friend: if you love her, and she returns your love, marry her, and she shall have a dowry that no gentleman's wife need be ashamed to bring to her husband."

There was no anger, no impatience in the banker's voice now, but a tone of deep feeling. Clement Austin looked at him, astonished by the change in his manner.

Henry Dunbar saw the look, and it seemed as if he endeavoured to answer it.

"You have no need to be surprised that I shrink from seeing Margaret Wilmot," he said. "Cannot you understand that my nerves may be none of the strongest, and that I cannot endure the idea of an interview with this girl, who, no doubt, by her persistent pursuit of me, suspects me of her father's murder? I am an old man, and I have been thirty-five years in India. My health is shattered, and I have a horror of all tragic scenes. I have not yet recovered from the shock of that horrible business at Winchester. Go and tell Margaret Wilmot this: tell her that I will be her true friend if she will accept that friendship, but that I will not see her until she has learned to think better of me."

There was something very straightforward, very simple, in all this. For a time, at least, Clement Austin's mind wavered. Margaret was, perhaps, wrong, after all, and Henry Dunbar might be an innocent man.

It was Clement who had informed Margaret of Mr. Dunbar's expected presence here upon this day; and it was on the strength of that information that the girl had come to St. Gundolph Lane, with the determination of seeing the man whom she believed to be the murderer of her father.

Clement returned to the office, where he had left Margaret, in order to repeat to her Mr. Dunbar's message.

No sooner had the door of the parlour closed upon the cashier than Henry Dunbar turned abruptly to his junior partner.

"There is a door leading from the yard into a court that connects St. Gundolph Lane with another lane at the back," he said, "is there not?"

He pointed to the dark little yard outside the window as he spoke.

"Yes, there is a door, I believe."

"Is it locked?"

"No; it is seldom locked till four o'clock; the clerks use it sometimes, when they go in and out."

"Then I shall go out that way," said Mr. Dunbar, who was almost breathless in his haste. "You can send the carriage back to the Clarendon by-and-by. I don't want to see that girl. Good morning."

He hurried out of the parlour, and into a passage leading to the yard, followed by Mr. Balderby, who wondered at his senior partner's excitement. The door in the yard was not locked. Henry Dunbar opened it, went out into the court, and closed the door behind him.

So, for the third time, he escaped from an interview with Margaret Wilmot.

- CHAPTER 27 -

CLEMENT AUSTIN'S WOOING

For the third time Margaret Wilmot was disappointed in the hope of seeing Henry Dunbar. Clement Austin had on the previous evening told her of the banker's intended visit to the office in St. Gundolph Lane, and the young music-mistress had made hasty arrangements for the postponement of her usual duties, in order that she might go to the City to see Henry Dunbar.

"He will not dare to refuse you," Clement Austin said; "for he must know that such a refusal would excite suspicion in the minds of the people about him."

"He must have known that at Winchester, and yet he avoided me there," answered Margaret Wilmot; "he must have known it when he refused to see me in Portland Place. He will refuse to see me to-day, if I ask for an interview with him. My only chance will be the chance of an accidental meeting with Him. Do you think that you can arrange this for me, Mr. Austin?"

Clement Austin readily promised to bring about an apparently accidental meeting between Margaret and Mr. Dunbar, and this is how it was that Joseph Wilmot's daughter had waited in the office in St. Gundolph Lane. She had arrived only five minutes after Mr. Dunbar entered the banking-house, and she waited very patiently, very resolutely, in the hope that when Henry Dunbar returned to his carriage she might snatch the opportunity of speaking to him, of seeing his face, and discovering whether he was guilty or not.

She clung to the idea that some indefinable expression of his countenance would reveal the fact of his guilt or innocence. But she could not dispossess herself of the belief that he was guilty. What other reason could there be for his persistent avoidance of her?

But, for the third time, she was baffled; and she went home very despondently, haunted by the image of her dead father; while Henry

Dunbar went back to the Clarendon in a common hack cab, which he picked up in Cornhill.

Margaret Wilmot found one of her pupils waiting in the pretty little parlour in the cottage at Clapham, and she was obliged to sit down to the piano and listen to a fantasia, very badly played, keeping sharp watch upon the pupil's fingers, for an hour or so, before she was free to think her own thoughts.

Margaret was very glad when the lesson was over. The pupil was a very vivacious young lady, who called her music-mistress "dear," and would have been glad to waste half an hour or so in an animated conversation about the last new style in bonnets, or the shape of the fashionable winter mantle, or the popular novel of the month. But Margaret's pale face seemed a mute appeal for compassion; so Miss Lamberton drew on her gloves, settled her bonnet before the glass over the mantel-piece, and tripped away.

Margaret sat by the little round table, with an open book before her. But she could not read, though the volume was one that had been lent her by Clement, and though she took a peculiar pleasure in reading any book that was a favourite of his. She did not read; she only sat with her eyes fixed, and her face very pale, in the dim light of two candles that flickered in the draught from the window.

She was aroused from her despondent reverie by a double knock at the door below, and presently the neat little maid-servant ushered Mr. Austin into the room.

Margaret started up, a little confused at the advent of this unexpected visitor. It was the first time that Clement had ever called upon her alone. He had often been her guest; but, until to-night, he had always come under his mother's wing to see the pretty music-mistress.

"I am afraid I startled you, Miss Wilmot," he said.

"Oh, no; not at all," answered Margaret; "I was sitting here, quite idle, thinking——"

"Thinking of your failure of to-day, I suppose?"

"Yes."

There was a pause, during which Margaret seated herself once more by the little table, while Clement Austin walked up and down the room thinking.

Presently he stopped suddenly, with his elbow leaning upon the corner of the mantel-piece, opposite Margaret, and looked down at the girl's thoughtful face. She had blushed when the cashier first entered the room; but she was very pale now.

"Margaret," said Clement Austin,—it was the first time he had called his mother's *protégée* by her Christian name, and the girl looked up at him with a surprised expression,—"Margaret, that which happened to-day makes me think that your conviction is only the horrible truth, and that Henry Dunbar, the sole surviving kinsman of those two men whom I learnt to honour and revere long ago, when I was a mere boy, is indeed guilty of your father's death. If so, the cause of justice demands that this man's crime should be brought to light. I am something of Shakespeare's opinion; I cannot but believe that 'murder will out,'[98] somehow or other, sooner or later. But I think that, in this business, the police have been culpably supine. It seems as if they feared to handle the case too closely, lest the clue they followed should lead them to Henry Dunbar."

"You think they have been bribed?"

"No; I don't think that. There seems to be a popular belief, all over the world, that a man with a million of money can do no wrong. I don't believe the police have been culpable; they have only been faint-hearted. They have suffered themselves to be discouraged by the difficulties of the case. Other crimes have been committed, other work has arisen for them to do, and they have been obliged to abandon an investigation which seemed hopeless. This is how criminals escape—this is how murderers are suffered to be at large; not because discovery is impossible, but because it can only be effected by a slow and wearisome process in which so few men have courage to persevere. While the country is ringing with the record of a great crime—while the murderer is on his guard night and day, waking and sleeping—the police watch and work: but by-and-by, when the crime is half forgotten—when security has made the criminal careless—when the chances of detection are ten-fold—the police have grown tired, and there is no eye to watch the guilty man's movements. I know nothing of the science of detection, Margaret; but I believe that Henry Dunbar was the murderer of your father; and I will do my uttermost, with God's help, to bring this crime home to him."

The girl's eyes flashed with a proud light, as Clement Austin finished speaking.

"Will you do this?" she said; "will you bring to light the mystery of my father's death? Will you bring punishment upon his murderer? It seems a horrible thing, perhaps, for a woman to wish detection to overtake any man, however base; but surely it would be more horrible if I were content to let my father's murder remain unavenged. My poor father! If he had been a good man, I do not think it would grieve me so

---

[98] "For murder, though it have no tongue, will speak with most miraculous organ" William Shakespeare, *Hamlet* II.ii.571-572. Cf. "Truth will come to light; murder cannot be hid long; a man's son may, but in the end truth will out", *The Merchant of Venice* II.ii.74-76. See also: *Macbeth*, III.iv.122-126, and *Richard II*, I.i.104-106.

much to remember his cruel death: but he was not a good man—he was not a good man."

"Let him have been what he may, Margaret, his murderer shall not go unpunished if I can aid the cause of justice," said Clement Austin. "But it was not to say this alone that I came here to-night, Margaret. I have something more to say to you."

There was a tenderness in the cashier's voice as he said these last words, that brought the blushes back to Margaret's pale cheeks.

"You know that I love you, Margaret," Clement said, in a low, earnest voice; "you must know that I love you: or if you do not, it is because there is no sympathy between us, and in that case my love is indeed hopeless. I have loved you from the first, dear—yes, from the very first summer twilight in which I saw your pale, pensive face in the dusky little garden at Wandsworth. The tender interest which I then felt in you was the first mysterious dawn of love, though I, in my infinite wisdom, put it down to an artistic admiration for your peculiar beauty. It was love, Margaret; and it has grown and strengthened in my heart ever since that summer evening, until it leads me here to-night to tell you all, and to ask you if there is any hope. Ah, Margaret, you must have known my love all along! You would have banished me had you felt that my love was hopeless: you could not have been so cruel as to deceive me."

Margaret looked up at her lover with a frightened face. Had she done wrong, then, to be happy in his society, if she did not love him—if she did not love him! But surely this sudden thrill of triumph and delight which filled her breast, as Clement spoke to her, must be in some degree akin to love.

Yes, she loved him; but the bright things of this world were not for her. Love and Duty fought for the mastery of her pure Soul: and Duty was the conqueror.

"Oh, Clement!" she said, "do you forget who I am? Do you forget that letter which I showed you long ago, a letter addressed to my father when he was a transported felon, suffering the penalty of his crime? Do you forget who I am, and the taint that is in my blood; the disgrace that stains my name? I am proud to think that you have loved me, Clement Austin; but I am no fitting wife for you!"

"You are a noble, true-hearted woman, Margaret; and as such you are a fitting wife for a king. Besides, I am not such a grandee that I need look for high lineage in the wife of my choice. I am only a working man, content to accept a salary for my services; and looking forward by-and-by to a junior partnership in the house I serve. Margaret, my mother loves you; and she knows that you are the woman I seek to win as my wife. Forget the taint upon your dead father's name as freely as I forget it, dearest; and only answer me one question: Is my love hopeless?"

"I will never consent to be your wife, Mr. Austin!" Margaret answered, in a low voice.

"Because you do not love me?"

"Because I will never cause you to blush for the history of your wife's girlhood."

"That is no answer to my question, Margaret," said Clement Austin, seating himself by her side, and taking both her hands in his. "I must ask you to look me full in the face, Miss Wilmot," he added, laughingly, drawing her towards him as he spoke; "for I begin to fancy you're addicted to prevarication. Look me in the face, Madge darling, and tell me that you love me."

But the blushing face would not be turned towards his own. Margaret's head was still averted.

"Don't ask me," she pleaded; "don't ask me. The day would come when you would regret your choice. I could not endure that. It would be too bitter. You have been very kind to me; and it would be a poor return for your kindness, if——"

"If you were to make me unutterably happy, eh, Margaret? I think it would be only a proper act of gratitude. Haven't I run all over Clapham, Brixton, and Wandsworth—to say nothing of an occasional incursion upon Putney—in order to procure you half-a-dozen pupils? And the very first favour I demand of you, which is only the gift of this clever little hand, you have the audacity to refuse me point-blank."

He waited for a few moments, in the hope that Margaret would say something; but her face was still averted, and the trembling hand which Mr. Austin was holding struggled to release itself from his grasp.

"Margaret," he said, very gravely, "perhaps I have been foolish and presumptuous in this business. In that case I fully deserve to be disappointed, however bitter the disappointment may be. If I have been wrong, Margaret; if I have been deceived by your sweet smile, your gentle words; for pity's sake tell me that it is so, and I will forgive you for having involuntarily deceived me, and will try to cure myself of my folly. But I will not leave this room, I will not abandon the dear hope that has brought me here to-night, until you tell me plainly that you do not love me. Speak, Margaret, and speak fearlessly."

But Margaret was still silent, only in the silence Clement Austin heard a low, sobbing sound.

"Margaret darling, you are crying. Ah! I know now that you love me, and I will not leave this room except as your plighted husband."

"Heaven help me!" murmured Joseph Wilmot's daughter; "Heaven lead me right! for I do love you, Clement, with all my heart."

- CHAPTER 28 -

BUYING DIAMONDS

M r. Dunbar did not waste much time before he began the grand
business which had brought him to London—that is to say,
the purchase of such a collection of diamonds as compose a
necklace second only to that which brought poor hoodwinked Cardinal
de Rohan and the unlucky daughter of the Caesars into such a morass of
trouble and slander.[99]

Early upon the morning after his visit to the bank, Mr. Dunbar went
out very plainly dressed, and hailed the first empty cab that he saw in
Piccadilly.

He ordered the cabman to drive straight to a street leading out of
Holborn, a very quiet-looking street, where you could buy diamonds
enough to set up all the jewellers in the Palais Royale and the Rue de la
Paix, and where, if you were so whimsical as to wish to transform a
service of plate into "white soup" at a moment's notice, you might
indulge your fancy in establishments of unblemished respectability.[100]

The gold and silver refiners, the diamond-merchants and wholesale
jewellers, in this quiet street, were a very superior class of people, and
you might dispose of a handful of gold chains and bangles without any
fear that one or two of them would find their way into the operator's
sleeve during the process of weighing. The great Mr. Krusible, who
thrust the last inch of an Eastern potentate's sceptre into the melting-pot

---

[99] Louis René Édouard de Rohan (1734-1803), Cardinal, politician, and prince of
Strasbourg. In the 1780s, de Rohan became embroiled in a scandal known as the affair of
the diamond necklace. The fabulous necklace was originally commissioned by Louis XV
for his mistress, Madame du Barry, but was not completed until after his death, whereby
the jewellers, who had not been paid, were left unable to sell it. De Rohan was duped by
an adventuress, Jeanne de la Motte, into believing that the Queen, Marie Antoinette,
intended to purchase the necklace and wished de Rohan to act as her intermediary.
Although de Rohan and Marie Antoinette were merely pawns in the convoluted plot
which followed, both suffered damage to their reputations when the scandal became
public.
[100] White soup is a delicate veal-based broth, which was very popular among the upper-
classes during the Regency period. It is frequently alluded to in Jane Austen's novels.
Braddon's euphemism implies that these are discreet establishments, used to catering to
the upper-classes who might find themselves in need of converting family heirlooms into
ready cash.

with the sole of his foot, as the detectives entered his establishment in search of the missing bauble, and walked lame for six months afterwards, lived somewhere in the depths of the city, and far away from this dull-looking Holborn street; and would have despised the even tenor of life, and the moderate profits of a business in this neighbourhood.

Mr. Dunbar left his cab at the Holborn end of the street, and walked slowly along the pavement till he came to a very dingy-looking parlour-window, which might have belonged to a lawyer's office but for some gilded letters on the wire blind, which, in a very pale and faded inscription, gave notice that the parlour belonged to Mr. Isaac Hartgold, diamond-merchant. A grimy brass plate on the door of the house bore another inscription to the same effect; and it was at this door that Mr. Dunbar stopped.

He rang a bell, and was admitted immediately by a very sharp-looking boy, who ushered him into the parlour, where he saw a mahogany counter, a pair of small brass scales, a horse-hair-cushioned office-stool considerably the worse for wear, and a couple of very formidable-looking iron safes deeply imbedded in the wall behind the counter. There was a desk near the window, at which a gentleman, with very black hair and whiskers was seated, busily engaged in some abstruse calculations between a pair of open ledgers.

He got off his high seat as Mr. Dunbar entered, and looked rather suspiciously at the banker. I suppose the habit of selling diamonds had made him rather suspicious of every one. Henry Dunbar wore a fashionable greatcoat with loose open cuffs, and it was towards these loose cuffs that Mr. Hartgold's eyes wandered with rapid and rather uneasy glances. He was apt to look doubtfully at gentlemen with roomy coat-sleeves, or ladies with long-haired muffs or fringed parasols. Unset diamonds are an eminently portable species of property, and you might carry a tolerably valuable collection of them in the folds of the smallest parasol that ever faded under the summer sunshine in the Lady's Mile.

"I want to buy a collection of diamonds for a necklace," Mr. Dunbar said, as coolly as if he had been talking of a set of silver spoons; "and I want the necklace to be something out of the common. I should order it of Garrard or Emanuel;[101] but I have a fancy for buying the diamonds upon paper, and having them made up after a design of my own. Can you supply me with what I want?"

"How much do you want? You may have what some people would call a necklace for a thousand pounds, or you may have one that'll cost

---

[101] London jewellers, catering to Royalty and the aristocracy. Queen Victoria appointed Garrard Crown Jewellers in 1843.

you twenty thousand. How far do you mean to go?"

"I am prepared to spend something between fifty and eighty thousand pounds."

The diamond merchant pursed up his lips reflectively. "You are aware that in these sort of transactions ready money is indispensable?" he said.

"Oh, yes, I am quite aware of that," Mr. Dunbar answered, coolly.

He took out his card-case as he spoke, and handed one of his cards to Mr. Isaac Hartgold. "Any cheques signed by that name," he said, "will be duly honoured in St. Gundolph Lane."

Mr. Hartgold bent his head reverentially to the representative of a million of money. He, in common with every business man in London, was thoroughly familiar with the names of Dunbar, Dunbar, and Balderby.

"I don't know that I can supply you with fifty thousand pounds' worth of such diamonds as you may require at a moment's notice," he said; "but I can procure them for you in a day or two, if that will do?"

"That will do very well. This is Tuesday; suppose I give you till Thursday?"

"The stones shall be ready for you by Thursday, sir."

"Very good. I will call for them on Thursday morning. In the meantime, in order that you may understand that the transaction is a *bonâ fide* one, I'll write a cheque for ten thousand, payable to your order, on account of diamonds to be purchased by me. I have my cheque-book in my pocket. Oblige me with pen and ink."

Mr. Hartgold murmured something to the effect that such a proceeding was altogether unnecessary; but he brought Mr. Dunbar his office inkstand, and looked on with an approving twinkle of his eyes while the banker wrote the cheque, in that slow, formal hand peculiar to him. It made things very smooth and comfortable, Mr. Hartgold thought, to say the least of it.

"And now, sir, with regard to the design of the necklace," said the merchant, when he had folded the cheque and put it into his waistcoat-pocket. "I suppose you've some idea that you'd like to carry out; and you'd wish, perhaps, to see a few specimens."

He unlocked one of the iron safes as he spoke, and brought out a lot of little paper packets, which were folded in a peculiar fashion, and which he opened with very gingerly fingers.

"I suppose you'd like some tallow-drops, sir?" he said. "Tallow-drops work-in better than anything for a necklace."

"What, in Heaven's name, are tallow-drops?"

Mr. Hartgold took up a diamond with a pair of pincers, and exhibited it to the banker.

"That's a tallow-drop, sir," he said. "It's something of a heart-shaped stone, you see; but we call it a tallow-drop, because it's very much the shape of a drop of tallow. You'd like large stones, of course, though they eat into a great deal of money? There are diamonds that are known all over Europe; diamonds that have been in the possession of royalty, and are as well known as the family they've belonged to. The Duke of Brunswick has pretty well cleared the market of that sort of stuff; but still they are to be had, if you've a fancy for anything of that kind?"

Mr. Dunbar shook his head.

"I don't want anything of that sort," he said; "the day may come when my daughter, or my daughter's descendants, may be obliged to realize the jewels. I'm a commercial man, and I want eighty thousand pounds' worth of diamonds that shall be worth the money I give for them to break up and sell again. I should wish you to choose diamonds of moderate size, but not small; worth, on an average, forty or fifty pounds apiece, we'll say."

"I shall have to be very particular about matching them in colour," said Mr. Hartgold, "as they're for a necklace." The banker shrugged his shoulders.

"Don't trouble yourself about the necklace," he said, rather impatiently. "I tell you again I'm a commercial man, and what I want is good value for my money."

"And you shall have it, sir," answered the diamond-merchant, briskly.

"Very well, then; in that case I think we understand each other, and there's no occasion for me to stop here any longer. You'll have eighty thousand pounds' worth of diamonds, at thereabouts, ready for me when I call here on Thursday morning. You can cash that cheque in the meantime, and ascertain with whom you have to deal. Good morning."

He left the diamond-merchant wondering at his sang froid, and returned to the cab, which had been waiting for him all this time.

He was just going to step into it, when a hand touched him lightly on the shoulder, and turning sharply and angrily round, he recognized the gentleman who called himself Major Vernon. But the Major was by no means the shabby stranger who had watched the marriage of Philip Jocelyn and Laura Dunbar in Lisford Church. Major Vernon had risen, resplendent as the phoenix, from the ashes of his old clothes.

The poodle collar was gone: the dilapidated boots had been exchanged for stout water-tight Wellingtons: the napless dirty white hat had given place to a magnificent beaver, with a broad trim curled at the sides. Major Vernon was positively splendid. He was as much wrapped up as ever; but his wrappings now were of a gorgeous, not to say gaudy, description. His thick greatcoat was of a dark olive-green, and the collar turned up over his ears was of a shiny-looking brown fur, which, to the confiding mind of the populace, is known as imitation sable. Inside this fur collar the Major wore a shawl-patterned scarf of all the colours in the prismatic scale, across which his nose lacked its usual brilliancy of hue by force of contrast. Major Vernon had a very big cigar in his mouth, and a very big cane in his hand, and the quiet City men turned to look at him as he stood upon the pavement talking to Henry Dunbar.

The banker writhed under the touch of his Indian acquaintance.

"What do you want with me?" he asked, in low angry tones; "why do you follow me about to play the spy upon me, and stop me in the public street? Haven't I done enough for you? Ain't you satisfied with what I have done?"

"Yes, dear boy," answered the Major, "perfectly satisfied, more than satisfied—for the present. But your future favours—as those low fellows, the butchers and bakers, have it—are respectfully requested for yours truly. Let me get into the cab with you, Mr. H.D., and take me back to the *casa*, and give me a comfortable little bit of per-rogg.[102] I haven't lost my aristocratic taste for seven courses, and an elegant succession of still fine sparkling wines, though during the last few years I've been rather frequently constrained to accept the shadowy hospitality of his grace of Humphrey.[103] '*Nante dinari, nante manjare*,' as we say in the Classics, which I translate, 'No credit at the butcher's or the baker's.'"[104]

"For Heaven's sake, stop that abominable slang!" said Henry Dunbar, impatiently.

"It annoys you, dear friend, eh? Well, I've known the time when—— But no matter, 'let what is broken, so remain,' as the poet observes; which is only an elegant way of saying, 'Let bygones be bygones.' And so you've been buying diamonds, dear boy?"

"Who told you so?"

"You did, when you came out of Mr. Isaac Hartgold's establishment. I happened to be passing the door as you went in, and I happened to be passing the door again as you came out."

"And playing the spy upon me."

"Not at all, dear boy. It was merely a coincidence, I assure you. I

---

[102] Casa: house (Spanish); Per-rogg: slang, perhaps deriving from Perrogate, a verb, for which *OED* has "*trans.* To desire (something) earnestly". The Major's use of the word as a noun may be meant in the sense of a thing he heartily desires, and, given the context, seems to relate to fine dining.

[103] "To dine with Duke Humphrey" was a common Elizabethan phrase, meaning to go without dinner. It features in several of Shakespeare's plays.

[104] '*Nante dinari, nante manjare*': loosely, no money, no eating.

called at the bank yesterday, cashed my cheques, ascertained your address; called at the Clarendon this morning, was told you'd that minute gone out; looked down Albemarle Street; there you were, sure enough; saw you get into a cab; got into another—a Hansom, and faster than yours—came behind you to the corner of this street."

"You followed me," said Henry Dunbar, bitterly.

"Don't call it *following*, dear friend, because that's low. Accident brought me into this neighbourhood at the very hour you were coming into this neighbourhood. If you want to quarrel with anything, quarrel with the doctrine of chances, not with me."

Henry Dunbar turned away with a sulky gesture. His friend watched him with very much the same malicious grin that had distorted his face under the lamp-lit porch at Maudesley. The Major looked like a vulgar-minded Mephistopheles: there was not even the "divinity of hell" about him.[105]

"And so you've been buying diamonds?" he repeated presently, after a considerable pause.

"Yes, I have. I am buying them for a necklace for my daughter."

"You are so dotingly fond of your daughter!" said the Major with a leer.

"It is necessary that I should give her a present."

"Precisely, and you won't even trust the business to a jeweller; you insist on doing it all yourself."

"I shall do it for less money than a jeweller."

"Oh, of course," answered Major Vernon; "the motive's as clear as daylight."

He was silent for a few minutes, then he laid his hand heavily upon his companion's shoulder, put his lips close to the banker's ear, and said, in a loud voice, for it was not easy for him to make himself heard above the jolting of the cab,—

"Henry Dunbar, you're a very clever fellow, and I dare say you think yourself a great deal sharper than I am; but, by Heaven, if you try any tricks with me, you'll find yourself mistaken! You must buy me an annuity. Do you understand? Before you move right or left, or say your soul's your own, you must buy me an annuity!"

The banker shook off his companion's hand, and turned round upon him, pale, stern, and defiant.

---

[105] Mephistopheles: demon in the Faust legend; the representative of the Devil. See Christopher Marlow, *The Tragicall History of Doctor Faustus* (1604). The term "Mephisto-phelean" has come to mean a fiendish person, one who tempts a person to destructive action.

"Take care, Stephen Vallance," he said; "take care how you threaten me. I should have thought you knew me of old, and would be wise enough to keep a civil tongue in your head, with *me*. As for what you ask, I shall do it, or I shall let it alone—as I think fit. If I do it, I shall take my own time about it, not yours."

"You're not afraid of me, then?" asked the other, recoiling a little, and much more subdued in his tone.

"No!"

"You are very bold."

"Perhaps I am. Do you remember the old story of some people who had a goose that laid golden eggs? They were greedy, and, in their besotted avarice, they killed the goose. But they have not gone down to posterity as examples of wisdom. No, Vallance, I'm not afraid of you."

Mr. Vallance leaned back in the cab, biting his nails savagely, and thinking. It seemed as if he was trying to find an answer for Mr. Dunbar's speech: but, if so, he must have failed, for he was silent for the rest of the drive: and when he got out of the vehicle, by-and-by, before the door of the Clarendon, his manner bore an undignified resemblance to that of a half-bred cur who carries his tail between his legs.

"Good afternoon, Major Vernon," the banker said, carelessly, as a liveried servant opened the door of the hotel: "I shall be very much engaged during the few days I am likely to remain in town, and shall be unable to afford myself the pleasure of your society."

The Major stared aghast at this cool dismissal.

"Oh," he murmured, vaguely, "that's it, is it? Well, of course, you know what's best for yourself—so, good afternoon!"

The door closed upon Major Vernon, alias Mr. Stephen Vallance, while he was still staring straight before him, in utter inability to realize his position. But he drew his cashmere shawl still higher up about his ears, took out a gaudy scarlet-morocco cigar-case, lighted another big cigar, and then strolled slowly down the quiet West-end street, with his bushy eyebrows contracted into a thoughtful frown.

"Cool," he muttered between his closed lips; "very cool, to say the least of it. Some people would call it audacious. But the story of the goose with the golden eggs is one of childhood's simple lessons that we're obliged to remember in after-life. And to think that the Government of this country should have the audacity to offer a measly hundred pounds or so for the discovery of a great crime! The shabbiness of the legislature must answer for it, if criminals remain at large. My friend's a deep one, a cursedly deep one; but I shall keep my eye upon him 'My faith is strong in time,' as the poet observes. My friend carries it with a high hand at present; but the day may come when he may want me; and if ever he does want me, egad, he shall pay me my own price, and it shall be rather a stiff one into the bargain."

- CHAPTER 29 -

GOING AWAY

At one o'clock on the appointed Thursday morning, Mr. Dunbar presented himself in the diamond-merchant's office. Henry Dunbar was not alone. He had called in St. Gundolph Lane, and asked Mr. Balderby to go with him to inspect the diamonds he had bought for his daughter.

The junior partner opened his eyes to the widest extent as the brilliants were displayed before him, and declared that big senior's generosity was something more than princely.

But perhaps Mr. Balderby did not feel so entirely delighted two or three hours afterwards, when Mr. Isaac Hartgold presented himself before the counter in St. Gundolph Lane, whence he departed some time afterwards carrying away with him seventy-five thousand eight hundred pounds in Bank-of-England notes.

Henry Dunbar walked away from the neighbourhood of Holborn with his coat buttoned tightly across his broad chest, and nearly eighty thousand pounds' worth of property hidden away in his breast-pockets. He did not go straight back to the Clarendon, but pierced his way across Smithfield, and into a busy smoky street, where he stopped by-and-by at a dingy-looking currier's shop.

He went in and selected a couple of chamois skins, very thick and strong. At another shop he bought some large needles, half-a-dozen skeins of stout waxed thread, a pair of large scissors, a couple of strong steel buckles, and a tailor's thimble. When he had made these purchases, he hailed the first empty cab that passed him, and went back to his hotel.

He dined, drank the best part of a bottle of Burgundy, and then ordered a cup of strong tea to be taken to his dressing-room. He had fires in his bedroom and dressing-room every night. To-night he retired very early, dismissed the servant who attended upon him, and locked the door of the outer room, the only door communicating with the corridor of the hotel.

He drank a cup of tea, bathed his head with cold water, and then sat down at a writing-table near the fire.

But he was not going to write; he pushed aside the writing-materials, and took his purchases of the afternoon from his pocket. He spread the chamois leather out upon the table, and cut the skins into two long strips, about a foot broad. He measured these round his waist, and then began to stitch them together, slowly and laboriously.

The work was not easy, and it took the banker a very long time to complete it to his own satisfaction. It was past twelve o'clock when he had stitched both sides and one end of the double chamois-leather belt; the other end he left open.

When he had completed the two sides and the end that was closed, he took four or five little canvas-bags from his pocket. Every one of these canvas-bags was full of loose diamonds.

A thrill of rapture ran through the banker's veins as he plunged his fingers in amongst the glittering stones. He filled his hands with the bright gems, and let them run from one hand to the other, like streams of liquid light. Then, very slowly and carefully, he began to drop the diamonds into the open end of the chamois-leather belt.

When he had dropped a few into the belt, he stitched the leather across and across, quilting-in the stones. This work took him so long, that it was four o'clock in the morning when he had quilted the last diamond into the belt. He gave a long sigh of relief as he threw the waste scraps of leather upon the top of the low fire, and watched them slowly smoulder away into black ashes. Then he put the chamois-leather belt under his pillow, and went to bed.

Henry Dunbar went back to Maudesley Abbey by the express on the morning after the day on which he had completed his purchase of the diamonds. He wore the chamois-leather belt buckled tightly round his waist next to his inner shirt, and was able to defy the swell-mob, had those gentry been aware of the treasures which he carried about with him.

He wrote from Warwickshire to one of the best and most fashionable jewellers at the West End, and requested that a person who was thoroughly skilled in his business might be sent down to Maudesley Abbey, duly furnished with drawings of the newest designs in diamond necklaces, earrings, &c.

But when the jeweller's agent came, two or three days afterwards, Mr. Dunbar could find no design that suited him; and the man returned to London without having received an order, and without having even seen the brilliants which the banker had bought.

"Tell your employer that I will retain two or three of these designs," Mr. Dunbar said, selecting the drawings as he spoke; "and if, upon consideration, I find that one of them will suit me, I will communicate with your establishment. If not, I shall take the diamonds to Paris, and get them made up there."

The jeweller ventured to suggest the inferiority of Parisian workmanship as compared with that of a first-rate English establishment; but Mr. Dunbar did not condescend to pay any attention to the young man's remonstrance.

"I shall write to your employer in due course," he said, coldly. "Good morning."

Major Vernon had returned to the Rose and Crown at Lisford. The deed which transferred to him the possession of Woodbine Cottage was speedily executed, and he took up his abode there. His establishment was composed of the old housekeeper, who had waited on the deceased admiral, and a young man-of-all-work, who was nephew to the housekeeper, and who had also been in the service of the late owner of the cottage.

From his new abode Mr. Vernon was able to keep a tolerably sharp look-out upon the two great houses in his neighbourhood—Maudesley Abbey and Jocelyn's Rock. Country people know everything about their neighbours; and Mrs. Manders, the housekeeper, had means of communication with both "the Abbey" and "the Rock;" for she had a niece who was under-housemaid in the service of Henry Dunbar, and a grandson who was a helper in Sir Philip Jocelyn's stables. Nothing could have better pleased the new inhabitant of Woodbine Cottage, who was speedily on excellent terms with his housekeeper.

From her he heard that a jeweller's assistant had been to Maudesley, and had submitted a portfolio of designs to the millionaire.

"Which they do say," Mrs. Manders continued, "that Mr. Dunbar had laid out nigh upon half-a-million of money in diamonds; and that he is going to give his daughter, Lady Jocelyn, a set of jewels such as the Queen upon her throne never set eyes on. But Mr. Dunbar is rare and difficult to please, it seems; for the young man from the jeweller's, he says to Mrs. Grumbleton at the western lodge, he says, 'Your master is not easy to satisfy, ma'am,' he says; from which Mrs. Grumbleton gathers that he had not took a order from Mr. Dunbar."

Major Vernon whistled softly to himself when Mrs. Manders retired, after having imparted this piece of information.

"You're a clever fellow, dear friend," he muttered, as he lighted his cigar; "you're a stupendous fellow, dear boy; but your friend can see through less transparent blinds than this diamond business. It's well planned—it's neat, to say the least of it. And you've my best wishes, dear boy; but—you must pay for them—you must pay for them, Henry Dunbar."

This little conversation between the new tenant of Woodbine Cottage

and his housekeeper occurred on the very evening on which Major
Vernon took possession of his new abode. The next day was Sunday—a
cold wintry Sunday; for the snow had been falling all through the last
three days and nights, and lay deep on the ground, hiding the low
thatched roofs, and making feathery festoons about the leafless branches,
until Lisford looked like a village upon the top of a twelfth-cake.[106] While
the Sabbath-bells were ringing in the frosty atmosphere, Major Vernon
opened the low white gate of his pleasant little garden, and went out
upon the high-road.

But not towards the church. Major Vernon was not going to church
on this bright winter's morning. He went the other way, tramping
through the snow, towards the eastern gate of Maudesley Park. He went
in by the low iron gate, for there was a bridle-path by this part of the
park—that very bridle-path by which Philip Jocelyn had ridden to
Lisford so often in the autumn weather.

Major Vernon struck across this path, following the tracks of late
footsteps in the deep snow, and thus took the nearest way to the Abbey.
There he found all very quiet. The supercilious footman who admitted
him to the hall seemed doubtful whether he should admit him any
farther.

"Mr. Dunbar are hup," he said; "and have breakfasted, to the best of
my knowledge, which the breakfast ekewpage have not yet been
removed."[107]

"So much the better," Major Vernon answered, coolly. "You may
bring up some fresh coffee, John; for I haven't made much of a
breakfast myself; and if you'll tell the cook to devil the thigh of a turkey,
with plenty of cayenne-pepper and a squeeze of lemon, I shall be obliged.
You needn't trouble yourself; I know my way."

The Major opened the door leading to Mr. Dunbar's apartments, and
walked without ceremony into the tapestried chamber, where he found
the banker sitting near a table, upon which a silver coffee service, a
Dresden cup and saucer, and two or three covered dishes gave evidence
that Mr. Dunbar had been breakfasting. Cold meats, raised pies, and
other comestibles were laid out upon the carved-oak sideboard.

---

[106] A part of traditional Twelfth Night celebrations, Twelfth-cake was originally baked
with a bean and a pea inside, and was accompanied by seasoned, sweetened ale and
sweetmeats. The persons who found the bean and pea in their portions of cake were
proclaimed King and Queen of the revels. In the 17th century, it was a simple plum-cake,
but by the nineteenth century had become more elaborate, consisting of a fruitcake,
decorated extravagantly with sugar confectionery.
[107] "ekewpage": the footman's pronunciation of "equipage", in the sense of a full
breakfast-service, china, silverware, glassware, etc.

The Major paused upon the threshold of the chamber and gravely contemplated his friend.

"It's comfortable!" he exclaimed; "to say the least of it, it's very comfortable, dear boy!"

The dear boy did not look particularly pleased as he lifted his eyes to his visitor's face.

"I thought you were in London?" he said.

"Which shows how very little you trouble yourself about the concerns of your neighbours," answered Major Vernon, "for if you had condescended to inquire about the movements of your humble friend, you would have been told that he had bought a comfortable little property in the neighbourhood, and settled down to do the respectable country gentleman for the remainder of his natural life—always supposing that the liberality of his honoured friend enables him to do the thing decently."

"Do you mean to say that you have bought property in this neighbourhood?"

"Yes! I am leasehold proprietor of Woodbine Cottage, near Lisford and Shorncliffe."

"And you mean to settle in Warwickshire?"

"I do."

Henry Dunbar smiled to himself as his friend said this.

"You're welcome to do so," he said, "as far as I am concerned."

The Major looked at him sharply.

"Your sentiments are liberality itself, my dear friend. But I must respectfully remind you that the expenses attendant upon taking possession of my humble abode have been very heavy. In plain English, the two thou' which you so liberally advanced as the first instalment of future bounties, has melted like snow in a rapid thaw. I want another two thou', friend of my youth and patron of my later years. What's a thousand or so, more or less, to the senior partner in the house of D., D., and B.? Make it two five this time, and your petitioner will ever pray, &c. &c. &c. Make it two five, Prince of Maudesley!"

There is no need for me to record the interview between these two men. It was rather a long one; for, in congenial companionship, Major Vernon had plenty to say for himself: it was only when he felt himself out of his element and unappreciated that the Major wrapped himself in the dignity of silence, as in some mystic mantle, and retired for the time being from the outer world.

He did not leave Maudesley Abbey until he had succeeded in the object of his visit, and he carried away in his pocket-book cheques to the amount of two thousand five hundred pounds.

"I flatter myself I was just in the nick of time," the Major thought, as he walked back to Woodbine Cottage, "for as sure as my name's what it is, my friend means a bolt. He means a bolt; and the money I've had to-day is the last I shall ever receive from that quarter."

Almost immediately after Major Vernon's departure, Henry Dunbar rang the bell for the servant who acted as his valet whenever he required the services of one, which was not often.

"I shall start for Paris to-night, Jeffreys," he said to this man. "I want to see what the French jewellers can do before I trust Lady Jocelyn's necklace into the hands of English workmen. I'm not well, and I want change of air and scene, so I shall start for Paris to-night. Pack a small portmanteau with everything that's indispensable, but pack nothing unnecessary."

"Am I to go with you, sir?" the man asked.

Henry Dunbar looked at his watch, and seemed to reflect upon this question some moments before he answered.

"How do the up-trains go on a Sunday?" he asked.

"There's an express from the north stops at Rugby at six o'clock, sir. You might meet that, if you left Shorncliffe by the 4:35 train."

"I could do that," answered the banker; "it's only three o'clock. Pack my portmanteau at once, Jeffreys, and order the carriage to be ready for me at a quarter to four. No, I won't take you to Paris with me. You can follow me in a day or two with some more things."

"Yes, sir."

There was no such thing as bustle and confusion in a household organized like that of Mr. Dunbar. The valet packed his master's portmanteau and dressing-case; the carriage came round to the gravel-drive before the porch at the appointed moment; and five minutes afterwards Mr. Dunbar came out into the hall, with his greatcoat closely buttoned over his broad chest, and a leopard-skin travelling-rug flung across his shoulder.

Round his waist he wore the chamois-leather belt which he had made with his own hands at the Clarendon Hotel. This belt had never quitted him since the night upon which he made it. The carriage conveyed him to the Shorncliffe station. He got out and went upon the platform. Although it was not yet five o'clock, the wintry light was fading in the gray sky, and in the railway station it was already dark. There were lamps here and there, but they only made separate splotches of light in the dusky atmosphere.

Henry Dunbar walked slowly up and down the platform. He was so deeply absorbed by his own thoughts that he was quite startled presently when a young man came close behind him, and addressed him eagerly.

"Mr. Dunbar," he said; "Mr. Dunbar!"

The banker turned sharply round, and recognized Arthur Lovell.

"Ah! my dear Lovell, is that you? You quite startled me."

"Are you going by the next train? I was so anxious to see you."

"Why so?"

"Because there's some one here who very much wishes to see you; quite an old friend of yours, he says. Who do you think it is?"

"I don't know, I can't guess—I've so many old friends. I can't see any one, Lovell. I'm very ill, I saw a physician while I was in London; and he told me that my heart is diseased, and that if I wish to live I must avoid any agitation, any sudden emotion, as I would avoid a deadly poison. Who is it that wants to see me?"

"Lord Herriston, the great Anglo-Indian statesman. He is a friend of my father's, and he has been very kind to me—indeed, he offered me an appointment, which I found it wisest to decline. He talked a great deal about you, when my father told him that you'd settled at Maudesley, and would have driven over to see you if he could have managed to spare the time, without losing his train. You'll see him, wont you?"

"Where is he?"

"Here, in the station—in the waiting-room. He has been visiting in Warwickshire, and he lunched with my father *en passant*;[108] he is going to Derby, and he's waiting for the down-train to take him on to the main line. You'll come and see him?"

"Yes, I shall be very glad; I——"

Henry Dunbar stopped suddenly, with his hand upon his side. The bell had been ringing while Lovell and the banker had stood upon the platform talking. The train came into the station at this moment.

"I shan't be able to see Lord Herriston to-night," Mr. Dunbar said, hurriedly; "I must go by this train, or I shall lose a day. Good-bye, Lovell. Make my best compliments to Herriston; tell him I have been very ill. Good-bye."

"Your portmanteau's in the carriage, sir," the servant said, pointing to the open door of a first-class compartment. Henry Dunbar got into the carriage. At the moment of his doing so, an elderly gentleman came out of the waiting-room.

"Is this my train, Lovell?" he asked.

"No, my Lord. Mr. Dunbar is here; he goes by this train. You'll have time to speak to him."

The train was moving. Lord Herriston was an active old fellow. He ran along the platform, looking into the carriages. But the old man's

---

108 In passing.

sight was not as good as his legs were; he looked eagerly into the carriage-windows, but he only saw a confusion of flickering lamplight, and strange faces, and newspapers unfurled in the hands of wakeful travellers, and the heads of sleepy passengers rolling and jolting against the padded sides of the carriage.

"My eyes are not what they used to be," he said, with a good-tempered laugh, when he went back to Arthur Lovell. "I didn't succeed in getting a glimpse of my old friend Henry Dunbar."

- CHAPTER 30 -

STOPPED UPON THE WAY

M r. Dunbar leant back in the corner of his comfortable seat, with his eyes closed. But he was not asleep, he was only thinking; and every now and then he bent forward, and looked out of the window into the darkness of the night. He could only distinguish the faint outline of the landscape as the train swept on upon its way, past low meadows, where the snow lay white and stainless, unsullied by a passing footfall; and scanty patches of woodland, where the hardy firs looked black against the glittering whiteness of the ground.

The country was all so much alike under its thick shroud of snow, that Mr. Dunbar tried in vain to distinguish any landmarks upon the way.

The train by which he travelled stopped at every station; and, though the journey between Shorncliffe and Rugby was only to last an hour, it seemed almost interminable to this impatient traveller, who was eager to stand upon the deck of Messrs. ——'s electric steamers, to feel the icy spray dashing into his face, and to see the town of Dover, shining like a flaming crescent against the darkness of the night, and the Calais lights in the distance rising up behind the black edge of the sea.[109]

The banker looked at his watch, and made a calculation about the time. It was now a quarter past five; the train was to reach Rugby at ten minutes to six; at six the London express left Rugby; at a quarter to eight it reached London; at half-past eight the Dover mail would leave London Bridge station; and at half-past seven, or thereabouts, next morning, Henry Dunbar would be rattling through the streets of Paris.

And then? Was his journey to end in that brilliant city, or was he to

---

[109] The first cross-channel passenger steamships between Dover and Calais began in the early 1820s.

go farther? That was a question whose answer was hidden in the traveller's own breast. He had not shown himself a communicative man at the best of times, and to-night he looked like a man whose soul is weighed down by the burden of a purpose which must he achieved at any cost of personal sacrifice.

He could not hear the names of the stations. He only heard those guttural and inarticulate sounds which railway officials roar out upon the darkness of the night, to the bewilderment of helpless travellers. His inability to distinguish the names of the stations annoyed him. The delay attendant upon every fresh stoppage worried him, as if the pause had been the weary interval of an hour. He sat with his watch in his hand; for every now and then he was seized with a sudden terror that the train had fallen out of its regular pace, and was crawling slowly along the rails.

What if it should not reach Rugby until after the London express had left the station?

Mr. Dunbar asked one of his fellow-travellers if this train was always punctual.

"Yes," the gentleman answered, coolly; "I believe it is generally pretty regular. But I don't know how the snow may affect the engine. There have been accidents in some parts of the country."

"In consequence of the depth of snow?"

"Yes. I understand so."

It was about ten minutes after this brief conversation, and within a quarter of an hour of the time at which the train was due at Rugby, when the carriage, which had rocked a good deal from the first, began to oscillate very violently. One meagre little elderly traveller turned rather pale, and looked nervously at his fellow-passengers; but the young man who had spoken to Henry Dunbar, and a bald-headed commercial-looking gentleman opposite to him, went on reading their newspapers as coolly as if the rocking of the carriage had been no more perilous than the lullaby motion of an infant's cradle, guided by a mother's gentle foot.

Mr. Dunbar never took his eyes from the dial of his watch. So the nervous traveller found no response to his look of terror.

He sat quietly for a minute or so, and then lowered the window near him, and let in a rush of icy wind, whereat the bald-headed commercial gentleman turned upon him rather fiercely, and asked him what he was about, and if he wanted to give them all inflammation of the lungs, by letting in an atmosphere that was two degrees below zero. But the little elderly gentleman scarcely heard this remonstrance; his head was out of the window, and he was looking eagerly Rugby-wards along the line.

"I'm afraid there's something wrong," he said, drawing in his head for a moment, and looking with a scared white face at his fellow-passengers;

"I'm really afraid there's something wrong. We're eight minutes behind our time, and I see the danger-signal up yonder, and the line seems blocked up with snow, and I really fear——"

He looked out again, and then drew in his head very suddenly.

"There's something coming!" he cried; "there's an engine coming—"

He never finished his sentence. There was a horrible smashing, tearing, grinding noise, that was louder than thunder, and more hideous than the crashing of cannon against the wooden walls of a brave ship.

That horrible sound was followed by a yell almost as horrible; and then there was nothing but death, and terror, and darkness, and anguish, and bewilderment; masses of shattered woodwork and iron heaped in direful confusion upon the blood-stained snow; human groans, stifled under the wrecks of shivered carriages: the cries of mothers whose children had been flung out of their arms into the very jaws of death; the piteous wail of children, who clung, warm and living, to the breasts of dead mothers, martyred in that moment of destruction; husbands parted from their wives; wives shrieking for their husbands; and, amidst all, brave men, with white faces, hurrying here and there, with lamps in their hands, half-maimed and wounded some of them, but forgetful of themselves in their care for the helpless wretches round them.

The express going northwards had run into the train from Shorncliffe, which had come upon the main line just nine minutes too late.

One by one the dead and wounded were carried away from the great heap of ruins; one by one the prostrate forms were borne away by quiet bearers, who did their duty calmly and fearlessly in that hideous scene of havoc and confusion. The great object to be achieved was the immediate clearance of the line; and the sound of pickaxes and shovels almost drowned those other dreadful sounds, the piteous moans of sufferers who were so little hurt as to be conscious of their sufferings.

The train from Shorncliffe had been completely smashed. The northern express had suffered much less; but the engine-driver had been killed, and several of the passengers severely injured.

Henry Dunbar was amongst those who were carried away helpless, and, to all appearance, lifeless from the ruin of the Shorncliffe train.

One of the banker's legs was broken, and he had received a blow upon the head, which had rendered him immediately unconscious.

But there were cases much worse than that of the banker; the surgeon who examined the sufferers said that Mr. Dunbar might recover from his injuries in two or three months, if he was carefully treated. The fracture of the leg was very simple; and if the limb was skilfully set, there would not be the least fear of contraction.

Half-a-dozen surgeons were busy in one of the waiting-rooms at the

Rugby station, whither the sufferers had been conveyed, and one of them took possession of the banker.

Mr. Dunbar's card-case had been found in the breast-pocket of his overcoat, and a great many people in the waiting-room knew that the gentleman with the white lace and grey moustache, lying so quietly upon one of the broad sofas, was no less a personage than Henry Dunbar, of Maudesley Abbey and St. Gundolph Lane. The surgeon knew it, and thought his good angel had sent this particular patient across his pathway.

He made immediate arrangements for bearing off Mr. Dunbar to the nearest hotel; he sent for his assistant; and in a quarter of an hour's time the millionaire was restored to consciousness, and opened his eyes upon the eager faces of two medical gentlemen, and upon a room that was strange to him.

The banker looked about him with an expression of perplexity, and then asked where he was. He knew nothing of the accident itself, and he had quite lost the recollection of all that had occurred immediately before the accident, or, indeed, from the time of his leaving Maudesley Abbey.

It was only little by little that the memory of the events of that day returned to him. He had wanted to leave Maudesley; he had wanted to go abroad—to go upon a journey—that was no new purpose in his mind. Had he actually set out upon that journey? Yes, surely, he must have started upon it; but what had happened, then?

He asked the surgeon what had happened, and why it was that he found himself in that strange place.

Mr. Daphney, the Rugby surgeon, told his patient all about the accident, in such a bland, pleasant way, that anybody might have thought the collision of a couple of engines rather an agreeable little episode in a man's life.

"But we are doing admirably, sir," Mr. Daphney concluded; "nothing could be more desirable than the way in which we are going on; and when our leg has been set, and we've taken a cooling draught, we shall be quite comfortable for the night. I really never saw a cleaner fracture—never, I can assure you."

But Mr. Dunbar raised himself into a sitting position, in spite of the remonstrances of his medical attendant, and looked anxiously about him.

"You say this place is Rugby?" he asked, moodily.

"Yes, this is Rugby," answered the surgeon, smiling, and rubbing his hands, almost as if he would have said, "Now, isn't *that* delightful?"

"Yes, this is the Queen's Hotel, Rugby; and I'm sure that every attention which the proprietor, Mr.——"

"I must get away from this place to-night," said Mr. Dunbar, interrupting the surgeon rather unceremoniously.

"To-night, my dear sir!" cried Mr. Daphney; "impossible—utterly impossible—suicide on your part, my dear sir, if you attempted it, and murder upon mine, if I allowed you to carry out such an idea. You will be a prisoner here for a month or so, sir, I regret to say; but we shall do all in our power to make your sojourn agreeable."

The surgeon could not help looking cheerful as he made this announcement; but seeing a very black and ominous expression upon the face of his patient, he contrived to modify the radiance of his own countenance.

"Our first proceeding, sir, must be to straighten this poor leg," he said, soothingly. "We shall place the leg in a cradle, from the thigh downwards: but I won't trouble you with technical details. I doubt if we shall be justified in setting the leg to-night; we must reduce the swelling before we can venture upon any important step. A cooling lotion, applied with linen cloths, must be kept on all night. I have made arrangements for a nurse, and my assistant will also remain here all night to supervise her movements."

The banker groaned aloud.

"I want to get to London," he said. "I must get to London!"

The surgeon and his assistant removed Mr. Dunbar's clothes. His trousers had to be cut away from his broken leg before anything could be done. Mr. Daphney removed his patient's coat and waistcoat; but the linen shirt was left, and the chamois-leather belt worn by the banker was under this shirt, next to and over a waistcoat of scarlet flannel.

"I wear a leather belt next my flannel waistcoat," Mr. Dunbar said, as the two men were undressing him; "I don't wish it to be removed."

He fainted away presently, for his leg was very painful; and on reviving from his fainting fit, he looked very suspiciously at his attendants, and put his hand to the buckle of his belt, in order to make himself sure that it had not been tampered with.

All through the long, feverish, restless night he lay pondering over this miserable interruption of his journey, while the sick-nurse and the surgeon's assistant alternately slopped cooling lotions about his wretched broken leg.

"To think that *this* should happen," he muttered to himself every now and then. "Amongst all the things I've ever dreaded, I never thought of this."

His leg was set in the course of the next day, and in the evening he had a long conversation with the surgeon.

This time Henry Dunbar did not speak so much of his anxiety to get away upon the second stage of his continental journey. His servant

Jeffreys arrived at Rugby in the course of the day; for the news of the accident had reached Maudesley Abbey, and it was known that Mr. Dunbar had been a sufferer.

To-night Henry Dunbar only spoke of the misery of being in a strange house.

"I want to get back to Maudesley," he said. "If you can manage to take me there, Mr. Daphney, and look after me until I've got over the effects of this accident, I shall be very happy to make you any compensation you please for whatever loss your absence from Rugby might entail upon you."

This was a very diplomatic speech: Mr. Dunbar knew that the surgeon would not care to let so rich a patient out of his hands; but he fancied that Mr. Daphney would have no objection to carrying his patient in triumph to Maudesley Abbey, to the admiration of the unprofessional public, and to the aggravation of rival medical men.

He was not mistaken in his estimate of human nature. At the end of the week he had succeeded in persuading the surgeon to agree to his removal; and upon the second Monday after the railway accident, Henry Dunbar was placed in a compartment which was specially prepared for him in the Shorncliffe train, and was conveyed from Shorncliffe station to Maudesley Abbey, without undergoing any change of position upon the road, and very carefully tended throughout the journey by Mr. Daphney and Jeffreys the valet.

They wheeled Mr. Dunbar's bed into his favourite tapestried chamber, and laid him there, to drag out long dreary days and nights, waiting till his broken bones should unite, and he should be free to go whither he pleased. He was not a very patient sufferer; he bore the pain well enough, but he chafed perpetually against the delay; and every morning he asked the surgeon the same question—

"When shall I be strong enough to walk about?"

- CHAPTER 31 -

CLEMENT AUSTIN MAKES A SACRIFICE

Margaret Wilmot had promised to become the wife of the man she loved; but she had given that promise very reluctantly, and only upon one condition. The condition was that, before her marriage with Clement Austin took place, the mystery of her father's death should be cleared up for ever.

"I cannot be your wife so long as the secret of that cruel deed remains unknown," she said to Clement. "It seems to me as if I have already been, wickedly neglectful of a solemn duty. Who had my father to love him and remember him in all the world but me? and who should avenge his death if I do not? He was an outcast from society; and people think it a very small thing that, after having led a reckless life, he should die a cruel death. If Henry Dunbar, the rich banker, had been murdered, the police would never have rested until the assassin had been discovered. But who cares what became of Joseph Wilmot, except his daughter? His death makes no blank in the world: except to me—except to me!"

Clement Austin did not forget his promise to do his uttermost towards the discovery of the banker's guilt. He believed that Henry Dunbar was the murderer of his old servant; and he had believed it ever since that day upon which the banker stole, like a detected thief, out of the house in St. Gundolph Lane.

It was just possible that Henry Dunbar might avoid Joseph Wilmot's daughter from a natural horror of the events connected with his return to England; but that the banker should resort to a cowardly stratagem to escape from an interview with the girl could scarcely be accounted for, except by the fact of his guilt.

He had an insurmountable terror of seeing this girl, because he was the murderer of her father.

The longer Clement Austin deliberated upon this business the more certainly he came to that one terrible conclusion: Henry Dunbar was guilty. He would gladly have thought otherwise: and he would have been very happy had he been able to tell Margaret Wilmot that the mystery of her father's death was a mystery that would never be solved upon this earth: but he could not do so; he could only bow his head before the awful necessity that urged him on to take his part in this drama of crime—the part of an avenger.

But a cashier in a London bank has very little time to play any part in life's history, except that quiet *rôle* which seems chiefly to consist in locking and unlocking iron safes, peering furtively into mysterious ledgers, and shovelling about new sovereigns as coolly as if they were Wallsend or Clay-Cross coals.[110]

Clement Austin's life was not an easy one, and he had no time to turn amateur detective, even in the service of the woman he loved.

He had no time to turn amateur detective so long as he remained at the banking-house in St. Gundolph Lane.

---

[110] Wallsend in North Tyneside and Clay-Cross in Derbyshire were well-known mining towns.

But could he remain there? That question arose in his mind, and took a very serious form. Was it possible to remain in that house when he believed the principal member of it to be one of the most infamous of men?

No; it was quite impossible for him to remain in his present situation. So long as he took a salary from Dunbar, Dunbar and Balderby, he was in a manner under obligation to Henry Dunbar. He could not remain in this man's service, and yet at the same time play the spy upon his actions, and work heart and soul to drag the dreadful secret of his life into the light of day.

Thus it was that towards the close of the week in which Henry Dunbar, for the first time after his return from India, visited the banking-offices, Clement Austin handed a formal notice of resignation to Mr. Balderby. The cashier could not immediately resign his situation, but was compelled to give his employers a month's notice of the withdrawal of his services.

A thunderbolt falling upon the morocco-covered writing-table in Mr. Balderby's private parlour could scarcely have been more astonishing to the junior partner than this letter which Clement Austin handed him very quietly and very respectfully.

There were many reasons why Clement Austin should remain in the banking-house. His father had lived for thirty years, and had eventually died, in the employment of Dunbar and Dunbar. He had been a great favourite with the brothers; and Clement had been admitted into the house as a boy, and had received much notice from Percival. More than this, he had every chance of being admitted ere long to a junior partnership upon very easy terms, which junior partnership would of course be the high-road to a great fortune.

Mr. Balderby sat with the letter open in his hands, staring at the lines before him as if he was scarcely able to comprehend their purport.

"Do you *mean* this, Austin?" he said at last.

"Yes, sir. Circumstances over which I have no control compel me to offer you my resignation."

"Have you quarrelled with anybody in the office? Has anything occurred in the house that has made you uncomfortable?"

"No, indeed, Mr. Balderby; I am very comfortable in my position."

The junior partner leaned back in his chair, and stared at the cashier as if he had been trying to detect the traces of incipient insanity in the young man's countenance.

"You are comfortable in your position, and yet you—Oh! I suppose the real truth of the matter is, that you have heard of something better, and you are ready to give us the go-by in order to improve your own circumstances?" said Mr. Balderby, with a tone of pique; "though I really don't see how you can very well be better off anywhere than you are here," he added, thoughtfully.

"You do me wrong, sir, when you think that I could willingly leave you for my own advantage," Clement answered, quietly. "I have no better engagement, nor have I even a prospect of any engagement."

"You haven't!" exclaimed the junior partner; "and yet you throw away such a chance as only falls to the lot of one man in a thousand! I don't particularly care about guessing riddles, Mr. Austin; perhaps you'll be kind enough to tell me frankly why you want to leave us?"

"I regret to say that it is impossible for me to do so, sir," replied the cashier; "my motive for leaving this house, which is a kind of second home to me, is no frivolous one, believe me. I have weighed well the step I am about to take, and I am quite aware that I sacrifice very excellent prospects in throwing up my present situation. But the reason of my resignation must remain a secret; for the present at least. If ever the day comes when I am able to explain my conduct, I believe that you will give me your hand, and say to me, 'Clement Austin, you only did your duty.'"

"Clement," said Mr. Balderby, "you are an excellent fellow; but you certainly must have got some romantic crotchet in your head, or you could never have thought of writing such a letter as this. Are you going to be married? Is that your reason for leaving us? Have you fascinated some wealthy heiress, and are you going to retire into splendid slavery?"

"No, sir. I am engaged to be married; but the lady whom I hope to call my wife is poor, and I have every necessity to be a working man for the rest of my life."

"Well, then, my dear fellow, it's a riddle; and, as I said before, I'm not good at guessing enigmas. There, my boy; go home and sleep upon this; and come back to me to-morrow morning, and tell me to throw this stupid letter in the fire—that's the wisest thing you can do. Good night."

But, in spite of all that Mr. Balderby could say, Clement Austin steadily adhered to his resolution. He worked early and late during the month in which he remained at his post, preparing the ledgers, balancing accounts, and making things straight and easy for the new cashier. He told Margaret Wilmot of what he had done, but he did not tell her the extent of the sacrifice which he had made for her sake. She was the only person who knew the real motive of his conduct, for to his mother he said very little more than he had said to Mr. Balderby.

"I shall be able to tell you my motives for leaving the banking-house at some future time, dear mother," he said; "until that time I can only entreat you to trust me, and to believe that I have acted for the best."

"I do believe it, my dear," answered the widow, cheerfully; "when did you ever do anything that wasn't wise and good?"

Her only son, Clement, was the god of this simple woman's idolatry; and if he had seen fit to turn her out of doors, and ask her to beg by his side in the streets of the city, I doubt if she would not have imagined some hidden wisdom lurking at the bottom of his apparently irrational proceedings. So she made no objection to his abandoning his desk in the house of Dunbar, Dunbar, and Balderby.

"We shall be poorer, I suppose, Clem," Mrs. Austin said; "but that's very little consequence, for your dear father left me so comfortably off that I can very well afford to keep house for my only son; and I shall have you more at home, dear, and that will indeed be happiness."

But Clement told his mother that he had some very important business on hand just then, which would occupy him a good deal; and indeed the first step necessary would be a journey to Shorncliffe, in Warwickshire.

"Why, that's where you went to school, Clem!"

"Yes, mother."

"And it's near Mr. Percival Dunbar—or, at least, Mr. Dunbar's country house."

"Yes, mother," answered Clement. "Now the business in which I am engaged is—is rather of a difficult nature, and I want legal help. My old schoolfellow, Arthur Lovell, who is as good a fellow as ever breathed, has been educated for the law, and is now a solicitor. He lives at Shorncliffe with his father, John Lovell, who is also a solicitor, and a man of some standing in the county. I shall run down to Shorncliffe, see my old friend, and get his advice; and if you'll bring Margaret down for a few days' change of air, we'll stop at the dear old Reindeer, where you used to come, mother, when I was at school, and where you used to give me such jolly dinners in the days when a good dinner was a treat to a hungry schoolboy."

Mrs. Austin smiled at her son; she smiled tenderly as she remembered his bright boyhood. Mothers with only sons are not very strong-minded. Had Clement proposed a trip to the moon, she would scarcely have known how to refuse him her company on the expedition.

She shivered a little, and looked rather doubtfully from the blazing fire which lit up the cosy drawing-room to the cold grey sky outside the window.

"The beginning of January isn't the pleasantest time in the year for a trip into the country, Clem, dear," she said; "but I should certainly be very lonely at home without you. And as to poor Madge, of course it would be a great treat to her to get away from her pupils and have a peep at the genuine country, even though there isn't a single leaf upon the trees. So I suppose I must say yes. But do tell me all about this business there's a dear good boy."

Unfortunately the dear good boy was obliged to tell his mother that the business in question was, like his motive for resigning his situation, a profound secret, and that it must remain so for some time to come.

"Wait, dear mother," he said; "you shall know all about it by and by. Believe me, when I tell you that it's not a very pleasant business," he added, with a sigh.

"It's not unpleasant for you, I hope, Clement?"

"It isn't pleasant for any one who is concerned in it, mother," answered the young man, thoughtfully; "it's altogether a miserable business; but I'm not concerned in it as a principal, you know, dear mother; and when it's all over we shall only look back upon it as the passing of a black cloud over our lives, and you will say that I have done my duty. Dearest mother, don't look so puzzled," added Clement; "this matter *must* remain a secret for the present. Only wait, and trust me."

"I will, my dear boy," Mrs. Austin said, presently. "I will trust you with all my heart; for I know how good you are. But I don't like secrets, Clem; secrets always make me uncomfortable."

No more was said upon this subject, and it was arranged by-and-by that Mrs. Austin and Margaret should prepare to start for Warwickshire at the beginning of the following week, when Clement would be freed from all engagements to Messrs. Dunbar, Dunbar, and Balderby.

Margaret had waited very patiently for this time, in which Clement would be free to give her all his help in that awful task which lay before her—the discovery of Henry Dunbar's guilt.

"You will go to Shorncliffe with my mother," Clement Austin said, upon the evening after his conversation with the widow; "you will go with her, Madge, ostensibly upon a little pleasure trip. Once there, we shall be able to contrive an interview with Mr. Dunbar. He is a prisoner at Maudesley Abbey, laid up by the effect of his accident the other day, but not too ill to see people, Balderby says; therefore I should think we may be able to plan an interview between you and him. You still hold to your original purpose? You wish to *see* Henry Dunbar?"

"Yes," answered Margaret, thoughtfully; "I want to see him. I want to look straight into the face of the man whom I believe to be my father's murderer. I don't know why it is, but this purpose has been uppermost in my mind ever since I heard of that dreadful journey to Winchester; ever since I first knew that my father had been murdered while travelling with Henry Dunbar. It might, as you have said, be wiser to watch and wait, and to avoid all chance of alarming this man. But I can't be wise. I want to see him. I want to look in his face, and see if his eyes can meet mine."

"You shall see him then, dear girl. A woman's instinct is sometimes worth more than a man's wisdom. You shall see Henry Dunbar. I know that my old schoolfellow Arthur Lovell will help me, with all his heart and soul. I have called again upon the Scotland-Yard people, and I gave them a minute description of the scene in St. Gundolph Lane; but they only shrugged their shoulders, and said the circumstances looked queer, but were not strong enough to act upon. If any body can help us, Arthur Lovell can; for he was present at the inquest and all further examination of the witnesses at Winchester."

If Margaret Wilmot and Clement Austin had been going upon any other errand than that which took them to Warwickshire, the journey to Shorncliffe might have been very pleasant to them.

To Margaret, this comfortable journey in the cushioned corner of a first-class carriage, respectfully waited upon by the man she loved, possessed at least the charm of novelty. Her journeys hitherto had been long wearisome pilgrimages in draughty third-class carriages, with noisy company, and in an atmosphere pervaded by a powerful effluvium of various kinds of alcohol.

Her life had been a very hard one, darkened by the ever-brooding shadow of disgrace. It was new to her to sit quietly looking out at the low meadows and glimmering white-walled villas, the patches of sparse woodland, the distant villages, the glimpses of rippling water, shining in the wintry sun. It was new to her to be loved by people whose minds were unembittered by the baneful memories of wrong and crime. It was new to her to hear gentle voices, sweet Christian-like words: it was new to her to breathe the bright atmosphere that surrounds those who lead a virtuous, God-fearing life.

But there is little sunshine without its attendant shadow. The shadow upon Margaret's life now was the shadow of that coming task—that horrible work which must be done—before she could be free to thank God for His mercies, and to be happy.

The London train reached Shorncliffe early in the afternoon. Clement Austin hired a roomy old fly,[111] and carried off his companions to the Reindeer.

The Reindeer was a comfortable old-fashioned hotel. It had been a very grand place in the coaching-days, and you entered the hostelry by a broad and ponderous archway, under which Highflyers and Electrics had

---

[111] A light, covered carriage, usually drawn by a single horse; often used for public conveyance or available for hire.

driven triumphantly in the days that were for ever gone.

The house was a roomy old place, with long corridors and wide staircases; noble staircases, with broad, slippery, oaken banisters and shallow steps. The rooms were grand and big, with bow windows so spotless in their cleanness that they had rather a cold effect on a January day, and were apt to inspire in the vulgar mind the fancy that a little dirt or smoke would look warmer and more comfortable. Certainly, if the Reindeer had a fault, it was that it was too clean. Everything was actually slippery with cleanness, from the newly-calendered chintz[112] that covered the sofa and the chair-cushions to the copper coal-scuttle that glittered by the side of the dazzling brass fender. There were faint odours of soft soap in the bed-chambers, which no amount of dried lavender could overcome. There was an effluvium of vitriol about all the brass-work, and there was a good deal of brass-work in the Reindeer: and if one species of decoration is more conducive to shivering than another, it certainly is brass-work in a state of high polish.

There was no dish ever devised by mortal cook which the sojourner at the Reindeer could not have, according to the preliminary statement of the landlord; but with whatever ambitious design the sojourner began to talk about dinner, it always ended, somehow or other, by his ordering a chicken, a little bit of boiled bacon, a dish of cutlets, and a tart. There were days upon which divers species of fish were to be had in Shorncliffe, but the sojourner at the Reindeer rarely happened to hit upon one of those days.

Clement Austin installed Margaret and the widow in a sitting-room which would have comfortably accommodated about forty people. There was a bow-window quite large enough for the requirements of a small family, and Mrs. Austin settled herself there, while the landlord was struggling with a refractory fire, and pretending not to know that the grate was damp.

Clement went through the usual fiction of deliberation as to what he should have for dinner, and of course ended with the perennial chicken and cutlets.

"I haven't the fine appetite I had fifteen years ago, Mr. Gilwood," he said to the landlord, "when my mother yonder, who hasn't grown fifteen days older in all those fifteen years,—bless her dear motherly heart!—used to come down to see me at the academy in the Lisford Road, and give me a dinner in this dear old room. I thought your cutlets the most ethereal morsels ever dished by mortal cook, Mr. Gilwood, and this

---

[112] Calendering is a process whereby cloth is passed through rollers to produce a smooth, stiff, or glazed finish.

room the best place in all the world. You know Mr. Lovell—Mr. Arthur Lovell?"

"Yes, sir; and a very nice young gentleman he is."

"He's settled in Shorncliffe, I suppose?"

"Well, I believe he is, sir. There was some talk of his going out to India, in a Government appointment, sir, or something of that sort; but I'm given to understand that it's all off now, and that Mr. Arthur is to go into partnership with his father; and a very clever young lawyer he is, I've been told."

"So much the better," answered Clement, "for I want to consult him upon a little matter of business. Good-bye, mother! Take care of Madge, and make yourselves as comfortable as you can. I think the fire will burn now, Mr. Gilwood. I shan't be away above an hour, I dare say; and then I'll come and take you for a walk before dinner. God bless you, my poor Madge!" Clement whispered, as Margaret followed him to the door of the room, and looked wistfully after him as he went down the staircase.

Mrs. Austin had once cherished ambitious views with regard to her son's matrimonial prospects; but she had freely given them up when she found that he had set his heart upon winning Margaret Wilmot for his wife. The good mother had made this sacrifice willingly and without complaint, as she would have made any other sacrifice for her dearly-beloved only son; and she found the reward of her devotion; for Margaret, this penniless, friendless girl, had become very dear to her—a real daughter, not in law, but bound by the sweet ties of gratitude and affection.

"And I was such a silly old creature, my dear," the widow said to Margaret, as they sat in the bow-window looking out into the quiet street; "I was so worldly-minded that I wanted Clement to marry a rich woman, so that I might have some stuck-up daughter-in-law, who would despise her husband's mother, and estrange my boy from me, and make my old age miserable. That's what I wanted, Madge, and what I might have had, perhaps, if Clem hadn't been wiser than his silly old mother. And, thanks to him, I've got the sweetest, truest, brightest girl that ever lived; though you are not as bright as usual to-day, Madge," Mrs. Austin added, thoughtfully. "You haven't smiled once this morning, my dear, and you seem as if you'd something on your mind."

"I've been thinking of my poor father," Margaret answered, quietly.

"To be sure, my dear; and I might have known as much, my poor tender-hearted lamb. I know how unhappy those thoughts always make you."

Clement Austin had not been at Shorncliffe for three years. He had visited Maudesley Abbey several times during the lifetime of Percival

Dunbar, for he had been a favourite with the old man; and he had been four years at a boarding-school kept by a clergyman of the Church of England in a fine old brick mansion on the Lisford Road.

The town of Shorncliffe was therefore familiar to Mr. Austin; and he looked neither to the right nor to the left as he walked towards the archway of St. Gwendoline's Church, near which Mr. Lovell's house was situated.

He found Arthur at home, and very delighted to see his old schoolfellow. The two young men went into a little panelled room, looking into the garden, a cosy little room which Arthur Lovell called his study; and here they sat together for upwards of an hour, discussing the circumstances of the murder at Winchester, and the conduct of Mr. Dunbar since that event.

In the course of that interview, Clement Austin plainly perceived that Arthur Lovell had come to the same conclusion as himself, though the young lawyer was slow to express his opinion.

"I cannot bear to think it," he said; "I know Laura Dunbar—that is to say, Lady Jocelyn—and it is too horrible to me to imagine that her father is guilty of this crime. What would be that innocent girl's feelings if it should be so, and if her father's guilt should be brought home to him!"

"Yes, it would be very terrible for Lady Jocelyn, no doubt," Clement answered; "but that consideration must not hinder the course of justice. I think this man's position has served him as a shield from the very first. People have thought it next to impossible that Henry Dunbar could be guilty of a crime, while they would have been ready enough to suspect some penniless vagabond of any iniquity."

Arthur Lovell told Clement that the banker was still at Maudesley, bound a prisoner by his broken leg, which was going on favourably enough, but very slowly.

Mr. Dunbar had expressed a wish to go abroad, in spite of his broken leg, and had only desisted from his design of being conveyed somehow or other from place to place, when he was told that any such imprudence might result in permanent lameness.

"Keep yourself quiet, and submit to the necessities of your accident, and you'll recover quickly," the surgeon told his patient. "Try to hurry the work of nature, and you'll have cause to repent your impatience for the remainder of your life."

So Henry Dunbar had been obliged to submit himself to the decrees of Fate, and to lie day after day, and night after night, upon his bed in the tapestried chamber, staring at the fire, or the figure of his valet and attendant; nodding in the easy-chair by the hearth; or listening to the cinders falling from the grate, and the moaning of the winter wind amongst the bare branches of the elms.

The banker was getting better and stronger every day, Arthur Lovell said. His attendants were able to remove him from one chamber to another; a pair of crutches had been made for him, but he had not yet been able to make his first feeble trial of them. He was fain to content himself with being carried to an easy-chair, to sit for a few hours, wrapped in blankets, with the leopard-skin rug about his legs. No man could have been more completely a prisoner than this man had become by the result of the fatal accident near Rugby.

"Providence has thrown him into my power," Margaret said, when Clement repeated to her the information which he had received from Arthur Lovell,—"Providence has thrown this man into my power; for he can no longer escape, and, surrounded by his own servants, he will scarcely dare to refuse to see me; he will surely never be so unwise as to betray his terror of me."

"And if he does refuse——"

"If he does, I'll invent some stratagem by which I may see him. But he will not refuse. When he finds that I am so resolute as to follow him here, he will not refuse to see me."

This conversation took place during a brief walk which the lovers took in the wintry dusk, while Mrs. Austin nodded by the fire in that comfortable half-hour which precedes dinner.

- CHAPTER 32 -

WHAT HAPPENED AT MAUDESLEY ABBEY

Early the next day Clement Austin walked to Maudesley Abbey, in order to procure all the information likely to facilitate Margaret Wilmot's grand purpose. He stopped at the gate of the principal lodge. The woman who kept it was an old servant of the Dunbar family, and had known Clement Austin in Percival Dunbar's lifetime. She gave him a hearty welcome, and he had no difficulty whatever in setting her tongue in motion upon the subject of Henry Dunbar.

She told him a great deal; she told him that the present owner of the Abbey never had been liked, and never would be liked: for his stern and gloomy manner was so unlike his father's easy, affable good-nature, that people were always drawing comparisons between the dead man and the living.

This, in a few words, is the substance of what the worthy woman said in a good many words. Mrs. Grumbleton gave Clement all the information he required as to the banker's daily movements at the present time. Henry Dunbar was now in the habit of rising about two o'clock in the day, at which time he was assisted from his bedroom to his sitting-room, where he remained until seven or eight o'clock in the evening. He had no visitors, except the surgeon, Mr. Daphney, who lived in the Abbey, and a gentleman called Vernon, who had bought Woodbine Cottage, near Lisford, and who now and then was admitted to Mr. Dunbar's sitting-room.

This was all Clement Austin wanted to know. Surely it might be possible, with a little clever management, to throw the banker completely off his guard, and to bring about the long-delayed interview between him and Margaret Wilmot.

Clement returned to the Reindeer, had a brief conversation with Margaret, and made all arrangements.

At four o'clock that afternoon, Miss Wilmot and her lover left the Reindeer in a fly; at a quarter to five the fly stopped at the lodge-gates.

"I will walk to the house," Margaret said; "my coming will attract less notice. But I may be detained for some time, Clement. Pray, don't wait for me. Your dear mother will be alarmed if you are very long absent. Go back to her, and send the fly for me by and by."

"Nonsense, Madge. I shall wait for you, however long you may be. Do you think my heart is not as much engaged in anything that may influence your fate as even your own can be? I won't go with you to the Abbey; for it will be as well that Henry Dunbar should remain in ignorance of my presence in the neighbourhood. I will walk up and down the road here, and wait for you."

"But you may have to wait so long, Clement."

"No matter how long. I can wait patiently, but I could not endure to go home and leave you, Madge."

They were standing before the great iron gates as Clement said this. He pressed Margaret's cold hand; he could feel how cold it was, even through her glove; and then rang the bell. She looked at him as the gate was opened; she turned and looked at him with a strangely earnest gaze as she crossed the boundary of Henry Dunbar's domain, and then walked slowly along the broad avenue.

That last look had shown Clement Austin a pale resolute face, something like the countenance of a fair young martyr going quietly to the stake.

He walked away from the gates, and they shut behind him with a loud clanging noise. Then he went back to them, and watched Margaret's figure growing dim and distant in the gathering dusk as she approached the Abbey. A faint glow of crimson firelight reddened the gravel-drive before the windows of Mr. Dunbar's apartments, and there was a footman airing himself under the shadow of the porch, with a glimmer of light shining out of the hall behind him.

"I do not suppose I shall have to wait very long for my poor girl," Clement thought, as he left the gates, and walked briskly up and down the road. "Henry Dunbar is a resolute man; he will refuse to see her today, as he refused before."

Margaret found the footman lolling against the clustered pillars of the gothic porch, staring thoughtfully at the low evening light, yellow and red behind the brown trunks of the elms, and picking his teeth with a gold toothpick.

The sight of the open hall-door, and this languid footman lolling in the porch, suddenly inspired Margaret Wilmot with a new idea. Would it not be possible to slip quietly past this man, and walk straight to the apartments of Mr. Dunbar, unquestioned, uninterrupted?

Clement had pointed out to her the windows of the rooms occupied by the banker. They were on the left-hand side of the entrance-hall. It would be impossible for her to mistake the door leading to them. It was dusk, and she was very plainly dressed, with a black straw bonnet, and a veil over her face. Surely she might deceive this languid footman by affecting to be some hanger-on of the household, which of course was a large one.

In that case she had no right to present herself at the front door, certainly; but then, before the languid footman could recover from the first shock of indignation at her impertinence, she might slip past him and reach the door leading to those apartments in which the banker hid himself and his guilt.

Margaret lingered a little in the avenue, watching for a favourable opportunity in which she might hazard this attempt. She waited five minutes or so.

The curve of the avenue screened her, in some wise, from the man in the porch, who never happened to roll his languid eyes towards the spot where she was standing.

A flight of rooks came scudding through the sky presently, very much excited, and cawing and screeching as if they had been an ornithological fire brigade hurrying to extinguish the flames of some distant rookery.

The footman, who was suffering acutely from the complaint of not knowing what to do with himself, came out of the porch and stood in the middle of the gravelled drive, with his back towards Margaret, staring at the birds as they flew westward.

This was her opportunity. The girl hurried to the door with a light step, so light upon the smooth solid gravel that the footman heard nothing until she was on the broad stone step under the porch, when the fluttering of her skirt, as it brushed against the pillars, roused him from a species of trance or reverie.

He turned sharply round, as upon a pivot, and stared aghast at the retreating figure under the porch.

"Hi, you there, young woman!" he exclaimed, without stirring from his post; "where are you going to? What's the meaning of your coming to this door? Are you aware that there's such a place as a servants' 'all and a servants' hentrance?"

But the languid retainer was too late. Margaret's hand was upon the massive knob of the door upon the left side of the hall before the footman had put this last indignant question.

He listened for an apologetic murmur from the young woman; but hearing none, concluded that she had found her way to the servants' hall, where she had most likely some business or other with one of the female members of the household.

"A dressmaker, I dessay," the footman thought. "Those gals spend all their earnings in finery and fallals, instead of behaving like respectable young women, and saving up their money against they can go into the public line with the man of their choice."

He yawned, and went on staring at the rooks, without troubling himself any further about the impertinent young person who had dared to present herself at the grand entrance.

Margaret opened the door, and went into the room next the hall.

It was a handsome apartment, lined with books from the floor to the ceiling; but it was quite empty, and there was no fire burning in the grate. The girl put up her veil, and looked about her. She was very, very pale now, and trembled violently; but she controlled her agitation by a great effort, and went slowly on to the next room.

The second room was empty like the first; but the door between it and the next chamber was wide open, and Margaret saw the firelight shining upon the faded tapestry, and reflected in the sombre depths of the polished oak furniture. She heard the low sound of the light ashes falling on the hearth, and the shorting breath of a dog.

She knew that the man she sought, and had so long sought without avail, was in that room. Alone; for there was no murmur of voices, no sound of any one moving in the apartment. That hour, to which Margaret Wilmot had looked as the great crisis of her life, had come; and her courage failed her all at once, and her heart sank in her breast on the very threshold of the chamber in which she was to stand face to face with Henry Dunbar.

"The murderer of my father!" she thought; "the man whose influence blighted my father's life, and made him what he was. The man through whose reckless sin my father lived a life that left him, oh! how sadly unprepared to die! The man who, knowing this, sent his victim before an offended God, without so much warning as would have given him time to think one prayer. I am going to meet *that* man face to face!"

Her breath came in faint gasps, and the firelit chamber swam before her eyes as she crossed the threshold of that door, and went into the room where Henry Dunbar was sitting alone before the low fire.

He was wrapped in crimson draperies of thick woollen stuff, and the leopard-skin railway rug was muffled about his knees A dog of the bull-dog breed was lying asleep at the banker's feet, half-hidden in the folds of the leopard-skin. Henry Dunbar's head was bent over the fire, and his eyes were closed in a kind of dozing sleep, as Margaret Wilmot went into the room.

There was an empty chair opposite to that in which the banker sat; an old-fashioned, carved oak-chair, with a high back and crimson-morocco cushions. Margaret went softly up to this chair, and laid her hand upon the oaken framework. Her footsteps made no sound on the thick Turkey carpet; the banker never stirred from his doze, and even the dog at his feet slept on.

"Mr. Dunbar!" cried Margaret, in a clear, resolute voice; "awake! it is I, Margaret Wilmot, the daughter of the man who was murdered in the grove near Winchester!"

The dog awoke, and snapped at her. The man lifted his head, and looked at her. Even the fire seemed roused by the sound of her voice! for a little jet of vivid light leaped up out of the smouldering log, and lighted the scared face of the banker.

Clement Austin had promised Margaret to wait for her, and to wait patiently; and he meant to keep his promise. But there are some limits even to the patience of a lover, though he were the veriest knight-errant who was ever eager to shiver a lance or hack the edge of a battle-axe for love of his liege lady. When you have nothing to do but to walk up and down a few yards of hard dusty high-road, upon a bleak evening in January, an hour more or less is of considerable importance. Five o'clock struck about ten minutes after Margaret Wilmot had entered the park, and Clement thought to himself that even if Margaret were successful in obtaining an interview with the banker, that interview would be over before six. But the faint strokes of Lisford-church clock died away upon the cold evening wind, and Clement was still pacing up and down, and the fly was still waiting; the horse comfortable enough, with a rug upon his back and his nose in a bag of oats; the man walking up and down by the side of the vehicle, slapping his gloved hands across his shoulders every now and then to keep himself warm. In that long hour between six and seven, Clement Austin's patience wore itself almost threadbare. It is one thing to ride into the lists on a prancing steed, caparisoned with embroidered trappings, worked by the fair hands of your lady-love, and with the trumpets braying, and the populace shouting, and the Queen of beauty smiling sweet approval of your prowess: but it is quite another thing to walk up and down a dusty country road, with the wind biting like some ravenous animal at the tip of your nose, and no more consciousness of your legs and arms than if you were a Miss Biffin.[113]

By the time seven o'clock struck, Clement Austin's patience had given up the ghost; and to impatience had succeeded a vague sense of alarm. Margaret Wilmot had gone to force herself into this man's presence, in spite of his reiterated refusal to see her. What if—what if, goaded by her persistence, maddened by the consciousness of his own guilt, he should attempt any violence.

Oh, no, no; that was quite impossible. If this man was guilty, his crime had been deliberately planned, and executed with such a diabolical cunning, that he had been able so far to escape detection. In his own house, surrounded by prying servants, he would never dare to assail this girl by so much as a harsh word.

But, notwithstanding this, Clement was determined to wait no longer. He would go to the Abbey at once, and ascertain the cause of Margaret's delay. He rang the bell, went into the park, and ran along the avenue to the perch. Lights were shining in Mr. Dunbar's windows, but the great hall-door was closely shut.

The languid footman came in answer to Clement's summons.

"There is a young lady here," Clement said, breathlessly; "a young lady—with Mr. Dunbar."

"Ho! is that hall?" asked the footman, satirically. "I thought Shorncliffe town-'all was a-fire, at the very least, from the way you rung. There *was* a young pusson with Mr. Dunbar above a hour ago, if *that's* what you mean?"

"Above an hour ago?" cried Clement Austin, heedless of the man's impertinence in his own growing anxiety; "do you mean to say that the young lady has left?"

"She *have* left, above a hour ago."

---

[113] Sarah Biffin (1784-1850) was a successful artist who, having been born without hands and arms, and with only vestigial legs, painted with her mouth. Charles Dickens mentions her in both *Nicholas Nickleby* and *Martin Chuzzlewit*.

"She went away from this house an hour ago?"

"More than a hour ago."

"Impossible!" Clement said; "impossible!"

"It may be so," answered the footman, who was of an ironical turn of mind; "but I let her out with my own hands, and I saw her go out with my own eyes, notwithstanding."

The man shut the door before Clement had recovered from his surprise, and left him standing in the porch; bewildered, though he scarcely knew why; frightened, though he scarcely knew what he feared.

- CHAPTER 33 -

MARGARET'S RETURN

For some minutes Clement Austin lingered in the porch at Maudesley Abbey, utterly at a loss as to what he should do next.

Margaret had left the Abbey an hour ago, according to the footman's statement; but, in that case, where had she gone? Clement had been walking up and down the road before the iron gates of the park, and they had not been opened once during the hours in which he had waited outside them. Margaret could not have left the park, therefore, by the principal entrance. If she had gone away at all, she must have gone out by one of the smaller gates—by the lodge-gate upon the Lisford Road, perhaps, and thus back to Shorncliffe.

"But then, why, in Heaven's name, had Margaret set out to walk home when the fly was waiting for her at the gates; when her lover was also waiting for her, full of anxiety to know the result of the step she had taken?

"She forgot that I was waiting for her, perhaps," Clement thought to himself. "She may have forgotten all about me, in the fearful excitement of this night's work."

The young man was by no means pleased by this idea.

"Margaret can love me very little, in that case," he said to himself. "My first thought, in any great crisis of my life, would be to go to her, and tell her all that had happened to me."

There were no less than four different means of exit from the park. Clement Austin knew this, and he knew that it would take him upwards of two hours to go to all four of them.

"I'll make inquiries at the gate upon the Lisford Road," he said to himself; "and if I find Margaret has left by that way, I can get the fly round there, and pick her up between this and Shorncliffe. Poor girl, in her ignorance of this neighbourhood, she has no idea of the distance she will have to walk!"

Mr. Austin could not help feeling vexed by Margaret's conduct; but he did all he could to save the girl from the fatigue she was likely to entail upon herself through her own folly. He ran to the lodge upon the Lisford Road, and asked the woman who kept it, if a lady had gone out about an hour before.

The woman told him that a young lady had gone out an hour and a half before.

This was enough. Clement ran across the park to the western entrance, got into the fly, and told the man to drive back to Shorncliffe, by the Lisford Road, as fast as he could go, and to look out on the way for the young lady whom he had driven to Maudesley Abbey that afternoon.

"You watch the left side of the road, I'll watch the right," Clement said.

The driver was cold and cross, but he was anxious to get back to Shorncliffe, and he drove very fast.

Clement sat with the window down, and the frosty wind blowing full upon his face as he looked out for Margaret.

But he reached Shorncliffe without having overtaken her, and the fly crawled under the ponderous archway beneath which the dashing mail-coaches had rolled in the days that were for ever gone.

"She must have got home before me," the cashier thought; "I shall find her up-stairs with my mother."

He went up to the large room with the bow-window. The table in the centre of the room was laid for dinner, and Mrs. Austin was nodding in a great arm-chair near the fire, with the county newspaper in her lap. The wax-candles were lighted, the crimson curtains were drawn before the bow-window, and the room looked altogether very comfortable: but there was no Margaret.

The widow started up at the sound of the opening of the door and her son's hurried footsteps.

"Why, Clement," she cried, "how late you are! I seem to have been sitting dozing here for full two hours; and the fire has been replenished three times since the cloth was laid for dinner. What have you been doing, my dear boy?"

Clement looked about him before he answered.

"Yes, I am very late, mother, I know," he said; "but where's Margaret?"

Mrs. Austin stared aghast at her son's question.

"Why, Margaret is with you, is she not?" she exclaimed.

"No, mother; I expected to find her here."

"Did you leave her, then?"

"No, not exactly; that is to say, I——"

Clement did not finish the sentence. He walked slowly up and down the room thinking, whilst his mother watched him very anxiously.

"My dear Clement," Mrs. Austin exclaimed at last, "you really quite alarm me. You set out this afternoon upon some mysterious expedition with Margaret; and though I ask you both where you are going, you both refuse to satisfy my very natural curiosity, and look as solemn as if you were about to attend a funeral. Then, after ordering dinner for seven o'clock, you keep it waiting nearly two hours; and you come in without Margaret, and seem alarmed at not seeing net here. What does it all mean, Clement?"

"I cannot tell you, mother."

"What! is this business of to-day, then, a part of your secret?"

"It is," answered the cashier. "I can only say again what I said before, mother—trust me!"

The widow sighed, and shrugged her shoulders with a deprecating gesture.

"I suppose I *must* be satisfied, Clem," she said. "But this is the first time there's ever been anything like a mystery between you and me."

"It is, mother; and I hope it may be the last."

The elderly waiter, who remembered the coaching days, and pretended to believe that the Reindeer was not an institution of the past, came in presently with the first course.

It happened to be one of those days on which fish was to be had in Shorncliffe; and the first course consisted of a pair of very small soles and a large cruet-stand. The waiter removed the cover with as lofty a flourish as if the small soles had been the noblest turbot that ever made the glory of an aldermannic feast.

Clement seated himself at the dinner-table, in deference to his mother, and went through the ceremony of dinner; but he scarcely ate half a dozen mouthfuls. His ears were strained to hear the sound of Margaret's footstep in the corridor without; and he rejected the waiter's fish-sauces in a manner that almost wounded the feelings of that functionary. His mind was racked by anxiety about the missing girl.

Had he passed her on the road? No, that was very improbable; for he had kept so sharp a watch upon the lonely highway that it was more than unlikely the familiar figure of her whom he looked for could have escaped his eager eyes. Had Mr. Dunbar detained her at Maudesley Abbey against her will? No, no, that was quite impossible; for the footman had distinctly declared that he had seen his master's visitor leave the house; and the footman's manner had been innocence itself.

The dinner-table was cleared by-and-by, and Mrs. Austin produced some coloured wools, and a pair of ivory knitting-needles, and set to work very quietly by the light of the tall wax-candles; but even she was beginning to be uneasy at the absence of her son's betrothed wife.

"My dear Clement," she said at last, "I'm really growing quite uneasy about Madge. How is it that you left her?"

Clement did not answer this question; but he got up and took his hat from a side-table near the door.

"I'm uneasy about her absence too, mother," he said, "I'll go and look for her."

He was leaving the room, but his mother called to him.

"Clement!" she cried, "you surely won't go out without your greatcoat—upon such a bitter night as this, too!"

But Mr. Austin did not stop to listen to his mother's remonstrance; he hurried out into the corridor, and shut the door of the room behind him. He wanted to run away and look for Margaret, though he did not know how or where to seek for her. Quiescence had become intolerable to him. It was utterly impossible that he should sit calmly by the fire, waiting for the coming of the girl he loved.

He was hurrying along the corridor, but he stopped abruptly, for a well-known figure appeared upon the broad landing at the top of the stairs. There was an archway at the end of the corridor, and a lamp hung under the archway. By the light of this lamp, Clement Austin saw Margaret Wilmot coming towards him slowly: as if she dragged herself along by a painful effort, and would have been well content to sink upon the carpeted floor and lie there helpless and inert.

Clement ran to meet her, with his face lighted up by that intense delight which a man feels when some intolerable fear is suddenly lifted off his mind.

"Margaret!" he cried; "thank God you have returned! Oh, my dear, if you only knew what misery your conduct has caused me!"

He held out his arms, but, to his unutterable surprise, the girl recoiled from him. She recoiled from him with a look of horror, and shrank against the wall, as if her chief desire was to avoid the slightest contact with her lover.

Clement was startled by the blank whiteness of her face, the fixed stare of her dilated eyes. The January wind had blown her hair about her forehead in loose disordered tresses; her shawl and dress were wet with melted snow; but the cashier scarcely looked at these. He only saw her face; his gaze was fascinated by the girl's awful pallor, and the strange

241

expression of her eyes.

"My darling," he said, "come into the parlour. My mother has been almost as much alarmed as I have been. Come, Margaret; my poor girl, I can see that this interview has been too much for you. Come, dear."

Once more he approached her, and again she shrank away from him, dragging herself along against the wall, and with her eyes still fixed in the same deathlike stare.

"Don't speak to me, Clement Austin," she cried; "don't approach me. There is contamination in me. I am no fit associate for an honest man. Don't come near me."

He would have gone to her, to clasp her in his arms, and comfort her with soothing, tender words; but there was something in her eyes that held him at bay, as if he had been rooted to the spot on which he stood.

"Margaret!" he cried.

He followed her, but she still recoiled from him, and, as he held out his hand to grasp her wrist, she slipped by him suddenly, and rushed away towards the other end of the corridor.

Clement followed her; but she opened a door at the end of the passage, and went into Mrs. Austin's room. The cashier heard the key turned hurriedly in the lock, and he knew that Margaret Wilmot had locked herself in. The room in which she slept was inside that occupied by Mrs. Austin.

Clement stood for some moments almost paralyzed by what had happened. Had he done wrong in seeking to bring about this interview between Margaret Wilmot and Henry Dunbar? He began to think that he had been most culpable. This impulsive and sensitive girl had seen her father's assassin: and the horror of the meeting had been too much for her impressionable nature, and had produced, for the time at least, a fearful effect upon her over-wrought brain.

"I must appeal to my mother," Clement thought; "she alone can give me any help in this business."

He hurried back to the sitting-room, and found his mother still watching the rapid movements of her ivory knitting-needles. The Reindeer was a well-built house, solid and old-fashioned, and listeners lurking in the long passages had small chance of reaping much reward for their pains unless they found a friendly keyhole.

Mrs. Austin looked up with an expression of surprise as her son re-entered the room.

"I thought you had gone to look for Margaret," she said.

"There was no occasion to do so, mother; she has returned."

"Thank Heaven for that! I have been quite alarmed by her strange absence."

"So have I, mother; but I am still more alarmed by her manner, now that she has returned. I asked you just now to trust me, mother," said Clement, very gravely. "It is my turn now to confide in you. The business in which Margaret has been engaged this evening was of a most painful nature—so painful that I am scarcely surprised by the effect that it has produced on her sensitive mind. I want you to go to her, mother. I want you to comfort my poor girl. She has locked herself in her own room; but she will admit you, no doubt. Go to her, dear mother, and try and quiet her excitement, while I go for a medical man."

"You think she is ill, then, Clement?"

"I don't know that, mother; but such violent emotion as she has evidently endured might produce brain-fever. I'll go and look for a doctor."

Clement hurried down to the hall of the hotel, while his mother went to seek Margaret. He found the landlord, who directed him to the favourite Shorncliffe medical man.

Luckily, Mr. Vincent, the surgeon, was at home. He received Clement very cordially, put on his hat without five minutes delay, and accompanied Margaret's lover back to the Reindeer.

"It is a case of mental excitement," Clement said. "There may be no necessity for medical treatment; but I shall feel more comfortable when you have seen this poor girl."

Clement conducted Mr. Vincent to the sitting-room, which was empty.

"I'll go and see how Miss Wilmot is now," the cashier said. The doctor gave a scarcely perceptible start as he heard that name of Wilmot. The murder of Joseph Wilmot had formed the subject of many a long discussion amongst the townspeople at Shorncliffe, and the familiar name struck the surgeon's ear.

"But what of that?" thought Mr. Vincent. "The name is not such a very uncommon one."

Clement went to his mother's room and knocked softly at the door. The widow came out to him presently.

"How is she now?" Clement asked.

"I can scarcely tell you. Her manner frightens me. She is lying on her bed as motionless as if she were a corpse, and with her eyes fixed upon the blank wall opposite to her. When I speak to her, she does not answer me by so much as a look; but if I go near her she shivers, and gives a long shuddering sigh. What does it all mean, Clement?"

"Heaven knows, mother. I can only tell you that she has gone through a meeting which was certainly calculated to have considerable effect upon her mind. But I had no idea that the effect would be anything like this. Can the doctor come?"

"Yes; he had better come at once."

Clement returned to the sitting-room, and remained there while Mr. Vincent went to see Margaret. To poor Clement it seemed as if the surgeon was absent nearly an hour, so intolerable was the anguish of that interval of suspense.

At last, however, the creaking footstep of the medical man sounded in the corridor. Clement hurried to the door to meet him.

"Well!" he cried, eagerly.

Mr. Vincent shook his head.

"It is a case in which my services can be of very little avail," he said; "the young lady is suffering from some mental uneasiness, which she refuses to communicate to her friends. If you could get her to talk to you, she would no doubt be very much benefited. If she were an ordinary person, she would cry, and the relief of tears would have a most advantageous effect upon her mind. Our patient is by no means an ordinary person. She has a very strong will."

"Margaret has a strong will!" exclaimed Clement, with a look of surprise; "why, she is gentleness itself."

"Very likely; but she has a will of iron, nevertheless. I implored her to speak to me just now; the tone of her voice would have been some slight diagnosis of her state; but I might as well have implored a statue. She only shook her head slowly, and she never once looked at me. However, I will send her a sedative draught, which had better be taken immediately, and I'll look round in the morning."

Mr. Vincent left the Reindeer, and Clement went to his mother's room. That loving mother was ready to sympathize with every trouble that affected her only son. She came out of Margaret's room and went to meet Clement.

"Is she still the same, mother?" he asked.

"Yes, quite the same. Would you like to see her?"

"Very much."

Mrs. Austin and her son went into the adjoining chamber. Margaret was lying, dressed in the damp, draggled gown which she had worn that afternoon, upon the outside of the bed. The dull stony look of her face filled Clement's mind with an awful terror. He began to fear that she was going mad.

He sat down upon a chair close by the bed, and watched her for some moments in silence, while his mother stood by, scarcely less anxious than himself.

Margaret's arm hung loosely by her side as lifeless in its attitude as if it had belonged to the dead. Clement took the slender hand in his. He had expected to find it dry and burning with feverish heat; but, to his surprise, it was cold as ice.

"Margaret," he said, in a low earnest voice, "you know how dearly I have loved and do love you; you know how entirely my happiness depends upon yours; surely, my dear one, you will not refuse—you cannot be so cruel as to keep your sorrow a secret from him who has so good a right to share it? Speak to me, my darling. Remember what suffering you are inflicting upon me by this cruel silence."

At last the hazel eyes lost their fixed look, and wandered for a moment to Clement Austin's face.

"Have pity upon me," the girl said, in a hoarse unnatural voice; "have compassion upon me, for I need man's mercy as well as the mercy of God. Have some pity upon me, Clement Austin, and leave me; I will talk to you to-morrow."

"You will tell me all that has happened?"

"I will talk to you to-morrow," answered Margaret, looking at her lover with a white, inflexible face; "but leave me now; leave me, or I will run out of this room, and away from this house. I shall go mad if I am not left alone!"

Clement Austin rose from his seat near the bedside.

"I am going, Margaret," he said, in a tone of wounded feeling; "but I leave you with a heavy heart. I did not think there would ever come a time in which you would reject my sympathy."

"I will talk to you to-morrow," Margaret said, for the second time.

She spoke in a strange mechanical way, as if this had been a set speech which she had arranged for herself.

Clement stood looking at her for some little time; but there was no change either in her face or attitude, and the young man went slowly and sorrowfully from the room.

"I leave her in your hands, mother," he said. "I know how tender and true a friend she has in you; I leave her in your care, under Providence. May Heaven have pity upon her and me!"

- CHAPTER 34 -

FAREWELL

M argaret submitted to take the sedative draught sent by the medical man. She submitted, at Mrs. Austin's request; but it seemed as if she scarcely understood why the medicine was offered to her. She was like a sleep-walker, whose brain is peopled by the creatures of a dream, and who has no consciousness of the substantial realities that surround him.

The draught Mr. Vincent had spoken of as a sedative turned out to be a very powerful opiate, and Margaret sank into a profound slumber about a quarter of an hour after taking the medicine.

Mrs. Austin went to Clement to carry him these good tidings.

"I shall sit up two or three hours, and see how the poor girl goes on, Clement," the widow said; "but I hope you'll go to bed; I know all this excitement has worn you out."

"No, mother; I feel no sense of fatigue."

"But you will try to get some rest, to please me? See, dear boy, it's already nearly twelve o'clock."

"Yes, if you wish it, mother, I'll go to my room," Mr. Austin answered, quickly.

His room was near those occupied by his mother and Margaret, much nearer than the sitting-room. He bade Mrs. Austin good night and left her; but he had no thought of going to bed, or even trying to sleep. He went to his own room, and walked up and down; going out into the corridor every now and then, to listen at the door of his mother's chamber.

He heard nothing. Some time between two and three o'clock Mrs. Austin opened the door of her room, and found her son lingering in the corridor.

"Is she still asleep, mother?" he asked.

"Yes, and she is sleeping very calmly. I am going to bed now; pray try to get some sleep yourself, Clem."

"I will, mother."

Clement returned to his room. He was thankful, as he thought that sleep would bring tranquillity and relief to Margaret's overwrought brain. He went to bed and fell asleep, for he was exhausted by the fatigue of the day and the anxiety of the night. Poor Clement fell asleep, and dreamt that he met Margaret Wilmot by moonlight in the park around

Maudesley Abbey, walking with a DEAD MAN, whose face was strange to him. This was the last of many dreams, all more or less grotesque or horrible, but none so vivid or distinct as this. The end of the vision woke Clement with a sudden shock, and he opened his eyes upon the cold morning light, which seemed especially cold in this chamber at the Reindeer, where the paper on the walls was of the palest grey, and every curtain or drapery of a spotless white.

Clement lost no time over his toilet. He looked at his watch while dressing, and found that it was between seven and eight. It wanted a quarter to eight when he left his room, and went to his mother's door to inquire about Margaret. He knocked softly, but there was no answer; then he tried the door, and finding it unlocked, opened it a few inches with a cautious hand, and listened to his mother's regular breathing.

"She is asleep, poor soul," he thought. "I won't disturb her, for she must want rest after sitting up half last night."

Clement closed the door as noiselessly as he had opened it, and then went slowly to the sitting-room. There was a struggling fire in the shining grate; and the indefatigable waiter, who refused to believe in the extinction of mail-coaches, had laid the breakfast apparatus—frosty-looking white-and-blue cups and saucers on a snowy cloth, a cut-glass cream-jug that looked as if it had been made out of ice, and a brazen urn in the last stage of polish. The breakfast service was harmoniously adapted to the season, and eminently calculated to produce a fit of shivering in the sojourner at the Reindeer.

But Clement Austin did not bestow so much as one glance upon the breakfast-table. He hurried to the bow-window, where Margaret Wilmot was sitting, neatly dressed in her morning garments, with her shawl on, and her bonnet lying on a chair near her.

"Margaret!" exclaimed Clement, as he approached the place where Joseph Wilmot's daughter was sitting; "my dear Margaret, why did you get up so early this morning, when you so much need rest?"

The girl rose and looked at her lover with a grave and quiet earnestness of expression; but her face was quite as colourless as it had been upon the previous night, and her lips trembled a little as she spoke to Clement.

"I have had sufficient rest," she said, in a low, tremulous voice; "I got up early because—because—I am going away."

Her two hands had been hanging loosely amongst the fringes of her shawl; she lifted them now, and linked her fingers together with a convulsive motion; but she never withdrew her eyes from Clement's face, and her glance never faltered as she looked at him.

"Going away, Margaret?" the cashier cried; "going away—to-day—

247

this morning?"

"Yes, by the half-past nine o'clock train."

"Margaret, you must be mad to talk of such a thing."

"No," the girl answered, slowly; "that is the strangest thing of all—I am not mad. I am going away, Clement—Mr. Austin. I wished to avoid seeing you. I meant to have written to you to tell you——"

"To tell me what, Margaret?" asked Clement. "Is it I who am going mad; or am I dreaming all this?"

"It is no dream, Mr. Austin. My letter would have only told you the truth. I am going away from here because I can never be your wife."

"You can never be my wife! Why not, Margaret?"

"I cannot tell you the reason."

"But you *shall* tell me, Margaret!" cried Clement, passionately. "I will accept no sentence such as this until I know the reason for pronouncing it; I will suffer no imaginary barrier to stand between you and me. There is some mystery, some mystification in all this, Margaret; some woman's fancy, which a few words of explanation would set at rest. Margaret, my pearl! do you think I will consent to lose you so lightly? My own dear love! do you know me so little as to think that I will part with you? My love is a stronger passion than you think, Madge; and the bondage you accepted when you promised to be my wife is a bondage that cannot so easily be shaken off!"

Margaret watched her lover's face with melancholy, tearless eyes.

"Fate is stronger than love, Clement," she said, mournfully, "I can never be your wife!"

"Why not?"

"For a reason which you can never know."

"Margaret, I will not submit——"

"You must submit," the girl said, holding up her hand, as if to stop her lover's passionate words. "You must submit, Clement. This world seems very hard sometimes, so hard that in a dreadful interval of dull despair the heavens are hidden from us, and we cannot recognize the Eternal wisdom guiding the hand that afflicts us. My life seems very hard to me to-day, Clement. Do not try to make it harder. I am a most unhappy woman; and in all the world there is only one favour you can grant me. Let me go away unquestioned; and blot my image from your heart for ever when I am gone."

"I will never consent to let you go," Clement Austin answered, resolutely. "You are mine by right of your own most sacred promise, Margaret. No womanish folly shall part us."

"Heaven knows it is no woman's folly that parts us, Clement," the girl answered, in a plaintive, tremulous voice.

"What is it, then, Margaret?"

"I can never tell you."

"You will change your mind."

"Never."

She looked at him with an air of quiet resolution stamped upon her colourless face.

Clement remembered what the doctor had said of his patient's iron will. Was it possible that Mr. Vincent had been right? Was this gentle girl's resolution to overrule a strong man's passionate vehemence?

"What is it that can part us, Margaret?" Mr. Austin cried. "What is it? You saw Mr. Dunbar yesterday?"

The girl shuddered, and over her colourless face there came a livid shade, which was more deathlike than the marble whiteness that had preceded it.

"Yes," Margaret Wilmot said, after a pause. "I was—very fortunate. I gained admission to—Mr. Dunbar's rooms."

"And you spoke to him?"

"Yes."

"Did your interview with him confirm or dissipate your suspicions? Do you still believe that Henry Dunbar murdered your unhappy father?"

"No," answered Margaret, resolutely; "I do not."

"You do not? The banker's manner convinced you of his innocence, then?"

"I do not believe that Henry Dunbar murdered my—my unhappy father."

It is impossible to describe the tone of anguish with which Margaret spoke those last three words.

"But something transpired in that interview at Maudesley Abbey, Margaret? Henry Dunbar told you something—perhaps something about your dead father—some disgraceful secret which you never heard before; and you think that the shame of that secret is a burden which I would fear to carry? You mistake my nature, Margaret, and you commit a cruel treason against my love. Be my wife, dear one; and if malicious people should point to you, and say, 'Clement Austin's wife is the daughter of a thief and a forger,' I would give them back scorn for scorn, and tell them that I honour my wife for virtues that have been sometimes missing in the consort of an emperor."

For the first time that morning Margaret's eyes grew dim, but she brushed away the gathering tears with a rapid movement of her trembling hand.

"You are a good man, Clement Austin," she said; "and I—wish that I were better worthy of you. You are a good man; but you are very cruel to

249

me to-day. Have pity upon me, and let me go."

She drew a pretty little watch from her waist, and looked at the dial. Then, suddenly remembering that the watch had been Clement's gift, she took the slender chain from her neck, and handed them both to him.

"You gave me these when I was your betrothed wife, Mr. Austin; I have no right to keep them now."

She spoke very mournfully; but poor Clement was only mortal. He was a good man, as Margaret had just declared; but, unhappily, good men are apt to fly into passions as well as their inferiors in the scale of morality.

Clement Austin threw the pretty little Genevese toy upon the floor, and ground it to atoms under the heel of his boot.

"You are cruel and unjust, Mr. Austin," Margaret said.

"I am a man, Miss Wilmot," Clement answered, bitterly; "and I have the feelings of a man. When the woman I have loved and believed in turns upon me, and coolly tells me that she means to break my heart, without so much as deigning to give me a reason for her conduct, I am not so much a gentleman as to be able to smile politely, and request her to please herself."

The cashier turned away from Margaret, and walked two at three times up and down the room. He was in a passion, but grief and indignation were so intermingled in his breast that he scarcely knew which was uppermost. But grief and love allied themselves presently, and together were much too strong for indignation.

Clement Austin went back to the window; Margaret was standing where he had left her, but she had put on her bonnet and gloves, and was quite ready to leave the house.

"Margaret," said Mr. Austin, trying to take her hand; but she drew herself away from him, almost as she had shrunk from him in the corridor on the previous night; "Margaret, once for all, listen to me. I love you, and I believe you love me. If this is true, no obstacle on earth shall part us so long as we live. There is only one condition upon which I will let you go this day."

"What is that condition?"

"Tell me that I have been fooled by my own egotism. I am twelve years older than you, Margaret, and there is nothing very romantic or interesting either in myself or my worldly position. Tell me that you do not love me. I am a proud man, I will not sue *in forma pauperis*.[114] If you

---

[114] Latin, meaning "in the character of a pauper". A legal term referring to the status granted to someone without funds to pay court costs, enabling them to pursue a legal claim. Clement simply means that he is too proud to beg in a degrading manner.

do not love me, Margaret, you are free to go."

Margaret bowed her head, and moved slowly towards the door.

"You are going—Miss Wilmot!"

"Yes, I am going. Farewell, Mr. Austin."

Clement caught the retreating girl by her wrist.

"You shall not go thus, Margaret Wilmot!" he cried, passionately—"not thus! You shall speak to me! You shall speak plainly! You shall speak the truth! You do not love me?"

"No; I do not love you."

"It was all a farce, then—a delusion—it was all falsehood and trickery from first to last. When you smiled at me, your smile was a mockery; when you blushed, your blushes were the simulated blushes of a professed coquette. Every tender word you have ever spoken to me—every tremulous cadence in your low voice—every tearful look in the eyes that have seemed so truthful—all—it has altogether been false—altogether a delusion—a——"

The strong man covered his face with his hands and sobbed aloud. Margaret watched him with tearless eyes; her lips were convulsively contracted, but there was no other evidence of emotion in her face.

"Why did you do this, Margaret?" Clement asked at last, in a heart-rending voice; "why did you do this cruel thing?"

"I will tell you why," the girl answered, slowly and deliberately; "I will tell you why, Mr. Austin; and then I shall seem utterly despicable in your eyes, and it will be a very easy thing for you to blot my image from your heart. I was a poor desolate girl; and I was worse than poor and desolate, for the stain of my father's shameful history blackened my name. It was a fine thing for such as me to win the love of an honest man—a gentleman—who could shelter me from all the troubles of life, and give me a stainless name and an honourable place in society. I was the daughter of a returned convict, an outcast, and your love offered me a splendid chance of redemption from the black depths of disgrace and misery in which I lived. I was only mortal, Clement Austin; what was there in my blood that should make me noble, or good, or strong to stand against temptation? I seized upon the one chance of my miserable life; I plotted to win your love. Step by step I lured you on until you offered to make me your wife. That was my end and aim. I triumphed; and for a time enjoyed my success, and the advantages that it brought me. But I suppose the worst sinners have some kind of conscience. Mine was awakened last night, and I resolved to spare you the misery of being married to a woman who comes of such a race as that from which I spring."

Nothing could be more callous than the manner with which Margaret

Wilmot had made this speech. Her tones had never faltered. She had spoken slowly, pausing before every fresh sentence; but she had spoken like a wretched creature, whose withered heart was almost incapable of womanly emotion. Clement Austin looked at her with a blank wondering stare.

"Oh! great heavens!" he cried at last; "how could I think it possible that any man could be as cruelly deceived as I have been by this woman!"

"I may go now, Mr. Austin?" said Margaret.

"Yes, you may go now—*you*, who once were the woman I loved; you, who have thrown away the beautiful mask I believed in, and revealed to me the face of a skeleton; you, who have lifted the silver veil of imagination to show me the hideous ghastliness of reality. Go, Margaret Wilmot; and may Heaven forgive you!"

"Do you forgive me, Mr. Austin?"

"Not yet. I will pray God to make me strong enough to forgive you!"

"Farewell, Clement!"

If my readers have seen *Manfred* at Drury Lane, let them remember the tone in which Miss Rose Leclercq breathed her last farewell to Mr. Phelps,[115] and they will know how Margaret Wilmot pronounced this mournful word—love's funeral bell,—

"Farewell, Clement!"

"One word, Miss Wilmot," cried Mr. Austin. "I have loved you too much in the past ever to become indifferent to your fate. Where are you going?"

"To London."

"To your old apartments at Clapham?"

"Oh, no, no!"

"Have you money—money enough to last you for some time?"

"Yes; I have saved money."

"If you should be in want of help, will you let me help you?"

"Willingly, Mr. Austin. I am not too proud to accept your help in the hour of my need."

"You will write to me, then, at my mother's, or you will write to my mother herself, if ever you require assistance. I shall tell my mother nothing of what has passed between us this day, except that we have parted. You are going by the half-past nine o'clock train, you say, Miss

[115] *Manfred* (written 1816-17) is a dramatic poem by Lord Byron (1788-1824). It was later adapted for the stage. Rose Leclercq (1843-1899, English actress) played Astarte in *Manfred* at Drury Lane on 10 October 1863, opposite Samuel Phelps (1804-1878, English actor and theatre manager) in the title role.

Wilmot?"

Clement had only spoken the truth when he said that he was a proud man. He asked this question in the same business-like tone in which he might have addressed a lady who was quite indifferent to him.

"Yes, Mr. Austin."

"I will order a fly for you, then. You have five minutes to spare. And I will send one of the waiters to the station, so that you may have no trouble about your luggage."

Clement rang the bell, and gave the necessary orders. Then he bowed gravely to Margaret, and wished her good morning as she left the room.

And this is how Margaret Wilmot parted from Clement Austin.[116]

- CHAPTER 35 -

A DISCOVERY AT THE LUXEMBOURG[117]

While Henry Dunbar sat in his lonely room at Maudesley Abbey, held prisoner by his broken leg, and waiting anxiously for the hour in which he should be allowed the privilege of taking his first experimental promenade upon crutches, Sir Philip Jocelyn and his beautiful young wife drove together on the crowded boulevards of the French capital.

They had been southward, and had returned to the gayest capital in all the world at the time when that capital is at its best and brightest.

They had returned to Paris for the early new year: and, as this year happened fortunately to be ushered into existence by a sharp frost and a bright sunny sky, the boulevards were not the black rivers of mud and slush that they are apt to be in the first days of the infantine year. Prince Louis Napoleon Buonaparte was only First President as yet; and Paris was by no means the wonderful city of endless boulevards and palatial edifices that it has since grown to be under the master hand which rules and beautifies it, as a lover adorns his mistress.[118] But it was not the less

---

[116] End of volume II in the original three-volume version.

[117] Chapter 1 of the third volume.

[118] Louis Napolean (1808–1873), President of the French Second Republic and ruler of the Second French Empire. He was elected President by popular vote in 1848, and proclaimed Emperor Napoleon III in December 1852. During his reign he extensively renovated and redesigned Paris, commissioning Baron Georges Eugène Haussmann to plan the alterations. Braddon's comment definitively locates the action of *Henry Dunbar* prior to 1852.

the most charming city in the universe; and Philip Jocelyn and his wife were as happy as two children in this paradise of brick and mortar.

They suited each other so well; they were never tired of each other's society, or at a stand-still for want of something to say to each other. They were rather frivolous, perhaps; but a little frivolity may be pardoned in two people who were so very young and so entirely happy. Sir Philip may have been a little too much devoted to horses and dogs, and Laura may have been a shade too enthusiastic upon the subject of new bonnets, and the jewellery in the Rue de la Paix.[119] But if they idled a little just now, in this delicious honeymoon-time, when it was so sweet to be together always, from morning till night, driving in a sleigh with jingling bells upon the snowy roads in the Bois, sitting on the balcony at Meurice's at night,[120] looking down into the long lamp-lit street and the misty gardens, where the trees were leafless and black against the dark blue sky, they meant to do their duty, and be useful to their fellow-creatures, when they were settled at Jocelyn's Rock. Sir Philip had half-a-dozen schemes for free schools, and model cottages with ovens that would bake everything in the world, and chimneys that would never smoke. And Laura had her own pet plans. Was she not an heiress, and therefore specially sent into the world to give happiness to people who had been born without that pleasant appendage of a silver spoon in their infantine mouths? She meant to be scrupulously conscientious in the administration of her talents; and sometimes at church on a Sunday, when the sermon was particularly awakening, she mentally debated the serious question as to whether new bonnets, and a pair of Jouvin's gloves daily, were not sinful; but I think she decided that the new bonnets and gloves were, on the whole, a pardonable weakness, as being good for trade.

The Warwickshire baronet knew a good many people in Paris, and he and his bride received a very enthusiastic welcome from these old friends, who pronounced that Miladi Jocelyn was *charmante* and *la belle des belles*; and that Sir Jocelyn was the most fortunate of men in having discovered this gay, lighthearted girl amongst the prudish and pragmatical *meess* of the *brumeuse Angleterre*.[121]

Laura made herself very much at home with her Parisian acquaintance; and in the grand house in the Rue Lepelletier many a glass was

---

[119] Fashionable shopping street in Paris, renowned for its jewellery shops.
[120] Le Meurice is a luxury Parisian hotel, established in 1817. It moved to its present location, overlooking the Tuileries Garden, in 1835.
[121] *Charmante*: charming; *la belle des belles*: the beauty of beauties; *brumeuse Angleterre*: foggy England.

turned full upon the beautiful English bride with the *chevelure doré* and the violet blue eyes.[122]

One morning Laura told her husband, with a gay laugh, that she was going to victimize him; but he was to promise to be patient and bear with her for once in a way.

"What is it you want me to do, my darling?"

"I want you to give me a long day in the Luxembourg. I want to see all the pictures—the modern pictures especially. I remember all the Rubenses at the Louvre, for I saw them three years ago, when I was staying in Paris with grandpapa. I like the modern pictures best, Philip: and I want you to tell me all about the artists, and what I ought to admire, and all that sort of thing."

Sir Philip never refused his wife anything; so he said, yes: and Laura ran away to her dressing-room like a school-girl who has been pleading for a holiday and has won her cause. She returned in a little more than ten minutes, in the freshest toilette, all pale shimmering blue, like the spring sky, with pearl-grey gloves and boots and parasol, and a bonnet that seemed made of azure butterflies.

It was drawing towards the close of this delightful honeymoon tour, and it was a bright sunshiny morning early in February; but February in Paris is sometimes better than April in London.

Philip Jocelyn's work that morning was by no means light, for Laura was fond of pictures, in a frivolous amateurish kind of way; and she ran from one canvas to another, like a fickle-minded bee that is bewildered by the myriad blossoms of a boundless parterre.[123] But she fixed upon a picture which she said she preferred to anything she had seen in the gallery.

Philip Jocelyn was examining some pictures on the other side of the room when his wife made this discovery. She hurried to him immediately, and led him off to look at the picture. It was a peasant-girl's head, very exquisitely painted by a modern artist, and the baronet approved his wife's taste.

"How I wish you could get me a copy of that picture, Philip," Laura said, entreatingly. "I should so like one to hang in my morning-room at Jocelyn's Rock. I wonder who painted that lovely face?"

There was a young artist hard at work at his easel, copying a large devotional subject that hung near the picture Laura admired. Sir Philip asked this gentleman if he knew the name of the artist who had painted the peasant-girl.

---

[122] *chevelure doré*: golden hair.
[123] Parterre: An ornamental flower garden.

"Ah, but yes, monsieur!" the painter answered, with animated politeness; "it is the work of one of my friends; a young Englishman, of a renown almost universal in Paris."

"And his name, monsieur?"

"He calls himself Kerstall—Frederick Kerstall; he is the son of an old monsieur, who calls himself also Kerstall, and who had much of celebrity in England it is many years."

"Kerstall!" exclaimed Laura, suddenly; "Mr. Kerstall! why, it was a Mr. Kerstall who painted papa's portrait; I have heard grandpapa say so again and again; and he took it away to Italy with him, promising to bring it back to London when he returned, after a year or two of study. And, oh, Philip, I should so like to see this old Mr. Kerstall; because, you know, he may have kept papa's portrait until this very day, and I should so like to have a picture of my father as he was when he was young, and before the troubles of a long life altered him," Laura said, rather mournfully.

She turned to the French artist presently, and asked him where the elder Mr. Kerstall lived, and if there was any possibility of seeing him.

The painter shrugged up his shoulders, and pursed up his mouth, thoughtfully.

"But, madame," he said, "this Monsieur Kerstall's father is very old, and he has ceased to paint it is a long time. They have said that he is even a little imbecile, that he does not remember himself of the most common events of his life. But there are some others who say that his memory has not altogether failed, and that he is still enough harshly critical towards the works of others."

The Frenchman might have run on much longer upon this subject, but Laura was too impatient to be polite. She interrupted him by asking for Mr. Kerstall's address.

The artist took out one of his own cards, and wrote the required address in pencil.

"It is in the neighbourhood of Notre Dame, madame, in the Rue Cailoux, over the office of a Parisian journal," he said, as he handed the card to Laura. "I don't think you will have any difficulty in finding the house."

Laura thanked the French artist and then took her husband's arm and walked away with him. "I don't care about looking at any more pictures to-day, Philip," she said; "but, oh, I do wish you would take me to this Mr. Kerstall's studio at once! You will be doing me such a favour, Philip, if you'll say yes."

"When did I ever say no to anything you asked me, Laura? We'll go to Mr. Kerstall immediately, if you like. But why are you so anxious to see this old portrait of your father, my dear?"

"Because I want to see what he was before he went to India. I want to see what he was when he was bright and young before the world had hardened him. Ah, Philip, since we have known and loved each other, it seems to me as if I had no thought or care for any one in all this wide world except yourself. But before that time I was very unhappy about my father. I had expected that he would be so fond of me. I had so built upon his return to England, thinking that we should be nearer and dearer to each other than any father and daughter ever were before. I had thought all this, Philip; night after night I had dreamt the same dream,— the bright happy dream in which my father came home to me, the fond foolish dream in which I felt his strong arms folded round me, and his true heart beating against my own. But when he did come at last, it seemed to me as if this father was a man of stone; his white fixed face repelled me; his cold hard voice turned my blood to ice. I was frightened of him, Philip; I was frightened of my own father; and little by little we grew to shun each other, till at last we met like strangers, or something worse than strangers; for I have seen my father look at me with an expression of absolute horror in his stern cruel eyes. Can you wonder, then, that I want to see what he was in his youth? I shall learn to love him, perhaps, if I can see the smiling image of his lost youth."

Laura said all this in a very low voice as she walked with her husband through the garden of the Luxembourg. She walked very fast; for she was as eager as a child who is intent upon some scheme of pleasure.

- CHAPTER 36 -

LOOKING FOR THE PORTRAIT

The Rue Cailoux was a very quiet little street—a narrow, winding street, with tall shabby-looking houses, and untidy-little green-grocers' shops peeping out here and there.

The pavement suggested the idea that there had just been an outbreak of the populace, and that the stones had been ruthlessly torn up to serve in the construction of barricades, and only very carelessly put down again. It was a street which seemed to have been built with a view to achieving the largest amount of inconvenience out of a minimum of materials; and looked at in this light the Rue Cailoux was a triumph: it was a street in which Parisian drivers clacked their whips to a running accompaniment of imprecations: it was a street in which you met dirty porters carrying six feet of highly-baked bread, and shrill old women with wonderful bandanas bound about their grisly heads: but above all, it was a street in which you were so shaken and jostled, and bumped and startled, by the ups and downs of the pavement, that you had very little leisure to notice the distinctive features of the neighbourhood.

The house in which Mr. Kerstall, the English artist, lived was a gloomy-looking building with a dingy archway, beneath which Sir Philip Jocelyn and his wife alighted.

There was a door under this archway, and there was a yard beyond it, with the door of another house opening upon it, and ranges of black curtainless windows looking down upon it, and an air of dried herbs, green-stuff, chickens in the moulting stage, and old women, generally pervading it. The door which belonged to Mr. Kerstall's house, or rather the house in which Mr. Kerstall lived in common with a colony of unknown number and various avocations, was open, and Sir Philip and his wife went into the hall.

There was no such thing as a porter or portress; but a stray old woman, hovering under the archway, informed Philip Jocelyn that Mr. Kerstall was to be found on the second story. So Laura and her husband ascended the stairs, which were bare of any covering except dirt, and went on mounting through comparative darkness, past the office of the Parisian journal, till they came to a very dingy black door.

Philip knocked, and, after a considerable interval, the door was opened by another old woman, tidier and cleaner than the old women who pervaded the yard, but looking very like a near relation to those ladies.

Philip inquired in French for the senior Mr. Kerstall; and the old woman told him, very much through her nose, that Mr. Kerstall father saw no one; but that Mr. Kerstall son was at his service.

Philip Jocelyn said that in that case he would be glad to see Mr. Kerstall junior; upon which the old woman ushered the baronet and his wife into a saloon, distinguished by an air of faded splendour, and in which the French clocks and ormolu candelabras were in the proportion of two to one to the chairs and tables.

Sir Philip gave his card to the old woman, and she carried it into the adjoining chamber, whence there issued a gush of tobacco-smoke, as the door between the two rooms was opened and then shut again.

In less than three minutes by the minute-hand of the only one of the ormolu clocks which made any pretence of going, the door was opened again, and a burly-looking, middle-aged gentleman, with a very black beard, and a dirty holland blouse all smeared with smudges of oil-colour, appeared upon the threshold of the adjoining chamber, surrounded by a cloud of tobacco-smoke—like a heathen deity, or a good-tempered-looking African genie newly escaped from his bottle.

This was Mr. Kerstall junior. He introduced himself to Sir Philip, and waited to hear what that gentleman required of him.

Philip Jocelyn explained his business, and told the painter how, more than five-and-thirty years before, the portrait of Henry Dunbar, only son of Percival Dunbar the great banker, had been painted by Mr. Michael Kerstall, at that time a fashionable artist.

"Five-and-thirty years ago!" said the painter, pulling thoughtfully at his beard; "five-and-thirty years ago! that's a very long time, my lord, and I'm afraid it's not likely my father will remember the circumstance; for I regret to say that he is slow to remember the events of a few days past. His memory has been failing a long time. You wish to know the fate of this portrait of Mr. Dunbar, I think you said?"

Laura answered this question, although it had been addressed to her husband.

"Yes, we want to see the picture, if possible," she said; "Mr. Dunbar is my father, and there is no other portrait of him in existence. I do so want to see this one, and to obtain possession of it, if it is possible for me to do so."

"And you are of opinion that my father took the picture to Italy with him when he left England more than five-and-thirty years ago?"

"Yes; I've heard my grandfather say so. He lost sight of Mr. Kerstall, and could never obtain any tidings of the picture. But I hope that, late as it is, we may be more fortunate now. You do not think the picture has been destroyed, do you?" Laura asked eagerly.

"Well," the artist answered, doubtfully, "I should be inclined to fear that the portrait may have been painted out: and yet, by the bye, as the picture belonged by right to Mr. Percival Dunbar, and not to my father, that circumstance may have preserved it uninjured through all these years. My father has a heap of unframed canvases, inches thick in dust, and littering every corner of his room. Mr. Dunbar's portrait may be amongst them."

"Oh, I should be so very much obliged if you would allow me to examine those pictures," said Laura.

"You think you would recognize the portrait?"

"Yes, surely; I could not fail to do so. I know my father's face so well as it is, that I must certainly have some knowledge of it as it was five-and-thirty years ago, however much he may have altered in the interval. Pray, Mr. Kerstall, oblige me by letting me see the pictures."

"I should be very churlish were I to refuse to do so," the painter answered, good-naturedly. "I will just go and see if my father is able to receive visitors. He has been a voluntary exile from England for the last five-and-thirty years, so I fear he will have forgotten the name of Dunbar; but he may by chance be able to give us some slight assistance."

Mr. Kerstall left his visitors for about ten minutes, and at the end of that time he returned to say that his father was quite ready to receive Sir Philip and Lady Jocelyn.

"I mentioned the name of Dunbar to him," the painter said; "but he remembers nothing. He has been painting a little this morning, and is in very high spirits about his work. It pleases him to handle the brushes, though his hand is terribly shaky, and he can scarcely hold the palette."

The artist led the way to a large room, comfortably but plainly furnished, and heated to a pitch of suffocation by a stove. There was a bed in a curtained alcove at the end of the apartment; an easel stood near the large window; and the proprietor of the chamber sat in a cushioned arm-chair close to the suffocating stove.

Michael Kerstall was an old man, who looked even older than he was. He was a picturesque-looking old man, with long white hair dropping down over his coat-collar, and a black-velvet skull-cap upon his head. He was a cheerful old man, and life seemed very pleasant to him; for Frenchmen have a habit of honouring their fathers and mothers, and Mr. Frederick Kerstall was a naturalized citizen of the French republic.

The old man nodded and smiled and chuckled as Sir Philip and Laura were presented to him, and pointed with a courtly grace to the chairs which his son set for his guests.

"You want to see my pictures, sir? Ah, yes; to be sure, to be sure! The modern school of painting, sir, is something marvellous to an old man, sir; an old man who remembers Sir Thomas Lawrence—ay, sir, I had the honour to know him intimately. No pre-Raphaelite theories in those days, sir;[124] no figures cut of coloured pasteboard and glued on to the canvas; no green trees and vermilion draperies, and chocolate-coloured streaks across an ultramarine background, sir; and I'm told the young people call that a sky. No pointed chins, and angular knees and elbows, and frizzy red hair—red, sir, and as frizzy as a blackamoor's—and I'm told the young people call that female beauty. No, sir; nothing of that sort in my day. There was a French painter in my day, sir, called David, and there was an English painter in my day called Lawrence; and they painted ladies and gentlemen, sir; and they instituted a gentlemanly school, sir. And you put a crimson curtain behind your subject, and you put a bran-

---

[124] The Pre-Raphaelite Brotherhood was an association of English artists and poets formed in 1848, which opposed the principles of the Royal Academy. Their paintings championed a return to detail, intensive colour, complexity of composition and use of symbolism. Subjects were often taken from literary or religious works.

new hat, or a roll of paper, in his right hand, and you thrust his left hand in his waistcoat—the best black satin, sir, with strong light in the texture—and you made your subject look like a gentleman. Yes, sir, if he was a chimney-sweep when he went into your studio, he went out of it a gentleman."

The old man would have gone on talking for any length of time, for pre-Raphaelitism was his favourite antipathy; and the black-bearded gentleman standing behind his chair was an enthusiastic member of the pre-Raphaelite brotherhood.

Mr. Kerstall senior seemed so thoroughly in possession of all his faculties while he held forth upon modern art, that Laura began to hope his memory could scarcely be so much impaired as his son had represented it to be.

"When you painted portraits in England, Mr. Kerstall," she said, "before you went to Italy, you painted a likeness of my father, Henry Dunbar, who was then a young man. Do you remember that circumstance?"

Laura asked this question very hopefully; but to her surprise, Mr. Kerstall took no notice whatever of her inquiry, but went rambling on about the degeneracy of modern art.

"I am told there is a young man called Millais, sir, and another young man called Holman Hunt, sir,—positive boys, sir; actually very little more than boys, sir; and I'm given to understand, sir, that when these young men's works are exhibited at the Royal Academy in London, sir, people crowd round them, and go raving mad about them; while a gentlemanly portrait of a county member, with a Corinthian pillar and a crimson curtain, gets no more attention than if it was a bishop's half-length of black canvas. I am told so, sir, and I am obliged to believe it, sir."[125]

Poor Laura listened very impatiently to all this talk about painters and their pictures. But Mr. Kerstall the younger perceived her anxiety, and came to her relief.

"Lady Jocelyn would very much like to see the pictures you have scattered about in this room, my dear father," he said, "if you have no objection to our turning them over?"

The old man chuckled and nodded.

"You'll find 'em gentlemanly," he said; "you'll find 'em all more or less gentlemanly."

---

[125] John Everett Millais (1829-1896) and William Holman Hunt (1827-1910) were both founding members, with Dante Gabriel Rossetti (1828-1882), of the PRB. See note above.

"You're sure you don't remember painting the portrait of a Mr. Dunbar?" Mr. Kerstall the younger said, bending over his father's chair as he spoke. "Try again, father—try to remember—Henry Dunbar, the son of Percival Dunbar, the great banker."

Mr. Kerstall senior, who never left off smiling, nodded and chuckled, and scratched his head, and seemed to plunge into a depth of profound thought.

Laura began to hope again.

"I remember painting Sir Jasper Rivington, who was Lord Mayor in the year—bless my heart how the dates do slip out of my mind, to be sure!—I remember painting *him*, in his robes too; yes, sir—by gad, sir, his official robes. He'd like me to have painted him looking out of the window of his state-coach, sir, bowing to the populace on Ludgate Hill, with the dome of St. Paul's in the background; but I told him the notion wasn't practicable, sir; I told him it couldn't be done, sir; I——"

Laura looked despairingly at Mr. Kerstall the younger.

"May we see the pictures?" she asked. "I am sure that I shall recognize my father's portrait, if by any chance it should be amongst them."

"We will set to work at once, then," the artist said, briskly. "We're going to look at your pictures, father."

Unframed canvases, and unfinished sketches on millboard, were lying about the room in every direction, piled against the wall, heaped on side-tables, and stowed out of the way upon shelves, and everywhere the dust lay thick upon them.

"It was quite a chamber of horrors," Mr. Kerstall the younger said, gaily: for it was here that he banished his own failures; his sketches for his pictures that were to be painted upon some future occasion; carelessly-drawn groups that he meant some day to improve upon; finished pictures that he had been unable to sell; and all the other useless litter of an artist's studio.

There were a great many dingy performances of Mr. Kerstall senior; very classical, and extremely uninteresting; studies from the life, grey and chalky and muscular, with here and there a knotty-looking foot or a lumpy arm, in the most unpleasant phases of foreshortening. There were a good many portraits, gentlemanly to the last degree; but poor Laura looked in vain for the face she wanted to see—the hard cold face, as she fancied it must have been in youth.

There were portraits of elderly ladies with stately head-gear, and simpering young ladies with innocent short-waisted bodices and flowers held gracefully, in their white-muslin draperies; there were portraits of stern clerical grandees, and parliamentary non-celebrities, with popular bills rolled up in their hands, ready to be laid upon the speaker's table, and with a tight look about the lips, that seemed to say the member was prepared to carry his motion, or perish on the floor of the House.

There were only a few portraits of young men of military aspect, looking fiercely over regulation stocks, and with forked lightning and little pyramids of cannon-balls in the background.

Laura sighed heavily at last, for amongst all these portraits there was not one which in the least possible degree recalled the hard handsome face with which she was familiar.

"I'm afraid my father's picture has been lost or destroyed," she said, mournfully.

But Mr. Kerstall would not allow this.

I have said that it was Laura's peculiar privilege to bewitch everybody with whom she came in contact, and to transform them, for the nonce, into her willing slaves, eager to go through fire and water in the service of this beautiful creature, whose eyes and hair were like blue skies and golden sunshine, and carried light and summer wherever they went.

The black-bearded artist in the paint-smeared holland blouse was in no manner proof against Lady Jocelyn's fascinations.

He had well-nigh suffocated himself with dust half-a-dozen times already in her service, and was ready to inhale as much more dust if she desired him so to do.

"We won't give it up just yet, Lady Jocelyn," he said, cheerfully; "there's a couple of shelves still to examine. Suppose we try shelf number one, and see if we can find Mr. Henry Dunbar up there."

Mr. Kerstall junior mounted upon a chair, and brought down another heap of canvases, dirtier than any previous collection. He brought these to a table by the side of his father's easel, and one by one he wiped them clean with a large ragged silk handkerchief, and then placed them on the easel.

The easel stood in the full light of the broad window. The day was bright and clear, and there was no lack of light, therefore, upon the portraits.

Mr. Kerstall senior began to be quite interested in his son's proceedings, and contemplated the younger man's operations with a perpetual chuckling and nodding of the head, that were expressive of unmitigated satisfaction.

"Yes, they're gentlemanly," the old man mumbled; "nobody can deny that they're gentlemanly. They may make a cabal against me in Trafalgar Square, and decline to hang 'em: but they can't say my pictures are ungentlemanly. No, no. Take a basin of water and a sponge, Fred, and wash the dust off. It pleases me to see 'em again—yes, by gad, sir, it

263

pleases me to see 'em again!"

Mr. Frederick Kerstall obeyed his father, and the pictures brightened wonderfully under the influence of a damp sponge. It was rather a slow operation; but Laura was bent upon seeing every picture, and Philip Jocelyn waited patiently enough until the inspection should be concluded.

The old man brightened up as much as his paintings, and began presently to call out the names of the subjects.

"The member for Slopton-on-the-Tees," he said, as his son placed a portrait on the easel; "that was a presentation picture, but the subscriptions were never paid up, and the committee left the portrait upon my hands. I don't remember the name of the member, because my memory isn't quite so good as it used to be; but the borough was Slopton-on-the-Tees—Slopton—yes, yes, I remember that."

The younger Kerstall took away the member for Slopton, and put another picture on the easel. But this was like the rest; the pictured face bore no trace of resemblance to that face for which Laura was looking.

"I remember him too," the old man cried, with a triumphant chuckle. "He was an officer in the East-India Company's service. I remember him; a dashing young fellow he was too. He had the picture painted for his mother: paid me a third of the money at the first sitting; never paid me a sixpence afterwards; and went off to India, promising to send me a bill of exchange for the balance by the next mail; but I never heard any more of him."

Mr. Kerstall removed the Indian officer, and substituted another portrait.

Sir Philip, who was sitting near the window, looking on rather listlessly, cried—

"What a handsome face!"

It *was* a handsome face—a bright young face, which smiled haughty defiance at the world—a splendid face, with perhaps a shade of insolence in the curve of the upper lip, sharply defined under a thick auburn moustache, with pointed ends that curled fiercely upwards. It was such a face as might have belonged to the favourite of a powerful king; the face of the Cinq Mars, on the very summit of his giddy eminence, with a hundred pairs of boots in his dressing-room, and quiet Cardinal Richelieu watching silently for the day of his doom.[126] English Bucking-ham may have worn the same insolent smile upon his lips, the same

---

[126] Henri Coiffier de Ruzé, Marquis de Cinq Mars (1620-1642) was a favourite of Louis XIII of France and an enemy of Cardinal Armand Jean du Plessis de Richelieu (1585-1642). His conspiracies against the Cardinal failed, however, and Richelieu was responsible for Cinq Mars' imprisonment and subsequent execution.

bright triumph in his glance, when he walked up to the throne of Louis the Just, with the pearls and diamonds dropping from his garments as he went along, and with forbidden love beaming on him out of Austrian Anne's blue eyes.[127] It was such a face as could only belong to some high favourite of fortune, defiant of all mankind in the consciousness of his own supreme advantages.

But Laura Jocelyn shook her head as she looked at the picture.

"I begin to despair of finding my father's portrait," she said; "I have seen nothing at all like it yet."

The old man lifted up his bony hand, and pointed to the picture on the easel.

"That's the best thing I ever did," he said, "the very best thing I ever did. It was exhibited in the Academy six-and-thirty years ago—yes, by gad, sir, six-and-thirty years ago! and the papers mentioned it very favourably, sir; but the man who commissioned it, sent it back to me for alteration. The expression of the face didn't please him; but he paid me two hundred guineas for the picture, so I had no reason to complain; and if I'd remained in England, the connection might have been advantageous to me; for they were rich city people, sir—enormously wealthy—something in the banking-line, and the name, the name—let me see—let me see!"

The old man tapped his forehead thoughtfully.

"I remember," he added presently: "it was a great name in the City—it was a well-known name—Dun—Dunbar—Dunbar."

"Why, father, that was the very name I was asking you about, half an hour ago!"

"I don't remember your asking me any such thing," the old man answered, rather snappishly; "but I do know that the picture on that easel is the portrait of Mr. Dunbar's only son."

Mr. Kerstall the younger looked at Laura Jocelyn, full; expecting to see her face beaming with satisfaction; but, to his own surprise, she looked more disappointed than ever.

"Your poor father's memory deceives him," she said, in a low voice; "that is not my father's portrait."

"No," said Philip Jocelyn, "that was never the likeness of Henry Dunbar."

Mr. Frederick Kerstall shrugged his shoulders.

"I told you as much," he murmured, confidentially. "I told you my

---

[127] George Villiers, first Duke of Buckingham (1592-1628), favourite of James I of England. In *The Three Musketeers* (serialized 1844), Alexandre Dumas pere represents him as being the lover of Anne of Austria, the queen of Louis XIV.

poor father's memory was gone. Would you like to see the rest of the pictures?"

"Oh, yes, if you do not mind all this trouble."

Mr. Kerstall brought down another heap of unframed canvases from shelf number two. Some of these were fancy heads, and some sketches for grand historical pictures. There were only about four portraits, and not one of them bore the faintest likeness to the face that Laura wanted to see.

The old man chuckled as his son exhibited the pictures, and every now and then volunteered some scrap of information about these various works of art, to which his son listened patiently and respectfully.

So at last the inspection was ended. The baronet and his wife thanked the artist very warmly for his politeness, and Philip gave him a commission for a replica of the picture which Laura had admired in the Luxembourg. Mr. Frederick Kerstall conducted his guests down the dingy staircase, and saw them to the hired carriage that was waiting under the archway.

And this was all that came of Laura Jocelyn's search for her father's portrait.

- CHAPTER 37 -

MARGARET'S LETTER

Life seemed very blank to Clement Austin when he returned to London a day or two after Margaret Wilmot's departure from the Reindeer. He told his mother that he and his betrothed had parted; but he would tell no more.

"I have been cruelly disappointed, mother, and the subject is very bitter to me," he said; and Mrs. Austin had not the courage to ask any further questions.

"I suppose I *must* be satisfied, Clement," she said. "It seems to me as if we had been living lately in an atmosphere of enigmas. But I can afford to be contented, Clement, so long as I have you with me."

Clement went back to London. His life seemed to have altogether slipped away from him, and he felt like an old man who has lost all the bright chances of existence; the hope of domestic happiness and a pleasant home; the opportunity of a useful career and an honoured name; and who has nothing more to do but to wait patiently till the slow current of his empty life drops into the sea of death.

"I feel so old, mother," he said, sometimes; "I feel so old."

To a man who has been accustomed to be busy there is no affliction so intolerable as idleness.

Clement Austin felt this, and yet he had no heart to begin life again, though tempting offers came to him from great commercial houses, whose chiefs were eager to secure the well-known cashier of Messrs. Dunbar, Dunbar, and Balderby's establishment.

Poor Clement could not go into the world yet. His disappointment had been too bitter, and he had no heart to go out amongst hard men of business, and begin life again. He wasted hour after hour, and day after day, in gloomy thoughts about the past. What a dupe he had been! what a shallow, miserable fool! for he had believed as firmly in Margaret Wilmot's truth, as he had believed in the blue sky above his head.

One day a new idea flashed into Clement Austin's mind; an idea which placed Margaret Wilmot's character even in a worse light than that in which she had revealed herself in her own confession.

There could be only one reason for the sudden change in her sentiments about Henry Dunbar: the millionaire had bribed her to silence! This girl, who seemed the very incarnation of purity and candour, had her price, perhaps, as well as other people, and Henry Dunbar had bought the silence of his victim's daughter.

"It was the knowledge of this business that made her shrink away from me that night when she told me that she was a contaminated creature, unfit to be the associate of an honest man Oh, Margaret, Margaret! poverty must indeed be a bitter school if it has prepared you for such degradation as this!"

The longer Clement thought of the subject, the more certainly he arrived at the conclusion that Margaret Wilmot had been, either bribed or frightened into silence by Henry Dunbar. It might be that the banker had terrified this unhappy girl by some awful threat that had preyed upon her mind, and driven her from the man who loved her, whom she loved perhaps, in spite of those heartless words which she had spoken in the bitter hour of their parting.

Clement could not thoroughly believe in the baseness of the woman he had trusted. Again and again he went over the same ground, trying to find some lurking circumstance, no matter how unlikely in its nature, which should explain and justify Margaret's conduct.

Sometimes in his dreams he saw the familiar face looking at him with pensive, half-reproachful glances; and then a dark figure that was strange to him came between him and that gentle shadow, and thrust the vision away with a ruthless hand. At last, by dint of going over the ground again and again, always pleading Margaret's cause against the stern witness of cruel facts, Clement came to look upon the girl's innocence as a settled thing.

There was falsehood and treachery in the business, but Margaret Wilmot was neither false nor treacherous. There was a mystery, and Henry Dunbar was at the bottom of it.

"It seems as if the spirit of the murdered man troubled our lives, and cried to us for vengeance," Clement thought. "There will be no peace for us until the secret of the deed done in the grove near Winchester has been brought to light."

This thought, working night and day in Clement Austin's brain, gave rise to a fixed resolve. Before he went back to the quiet routine of life, he set himself a task to accomplish, and that task was the solution of the Winchester mystery.

On the very day after this resolution took a definite form, Clement received a letter from Margaret Wilmot. The sight of the well-known writing gave him a shock of mingled surprise and hope, and his fingers were faintly tremulous as they tore open the envelope. The letter was carefully worded, and very brief.

"You are a good man, Mr. Austin," Margaret wrote; *"and though you have reason to despise me, I do not think you will refuse to receive my testimony in favour of another who has been falsely suspected of a terrible crime, and who has need of justification. Henry Dunbar was not the murderer of my father. As Heaven is my witness, this is the truth, and I know it to be the truth. Let this knowledge content you, and allow the secret of the murder to remain for ever a mystery upon earth, God knows the truth, and has doubtless punished the wretched sinner who was guilty of that crime, as He punishes every other sinner, sooner or later, in the course of His ineffable wisdom. Leave the sinner, wherever he may be hidden, to the judgment of God, which penetrates every hiding-place; and forget that you have ever known me, or my miserable story.*

"MARGARET WILMOT."

Even this letter did not shake Clement Austin's resolution.

"No, Margaret," he thought; "even your pleading shall not turn me from my purpose. Besides, how can I tell in what manner this letter may have been written? It may have been written at Henry Dunbar's dictation, and under coercion. Be it as it may, the mystery of the Winchester murder shall be set at rest, if patience or intelligence can solve the enigma. No mystery shall separate me from the woman I love."

Clement put Margaret's letter in his pocket, and went straight to Scotland Yard, where he obtained an introduction to a businesslike-looking man, short and stoutly built, with close-cropped hair, very little shirt-collar, a shabby black satin stock, and a coat buttoned tightly across the chest. He was a man whose appearance was something between the aspect of a shabby-genteel half-pay captain and an unlucky stockbroker: but Clement liked the steady light of his small grey eyes, and the decided expression of his thin lips and prominent chin.

The detective business happened to be rather dull just now. There was nothing stirring but a Bank-of-England forgery case; and Mr. Carter informed Clement that there were more cats in Scotland Yard than could find mice to kill. Under these circumstances, Mr. Carter was able to enter into Clement's views, and sequestrate himself for a short period for the more deliberate investigation of the Winchester business.

"I'll look up a file of newspapers, and run my eye over the details of the case," said the detective. "I was away in Glasgow, hunting up the particulars of the great Scotch-plaid robberies, all last summer, and I can't say I remember much of what was done in the Wilmot business. Mr. Dunbar himself offered a reward for the apprehension of the guilty party, didn't he?"

"Yes; but that might be a blind."

"Oh, of course it might; but then, on the other hand, it mightn't. You must always look at these sort of things from every point of view. Start with a conviction of the man's guilt, and you'll go hunting up evidence to bolster that conviction. My plan is to begin at the beginning; learn the alphabet of the case, and work up into the syntax and prosody."

"I should like to help you in this business," Clement Austin said, "for I have a vital interest in the issue of the case."

"You're rather more likely to hinder than help, sir," Mr. Carter answered, with a smile; "but you're welcome to have a finger in the pie if you like, as long as you'll engage to hold your tongue when I tell you."

Clement promised to be the very spirit of discretion. The detective called upon him two days after the interview at Scotland Yard.

"I've read-up the Wilmot case, sir," Mr. Carter said; "and I think the next best thing I can do is to see the scene of the murder. I shall start for Winchester to-morrow morning."

"Then I'll go with you," Clement said, promptly.

"So be it, Mr. Austin. You may as well bring your cheque-book while you're about it, for this sort of thing is apt to come rather expensive."

- CHAPTER 38 -

NOTES FROM A JOURNAL KEPT BY CLEMENT AUSTIN
DURING HIS JOURNEY TO WINCHESTER

"If I had been a happy man, with no great trouble weighing upon my mind, and giving its own dull colour to every event of my life, I think I might have been considerably entertained by the society of Mr. Carter, the detective. The man had an enthusiastic love of his profession; and if there is anything degrading in the office, that degradation had in no way affected him. It may be that Mr. Carter's knowledge of his own usefulness was sufficient to preserve his self-respect. If, in the course of his duty, he had unpleasant things to do; if he had to affect friendly acquaintanceship with the man whom he was hunting to the gallows; if he was called upon to worm-out chance clues to guilty secrets in the careless confidence that grows out of a friendly glass; if at times he had to stoop to acts which, in other men, would be branded as shameful and treacherous, he knew that he did his duty, and that society could not hold together unless some such men as himself—clear-headed, brave, resolute, and unscrupulous in the performance of unpleasant work—were willing to act as watch-dogs for the protection of the general fold, and to the terror of savage and marauding beasts.

"Mr. Carter told me a great deal of his experience during our journey down to Winchester. I listened to him, and understood what he said to me; but I could not take any interest in his conversation. I could not remember anything, or think of anything, except the mystery which separates me from the woman I love.

"The more I think of this, the stronger becomes my conviction that I have not been the dupe of a heartless or mercenary woman. Margaret has not acted as a free agent. She has paid the penalty of her determination to force herself into the presence of Henry Dunbar. By some inexplicable means, by some masterpiece of villainy and cunning, this man has induced his victim's daughter to become the champion of his innocence, instead of the denouncer of his guilt.

"There must be some hopeless entanglement, some cruel involvement, by reason of which Margaret is compelled to falsify her nature, and sacrifice her own happiness as well as mine. When she left me that day at Shorncliffe, she suffered as cruelly as I could suffer: I know now that it was so. But I was blinded then by pride and anger: I was conscious of nothing but my own wrongs.

"Three times in the course of my journey from London to Winchester I have taken Margaret's strange letter from my pocket-book, and have read the familiar lines, with the idea of putting entire confidence in my companion, and placing the letter in his hands. But in order to do this I must tell him the story of my love and my disappointment; and I cannot bring myself to do that. It may be that this man could discover hidden meanings in Margaret's words—meanings that are utterly dark to me. I suppose the science of detection includes the power to guess at thoughts that lurk behind expressions which are simple enough in themselves."

*   *   *   *   *

"We got into Winchester at twelve o'clock in the day; and Mr. Carter proposed that we should come straight to the George Hotel, at which house Henry Dunbar stayed after the murder in the grove.

"'We can't do better than put up at the hotel where the suspected party was stopping at the time of the event we're looking up,' Mr. Carter said to me, as we strolled away from the station, after giving our small amount of luggage into the care of a porter; 'we shall pick up all manner of information in a promiscuous way, if we're staying in the house; little bits that will seem nothing at all till you put them all together, and begin at the beginning, and read them off the right way. Now, Mr. Austin, there's a few words I must say before we begin business; for you're an amateur at this kind of work, and it's just possible that, with the best intentions, you may go and spoil my game. Now I've undertaken this affair, and I want to go through with it conscientiously; under which circumstances I'm obliged to be candid. Are you willing to act under orders?'

"I told Mr. Carter that I was perfectly willing to obey his orders in everything, so long as what I did helped the purposes of our journey.

"'That's all square and pleasant,' he answered; 'so now for it. First and foremost, you and me are two gentlemen that have got more time than we know what to do with, and more money than we know how to spend. We've heard a great deal about the fishing round Winchester; and we've come down to spend an idle week or so, and have a look about the place against next summer; and if we like the looks of the place, why, we shall come and spend the summer months at the George, where we find the accommodation in general, and say the fried soles, or the mock-turtle, in particular, better than at any hotel in the three kingdoms. That's number one; and that places us at once on the footing of good customers, who are likely to be better customers. This will square the landlord and the waiters, and there's nothing they can tell us that they won't tell us willingly. So much for the first place. Now point number two is, that we know nothing whatever of the man that was murdered. We know Mr. Dunbar because he's a great man, a public character, and all that sort of thing. We did see something about the murder in the papers, but didn't take any interest in it. This will draw out the landlord or the waiters, as the case may be, and we shall get the history of the murder, with all that was said, and done, and thought, and suspected and hinted, and whispered about it. When the landlord and the waiters have talked about it a good deal, we begin to warm up, and take a kind of morbid interest in the business; and then, little by little, I put in my questions, and keep on putting 'em till every bit of information upon this particular subject is picked away as clean as the meat that's torn off a bone by a hungry dog. Now you'd like to help me in this business, I dare say, Mr. Austin; and if you would, I think I can hit upon a plan by which you might make yourself uncommonly useful.'

"I told my companion that I was very anxious to give him any help I could afford, however insignificant that help might be.

"'Then, I'll tell you what you can do. I shan't go at the subject we want to talk about at once; because, if I did, I should betray my interest in the business and spoil my game; not that anybody would try to thwart me, you understand, if they knew that I was detective officer Henry Carter, of Scotland Yard. They'd be all on the *qui vive*[128] directly they found out who I was, and what I was after, and they'd try to help me. That's what they'd do; and Tom would tell me this, and Dick would explain that, and Harry would remember the other; and among them they'd contrive to muddle the clearest head that ever worked a difficult problem in criminal Euclid.[129] My game is to keep myself dark, and get all the light I can from other people. I shan't ask any leading question, but I shall wait quietly till the murder of Joseph Wilmot crops up in the conversation; and I don't suppose I shall have to wait long. Your business will be easy enough. You'll have letters to write, you will; and as soon as ever you hear me and the landlord, or me and the waiter, as the case may be, working round to the murder, you'll take out your desk and begin to write.'

"'You want me to take notes of the conversation,' I said.

"'You've hit it. You won't appear to take any interest in the talk about

---

[128] To be on guard, on the alert.
[129] Greek mathematician, known as the "father of geometry". Carter's allusion echoes many other such analogies in Braddon's work, which suggest that detection is a kind of science.

Henry Dunbar and the murder of his valet. You'll be altogether wrapped up in those letters of yours, which must be written before the London post goes out; but you'll contrive to write down every word that's said by the people at the George bearing upon the business we're hunting up. Never mind my questions; don't write them down, for they're of no account. Write down the answers as plain as you can. They'll come all of a heap, or anyhow; but that's no matter. It'll be my business to sort 'em, and put 'em ship-shape afterwards. You just keep your mouth shut, and take notes, Mr. Austin; that's all you've got to do.'

"I promised to do this to the best of my ability. We were close to the George by this time, and I could not help thinking of that bright summer's day upon which Henry Dunbar and his victim had driven into Winchester on the first stage of a journey which one of them was never to finish. The conviction of the banker's guilt had so grown upon me since that scene in St. Gundolph Lane, that I thought of the man now almost as if he had been fairly tried and deliberately found guilty. It surprised me when the detective talked of his guilt as open to question, and yet to be proved. In my mind Henry Dunbar stood self-condemned, by the evidence of his own conduct, as the murderer of his old servant Joseph Wilmot.

"The weather was bleak and windy, and there were very few wanderers in the hilly High Street of Winchester. We were received with very courteous welcome at the George, and were conducted to a comfortable sitting-room upon the first-floor, with windows looking out upon the street. Two bedrooms in the vicinity of the sitting-room were assigned to us. I ordered dinner for six o'clock, having ascertained that hour to be agreeable to Mr. Carter, who was slowly removing his wrappings, and looking deliberately at every separate article in the room; as if he fancied there might be some scrap of information to be picked up from a window-blind, or a coal-scuttle, or lurking mysteries hidden in a sideboard-drawer. I have no doubt the habit of observation was so strong upon this man that he observed the most insignificant things involuntarily.

"It was a very dull unpleasant day, and I was glad to draw my chair to the fire and make myself comfortable, while the waiter went to fetch a bottle of soda-water and sixpenn'orth of 'best French' for my companion, who was walking about the room with his hands in his pockets, and his grizzled eyebrows knotted together.

"The reward which Government had offered for the arrest of Joseph Wilmot's murderer was the legitimate price usually bidden for the head of an assassin. The Government had offered to pay one hundred pounds to any person or persons who should give such information as would lead to the apprehension of the guilty party or parties. I had promised Mr. Carter that I would give him another hundred pounds on my own account if he succeeded in solving the mystery of Joseph Wilmot's death. The reward at stake was therefore two hundred pounds; and this was a pretty high stake, Mr. Carter told me, as the detective business went. I had given him my written engagement to pay the hundred pounds upon the day of the murderer's arrest, and I was very well able to do so without fear of being compelled to ask help of my mother; for I had saved upwards of a thousand pounds during my twelve years' service in the house of Dunbar, Dunbar, and Balderby.

"I saw from Mr. Carter's countenance that he was thinking, and thinking very earnestly. He drank the soda-water and brandy; but he said nothing to the waiter who brought him that popular beverage. When the man was gone, he came and planted himself opposite to me upon the hearth-rug.

"'I'm going to talk to you very seriously, sir,' he said.

"I assured him that I was quite ready to listen to anything he might have to say.

"'When you employ a detective officer, sir,' he began, 'don't employ a man you can't put entire confidence in. If you can't trust him don't have anything to do with him; for if he isn't to be trusted with the dearest family secret that ever was kept sacred by an honest man, why he's a scoundrel, and you're much better off without his help. But when you've got a man that has been recommended to you by those who know him, trust him, and don't be afraid to trust him, don't confide in him by halves; don't tell him one part of your story, and keep the other half hidden from him; because, you see, working in the twilight isn't much more profitable than working in the dark. Now, why do I say this to you, Mr. Austin? You know as well as I do. I say it because I know you haven't trusted me.'

"'I have told you all that was absolutely necessary for you to know,' I said.

"'Not a bit of it, sir. It's absolutely necessary for me to know everything: that is, if you want me to succeed in the business I'm engaged upon. You're afraid to give me your confidence out and out, without reserve. Lor' bless your innocence, sir; in my profession a man learns the use of his eyes; and when once he's learnt how to use them, it ain't easy for him to keep them shut. I know as well as you do that you're hiding something from me: you're keeping something back, though you've half a mind to trust me. You took out a letter three times while we were sitting opposite to each other in the railway carriage; and you read the letter; and every now and then, while you were reading it, you looked up at me with a hesitating you-would-and-you-wouldn't sort of look. You thought I was looking out of the window all the time; and so I was, being uncommonly interested in the corn-fields we were passing just then, so flat and stumpy and picturesque they looked; but, lor', Mr. Austin, if I couldn't look out of the window and watch you at the same time, I shouldn't be worth my salt to you or any one else. I saw plain enough that you had half a mind to show me that letter; and it wasn't very difficult to guess that the letter had some bearing upon the business that has brought us to Winchester.'

"Mr. Carter paused, and settled himself comfortably against the corner of the chimney-piece. I was not surprised that he should have read my thoughts in the railway carriage. I pondered the matter seriously. He was right in the main, no doubt; but how could I tell a detective officer my dearest secret—the sad story of my only love?

"'Trust me, Mr. Austin,' my companion said; 'if you want me to be of use to you, trust me thoroughly. The very thing you are hiding from me may be the clue I most want to get hold of.'

"'I don't think that,' I said. 'However, I have every reason to believe you to be an honest, conscientious fellow, and I will trust you. I dare say you wonder why I am so much interested in this business?'

"'Well, to tell the honest truth, sir, it does seem rather out of the common to see an independent gentleman like you taking all this trouble to find out the rights and wrongs of a murder committed going on for a twelvemonth ago: unless you're any relation of the murdered man: and even if you're that, you're very unlike the common run of relations, for they generally take such things quieter than anybody else,' answered Mr. Carter.

"I told the detective that I had never seen the murdered man in the course of my life, and had never heard his name until after the murder.

"'Well, sir, then all I can say is, I don't understand your motive,' returned, Mr. Carter.

"'Well, Carter, I think you're a good fellow, and I'll trust you,' I said; 'but, in order to do that, I must tell you a long story, and what's worse still, a love-story.'

"I felt that I blushed a little as I said this, and was ashamed of the false shame that brought that missish glow into my cheeks. Mr. Carter perceived my embarrassment, and was kind enough to encourage me.

"'Don't you be afraid of telling the story, because it's a sentimental one,' he said: 'Lor' bless you, I've heard plenty of love-stories. There ain't many bits of business come our way but what, if you sift 'em to the bottom, you find a petticoat. You remember the Oriental bloke that always asked, 'Who is she?' when he heard of a fight, or a fire, or a mad bull broke loose, or any trifling calamity of that sort; because, according to his views, a female was at the bottom of everything bad that ever happened upon this earth. Well, sir, if that Oriental potentate had lived in our times, and been brought up to the detective line, I'm blest if he need have changed his opinions. So don't you be ashamed of telling a love-story, sir. I was in love myself once, though I do seem such a dry old chip; and I married the woman I loved too; and she was a pretty little country girl, as fresh and innocent as the daisies in her father's paddocks; and to this day she don't know what my business really is. She thinks I'm something in the City, bless her dear little heart!'

"This touch of sentiment in Mr. Carter's conversation was quite unaffected, and I felt all the more inclined to trust him after this little revelation of his domestic life. I told him the story of my acquaintance with Margaret, very briefly giving him only the necessary details. I told him of the girl's several efforts to see Henry Dunbar, and the banker's persistent avoidance of her. I told him then of our journey to Shorncliffe, and Margaret's strange conduct after her interview with the man she had been so eager to see.

"The telling of this, though I told it briefly, occupied nearly an hour. Mr. Carter sat opposite me all the time, listening intently; staring at me with one fixed unvarying stare, and fingering musical passages upon his knees, with slow cautious motions of his fingers and thumbs. But I could see that he was not listening only: he was pondering and reasoning upon what I told him. When I had finished my story, he remained silent for some minutes: but he still stared at me with the same relentless and stony gaze, and he still fingered his knees, following up his right hand with his left, as slowly and deliberately as if he had been composing a fugue after the manner of Mendelssohn.[130]

"'And up to the time of that interview at Maudesley Abbey, Miss Wilmot had stuck to the idea that Henry Dunbar was the murderer of her father?' he said, at last.

"'Most resolutely.'

"'And after that interview the young lady changed her opinion all of a sudden, and would have it that the banker was innocent?' asked Mr. Carter.

"'Yes; when Margaret returned from Maudesley Abbey she declared her conviction of Henry Dunbar's innocence.'

"'And she refused to fulfil her engagement with you?'

"'She did.'

---

[130] Jakob Ludwig Felix Mendelssohn Bartholdy (1809-1847), German composer and pianist.

"The detective left off fingering fugues upon his knees, and began to scratch his head, slowly pushing his hand up and down amongst his iron-grey hair, and staring at me. I saw now that this stony glare was only the fixed expression of Mr. Carter's face when he was thinking profoundly, and that the relentlessness of his gaze had very little relation to the object at which he gazed.

"I watched his face as he pondered, in the hope of seeing some sudden mental illumination light up his stolid countenance: but I watched in vain. I saw that he was at fault: I saw that Margaret Wilmot's conduct was quite as inexplicable to him as it had been to me.

"'Mr. Dunbar's a very rich man,' he said, at last; 'and money generally goes a good way in these cases. There was a political party, Sir Robert somebody—but not Sir Robert Peel—who said, 'Every man has his price.'[131] Now, do you think it possible that Miss Wilmot would take a bribe, and hold her tongue?'

"'Do I think that she would take money from the man she suspected as the murderer of her father—the man she knew to have been the enemy of her father? No,' I answered, resolutely; 'I am certain that she is incapable of any such baseness. The idea that she had been bribed flashed across me in the first bitterness of my anger: but even then I dismissed it as incredible. Now that I can think coolly of the business, I know that such an alternative is impossible. If Margaret Wilmot has been influenced by Henry Dunbar, it is upon her terror that he has acted. Heaven knows how he may have threatened her! The man who could lure his old servant into a lonely wood and there murder him—the man who, neither early nor late, had one touch of pity for the tool and accomplice of his youthful crime—not one lingering spark of compassion for the humble friend who sacrificed an honest name in order to serve his master—would have little compunction in torturing a friendless girl who dared to come before him in the character of an accuser.'

"'But you say that Miss Wilmot was resolute and high-spirited. Is she a likely person to be governed by her terror of Mr. Dunbar? What threat could he use to terrify her?'

"I shook my head hopelessly.

"'I am as ignorant as you are,' I said; 'but I have strong reason to believe that Margaret Wilmot was under the influence of some great terror when she returned from Maudesley Abbey.'

"'What reason?' asked Mr. Carter.

---

[131] Carter is referring to Sir Robert Walpole, 1st Earl of Oxford (1676-1745), British statesman, Whig politician, and de facto Prime Minister between 1721 and 1745.

"'Her manner was sufficient evidence that she had been frightened. Her face was as white as a sheet of paper when I met her, and she trembled and shrank away from me, as if even my presence was horrible to her.'

"'Could you manage to repeat what she said that night and the next morning?'

"It was not very pleasant to me to re-open my wounds for the benefit of Mr. Carter the detective; but it would have been absurd to thwart the man when he was working in my interests. I loved Margaret too well to forget anything she ever said to me, even in our happiest and most careless hours: and I had special reason to remember that cruel farewell interview, and the strange scene in the corridor at the Reindeer, on the night of her return from Maudesley Abbey. I went over all this ground again, therefore, for Mr. Carter's edification, and told him, word for word, all that Margaret had said to me. When I had finished, he relapsed once more into a reverie, during which I sat listening to the ticking of an eight-day clock in the passage outside our sitting-room, and the occasional tramp of a passing footstep on the pavement below our windows.

"'There's only one thing strikes me very particular in all you've told me,' the detective said, by-and-by, when I had grown tired of watching him, and had suffered my thoughts to wander back to the happy time in which Margaret and I had loved and trusted each other; 'there's only one thing strikes me in all the young lady said to you, and that is these words—'There is contamination in my touch,' Miss Wilmot says to you. 'I am unfit to be the associate of an honest man,' Miss Wilmot says to you. Now, that looks as if she had been bought over somehow or other by Mr. Dunbar. I've turned it over in my mind every way; and however I reckon it up, that's about what it comes to. The young woman was bought over, and she was ashamed of herself for being bought over.'

"I told Mr. Carter that I could never bring myself to believe this.

"'Perhaps not, sir, but it may be gospel truth for all that. There's no other way I can account for the young woman's carryings on. If Mr. Dunbar was innocent, and had contrived, somehow or other, to convince the young woman of his innocence, why, she'd have come to you free and open, and would have said, 'My dear, I've made a mistake about Mr. Dunbar, and I'm very sorry for it; but we must look somewhere else for my poor pa's murderer.' But what does the young woman do? She goes and scrapes herself along the passage-wall, and shudders and shivers, and says, 'I'm a wretch; don't touch me—don't come near me.' It's just like a woman, to take the bribe, and then be sorry for having taken it.'

"I said nothing in answer to this. It was inexpressibly obnoxious to me to hear my poor Margaret spoken of as 'a young woman' by my business-like companion. But there was no possibility of keeping any veil over the sacred mysteries of my heart. I wanted Mr. Carter's help. For the present Margaret was lost to me; and my only hope of penetrating the hidden cause of her conduct lay in Mr. Carter's power to solve the dark enigma of Joseph Wilmot's death.

"'Oh, by the bye,' exclaimed the detective, 'there was a letter, wasn't there?'

"He held out his hand as I searched for the letter in my pocket-book. What a greedy, inquisitive-looking palm it seemed! and how I hated Mr. Henry Carter, detective officer, at that particular moment!

"I gave him the letter; and I did not groan aloud as I handed it to him. He read it slowly, once, twice, three times—half-a-dozen times, I think, in all—pushing the fingers of his left hand through his hair as he read, and frowning at the paper before him. It was while he was reading the letter for the last time that I saw a sudden glimmer of light in his hard eyes, and a half-smile playing round his thin lips.

"'Well?' I said, interrogatively, as he gave me back the letter.

"'Well, sir, the young lady,'—Mr. Carter called Margaret a young lady this time, and I could not help thinking that her letter had revealed her to him as something different from the ordinary class of female popularly described as a young woman,—'the young lady was in earnest when she wrote that letter, sir,' he said; 'it wasn't written under dictation, and she wasn't bribed to write it. There's heart in it, sir, if I may be allowed the expression: there's a woman's heart in that letter: and when a woman's heart is once allowed scope, a woman's brains shrivel up like so much tinder. I put this letter to that speech in the corridor at the Reindeer, Mr. Austin; and out of those two twos I verily believe I can make the queerest four that was ever reckoned up by a first-class detective.'

"A faint flush, which looked like a glow of pleasure, kindled all over Mr. Carter's sallow face as he spoke, and he got up and walked about the room; not slowly or thoughtfully, but with a brisk eager tread that was new to me. I could see that his spirits had risen a great many degrees since the reading of the letter.

"'You have got some clue,' I said; 'you see your way——'

"He turned round and checked my eager curiosity by a warning gesture of his uplifted hand.

"'Don't be in a hurry, sir,' he said, gravely; 'when you lose your way of a dark night, in a swampy country, and see a light ahead, don't begin to clap your hands and cry hooray till you know what kind of light it is. It may be a Jack-o'-lantern; or it may be the identical lamp over the door of the house you're bound for. You leave this business to me, Mr. Austin, and don't you go jumping at conclusions. I'll work it out quietly: and when I've worked it out I'll tell you what I think of it. And now suppose we take a stroll through the cathedral-yard, and have a look at the place where the body was found.'

"'How shall we find out the exact spot?' I asked, while I was putting on my hat and overcoat.

"'Any passer-by will point it out,' Mr. Carter answered; 'they don't have a popular murder in the neighbourhood of Winchester every day; and when they do, I make not the least doubt they know how to appreciate the advantage. You may depend upon it, the place is pretty well known.'

"It was nearly five o'clock by this time. We went down the slippery oak-staircase, and out into the quiet street. A bleak wind was blowing down from the hills, and the rooks' nests high up in the branches of the old trees about the cathedral were rocking like that legendary cradle in the tree-top. I had never been in Winchester before, and I was pleased with the quaint old houses, the towering cathedral, the flat meadows, and winding streams of water rippled by the wind. I was soothed, somehow or other, by the peculiar quiet of the scene; and I could not help thinking that, if a man's life was destined to be miserable, Winchester would be a nice place for him to be miserable in. A dreamy, drowsy, forgotten city, where the only changes of the slow day would be the varying chimes of the cathedral clock, the different tones of the cathedral bells.

"Mr. Carter had studied every scrap of evidence connected with the murder of Joseph Wilmot. He pointed out the door at which Henry Dunbar had gone into the cathedral, the pathway which the two men had taken as they went towards the grove. We followed this pathway, and walked to the very place in which the murdered man had been found.

"A lad who was fishing in one of the meadows near the grove went with us to show us the exact spot. It was between an elm and a beech.

"'There's not many beeches in the grove,' the lad said, 'and this is the biggest of them. So that it's easy enough for any one to pick out the spot. It was very dry weather last August at the time of the murder, and the water wasn't above half as deep as it is now.'

"'Is it the same depth every where?' Mr. Carter asked.

"'Oh, dear no,' the boy said; 'that's what makes these streams so dangerous for bathing: they're shallow enough in some places; but there's all manner of holes about; and unless you're a good swimmer, you'd better not try it on.'

"Mr. Carter gave the boy sixpence and dismissed him. We strolled a little farther on, and then turned and went back towards the cathedral. My companion was very silent, and I could see that he was still thinking. The change that had taken place in his manner after he had read Margaret's letter had inspired me with new confidence in him, and I was better able to await the working out of events. Little by little the solemn nature of the business in which I was engaged grew and gathered force in my mind, and I felt that I had something more to do than to solve the mystery of Margaret's conduct to myself: I had to perform a duty to society, by giving my uttermost help towards the discovery of Joseph Wilmot's murderer.

"If the heartless assassin of this wretched man was suffered to live and prosper, to hold up his head as the master of Maudesley Abbey, the chief partner in a great City firm that had borne an honourable name for a century and a half, a kind of premium was offered to crime in high places. If Henry Dunbar had been some miserable starving creature, who, in a fit of mad fury against the inequalities of life, had lifted his gaunt arm to slay his prosperous brother for the sake of bread—detectives would have dogged his sneaking steps, and watched his guilty face, and hovered round and about him till they tracked him to his doom. But because in this case the man to whom suspicion pointed had the supreme virtues comprised in a million of money, Justice wore her thickest bandage, and the officials, who are so clever in tracking a low-born wretch to the gallows, held aloof, and said respectfully, 'Henry Dunbar is too great a man to be guilty of a diabolical crime.'

"These thoughts filled my mind as I walked back to the George Hotel with Mr. Carter.

"It was half-past six when we entered the house, and we had kept dinner waiting half an hour, much to the regret of the most courteous of waiters, who expressed intense anxiety about the condition of the fish.

"As the man hovered about us at dinner, I expected every moment that Mr. Carter would lead up to the only topic which had any interest either for himself or me. But he was slow to do this; he talked of the town, the last assizes, the state of the country, the weather, the prosperity of the trout-fishing season—everything except the murder of Joseph Wilmot. It was only after dinner, when some petrified specimens of dessert, in the shape of almonds and raisins, figs and biscuits, had been arranged on the table, that any serious business began. The preliminary skirmishing had not been without its purpose, however; for the waiter had been warmed into a communicative and confidential mood, and was now ready to tell us anything he knew.

"I delegated all our arrangements to my companion; and it was something wonderful to see Mr. Carter lolling in his arm-chair with what he called the 'wine-cart' in his hand, deliberating between a forty-two port, 'light and elegant,' and a forty-five port, 'tawny and rich bouquet.'

"'I think we may as well try number fifteen,' he said, handing the list of wines to the waiter after due consideration; 'and decant it carefully, whatever you do. I hope your cellar isn't cold.'

"'Oh, no, sir; master's very careful of his cellar, sir.'

"The waiter went away impressed with the idea that he had to deal with a couple of connoisseurs.

"'You've got those letters to write before ten o'clock, eh, Mr. Austin?' said the detective, as the waiter re-entered the room with a decanter on a silver salver.

"I understood the hint, and accordingly took my travelling-desk to a side-table near the fireplace. Mr. Carter handed me one of the wax-candles, and I sat down before the little table, unlocked my desk, and began to write a few lines to my mother; while the detective smacked his lips and knowingly deliberated over his first glass of port.

"'Very decent quality of wine,' he said, 'very decent. Do you know where your master got it, eh? No, you don't. Ah! bottled it himself, I suppose. I thought he might have got it at the Warren-Court sale the other day, at the other end of the county. Fill a glass for yourself, waiter, and put the decanter down by the fender; the wine's rather cold. By the bye, I heard your wines very well spoken of the other day, by a person of some importance, too—of considerable importance, I may say.'

"'Indeed, sir,' murmured the waiter, who was standing at a respectful distance from the table, and was sipping his wine with deferential slowness.

"'Yes; I heard your house spoken of by no less a person than Mr. Dunbar, the great banker.'

"The waiter pricked up his ears. I pushed aside the letter to my mother, and waited with a blank sheet of paper before me.

"'That was a very strange affair, by the by,' said Mr. Carter. 'Fill yourself another glass of wine, waiter; my friend here doesn't drink port; and if you don't help me to put away that bottle, I shall take too much. Were you examined at the inquest on Joseph Wilmot?'

"'No, sir,' answered the waiter, eagerly. 'I were not, sir; and they do say as we ought every one of us to have been examined; for you see there's little facks as one person will notice and as another won't notice, and it isn't a man's place to come forward with every little trivial thing, you see, sir; but if little trivial things was drawn out of one and another, they might help, you see, sir.'

"There could be no end gained by taking notes of this reply, so I amused myself by making a good nib to my pen while I waited for something better worth jotting down.

"'Some of your people were examined, I suppose?' said Mr. Carter.

"'Oh, yes, sir,' answered the waiter; 'master, he were examined, to begin with; and then Brigmawl, the head-waiter, he give his evidence; but, lor', sir, without unfriendliness to William Brigmawl, which me and Brigmawl have been fellow-servants these eleven year, our head-waiter is that wrapped up in hisself, and his own cravats, and shirt-fronts, and gold studs, and Albert chain, that he'd scarcely take notice of an earthquake swallering up half the world before his eyes, unless the muck and dirt of that earthquake was to spoil his clothes. William Brigmawl has been head-waiter in this house nigh upon thirty year; and beyond a stately way of banging-to a carriage-door, or showing visitors to their rooms, or poking a fire, and a kind of knack of leading on timid people to order expensive wines, I really don't see Brigmawl's great merit. But as to Brigmawl at an inquest, he's about as much good as the Pope of Rome.'

"'But why was Brigmawl examined in preference to any one else?'

"'Because he was supposed to know more of the business than any of us, being as it was him that took the order for the dinner. But me and Eliza Jane, the under-chambermaid, was in the hall at the very moment when the two gentlemen came in.'

"'You saw them both, then?'

"'Yes, sir, as plain as I now see you. And you might have knocked me down with a feather when I was told afterwards that the one who was murdered was nothing more than a valet.'

"'You're not getting on very fast with your letters,' said Mr. Carter, looking over his shoulder at me.

"'I had written nothing yet, and I understood this as a hint to begin. I wrote down the waiter's last remark.

"'Why were you so surprised to find he was a valet?' Mr. Carter asked of the waiter.

"'Because, you see, sir, he had the look of a gentleman,' the man answered; 'an out-and-out gentleman. It wasn't that he held his head higher than Mr. Dunbar, or that he was better dressed—for Mr. Dunbar's clothes looked the newest and best; but he had a kind of languid don't-careish way that seems to be peculiar to first-class gentlemen.'

"'What sort of a looking man was he?'

"'Paler than Mr. Dunbar, and thinner built, and fairer.'

"I jotted down the waiter's remarks; but I could not help thinking that this talk about the murdered man's manner and appearance was about as useless as anything could be.

"'Paler and thinner than Mr. Dunbar,' repeated the detective; 'paler and thinner, eh? This was one thing you noticed; but what was it, now, that you could have said at the inquest if you had been called as a witness?'

"'Well, sir, I'll tell you. It's a small matter, and I've mentioned it many a time, both to William Brigmawl and to others; but they talk me down, and say I was mistaken; and Eliza Jane being a silly giggling hussey, can't bear me out in what I say. But I do most solemnly declare that I speak the truth, and am not deceived. When the two gentlemen—which gentlemen they both was to look at—came into our hall, the one that was murdered had his coat buttoned tight across his chest, except one button; and through the space left by that one button I saw the glitter of a gold chain.'

"'Well, what then?'

"'The other gentleman, Mr. Dunbar, had his coat open as he got out of the carriage, and I saw as plain as ever I saw anything, that he had no gold-chain. But two minutes after he had come into the hall, and while he was ordering dinner, he took and buttoned his coat. Well, sir, when he came in, after visiting the cathedral, his coat was partially unbuttoned and I saw that he wore a gold-chain, and, unless I am very much mistaken, the same gold-chain that I had seen peeping out of the breast of the murdered man. I could almost have sworn to that chain because of the colour of the gold, which was a particular deep yaller. It was only afterwards that these things came back to my mind, and I certainly thought them very strange.'

"'Was there anything else?'

"'Nothing; except what Brigmawl dropped out one night at supper, some weeks after the inquest, about his having noticed Mr. Dunbar opening his desk while he was waiting for Joseph Wilmot to come home to dinner; and Brigmawl do say, now that it ain't a bit of use, that Mr. Dunbar, do what he would, couldn't find the key of his own desk for ever so long.'

"'He was confused, I suppose; and his hands trembled, eh?' asked the detective.

"'No, sir; according to what Brigmawl said, Mr. Dunbar seemed as cool and collected as if he was made of iron. But he kept trying first one key and then another, for ever so long, before he could find the right one.'

"'Did he now? that was queer.'

"'But I hope you won't think anything of what I've let drop, sir,' said the waiter, hastily. 'I'm sure I wouldn't say any thing disrespectful against Mr. Dunbar; but you asked me what I saw, sir, and I have told you candid, and——'

"'My good fellow, you're perfectly safe in talking to me,' the detective answered, heartily. 'Suppose you bring us a little strong tea, and clear away this dessert; and if you've anything more to tell us, you can say it while you're pouring out the tea. There's so much connected with these sort of things that never gets into the papers, that really it's quite interesting to hear of 'em from an eye-witness.'

"The waiter went away, pleased and re-assured, after clearing the table very slowly. I was impatient to hear what Mr. Carter had gathered from the man's talk.

"'Well,' he said, 'unless I'm very much mistaken, I think I've got my friend the master of Maudesley Abbey.'

"'You do; but how so?' I asked. 'That talk about the gold-chain having changed hands must be utterly absurd. What should Henry Dunbar want with Joseph Wilmot's watch and chain?'

"'Ah, you're right there,' answered Mr. Carter. 'What should Henry Dunbar want with Joseph Wilmot's gold chain? That's one question. Why should Joseph Wilmot's daughter be so anxious to screen Henry Dunbar now that she has seen him for the first time since the murder? There's another question for you. Find the answer for it, if you can.

"I told the detective that he seemed bent upon mystifying me, and that he certainly succeeded to his heart's content.

"Mr. Carter laughed a triumphant little laugh.

"'Never you mind, sir,' he said; you leave it to me, and you watch it well, sir. It'll work out very neatly, unless I'm altogether wrong. Wait for the end, Mr. Austin, and wait patiently. Do you know what I shall do to-morrow?'

"'I haven't the faintest idea.'

"'I shall waste no more time in asking questions. I shall have the water near the scene of the murder dragged. I shall try and find the clothes that were stripped off the man who was murdered last August!'"

- CHAPTER 39 -

CLEMENT AUSTIN'S JOURNAL CONTINUED

"The rest of the evening passed quietly enough. Mr. Carter drank his strong tea, and then asked my permission to go out and smoke a couple of cigars in the High Street. He went, and I finished my letter to my mother. There was a full moon, but it was obscured every now and then by the black clouds that drifted across it. I went out myself to post the letter, and I was glad to feel the cool breeze blowing the hair away from my forehead, for the excitement of the day had given me a nervous headache.

"I posted my letter in a narrow street near the hotel. As I turned away from the post-office to go back to the High Street, I was startled by the apparition of a girlish figure upon the other side of the street—a figure so like Margaret's that its presence in that street filled me with a vague sense of fear, as if the slender figure, with garments fluttering in the wind, had been a phantom.

"Of course I attributed this feeling to its right cause, which was doubtless neither more nor less than the over-excited state of my own brain. But I was determined to set the matter quite at rest, so I hurried across the way and went close up to the young lady, whose face was completely hidden by a thick veil.

"'Miss Wilmot—Margaret,' I said.

"I had thought it impossible that Margaret should be in Winchester, and I was only right, it seemed, for the young lady drew herself away from me abruptly and walked across the road, as if she mistook my error in addressing her for an intentional insult. I watched her as she walked rapidly along the narrow street, until she turned sharply away at a corner and disappeared. When I first saw her, as I stood by the post-office, the moonlight had shone full upon her. As she went away the moon was hidden by a fleecy grey cloud, and the street was wrapped in shadow. Thus it was only for a few moments that I distinctly saw the outline of her figure. Her face I did not see at all.

"I went back to the hotel and sat by the fire trying to read a newspaper, but unable to chain my thoughts to the page. Mr. Carter came in a little before eleven o'clock. He was in very high spirits, and drank a tumbler of steaming brandy-and-water with great gusto. But question him how I might, I could get nothing from him except that he meant to have a search made for the dead man's clothes.

"I asked him why he wanted them, and what advantage would be gained by the finding of them, but he only nodded his head significantly, and told me to wait.

*   *   *   *   *

"To-day has been most wretched—a day of miserable discoveries; and yet not altogether miserable, for the one grand discovery of the day has justified my faith in the woman I love.

"The morning was cold and wet. There was not a ray of sunshine in the dense grey sky, and the flat landscape beyond the cathedral seemed almost blotted out by the drizzling rain; only the hills, grand and change-less, towered above the mists, and made the landmarks of the soddened country.

"We took an early and hasty breakfast. Quiet and business-like as the detective's manner was even to-day, I could see that he was excited. He took nothing but a cup of strong tea and a few mouthfuls of dry toast, and then put on his coat and hat.

"'I'm going down to the chief quarters of the county constabulary, he said. 'I shall be obliged to tell the truth about my business down there, because I want every facility for what I'm going to do. If you'd like to see the water dragged, you can meet me at twelve o'clock in the grove. You'll find me superintending the work.'

"It was about half-past eight when Mr. Carter left me. The time hung very heavily on my hands between that time and eleven o'clock. At eleven I put on my hat and overcoat and went out into the rain.

"I found my friend the detective standing in one of the smaller entrances of the cathedral, in very earnest conversation with an old man. As Mr. Carter gave me no token of recognition, I understood that he did not want me to interrupt his companion's talk, so I walked slowly on by the same pathway along which we had gone on the previous afternoon; the same pathway by which the murdered man had gone to his death.

"I had not walked half a mile before I was joined by the detective.

"'I gave you the office just now,' he said, 'because I thought if you spoke to me, that old chap would leave off talking, and I might miss something that was on the tip of his tongue.'

"'Did he tell you much?'

"'No; he's the man who gave his evidence at the inquest. He gave me a minute description of Henry Dunbar's watch and chain. The watch didn't open quite in the usual manner, and the gentleman was rather awkward in opening it, my friend the verger tells me. He was awkward with the key of his desk. He seems to have had a fit of awkwardness that day.'

"'You think that he was guilty, and that he was confused and agitated by the hideous business he had been concerned in?'

"Mr. Carter looked at me with a very queer smile on his face.

"'You're improving, Mr. Austin,' he said; 'you'd make a first-class detective in next to no time.'

"I felt rather doubtful as to the meaning of this compliment, for there was something very like irony in Mr. Carter's tone.

"'I'll tell you what I think,' he said, stopping presently, and taking me by the button-hole. 'I think that I know why the murdered man's coat, waistcoat, and shirt were stripped off him.'

"I begged the detective to tell me what he thought upon this subject; but he refused to do so.

"'Wait and see,' he said; 'if I'm right, you'll soon find out what I mean; if I'm wrong, I'll keep my thoughts to myself. I'm an old hand, and I don't want to be found out in a mistake.'

"I said no more after this. The disappearance of the murdered man's clothes had always appeared to me the only circumstance that was irreconcilable with the idea of Henry Dunbar's guilt. That some brutal wretch, who stained his soul with blood for the sake of his victim's poor possessions, should strip off the clothes of the dead, and make a market even out of them, was probable enough. But that Henry Dunbar, the wealthy, hyper-refined Anglo-Indian, should linger over the body of his valet and offer needless profanation to the dead, was something incredible, and not to be accounted for by any theory whatever.

"This was the one point which, from first to last, had completely baffled me.

"We found the man with the drags waiting for us under the dripping trees. Mr. Carter had revealed himself to the constabulary as one of the chief luminaries of Scotland Yard; and if he had wanted to dig up the foundations of the cathedral, they would scarcely have ventured to interfere with his design. One of the constables was lounging by the water's edge, watching the men as they prepared for business.

"I have no need to write a minute record of that miserable day. I know that I walked up and down, up and down, backwards and forwards, upon the soddened grass, from noon till sundown, always thinking that I would go away presently, always lingering a little longer; hindered by the fancy that Mr. Carter's search was on the point of being successful. I know that for hour after hour the grating sound of the iron drags grinding on the gravelly bed of the stream sounded in my tired ears, and yet there was no result. I know that rusty scraps of worn-out hardware, dead bodies of cats and dogs, old shoes laden with pebbles, rank entanglements of vegetable corruption, and all manner of likely and unlikely rubbish, were dragged out of the stream, and thrown aside upon the bank.

"The detective grew dirtier and slimier and wetter as the day wore on; but still he did not lose heart.

"'I'll have every inch of the bed of the stream, and every hidden hole in the bottom, dragged ten times over, before I'll give it up,' he said to me, when he came to me at dusk with some brandy that had been brought by a boy who had been fetching beer, more or less, all the afternoon.

"When it grew dark, the men lighted a couple of flaring resinous torches, which Mr. Carter had sent for towards dusk, and worked, by the patches of fitful light which these torches threw upon the water. I still walked up and down under the dripping trees, in the darkness, as I had walked in the light; and once when I was farthest from the red glare of the torches, a strange fancy took possession of me. In amongst the dim branches of the trees I thought I saw something moving, something that reminded me of the figure I had seen opposite the post-office on the previous night.

"I ran in amongst the trees; and as I did so, the figure seemed to me to recede, and disappear; a faint rustling of a woman's dress sounded in my ears, or seemed so to sound, as the figure melted from my sight. But again I had good reason to attribute these fancies to the state of my own brain, after that long day of anxiety and suspense.

"At last, when I was completely worn out by my weary day, Mr. Carter came to me.

"'They're found!' he cried. 'We've found 'em! We've found the murdered man's clothes! They've been drifted away into one of the deepest holes there is, and the rats have been gnawing at 'em. But, please Providence, we shall find what we want. I'm not much of a church-goer, but I do believe there's a Providence that lies in wait for wicked men, and catches the very cleverest of them when they least expect it.'

"I had never seen Mr. Carter so much excited as he seemed now. His face was flushed, and his nostrils quivered nervously.

"I followed him to the spot where the constable and two men, who had been dragging the stream, were gathered round a bundle of wet rubbish lying on the ground.

"Mr. Carter knelt down before this bundle, which was covered with trailing weeds and moss and slime, and the constable stooped over him with a flaming torch in his hand.

"'These are somebody's clothes, sure enough,' the detective said; 'and, unless I'm very much mistaken, they're what I want. Has anybody got a basket?'

"Yes. The boy who had fetched beer had a basket. Mr. Carter stuffed the slimy bundle into this basket, and put his arm through the handle.

"'You're not going to look 'em over here, then?' said the local constable, with an air of disappointment.

"'No, I'll take them straight to my hotel; I shall have plenty of light there. You can come with me, if you like,' Mr. Carter answered.

"He paid the men, who had been at work all day, and paid them liberally, I suppose, for they seemed very well satisfied. I had given him money for any expenses such as these; for I knew that, in a case of this kind, every insignificant step entailed the expenditure of money.

"We walked homewards as rapidly as the miserable state of the path, the increasing darkness, and the falling rain would allow us to walk. The constable walked with us. Mr. Carter whistled softly to himself as he went along, with the basket on his arm. The slimy green stuff and muddy water dripped from the bottom of the basket as he carried it.

"I was still at a loss to understand the reason of his high spirits; I was still at a loss to comprehend why he attached so much importance to the finding of the dead man's clothes.

"It was past eight o'clock when we three men—the detective, the Winchester constable, and myself—entered our sitting-room at the George Hotel. The principal table was laid for dinner; and the waiter, our friend of the previous evening, was hovering about, eager to receive us. But Mr. Carter sent the waiter about his business.

"'I've got a little matter to settle with this gentleman,' he said, indicating the Winchester constable with a backward jerk of his thumb; 'I'll ring when I want dinner.'

"I saw the waiter's eyes open to an abnormal extent, as he looked at the constable, and I saw a sudden blank apprehension creep over his face, as he retired very slowly from the room.

"'Now,' said Mr. Carter, 'we'll examine the bundle.'

"He pushed away the dinner-table, and drew forward a smaller table. Then he ran out of the room, and returned in about two minutes, carrying with him all the towels he had been able to find in my room and his own, which were close at hand. He spread the towels on the table, and then took the slimy bundle from the basket.

"'Bring me the candles—both the candles,' he said to the constable.

"The man held the two wax-candles on the right hand of the detective, as he sat before the table. I stood on his left hand, watching him intently.

"He touched the ragged and mud-stained bundle as carefully as if it had been some living thing. Foul river-insects crept out of the weeds, which were so intermingled with the tattered fabrics that it was difficult to distinguish one substance from the other.

"Mr. Carter was right: the rats had been at work. The outer part of the bundle was a coat—a cloth coat, gnawed into tatters by the sharp teeth of water-rats.

"Inside the coat there was a waistcoat, a satin scarf that was little better than a pulp, and a shirt that had once been white. Inside the white shirt there was a flannel shirt, out of which there rolled half-a-dozen heavy stones. These had been used to sink the bundle, but were not so heavy as to prevent its drifting into the hole where it had been found.

"The bundle had been rolled up very tightly, and the outer garment was the only one which had been destroyed by the rats. The inner garment—the flannel shirt—was in a very tolerable state of preservation.

"The detective swept the coat and waistcoat and the pebbles back into the basket, and then rolled both of the shirts in a towel, and did his best to dry them. The constable watched him with open eyes, but with no ray of intelligence in his stolid face.

"'Well,' said Mr. Carter,' there isn't much here, is there? I don't think I need detain you any longer. You'll be wanting your tea, I dare say.'

"'I didn't think there would be much in them,' the constable said, pointing contemptuously to the wet rags; his reverential awe of Scotland Yard had been considerably lessened during that long tiresome day. 'I didn't see your game from the first, and I don't see it now. But you wanted the things found, and you've had 'em found.'

"'Yes; and I've paid for the work being done,' Mr. Carter answered briskly; 'not but what I'm thankful to you for giving me your help, and I shall esteem it a favour if you'll accept a trifle, to make up for your lost day. I've made a mistake, that's all; the wisest of us are liable to be mistaken once in a way.'

"The constable grinned as he took the sovereign which Mr. Carter offered him. There was something like triumph in the grin of that Winchester constable—the triumph of a country official who was pleased to see a Londoner at fault.

"I confess that I groaned aloud when the door closed upon the man, and I found myself alone with the detective, who had seated himself at the little table, and was poring over one of the shirts outspread before him.

"'All this day's labour and weariness has been so much wasted trouble,' I said; 'for it seems to have brought us no step nearer to the point we wanted to reach."

"'Hasn't it, Mr. Austin?" cried the detective, eagerly. 'Do you think I am such a fool as to speak out before the man who has just left this room? Do you think I'm going to tell him my secret, or let him share my gains? The business of to-day has brought us to the very end we want to reach. It has brought about the discovery to which Margaret Wilmot's letter was the first indication—the discovery pointed to by every word that man told us last night. Why did I want to find the clothes worn by the murdered man? Because I knew that those garments must contain a secret, or they never would have been stripped from the corpse. It ain't often that a murderer cares to stop longer than he's obliged by the side of his victim; and I knew all along that whoever stripped off those clothes must have had a very strong reason for doing it. I have worked this business out by my own lights, and I've been right. Look there, Mr.

Austin.'

"He handed me the wet discoloured shirt, and pointed with his finger to one particular spot.

"There, amidst the stains of mud and moss, I saw something which was distinct and different from them. A name, neatly worked in dark crimson thread—a Christian and surname, in full.

"'How do you make that out?' Mr. Carter asked, looking me full in the face.

"Neither I nor any rational creature upon this earth able to read English characters could have well made out that name otherwise than I made it out.

"It was the name of Henry Dunbar.

"'You see it all now, don't you?' said Mr. Carter; 'that's why the clothes were stripped off the body, and hidden at the bottom of the stream, where the water seemed deepest; that's why the watch and chain changed hands; that's why the man who came back to this house after the murder was slow to select the key of the desk. You understand now why it was so difficult for Margaret Wilmot to obtain access to the man at Maudesley Abbey; and why, when she had once seen that man, she tried to shield him from inquiry and pursuit. When she told you that Henry Dunbar was innocent of her father's murder, she only told you the truth. The man who was murdered was Henry Dunbar; the man who murdered him was——'

"I could hear no more. The blood surged up to my head, and I staggered back and dropped into a chair.

"When I came to myself, I found the detective splashing cold water in my face. When I came to myself, and was able to think steadily of what had happened, I had but one feeling in my mind; and that was pity, unutterable pity, for the woman I loved."

*   *   *   *   *

"Mr. Carter carried the bundle of clothes to his own room, and returned by and by, bringing his portmanteau with him. He put the portmanteau in a corner near the fireplace.

"'I've locked the clothes safely in that,' he said; 'and I don't mean to let it out of my sight till it's lodged in very safe hands. That mark upon Henry Dunbar's shirt will hang his murderer.'

"'There may have been some mistake,' I said; 'the clothes marked with the name of Henry Dunbar may not have really belonged to Henry Dunbar. He may have given those clothes to his old valet.'

"'That's not likely, sir; for the old valet only met him at Southampton two or three hours before the murder was committed. No; I can see it all now. It's the strangest case that ever came to my knowledge, but it's simple enough when you've got the right clue to it. There was no probable motive which could induce Henry Dunbar, the very pink of respectability, and sole owner of a million of money, to run the risk of the gallows; there were very strong reasons why Joseph Wilmot, a vagabond and a returned criminal, should murder his late master, if by so doing he could take the dead man's place, and slip from the position of an outcast and a penniless reprobate into that of chief partner in the house of Dunbar and Company. It was a bold game to hazard, and it must have been a fearfully perilous and difficult game to play, and the man has played it well, to have escaped suspicion so long. His daughter's conscientious scruples have betrayed him."

"Yes, Mr. Carter spoke the truth. Margaret's refusal to fulfil her engagement had set in motion the machinery by means of which the secret of this foul murder had been discovered.

"I thought of the strange revelation, still so new to me, until my brain grew dazed. How had it been done? How had it been managed? The man whom I had seen and spoken with was not Henry Dunbar, then, but Joseph Wilmot, the murderer of his master—the treacherous and deliberate assassin of the man he had gone to meet and welcome after his five-and-thirty years' absence from England!

"'But surely such a conspiracy must be impossible,' I said, by and by; 'I have seen letters in St. Gundolph Lane, letters in Henry Dunbar's hand, since last August.'

"'That's very likely, sir,' the detective answered, coolly. 'I turned up Joseph Wilmot's own history while I was making myself acquainted with the details of this murder. He was transported thirty years ago for forgery: he made a bold attempt at escape, but he was caught in the act, and removed to Norfolk Island. He was one of the cleverest chaps at counterfeiting any man's handwriting that was ever tried at the Old Bailey. He was known as one of the most daring scoundrels that ever stepped on board a convict-ship; a clever villain, and a bold one, but not without some touches of good in him, I'm told. At Norfolk Island he worked so hard and behaved so well that he got set free before he had served half his time. He came back to England, and was seen about London, and was suspected of being concerned in all manner of criminal offences, from card-sharping to coining, but nothing was ever brought home to him. I believe he tried to make an honest living, but couldn't: the brand of the gaol-bird was upon him; and if he ever did get a chance, it was taken away from him before the sincerity of any apparent reformation had been tested. This is his history, and the history of many other men like him.'

"And Margaret was the daughter of this man. An inexpressible feeling of melancholy took possession of me as I thought of this. I understood everything now. This noble girl had heroically put away from her the one chance of bright and happy life, rather than bring upon her husband the foul taint of her father's crime. I could understand all now. I looked back at the white face, rigid in its speechless agony; the fixed, dilated eyes; and I pictured to myself the horror of that scene at Maudesley Abbey, when the father and daughter stood opposite to each other, and Margaret Wilmot discovered *why* the murderer had persistently hidden himself from her.

"The mystery of my betrothed wife's renunciation of my love had been solved; but the discovery was so hideous that I looked back now and regretted the time of my ignorance and uncertainty. Would it not have been better for me if I had let Margaret Wilmot go her own way, and carry out her sublime scheme of self-sacrifice? Would it not have been better to leave the dark secret of the murder for ever hidden from all but that one dread Avenger whose judgments reach the sinner in his remotest hiding-place, and follow him to the grave? Would it not have been better to do this?

"No! my own heart told me the argument was false and cowardly. So long as man deals with his fellow-man, so long as laws endure for the protection of the helpless and the punishment of the wicked, the course of justice must know no hindrance from any personal consideration.

"If Margaret Wilmot's father had done this hateful deed, he must pay the penalty of his crime, though the broken heart of his innocent daughter was a sacrifice to his iniquity. If, by a strange fatality, I, who so dearly loved this girl, had urged on the coming of this fatal day, I had only been a blind instrument in the mighty hand of Providence, and I had no cause to regret the revelation of the truth.

"There was only one thing left me. The world would shrink away, perhaps, from the murderer's daughter; but I, who had seen her nature proved in the fiery furnace of affliction, knew what a priceless pearl Heaven had given me in this woman, whose name must henceforward sound vile in the ears of honest men, and I did not recoil from the horror of my poor girl's history.

"'If it has been my destiny to bring this great sorrow upon her,' I thought, 'it shall be my duty to make her future safe and happy."

"But would Margaret ever consent to be my wife, if she discovered that I had been the means of bringing about the discovery of her father's crime?

"This was not a pleasant thought, and it was uppermost in my mind while I sat opposite to the detective, who ate a very hearty dinner, and whose air of suppressed high spirits was intolerable to me.

"Success is the very wine of life, and it was scarcely strange that Mr. Carter should feel pleased at having succeeded in finding a clue to the mystery that had so completely baffled his colleagues. So long as I had believed in Henry Dunbar's guilt, I had felt no compunction as to the task I was engaged in. I had even caught something of the detective's excitement in the chase. But now, now that I knew the shame and anguish which our discovery must inevitably entail upon the woman I loved, my heart sank within me, and I hated Mr. Carter for his ardent enjoyment of his triumph.

"'You don't mind travelling by the mail-train, do you, Mr. Austin?' the detective said, presently.

"'Not particularly; but why do you ask me?'

"'Because I shall leave Winchester by the mail to-night.'

"'What for?'

"'To get as fast as I can to Maudesley Abbey, where I shall have the honour of arresting Mr. Joseph Wilmot.'

"So soon! I shuddered at the rapid course of justice when once a criminal mystery is revealed.

"'But what if you should be mistaken! What if Joseph Wilmot was the victim and not the murderer?'"

"'In that case I shall soon discover my mistake. If the man at Maudesley Abbey is Henry Dunbar, there must be plenty of people able to identify him.'

"'But Henry Dunbar has been away five-and-thirty years.'

"'He has; but people don't think much of the distance between England and Calcutta nowadays. There must be people in England now who knew the banker in India. I'm going down to the resident magistrate, Mr. Austin; the man who had Henry Dunbar, or the supposed Henry Dunbar, arrested last August. I shall leave the clothes in his care, for Joseph Wilmot will be tried at the Winchester assizes. The mail leaves Winchester at a quarter before eleven,' added Mr. Carter, looking at his watch as he spoke; 'so I haven't much time to lose.'

"He took the bundle from the portmanteau, wrapped it in a sheet of brown paper which the waiter had brought him a few minutes before, and hurried away. I sat alone brooding over the fire, and trying to reason upon the events of the day.

"The waiter was moving softly about the room; but though I saw him look at me wistfully once or twice, he did not speak to me until he was about to leave the room, when he told me that there was a letter on the mantelpiece; a letter which had come by the evening post.

"The letter had been staring me in the face all the evening, but in my abstraction I had never noticed it.

"It was from my mother. I opened it when the waiter had left me, and read the following lines:

"'MY DEAREST CLEM,—*I was very glad to get your letter this morning, announcing your safe arrival at Winchester. I dare say I am a foolish old woman, but I always begin to think of railway collisions, and all manner of possible and impossible calamities, directly you leave me on ever so short a journey.*

"'*I was very much surprised yesterday morning by a visit from Margaret Wilmot. I was very cool to her at first; for though you never told me why your engagement to her was so abruptly broken off, I could not but think she was in some manner to blame, since I knew you too well, my darling boy, to believe you capable of inconstancy or unkindness. I thought, therefore, that her visit was very ill-timed, and I let her see that my feelings towards her were entirely changed.*

"'*But, oh, Clement, when I saw the alteration in that unhappy girl, my heart melted all at once, and I could not speak to her coldly or unkindly. I never saw such a change in any one before. She is altered from a pretty girl into a pale haggard woman. Her manners are as much changed as her personal appearance. She had a feverish restlessness that fidgeted me out of my life; and her limbs trembled every now and then while she was speaking, and her words seemed to die away as she tried to utter them. She wanted to see you, she said; and when I told her that you were out of town, she seemed terribly distressed. But afterwards, when she had questioned me a good deal, and I told her that you had gone to Winchester, she started suddenly to her feet, and began to tremble from head to foot.*

"'*I rang for wine, and made her take some. She did not refuse to take it; on the contrary, she drank the wine quite eagerly, and said, 'I hope it will give me strength. I am so feeble, so miserably weak and feeble, and I want to be strong.' I persuaded her to stop and rest; but she wouldn't listen to me. She wanted to go back to London, she said; she wanted to be in London by a particular time. Do what I would, I could not detain her. She took my hands, and pressed them to her poor pale lips, and then hurried away, so changed from the bright Margaret of the past, that a dreadful thought took possession of my mind, and I began to fear that she was mad.*'

"The letter went on to speak of other things; but I could not think of anything but my mother's description of Margaret's visit. I understood her agitation at hearing of my journey to Winchester. She knew that only one motive could lead me to that place. I knew now that the familiar figure I had seen in the moonlit street and in the dusky grove was no phantasm of my over-excited brain. I knew now that it was the figure of the noble-hearted woman I loved—the figure of the heroic daughter, who had followed me to Winchester, and dogged my footsteps, in the vain effort to stand between her father and the penalty of his crime.

"As I had been watched in the street on the previous night, I had been watched to-night in the grove. The rustling dress, the shadowy figure melting in the obscurity of the rain-blotted landscape had belonged to Margaret Wilmot!

"Mr. Carter came in while I was still pondering over my mother's letter.

"'I'm off,' he said, briskly. 'Will you settle the bill, Mr. Austin? I suppose you'd like to be with me to the end of this business. You'll go down to Maudesley Abbey with me, won't you?'

"'No,' I said; 'I will have no farther hand in this matter. Do your duty, Mr. Carter; and the reward I promised shall be faithfully paid to you. If Joseph Wilmot was the treacherous murderer of his old master, he must pay the penalty of his crime; I have neither the power nor the wish to shield him. But he is the father of the woman I love. It is not for me to help in hunting him to the gallows.'

"Mr. Carter looked very grave.

"'To be sure, sir,' he said; 'I recollect now. I've been so wrapt up in this business that I forgot the difference it would make to you; but many a good girl has had a bad father, you know, sir, and——'

"I put up my hand to stop him.

"'Nothing that can possibly happen will lessen my esteem for Miss Wilmot,' I said. 'That point admits of no discussion.'

"I took out my pocket-book, gave the detective money for his expenses, and wished him good night.

"When he had left me, I went out into the High Street. The rain was over, and the moon was shining in a cloudless sky. Heaven knows how I should have met Margaret Wilmot had chance thrown her in my way to-night. But my mind was filled with her image; and I walked about the quiet town, expecting at every turn in the street, at every approaching footstep sounding on the pavement, to see the figure I had seen last night. But go where I would I saw no sign of her; so I came back to the hotel at last, to sit alone by the dull fire, and write this record of my day's work."

*   *   *   *   *

While Clement Austin sat in the lonely sitting-room at the George Inn, with his rapid pen scratching along the paper before him, a woman walked up and down the lamp-lit platform at Rugby, waiting for the branch train which was to take her on to Shorncliffe.

This woman was Margaret Wilmot—the haggard, trembling girl whose altered manner had so terrified simple-hearted Mrs. Austin.

But she did not tremble now. She had pushed her thick black veil away from her face, and though no vestige of healthy colour had come back to her cheeks or lips, her features had a set look of steadfast resolution, and her eyes looked straight before her, like the eyes of a person who has one special purpose in view, and will not swerve or falter until that purpose has been carried out.

There was only one elderly gentleman in the first-class carriage in which Margaret Wilmot took her seat when the branch train for Shorncliffe was ready; and as this one fellow-passenger slept throughout the journey, with his face covered by an expansive silk handkerchief, Margaret was left free to think her own thoughts.

The girl was scarcely less quiet than her slumbering companion; she sat in one changeless attitude, with her hands clasped together in her lap, and her eyes always looking straight forward, as they had looked when she walked upon the platform. Once she put her hand mechanically to the belt of her dress, and then shook her head with a sigh as she drew it away.

"How long the time seems!" she said; "how long! and I have no watch now, and I can't tell how late it is. If they should be there before me. If they should be travelling by this train. No, that's impossible. I know that neither Clement, nor the man that was with him, left Winchester by the train that took me to London. But if they should telegraph to London or Shorncliffe?"

She began to tremble at the thought of this possibility. If that grand wonder of science, the electric telegraph, should be made use of by the men she dreaded, she would be too late upon the errand she was going on.

The mail train stopped at Shorncliffe while she was thinking of this fatal possibility. She got out and asked one of the porters to get her a fly; but the man shook his head.

"There's no flies to be had at this time of night, miss," he said, civilly enough. "Where do you want to go?"

She dared not tell him her destination; secrecy was essential to the fulfilment of her purpose.

"I can walk," she said; "I am not going very far." She left the station before the man could ask her any further questions, and went out into the moonlit country road on which the station abutted. She went through the town of Shorncliffe, where the diamond casements were all darkened for the night, and under the gloomy archway, past the dark shadows which the ponderous castle-towers flung across the rippling water. She left the town, and went out upon the lonely country road, through patches of moonlight and shadow, fearless in her self-abnegation, with only one thought in her mind: "Would she be in time?"

She was very tired when she came at last to the iron gates at the principal entrance of Maudesley Park. She had heard Clement Austin speak of a bridle-path through the park to Lisford, and he had told her that this bridle-path was approached by a gate in the park-fence upwards of a mile from the principal lodge.

She walked along by this fence, looking for the gate.

She found it at last; a little low wooden gate, painted white, and only fastened by a latch. Beyond the gate there was a pathway winding in and out among the trunks of the great elms, across the dry grass.

Margaret Wilmot followed this winding path, slowly and doubtfully, till she came to the margin of a vast open lawn. Upon the other side of this lawn she saw the dark frontage of Maudesley Abbey, and three tall lighted windows gleaming through the night.

- CHAPTER 40 -

FLIGHT

The man who called himself Henry Dunbar was lying on the tapestried cushions of a carved oaken couch that stood before the fire in his spacious sitting-room. He lay there, listening to the March wind roaring in the broad chimney, and watching the blazing coals and the crackling logs of wood.

It was three o'clock in the morning now, and the servants had left the room at midnight; but the sick man had ordered a huge fire to be made up—a fire that promised to last for some hours.

The master of Maudesley Abbey was in no way improved by his long imprisonment. His complexion had faded to a dull leaden hue; his cheeks were sunken; his eyes looked unnaturally large and unnaturally bright. Long hours of loneliness, long sleepless nights, and thoughts that from every diverging point for ever narrowed inwards to one hideous centre, had done their work of him. The man lying opposite the fire to-night looked ten years older than the man who gave his evidence so boldly and clearly before the coroner's jury at Winchester.

The crutches—they were made of some light, polished wood, and were triumphs of art in their way—leaned against a table close to the couch, and within reach of the man's hand. He had learned to walk about the rooms and on the gravel-drive before the Abbey with these crutches, and had even learned to do without them, for he was now able to set the lamed foot upon the ground, and to walk a few paces pretty steadily, with no better support than that of his cane; but as yet he

299

walked slowly and doubtfully, in spite of his impatience to be about once
more.

Heaven knows how many different thoughts were busy in his restless
brain that night. Strange memories came back to him, as he lay staring at
the red chasms and craggy steeps in the fire—memories of a time so
long gone by, that all the personages of that period seemed to him like
the characters in a book, or the figures in a picture. He saw their faces,
and he remembered how they had looked at him; and among these other
faces he saw the many semblances which his own had worn.

O God, how that face had changed! The bright, frank, boyish countenance, looking eagerly out upon a world that seemed so pleasant; the
young man's hopeful smile; and then—and then, the hard face that grew
harder with the lapse of years; the smile that took no radiance from a
light within; the frown that blackened as the soul grew darker. He saw all
these, and still for ever, amid a thousand distracting ideas, his thoughts,
which were beyond his own volition, concentrated in the one plague-
spot of his life, and held him there, fixed as a wretch bound hand and
foot upon the rack.

"If I could only get away from this place," he said to himself; "if I
could get away, it would all be different. Change of scene, activity, hurrying from place to place in new countries and amongst strange people,
would have the usual influence upon me. That memory would pass away
then, as other memories have passed; only to be recalled, now and then,
in a dream; or conjured up by some chance allusion dropped from the
lips of strangers, some coincidence of resemblance in a scene, or face, or
tone, or look. *That* memory cannot be so much worse than the rest that
it should be ineffaceable, where they have been effaced. But while I stay
here, here in this dismal room, where the dropping of the ashes on the
hearth, the ticking of the clock upon the chimney-piece, are like that
torture I have read of somewhere—the drop of water falling at intervals
upon the victim's forehead until the anguish of its monotony drives him
raving mad—while I stay here there is no hope of forgetfulness, no
possibility of peace. I saw him last night, and the night before last, and
the night before that. I see him always when I go to sleep, smiling at me,
as he smiled when we went into the grove. I can hear his voice, and the
words he said, every syllable of those insignificant words, selfish mur-
murs about the probability of his being fatigued in that long walk, the
possibility that it would have been better to hire a fly, and to have driven
by the road—bah! What was he that I should be sorry for him? Am I
sorry for him? No! I am sorry for myself, and for the torture which I
have created for myself. O God! I can see him now as he looked up at
me out of the water. The motion of the stream gave a look of life to his

face, and I almost thought he was still alive, and I had never done that deed."

These were the pleasant fireside thoughts with which the master of Maudesley Abbey beguiled the hours of his convalescence. Heaven keep our memories green! exclaims the poet novelist;[132] and Heaven preserve us from such deeds as make our memories hideous to us!

From such a reverie as this the master of Maudesley Abbey was suddenly aroused by the sound of a light knocking against one of the windows of his room—the window nearest him as he lay on the couch.

He started, and lifted himself into a sitting posture.

"Who is there?" he cried, impatiently.

He was frightened, and clasped his two hands upon his forehead, trying to think who the late visitant could be. Why should any one come to him at such an hour, unless—unless *it* was discovered? There could be no other justification for such an intrusion.

His breath came short and thick as he thought of this. Had it come at last, then, that awful moment which he had dreamed of so many times— that hideous crisis which he had imagined under so many different aspects? Had it come at last, like this?—quietly, in the dead of the night, without one moment's warning?—before he had prepared himself to escape it, or hardened himself to meet it? Had it come now? The man thought all this while he listened, with his chest heaving, his breath coming in hoarse gasps, waiting for the reply to his question.

There was no reply except the knocking, which grew louder and more hurried.

If there can be expression in the tapping of a hand against a pane of glass, there was expression in that hand—the expression of entreaty rather than of demand, as it seemed to that white and terror-stricken listener.

His heart gave a great throb, like a prisoner who leaps away from the fetters that have been newly loosened.

"What a fool I have been!" he thought. "If it was that, there would be knocking and ringing at the hall-door, instead of that cautious summons. I suppose that fellow Vallance has got into some kind of trouble, and has come in the dead of the night to hound me for money. It would be only like him to do it. He knows he must be admitted, let him come when he may."

The invalid gave a groan as he thought this. He got up and walked to the window, leaning upon his cane as he went.

The knocking still sounded. He was close to the window, and he

---

[132] See note 26, p.57 above.

heard something besides the knocking—a woman's voice, not loud, but peculiarly audible by reason of its earnestness.

"Let me in; for pity's sake let me in!"

The man standing at the window knew that voice: only too well, only too well. It was the voice of the girl who had so persistently followed him, who had only lately succeeded in seeing him. He drew back the bolts that fastened the long French window, opened it, and admitted Margaret Wilmot.

"Margaret!" he cried; "what, in Heaven's name, brings you here at such an hour as this?"

"Danger!" answered the girl, breathlessly. "Danger to you! I have been running, and the words seem to choke me as I speak. There's not a moment to be lost, not one moment. They will be here directly; they cannot fail to be here directly. I felt as if they had been close behind me all the way—they may have been so. There is not a moment—not one moment!"

She stopped, with her hands clasped upon her breast. She was incoherent in her excitement, and knew that she was so, and struggled to express herself clearly.

"Oh, father!" she exclaimed, lifting her hands to her head, and pushing the loose tangled hair away from her face; "I have tried to save you—I have tried to save you! But sometimes I think that is not to be. It may be God's mercy that you should be taken, and your wretched daughter can die with you!"

She fell upon her knees, suddenly, in a kind of delirium, and lifted up her clasped hands.

"O God, have mercy upon him!" she cried. "As I prayed in this room before—as I have prayed every hour since that dreadful time—I pray again to-night. Have mercy upon him, and give him a penitent heart, and wash away his sin. What is the penalty he may suffer here, compared to that Thou canst inflict hereafter? Let the chastisement of man fall upon him, so as Thou wilt accept his repentance!"

"Margaret," said Joseph Wilmot, grasping the girl's arm, "are you praying that I may be hung? Have you come here to do that? Get up, and tell me what is the matter!"

Margaret Wilmot rose from her knees shuddering, and looking straight before her, trying to be calm—trying to collect her thoughts.

"Father," she said, "I have never known one hour's peaceful sleep since the night I left this room. For the last three nights I have not slept at all. I have been travelling, walking from place to place, until I could drop on the floor at your feet. I want to tell you—but the words—the words—won't come—somehow——"

She pointed to her dry lips, which moved, but made no sound. There was a bottle of brandy and a glass on the table near the couch. Joseph Wilmot was seldom without that companion. He snatched up the bottle and glass, poured out some of the brandy, and placed it between his daughter's lips. She drank the spirit eagerly. She would have drunk living fire, if, by so doing, she could have gained strength to complete her task.

"You must leave this house directly!" she gasped. "You must go abroad, anywhere, so long as you are safe out of the way. They will be here to look for you—Heaven only knows how soon!"

"They! Who?"

"Clement Austin, and a man—a detective——"

"Clement Austin—your lover—your confederate? You have betrayed me, Margaret!"

"I!" cried the girl, looking at her father.

There was something sublime in the tone of that one word—something superb in the girl's face, as her eyes met the haggard gaze of the murderer.

"Forgive me, my girl! No, no, you wouldn't do that, even to a loathsome wretch like me!"

"But you will go away—you will escape from them?"

"Why should I be afraid of them? Let them come when they please, they have no proof against me."

"No proof? Oh, father, you don't know—you don't know. They have been to Winchester. I heard from Clement's mother that he had gone there; and I went after him, and found out where he was—at the inn where you stayed, where you refused to see me—and that there was a man with him. I waited about the streets; and at night I saw them both, the man and Clement. Oh! father, I knew they could have only one purpose in coming to that place. I saw them at night; and the next day I watched again—waiting about the street, and hiding myself under porches or in shops, when there was any chance of my being seen. I saw Clement leave the George, and take the way towards the cathedral. I went to the cathedral-yard afterwards, and saw the strange man talking in a doorway with an old man. I loitered about the cathedral-yard, and saw the man that was with Clement go away, down by the meadows, towards the grove, to the place where——"

She stopped, and trembled so violently that she was unable to speak.

Joseph Wilmot filled the glass with brandy for the second time, and put it to his daughter's lips.

She drank about a teaspoonful, and then went on, speaking very rapidly, and in broken sentences—

"I followed the man, keeping a good way behind, so that he might

303

not see that he was followed. He went straight down to the very place where—the murder was done. Clement was there, and three men. They were there under the trees, and they were dragging the water."

"Dragging the water! Oh, my God, why were they doing that?" cried the man, dropping suddenly on the chair nearest to him, and with his face livid.

For the first time since Margaret had entered the room terror took possession of him. Until now he had listened attentively, anxiously; but the ghastly look of fear and horror was new upon his face. He had defied discovery. There was only one thing that could be used against him—the bundle of clothes, the marked garments of the murdered man—those fatal garments which he had been unable to destroy, which he had only been able to hide. These things alone could give evidence against him; but who should think of searching for these things? Again and again he had thought of the bundle at the bottom of the stream, only to laugh at the wondrous science of discovery which had slunk back baffled by so slight a mystery, only to fancy the water-rats gnawing the dead man's garments, and all the oose and slime creeping in and out amongst the folds until the rotting rags became a very part of the rank river-weeds that crawled and tangled round them.

He had thought this, and the knowledge that strangers had been busy on that spot, dragging the water—the dreadful water that had so often flowed through his dreams—with, not one, but a thousand dead faces looking up and grinning at him through the stream—the tidings that a search had been made there, came upon him like a thunderbolt.

"Why did they drag the water?" he cried again.

His daughter was standing at a little distance from him. She had never gone close up to him, and she had receded a little—involuntarily, as a woman shrinks away from some animal she is frightened of—whenever he had approached her. He knew this—yes, amidst every other con-flicting thought, this man was conscious that his daughter avoided him.

"They dragged the water," Margaret said; "I walked about—that place—under the elms—all the day—only one day—but it seemed to last for ever and ever. I was obliged to hide myself—and to keep at a distance, for Clement was there all day; but as it grew dusk I ventured nearer, and found out what they were doing, and that they had not found what they were searching for; but I did not know yet what it was they wanted to find."

"But they found it!" gasped the girl's father; "did they find it? Come to that."

"Yes, they found it by-and-by. A bundle of rags, a boy told me—a boy who had been about with the men all day—'a bundle of rags, it looked like,' he said; but he heard the constable say that those rags were the clothes that had belonged to the murdered man."

"What then? What next?"

"I waited to hear no more, father; I ran all the way to Winchester to the station—I was in time for a train, which brought me to London—I came on by the mail to Rugby—and——"

"Yes, yes; I know—and you are a brave girl, a noble girl. Ah! my poor Margaret, I don't think I should have hated that man so much if it hadn't been for the thought of you—your lonely girlhood—your hopeless, joyless existence—and all through him—all through the man who ruined me at the outset of my life. But I won't talk—I daren't talk: they have found the clothes; they know that the man who was murdered was Henry Dunbar—they will be here—let me think—let me think how I can get away!"

He clasped both his hands upon his head, as if by force of their iron grip he could steady his mind, and clear away the confusion of his brain.

From the first day on which he had taken possession of the dead man's property until this moment he had lived in perpetual terror of the crisis which had now arrived. There was no possible form or manner in which he had not imagined the situation. There was no preparation in his power to make that he had left unmade. But he had hoped to anticipate the dreaded hour. He had planned his flight, and meant to have left Maudesley Abbey for ever, in the first hour that found him capable of travelling. He had planned his flight, and had started on that wintry afternoon, when the Sabbath bells had a muffled sound, as their solemn peals floated across the snow—he had started on his journey with the intention of never again returning to Maudesley Abbey. He had meant to leave England, and wander far away, through all manner of unfrequented districts, choosing places that were most difficult of approach, and least affected by English travellers.

He had meant to do this, and had calculated that his conduct would be, at the worst, considered eccentric; or perhaps it would be thought scarcely unnatural in a lonely man, whose only child had married into a higher sphere than his own. He had meant to do this, and by-and-by, when he had been lost sight of by the world, to hide himself under a new name and a new nationality, so that if ever, by some strange fatality, by some awful interposition of Providence, the secret of Henry Dunbar's death should come to light, the murderer would be as entirely removed from human knowledge as if the grave had closed over him and hidden him for ever.

This is the course that Joseph Wilmot had planned for himself. There had been plenty of time for him to think and plot in the long nights that he had spent in those splendid rooms—those noble chambers, whose grandeur had been more hideous to him than the blank walls of a condemned cell; whose atmosphere had seemed more suffocating than the foetid vapours of a fever-tainted den in St. Giles's.[133] The passionate, revengeful yearning of a man who has been cruelly injured and betrayed, the common greed of wealth engendered out of poverty's slow torture, had arisen rampant in this man's breast at the sight of Henry Dunbar. By one hideous deed both passions were gratified; and Joseph Wilmot, the bank-messenger, the confidential valet, the forger, the convict, the ticket-of-leave man, the penniless reprobate, became master of a million of money.

Yes, he had done this. He had entered Winchester upon that August afternoon, with a few sovereigns and a handful of silver in his pocket, and with a life of poverty and degradation, before him. He had left the same town chief partner in the firm of Dunbar, Dunbar, and Balderby, and sole owner of Maudesley Abbey, the Yorkshire estates, and the house in Portland Place.

Surely this was the very triumph of crime, a master-stroke of villany. But had the villain ever known one moment's happiness since the commission of that deed—one moment's peace—one moment's freedom from a slow, torturing anguish that was like the gnawing of a ravenous beast for ever preying on his entrails? The author of the *Opium-Eater* suffered so cruelly from some internal agony that he grew at last to fancy there was indeed some living creature inside him, for ever torturing and tormenting him.[134] This doubtless was only the fancy of an invalid: but what of that undying serpent called Remorse, which coils itself about the heart of the murderer and holds it for ever in a deadly grip—never to beat freely again, never to know a painless throb, or feel a sweet emotion?

In a few minutes—while the rooks were cawing in the elms, and the green leaves fluttering in the drowsy summer air, and the blue waters rippling in the sunshine and flecked by the shadows—Joseph Wilmot had done a deed which had given him the richest reward that a murderer ever hoped to win; and had so transformed his life, so changed the very current of his being, that he went away out of that wood, not alone, but dogged step by step by a gaunt, stalking creature, a hideous monster that echoed his every breath, and followed at his shoulder, and clung about

---

[133] A notorious slum district of London, renowned for poverty, overcrowding, crime, and disease. William Hogarth depicted the area in his engraving *Gin Lane* (1751).
[134] Thomas de Quincy (1785-1859), author of the autobiographical *Confessions of an English Opium Eater*, first published anonymously in the *London Magazine* (1821).

him, and grappled his throat, and weighed him down; a horrid thing, which had neither shape nor name, and yet wore every shape, and took every name, and was the ghost of the deed that he had done.

Joseph Wilmot stood for a few moments with his hands clasped upon his head, and then the shadows faded from his face, which suddenly became fixed and resolute-looking. The first thrill of terror, the first shock of surprise, were over. This man never had been and never could be a coward. He was ready now for the worst. It may be that he was glad the worst had come. He had suffered such unutterable anguish, such indescribable tortures, during the time in which his guilt had been unsuspected, that it may have been a kind of relief to know that his secret was discovered, and that he was free to drop the mask.

While he paused, thinking what he was to do, some lucky thought came to him, for his face brightened suddenly with a triumphant smile.

"The horse!" he said. "I may ride, though I can't walk."

He took up his cane, and went to the next room, where there was a door that opened into the quadrangle, in which the master of the Abbey had caused a loose box to be built for his favourite horse. Margaret followed her father, not closely, but at a little distance, watching him with anxious, wondering eyes.

He unfastened the half-glass door, opened it, and went out into the quadrangular garden, the quaint old-fashioned garden, where the flower-beds were primly dotted on the smooth grass-plot, in the centre of which there was a marble basin, and the machinery of a little fountain that had never played within the memory of living man.

"Go back for the lamp, Margaret," Joseph Wilmot whispered. "I must have light."

The girl obeyed. She had left off trembling now, and carried the shaded lamp as steadily as if she had been bent on some simple womanly errand. She followed her father into the garden, and went with him to the loose box where the horse was to be found.

The animal knew his master, even in that uncertain light. There was gas laid on in the millionaire's stables, and a low jet had been left burning by the groom.

The horse plunged his head about his master's shoulders, and shook his mane, and reared, and disported himself in his delight at seeing his old friend once more, and it was only Joseph Wilmot's soothing hand and voice that subdued the animal's exuberant spirits.

"Steady, boy, steady! quiet, old fellow!" Joseph said, in a whisper.

Three or four saddles and bridles hung upon a rack in one corner of the small stable. Joseph Wilmot selected the things he wanted, and began to saddle the horse, supporting himself on his cane as he did so.

The groom slept in the house now, by his master's orders, and there was no one within hearing.

The horse was saddled and bridled in five minutes, and Joseph Wilmot led him out of the stable, followed by Margaret, who still carried the lamp. There was a low iron gate leading out of the quadrangle into the grounds. Joseph led the horse to this gate.

"Go back and get me my coat," he said to Margaret; "you'll go faster than I can. You'll find a coat lined with fur on a chair in the bedroom."

His daughter obeyed, silently and quietly, as she had done before. The rooms all opened one into the other. She saw the bedroom with the tall, gloomy bedstead, the light of the fire flickering here and there. She set the lamp down upon a table in this room, and found the fur-lined coat her father had sent her to fetch. There was a purse lying on a dressing-table, with sovereigns glittering through the silken network, and the girl snatched it up as she hurried away, thinking, in her innocent simplicity, that her father might have nothing but those few sovereigns to help him in his flight. She went back to him, carrying the bulky overcoat, and helped him to put it on in place of the dressing-grown he had been wearing. He had taken his hat before going to the stable.

"Here is your purse, father," she said, thrusting it into his hand; "there is something in it, but I'm afraid there's not very much. How will you manage for money where you are going?"

"Oh, I shall manage very well."

He had got into the saddle by this time, not without considerable difficulty; but though the fresh air made him feel faint and dizzy, he felt himself a new man now that the horse was under him—the brave horse, the creature that loved him, whose powerful stride could carry him almost to the other end of the world; as it seemed to Joseph Wilmot in the first triumph of being astride the animal once more. He put his hand involuntarily to the belt that was strapped round him, as Margaret asked that question about the money.

"Oh, yes," he said, "I've money enough—I am all right."

"But where are you going?" she asked, eagerly.

The horse was tearing up the wet gravel, and making furious champing noises in his impatience of all this delay.

"I don't know," Joseph Wilmot answered; "that will depend upon—I don't know. Good night, Margaret. God bless you! I don't suppose He listens to the prayers of such as me. If He did, it might have been all different long ago—when I tried to be honest!"

Yes, this was true; the murderer of Henry Dunbar had once tried to be honest, and had prayed God to prosper his honesty; but then he only tried to do right in a spasmodic, fitful kind of way, and expected his prayers to be granted as soon as they were asked, and was indignant with a Providence that seemed to be deaf to his entreaties. He had always lacked that sublime quality of patience, which endures the evil day, and calmly breasts the storm.

"Let me go with you, father," Margaret said, in an entreating voice, "let me go with you. There is nothing in all the world for me, except the hope of God's forgiveness for you. I want to be with you. I don't want you to be amongst bad men, who will harden your heart. I want to be with you—far away—where——"

"*You* with me?" said Joseph Wilmot, slowly; "you wish it?"

"With all my heart!"

"And you're true," he cried, bending down to grasp his daughter's shoulder and look her in the face, "you're true, Margaret, eh?—true as steel; ready for anything, no flinching, no quailing or trembling when the danger comes. You've stood a good deal, and stood it nobly. Can you stand still more, eh?"

"For your sake, father, for your sake! yes, yes, I will brave anything in the world, do anything to save you from——"

She shuddered as she remembered what the danger was that assailed him, the horror from which flight alone could save him. No, no, no! *that* could never be endured at any cost; at any sacrifice he must be saved from *that*. No strength of womanly fortitude, no trust in the mercy of God, could even make her resigned to *that*.

"I'll trust you, Margaret," said Joseph Wilmot, loosening his grasp upon the girl's shoulder; "I'll trust you. Haven't I reason to trust you? Didn't I see your mother, on the day when she found out what my history was; didn't I see the colour fade out of her face till she was whiter than the linen collar round her neck, and in the next moment her arms were about me, and her honest eyes looking up in my face, as she cried, 'I shall never love you less, dear; there's nothing in this world can make me love you less!'"

He paused for a moment. His voice had grown thick and husky; but he broke out violently in the next instant.

"Great Heaven! why do I stop talking like this? Listen to me, Margaret; if you want to see the last of me, you must find your way, somehow or other, to Woodbine Cottage, near Lisford—on the Lisford Road, I think. Find your way there—I'm going there now, and shall be there long before you—you understand?"

"Yes; Woodbine Cottage, Lisford—I shan't forget! God speed you, father!—God help you!"

"He is the God of sinners," thought the wretched girl. "He gave Cain a long lifetime in which to repent of his sins."

Margaret thought this as she stood at the gate, listening to the horse's hoofs upon the gravel road that wound through the grounds away into the park.

She was very, very tired, but had little sense of her fatigue, and her journey was by no means finished yet. She did not once look back at Maudesley Abbey—that stately and splendid mansion, in which a miserable wretch had acted his part, and endured the penalty of his guilt, for many wearisome months She went away—hurrying along the lonely pathways, with the night breezes blowing her loose hair across her eyes, and half-blinding her as she went—to find the gate by which she had entered the park.

She went out at this gateway because it was the only point of egress by which she could leave the park without being seen by the keeper of a lodge. The dim morning light was grey in the sky before she met any one whom she could ask to direct her to Woodbine Cottage; but at last a man came out of a farmyard with a couple of milk-pails, and directed her to the Lisford Road.

It was broad daylight when she reached the little garden-gate before Major Vernon's abode. It was broad daylight, and the door leading into the prim little hall was ajar. The girl pushed it open, and fell into the arms of a man, who caught her as she fainted.

"Poor girl, poor child!" said Joseph Wilmot; "to think what she has suffered. And I thought that she would profit by that crime; I thought that she would take the money, and be content to leave the mystery unravelled. My poor child! my poor, unhappy child!"

The man who had murdered Henry Dunbar wept aloud over the white face of his unconscious daughter.

"Don't let's have any of that fooling," cried a harsh voice from the little parlour; "we've no time to waste on snivelling!"

- CHAPTER 41 -

AT MAUDESLEY ABBEY

M r. Carter the detective lost no time about his work; but he did not employ the telegraph, by which means he might perhaps have expedited the arrest of Henry Dunbar's murderer. He did not avail himself of the facilities offered by that wonderful electric telegraph, which was once facetiously called the rope that hung Tawell the Quaker,[135] because in so doing he must have taken the local police into his confidence, and he wished to do his work quietly, only aided by a companion and humble follower, whom he was in the habit of employing.

He went up to London by the mail-train after parting from Clement Austin; took a cab at the Waterloo station, and drove straight off to the habitation of his humble assistant, whom he most unceremoniously roused from his bed. But there was no train for Warwickshire before the six-o'clock parliamentary, and there was a seven-o'clock express, which would reach Rugby ten minutes after that miserably slow conveyance; so Mr. Carter naturally elected to sacrifice the ten minutes, and travel by the express. Meanwhile he took a hearty breakfast, which had been hastily prepared by the wife of his friend and follower, and explained the nature of the business before them.

It must be confessed that, in making these explanations to his humble friend, Mr. Carter employed a tone that implied no little superiority, and that the friendliness of his manner was tempered by condescension.

The friend was a middle-aged and most respectable-looking ind-ividual, with a turnip-hued skin relieved by freckles, dark-red eyes, and pale-red hair. He was not a very prepossessing person, and had a habit of working about his lips and jaws when he was neither eating nor talking, which was far from pleasant to behold. He was very much esteemed by Mr. Carter, nevertheless; not so much because he was clever, as because he looked so eminently stupid. This last characteristic had won for him the *sobriquet* of Sawney Tom, and he was considered worth his weight in sovereigns on certain occasions, when a simple country lad or a verdant-looking linen-draper's apprentice was required to enact some little part in

---

[135] John Tawell (1784-1845) was executed in 1845 for poisoning his mistress, Sarah Hart, with prussic acid. Tawell, like Joseph Wilmot, had previously been transported for forgery. After the murder, he was apprehended due to a telegraph being sent from Slough to Paddington. See "The Salt Hill Murder: Execution of John Tawell", *The Times*, Saturday 29 March 1845: 5.

the detective drama.

"You'll bring some of your traps with you, Sawney," said Mr. Carter.—"I'll take another, ma'am, if you please. Three minutes and a half this time, and let the white set tolerably firm." This last remark was addressed to Mrs. Sawney Tom, or rather Mrs. Thomas Tibbles— Sawney Tom's name was Tibbles—who was standing by the fire, boiling eggs and toasting bread for her husband's patron. "You'll bring your traps, Sawney," continued the detective, with his mouth full of buttered toast; "there's no knowing how much trouble this chap may give us; because you see a chap that can play the bold game he has played, and keep it up for nigh upon a twelvemonth, could play any game. There's nothing out that he need look upon as beyond him. So, though I've every reason to think we shall take my friend at Maudesley as quietly as ever a child in arms was took out of its cradle, still we may as well be prepared for the worst."

Mr. Tibbles, who was of a taciturn disposition, and who had been busily chewing nothing while listening to his superior, merely gave a jerk of acquiescence in answer to the detective's speech.

"We start as solicitor and clerk," said Mr. Carter. "You'll carry a blue bag. You'd better go and dress: the time's getting on. Respectable black and a clean shave, you know, Sawney. We're going to an old gentleman in the neighbourhood of Shorncliffe, that wants his will altered all of a hurry, having quarrelled with his three daughters; that's what *we're* goin' to do, if anybody's curious about our business."

Mr. Tibbles nodded, and retired to an inner apartment, whence he emerged by-and-by dressed in a shabby-genteel costume of somewhat funereal aspect, and with the lower part of his face rasped like a French roll, and somewhat resembling that edible in colour.

He brought a small portmanteau with him, and then departed to fetch a cab, in which vehicle the two gentlemen drove away to the Euston-Square station.

It was one o'clock in the day when they reached the great iron gates of Maudesley Abbey in a fly which they had chartered at Shorncliffe. It was one o'clock on a bright sunshiny day, and the heart of Mr. Carter the detective beat high with expectation of a great triumph.

He descended from the fly himself, in order to question the woman at the lodge.

"You'd better get out, Sawney," he said, putting his head in at the window, in order to speak to his companion; "I shan't take the vehicle into the park. It'll be quieter and safer for us to walk up to the house."

Mr. Tibbles, with his blue-bag on his arm, got out of the fly, prepared to attend his superior whithersoever that luminary chose to lead him.

The woman at the lodge was not alone; a little group of gossips were gathered in the primly-furnished parlour, and the talk was loud and animated.

"Which I was that took aback like, you might have knocked me down with a feather," said the proprietress of the little parlour, as she went out of the rustic porch to open the gate for Mr. Carter and his companion.

"I want to see Mr. Dunbar," he said, "on particular business. You can tell him I come from the banking-house in St. Gundolph Lane. I've got a letter from the junior partner there, and I'm to deliver it to Mr. Dunbar himself!"

The keeper of the lodge threw up her hands and eyes in token of utter bewilderment.

"Begging your pardon, sir," she said, "but I've been that upset, I don't know scarcely what I'm a-doing of. Mr. Dunbar have gone, sir, and nobody in that house don't know why he went, or when he went, or where he's gone. The man-servant as waited on him found the rooms all empty the first thing this morning; and the groom as had charge of Mr. Dunbar's horse, and slep' at the back of the house, not far from the stables, fancied as how he heard a trampling last night where the horse was kep', but put it down to the animal bein' restless on account of the change in the weather; and this morning the horse was gone, and the gravel all trampled up, and Mr. Dunbar's gold-headed cane (which the poor gentleman was still so lame it was as much as he could do to walk from one room to another) was lying by the garden-gate; and how he ever managed to get out and about and saddle his horse and ride away like that without bein' ever heard by a creetur, nobody hasn't the slightest notion; and everybody this morning was distracted like, searchin' 'igh and low; but not a sign of Mr. Dunbar were found nowhere."

Mr. Carter turned pale, and stamped his foot upon the gravel-drive. Two hundred pounds is a large stake to a poor man; and Mr. Carter's reputation was also trembling in the balance. The very man he wanted gone—gone away in the dead of the night, while all the household was sleeping!

"But he was lame," he cried. "How about that?—the railway accident—the broken leg——"

"Yes, sir," the woman answered, eagerly, "that's the very thing, sir; which they're all talkin' about it at the house, sir, and how a poor invalid gentleman, what could scarce stir hand or foot, should get up in the middle of the night and saddle his own horse, and ride away at a rampageous rate; which the groom says he *have* rode rampageous, or the gravel wouldn't be tore up as it is. And they do say, sir, as Mr. Dunbar must have been took mad all of a sudden, and the doctor was in an awful way when he heard it; and there's been people riding right and left lookin' for him, sir. And Miss Dunbar—leastways Lady Jocelyn—was sent for early this morning, and she's at the house now, sir, with her husband Sir Philip; and if your business is so very important, perhaps you'd like to see her——"

"I should," answered the detective, briskly. "You stop here, Sawney," he added, aside to his attendant; "you stop here, and pick up what you can. I'll go up to the house and see the lady."

Mr. Carter found the door open, and a group of servants clustered in the gothic porch. Lady Jocelyn was in Mr. Dunbar's rooms, a footman told him. The detective sent this man to ask if Mr. Dunbar's daughter would receive a stranger from London, on most important business.

The man came back in five minutes to say yes, Lady Jocelyn would see the strange gentleman.

The detective was ushered through the two outer rooms leading to that tapestried apartment in which the missing man had spent so many miserable days, so many dismal nights. He found Laura standing in one of the windows looking out across the smooth lawn, looking anxiously out towards the winding gravel-drive that led from the principal lodge to the house.

She turned away from the window as Mr. Carter approached her, and passed her hand across her forehead. Her eyelids trembled, and she had the look of a person whose senses had been dazed by excitement and confusion.

"Have you come to bring me any news of my father?" she said. "I am distracted by this serious calamity."

Laura looked imploringly at the detective. Something in his grave face frightened her.

"You have come to tell me of some new trouble," she cried.

"No, Miss Dunbar—no, Lady Jocelyn, I have no new trouble to announce to you. I have come to this house in search of—of the gentleman who went away last night. I must find him at any cost. All I want is a little help from you. You may trust to me that he shall be found, and speedily, if he lives."

"If he lives!" cried Laura, with a sudden terror in her face.

"Surely you do not imagine—you do not fear that——"

"I imagine nothing, Lady Jocelyn. My duty is very simple, and lies straight before me. I must find the missing man."

"You will find my father," said Laura, with a puzzled expression.

"Yes, I am most anxious that he should be found; and if—if you will accept any reward for your efforts, I shall be only too glad to give all you can ask. But how is it that you happen to come here, and to take this interest in my father? You come from the banking-house, I suppose?"

"Yes," the detective answered, after a pause, "yes, Lady Jocelyn, I come from the office in St. Gundolph Lane."

Mr. Carter was silent for some few moments, during which his eyes wandered about the apartment in that professional survey which took in every detail, from the colour of the curtains and the pattern of the carpets, to the tiniest porcelain toy in an antique cabinet on one side of the fireplace. The only thing upon which the detective's glance lingered was the lamp, which Margaret had extinguished.

"I'm going to ask your ladyship a question," said Mr. Carter, presently, looking gravely, and almost compassionately, at the beautiful face before him; "you'll think me impertinent, perhaps, but I hope you'll believe that I'm only a straightforward business man, anxious to do my duty in my own line of life, and to do it with consideration for all parties. You seem very anxious about this missing gentleman; may I ask if you are very fond of him? It's a strange question, I know, my lady—or it seems a strange question—but there's more in the answer than you can guess, and I shall be very grateful to you if you'll answer it candidly."

A faint flush crept over Laura's face, and the tears started suddenly to her eyes. She turned away from the detective, and brushed her handkerchief hastily across those tearful eyes. She walked to the window, and stood there for a minute or so, looking out.

"Why do you ask me this question?" she asked, rather haughtily.

"I cannot tell you that, my lady, at present," the detective answered; "but I give you my word of honour that I have a very good reason for what I do."

"Very well then, I will answer you frankly," said Laura, turning and looking Mr. Carter full in the face. "I will answer you, for I believe that you are an honest man. There is very little love between my father and me. It is our misfortune, perhaps: and it may be only natural that it should be so, for we were separated from each other for so many years, that, when at last the day of our meeting came, we met like strangers, and there was a barrier between us that could never be broken down. Heaven knows how anxiously I used to look forward to my father's return from India, and how bitterly I felt the disappointment when I discovered, little by little, that we should never be to one another what other fathers and daughters, who have never known the long bitterness of separation, are to each other. But pray remember that I do not complain; my father has been very good to me, very indulgent, very generous. His last act, before the accident which laid him up so long, was to take a journey to London on purpose to buy diamonds for a necklace, which was to be his wedding present to me. I do not speak of this because I care for the

315

jewels; but I am pleased to think that, in spite of the coldness of his manner, my father had some affection for his only child."

Mr. Carter was not looking at Laura, he was staring out of the window, and his eyes had that stolid glare with which they had gazed at Clement Austin while the cashier told his story.

"A diamond necklace!" he said; "humph—ha, ha—yes!" All this was in an undertone, that hummed faintly through the detective's closed teeth. "A diamond-necklace! You've got the necklace, I suppose, eh, my lady?"

"No; the diamonds were bought, but they were never made up."

"The unset diamonds were bought by Mr. Dunbar?"

"Yes, to an enormous amount, I believe. While I was in Paris, my father wrote to tell me that he meant to delay the making of the necklace until he was well enough to go on the Continent. He could see no design in England that at all satisfied him."

"No, I dare say not," answered the detective, "I dare say he'd find it rather difficult to please himself in that matter."

Laura looked inquiringly at Mr. Carter. There was something disrespectful, not to say ironical, in his tone.

"I thank you heartily for having been so candid with me, Lady Jocelyn," he said; "and believe me I shall have your interests at heart throughout this matter. I shall go to work immediately; and you may rely upon it, I shall succeed in finding the missing man."

"You do not think that—that under some terrible hallucination, the result of his long illness—you don't think that he has committed suicide?"

"No, Lady Jocelyn," answered the detective, decisively, "there is nothing further from my thoughts now."

"Thank Heaven for that!"

"And now, my lady, may I ask if you'll be kind enough to let me see Mr. Dunbar's valet, and to leave me alone with him in these rooms? I may pick up something that will help me to find your father. By the by, you haven't a picture of him—a miniature, a photograph, or anything of that sort, eh?"

"No, unhappily I have no portrait whatever of my father."

"Ah, that is unlucky; but never mind, we must contrive to get on without it."

Laura rang the bell. One of the superb footmen, the birds of paradise who consented to glorify the halls and passages of Maudesley Abbey, appeared in answer to the summons, and went in search of Mr. Dunbar's own man—the man who had waited on the invalid ever since the accident.

Having sent for this person, Laura bade the detective good morning, and went away through the vista of rooms to the other side of the hall, to that bright modernized wing of the house which Percival Dunbar had improved and beautified for the granddaughter he idolized.

Mr. Dunbar's own man was only too glad to be questioned, and to have a good opportunity of discoursing upon the event which had caused such excitement and consternation. But the detective was not a pleasant person to talk to, as he had a knack of cutting people short with a fresh question at the first symptom of rambling; and, indeed, so closely did he keep his companion to the point, that a conversation with him was a kind of intellectual hornpipe between a set of fire-irons.

Under this pressure the valet told all he knew about his master's departure, with very little loss of time by reason of discursiveness.

"Humph!—ha!—ah, yes!" muttered the detective between his teeth; "only one friend that was at all intimate with your master, and that was a gentleman called Vernon, lately come to live at Woodbine Cottage, Lisford Road; used to come at all hours to see your master; was odd in his ways, and dressed queer; first came on Miss Laura's wedding-day; was awful shabby then; came out quite a swell afterwards, and was very free with his money at Lisford. Ah!—humph! You've heard your master and this gentleman at high words—at least you've fancied so; but, the doors being very thick, you ain't certain. It might have been only telling anecdotes. Some gentlemen do swear and row like in telling anecdotes. Yes, to be sure! You've felt a belt round your master's waist when you've been lifting him in and out of bed. He wore it under his shirt, and was always fidgety in changing his shirt, and didn't seem to want you to see the belt. You thought it was a galvanic belt, or something of that sort. You felt it once, when you were changing your master's shirt, and it was all over little knobs as hard as iron, but very small. That's all you've got to say, except that you've always fancied your master wasn't quite easy in his mind, and you thought that was because of his having been suspected in the first place about the Winchester murder."

Mr. Carter jotted down some pencil-notes in his pocket-book while making this little summary of his conversation with the valet.

Having done this and shut his book, he prowled slowly through the sitting-room, bed-room, and dressing-room, looking about him, with the servant close at his heels.

"What clothes did Mr. Dunbar wear when he went away?"

"Grey trousers and waistcoat, small shepherd's plaid, and he must have taken a greatcoat lined with Russian sable."

"A black coat?"

"No; the coat was dark blue cloth outside."

Mr. Carter opened his pocket-book in order to add another memorandum—

Trousers and waistcoat, shepherd's plaid; coat, dark blue cloth lined with sable. "How about Mr. Dunbar's personal appearance, eh?"

The valet gave an elaborate description of his master's looks.

"Ha!—humph!" muttered Mr. Carter; "tall, broad-shouldered, hook-nose, brown eyes, brown hair mixed with grey."

The detective put on his hat after making this last memorandum: but he paused before the table, on which the lamp was still standing.

"Was this lamp filled last night?" he asked.

"Yes, sir; it was always fresh filled every day."

"How long does it burn?"

"Ten hours."

"When was it lighted?"

"A little before seven o'clock."

Mr. Carter removed the glass shade, and carried the lamp to the fire-place. He held it up over the grate, and drained the oil.

"It must have been burning till past four this morning," he said.

The valet stared at Mr. Carter with something of that reverential horror with which he might have regarded a wizard of the middle ages. But Mr. Carter was in too much haste to be aware of the man's admiration. He had found out all he wanted to know, and now there was no time to be lost.

He left the Abbey, ran back to the lodge, found his assistant, Mr. Tibbles, and despatched that gentleman to the Shorncliffe railway station, where he was to keep a sharp look out for a lame traveller in a blue cloth coat lined with brown fur. If such a traveller appeared, Sawney Tom was to stick to him wherever he went; but was to leave a note with the station-master for his chief's guidance, containing information as to what he had done.

- CHAPTER 42 -

THE HOUSEMAID AT WOODBINE COTTAGE

In less than a quarter of an hour after leaving the gate of Maudesley Park, the fly came to a stand-still before Woodbine Cottage. Mr. Carter paid the man and dismissed the vehicle, and went alone into the little garden.

He rang a bell on one side of the half-glass door, and had ample leisure to contemplate the stuffed birds and marine curiosities that adorned the little hall of the cottage before any one came to answer his summons. He rang a second time before anyone came, but after a delay of about five minutes a young woman appeared, with her face tied up in a coloured handkerchief. The detective asked to see Major Vernon, and the young woman ushered him into a little parlour at the back of the cottage, without either delay or hesitation.

The occupant of the cottage was sitting in an arm-chair by the fire.

There was very little light in the room, for the only window looked into a miniature conservatory, where there were all manner of prickly and spiky plants of the cactus kind, which had been the delight of the late owner of Woodbine Cottage.

Mr. Carter looked very sharply at the gentleman sitting in the easy-chair; but the closest inspection showed him nothing but a good-looking man, between fifty and sixty years of age, with a determined-looking mouth, half shaded by a grey moustache.

"I've come to make a few inquiries about a friend of yours, Major Vernon," the detective said; "Mr. Dunbar, of Maudesley Abbey, who has been missing since four o'clock this morning."

The gentleman in the easy-chair was smoking a meerschaum. As Mr. Carter said those two words, "four o'clock," his teeth made a little clicking noise upon the amber mouthpiece of the pipe.

The detective heard the sound, slight as it was, and drew his inference from it. Major Vernon had seen Joseph Wilmot, and knew that he had left the Abbey at four o'clock, and thus gave a little start of surprise when he found that the exact hour was known to others.

"You know where Mr. Dunbar has gone?" said Mr. Carter, looking still more sharply at the gentleman in the easy-chair.

"On the contrary, I was thinking of looking in upon him at the Abbey this evening."

"Humph!" murmured the detective, "then it's no use my asking you any questions on the subject?"

"None whatever. Henry Dunbar is gone away from the Abbey, you say? Why, I thought he was still under medical supervision—couldn't move off his sofa, except to take a turn upon a pair of crutches."

"I believe it was so, but he has disappeared notwithstanding."

"What do you mean by disappeared? He has gone away, I suppose, and he was free to go away, wasn't he?"

"Oh! of course; perfectly free."

"Then I don't so much wonder that he went," exclaimed the occupant of the cottage, stooping over the fire, and knocking the ashes out of his meerschaum. "He'd been tied by the leg long enough, poor

319

devil! But how is it you're running about after him, as if he was a little boy that had bolted from his precious mother? You're not the surgeon who was attending him?"

"No, I'm employed by Lady Jocelyn; in fact, to tell you the honest truth," said the detective, with a simplicity of manner that was really charming: "to tell you the honest truth, I'm neither more nor less than a private detective, and I have come down from London direct to look after the missing gentleman. You see, Lady Jocelyn is afraid the long illness and fever, and all that sort of thing, may have had a very bad effect upon her poor father, and that he's a little bit touched in the upper story, perhaps;—and, upon my word," added the detective, frankly, "I think this sudden bolt looks very like it. In which case I fancy we may look for an attempt at suicide. What do you think, now, Major Vernon, as a friend of the missing gentleman, eh?"

The Major smiled.

"Upon my word," he said, "I don't think you're so very far away from the mark. Henry Dunbar has been rather queer in his ways since that railway smash."

"Just so. I suppose you wouldn't have any objection to my looking about your house, and round the garden and outbuildings? Your friend *might* hide himself somewhere about your place. When once they take an eccentric turn, there's no knowing where to have 'em."

Major Vernon shrugged his shoulders.

"I don't think Dunbar's likely to have got into my house without my knowledge," he said; "but you are welcome to examine the place from garret to cellar if that's any satisfaction to you."

He rang a bell as he spoke. It was answered by the girl whose face was tied up.

"Ah, Betty, you've got the toothache again, have you? A nice excuse for slinking your work, eh, my girl? That's about the size of your tooth-ache, I expect! Look here now, this gentleman wants to see the house, and you're to show him over it, and over the garden too, if he likes—and be quick about it, for I want my dinner."

The girl curtseyed in an awkward countrified manner, and ushered Mr. Carter into the hall.

"Betty!" roared the master of the house, as the girl reached the foot of the stair with the detective; "Betty, come here!"

She went back to her master, and Mr. Carter heard a whispered conversation, very brief, of which the last sentence only was audible.

That last sentence ran thus:

"And if you don't hold your tongue, I'll make you pay for it."

"Ho, ho!" thought the detective; "Miss Betsy is to hold her tongue, is she? We'll see about that."

The girl came back to the hall, and led Mr. Carter into the two sitting-rooms in the front of the house. They were small rooms, with small furniture. They were old-fashioned rooms, with low ceilings, and queer cupboards nestling in out-of-the-way holes and corners: and Mr. Carter had enough work to do in squeezing himself into the interior of these receptacles, which all smelt, more or less, of chandlery and rum,—that truly seaman-like spirit having been a favourite beverage with the late inhabitant of the cottage.

After examining half-a-dozen cupboards in the lower regions, Mr. Carter and his guide ascended to the upper story.

The girl called Betsy[136] ushered the detective into a bedroom, which she said was her master's, and where the occupation of the Major was made manifest by divers articles of apparel lying on the chairs and hanging on the pegs, and, furthermore, by a powerful effluvium of stale tobacco, and a collection of pipes and cigar-boxes on the chimney-piece.

The girl opened the door of an impossible-looking little cupboard in a corner behind a four-post bed; but instead of inspecting the cupboard, Mr. Carter made a sudden rush at the door, locked it, and then put the key in his pocket.

"No, thank you, Miss Innocence," he said; "I don't crick my neck, or break my back, by looking into any more of your cupboards. Just you come here."

"Here," was the window, before which Mr. Carter planted himself.

The girl obeyed very quietly. She would have been a pretty-looking girl but for her toothache, or rather, but for the coloured handkerchief which muffled the lower part of her face, and was tied in a knot at the top of her head. As it was, Mr. Carter could only see that she had pretty brown eyes, which shifted left and right as he looked at her.

"Oh, yes, you're an artful young hussy, and no mistake," he said; "and that toothache's only a judgment upon you. What was that your master said to you in the parlour just now, eh? What was that he told you to hold your tongue about, eh?"

Betty shook her head, and began to twist the corner of her apron in her hands.

"Master didn't say nothing, sir," she said.

"Master didn't say nothing! Your morals and your grammar are about a match, Miss Betsy; but you'll find yourself rather in the wrong box by and by, my young lady, when you find yourself committed to prison for

---

[136] It may be an oversight on the part of Braddon that the girl is called "Betty" by her master, and "Betsy" by Carter and the narrator.

perjury; which crime, in a young female, is transportation for life," added Mr. Carter, in an awful tone.

"Oh, sir!" cried Betty, "it isn't me; it's master: and he do swear so when he's in his tantrums. If the 'taters isn't done to his likin', sir, he'll grumble about them quite civil at first, and then he'll work hisself up like, and take and throw them at me one by one, and his language gets worse with every 'tater. Oh, what am I to do, sir! I daren't go against him. I'd a'most sooner be transported, if it don't hurt much."

"Don't hurt much!" exclaimed Mr. Carter; "why, there's a ship-load of cat-o'-nine-tails goes out to Van Diemen's Land every quarter, and reserved specially for young females!" [137]

"Oh! I'll tell you all about it, sir," cried Mr. Vernon's housemaid; "sooner than be took up for perjuring, I'll tell you everything."

"I thought so," said Mr. Carter; "but it isn't much you've got to tell me. Mr. Dunbar came here this morning on horseback, between five and six?"

"It was ten minutes past six, sir, and I was opening the shutters."

"Precisely."

"And the gentleman came on horseback, sir, and was nigh upon fainting with the pain of his leg; and he sent me to call up master, and master helped him off the horse, and took the horse to the stable; and then the gentleman sat and rested in master's little parlour at the back of the house; and then they sent me for a fly, and I went to the Rose and Crown at Lisford, and fetched a fly; and before eight o'clock the gentleman went away."

Before eight, and it was now past three. Mr. Carter looked at his watch while the girl made her confession.

"And, oh, please don't tell master as I told you," she said; "oh, please don't, sir."

There was no time to be lost, and yet the detective paused for a minute, thinking of what he had just heard.

Had the girl told him the truth; or was this a story got up to throw him off the scent? The girl's terror of her master seemed genuine. She was crying now, real tears, that streamed down her pale cheeks, and wetted the handkerchief that covered the lower part of her face.

"I can find out at the Rose and Crown whether anybody did go away

[137] Van Diemen's Land was the original name for Tasmania used by Europeans, so named after Anthony van Diemen, the Governor-General of the Dutch East Indies who commissioned the voyage on which Abel Tasman discovered the island in the 17th century. The British established a penal colony on Van Diemen's Land in 1803.

in a fly," the detective thought.

"Tell your master I've searched the place, and haven't found his friend," he said to the girl; "and that I haven't got time to wish him good morning."

The detective said this as he went down stairs. The girl went into the little rustic porch with him, and directed him to the Rose and Crown at Lisford.

He ran almost all the way to the little inn; for he was growing desperate now, with the idea that his man had escaped him.

"Why, he can do anything with such a start," he thought to himself. "And yet there's his lameness—that'll go against him."

At the Rose and Crown Mr. Carter was informed that a fly had been ordered at seven o'clock that morning by a young person from Woodbine Cottage; that the vehicle had not long come in, and that the driver was somewhere about the stables. The driver was summoned at Mr. Carter's request, and from him the detective ascertained that a gentleman, wrapped up to the very nose, and wearing a coat lined with fur, and walking very lame, had been taken up by him at Woodbine Cottage. This gentleman had ordered the driver to go as fast as he could to Shorncliffe station; but on reaching the station, it appeared the gentleman was too late for the train he wanted to go by, for he came back to the fly, limping awful, and told the man to drive to Maningsly. The driver explained to Mr. Carter that Maningsly was a little village three miles from Shorncliffe, on a by-road. Here the gentleman in the fur coat had alighted at an ale-house, where he dined, and stopped, reading the paper and drinking hot brandy-and-water till after one o'clock. He acted altogether quite the gentleman, and paid for the driver's dinner and brandy-and-water, as well as his own. At half-after one he got into the fly, and ordered the man to go back to Shorncliffe station. At five minutes after two he alighted at the station, where he paid and dismissed the driver.

This was all Mr. Carter wanted to know.

"You get a fresh horse harnessed in double-quick time," he said, "and drive me to Shorncliffe station."

While the horse and fly were being got ready, the detective went into the bar, and ordered a glass of steaming brandy-and-water. He was accustomed to take liquids in a boiling state, as the greater part of his existence was spent in hurrying from place to place, as he was hurrying now.

"Sawney's got the chance this time," he thought. "Suppose he was to sell me, and go in for the reward?"

The supposition was not a pleasant one, and Mr. Carter looked grave for a minute or so; but he quickly relapsed into a grim smile.

"I think Sawney knows me too well for that," he said; "I think Sawney is too well acquainted with me to try *that* on."

The fly came round to the inn-door while Mr. Carter reflected upon this. He sprang into the vehicle, and was driven off to the station.

At the Shorncliffe station he found everything very quiet. There was no train due for some time yet; there was no sign of human life in the ticket-office or the waiting-rooms.

There was a porter asleep upon his truck on the platform, and there was one solitary young female sitting upon a bench against the wall, with her boxes and bundles gathered round her, and an umbrella and a pair of clogs on her lap.

Upon all the length of the platform there was no sign of Mr. Tibbles, otherwise Sawney Tom.

Mr. Carter awoke the porter, and sent him to the station-master to ask if any letter addressed to Mr. Henry Carter had been left in that functionary's care. The porter went yawning to make this inquiry, and came back by-and-by, still yawning, to say that there was such a letter, and would the gentleman please step into the station-master's office to claim and receive it.

The note was not a long one, nor was it encumbered by any ceremonious phraseology.

"Gent in furred coat turned up 2.10, took a ticket for Derby, 1 class, took ticket for same place self, 2 class.—Yrs to commd, T.T."

Mr. Carter crumpled up the note and dropped it into his pocket. The station-master gave him all the information about the trains. There was a train for Derby at seven o'clock that evening; and for the three and a half weary hours that must intervene, Mr. Carter was left to amuse himself as best he might.

"Derby," he muttered to himself, "Derby. Why, he must be going north; and what, in the name of all that's miraculous, takes him that way?"

- CHAPTER 43 -

ON THE TRACK

The railway journey between Shorncliffe and Derby was by no means the most pleasant expedition for a cold spring night, with the darkness lying like a black shroud on the flat fields, and a melancholy wind howling over those desolate regions, across which all night-trains seem to wend their way. I think that flat and darksome land which we look upon out of the window of a railway carriage in the dead of the night must be a weird district, conjured into existence by the potent magic of an enchanter's wand,—a dreary desert transported out of Central Africa, to make the night-season hideous, and to vanish at cock-crow.

Mr. Carter never travelled without a railway rug and a pocket brandy-flask; and sustained by these inward and outward fortifications against the chilling airs of the long night, he established himself in a corner of the second-class carriage, and made the best of his situation.

Fortunately there was no position of hardship to which the detective was unaccustomed; indeed, to be rolled up in a railway rug in the corner of a second-class carriage, was to be on a bed of down as compared with some of his experiences. He was used to take his night's rest in brief instalments, and was snoring comfortably three minutes after the guard had banged-to the door of his carriage.

But he was not permitted to enjoy any prolonged rest. The door was banged open, and a stentorian voice bawled into his ear that hideous announcement which is so fatal to the repose of travellers, "Change here!" &c., &c. The journey from Shorncliffe to Derby seemed almost entirely to consist of "changing here;" and poor Mr. Carter felt as if he had passed a long night in being hustled out of one carriage into another, and off one line of railway on to another, with all those pauses on draughty platforms which are so refreshing to the worn-out traveller who works his weary way across country in the dead of the night.

At last, however, after a journey that seemed interminable by reason of those short naps, which always confuse the sleeper's estimate of time, the detective found himself at Derby still in the dead of the night; for to the railway traveller it is all of night after dark. Here he applied immediately to the station-master, from whom he got another little note directed to him by Mr. Tibbles, and very much resembling that which he had received at Shorncliffe.

"*All right up to Derby,*" wrote Sawney Tom. "*Gent in furred coat took a ticket through to Hull. Have took the same, and go on with him direct.—Yours to command, T.T.*"

Mr. Carter lost no time after perusing this communication. He set to work at once to find out all about the means of following his assistant and the lame traveller.

Here he was told that he had a couple of hours to wait for the train that was to take him on to Normanton, and at Normanton he would have another hour to wait for the train that was to carry him to Hull.

"Ah, go it, do, while you're about it!" he exclaimed, bitterly, when the railway official had given him this pleasing intelligence. "Couldn't you make it a little longer? When your end and aim lies in driving a man mad, the quicker you drive the better, I should think!"

All this was muttered in an undertone, not intended for the ear of the railway official. It was only a kind of safety-valve by which the detective let off his superfluous steam.

"Sawney's got the chance," he thought, as he paced up and down the platform; "Sawney's got the trump cards this time; and if he's knave enough to play them against me——But I don't think he'll do that; our profession's a conservative one, and a traitor would have an uncommon good chance of being kicked out of it. We should drop him a hint that, considering the state of his health, we should take it kindly of him if he would hook it; or send him some polite message of that kind; as the military swells do when they want to get rid of a pal."

There were plenty of refreshments to be had at Derby, and Mr. Carter took a steaming cup of coffee and a formidable-looking pile of sandwiches before retiring to the waiting-room to take what he called "a stretch." He then engaged the services of a porter, who was to call him five minutes before the starting of the Normanton train, and was to receive an illegal douceur for that civility.

In the waiting-room there was a coke fire, very red and hollow, and a dim lamp. A lady, half buried in shawls, and surrounded by a little colony of small packages, was sitting close to the fire, and started out of her sleep to make nervous clutches at her parcels as the detective entered, being in that semi-conscious state in which the unprotected female is apt to mistake every traveller for a thief.

Mr. Carter made himself very comfortable on one of the sofas, and snored on peacefully until the porter came to rouse him, when he sprang up refreshed to continue his journey.

"Hull, Hull!" he muttered to himself. "His game will be to get off to Rotterdam, or Hamburgh, or St. Petersburg, perhaps; any place that there's a vessel ready to take him. He'll get on board the first that sails. It's a good dodge, a very neat dodge, and if Sawney hadn't been at the station, Mr. Joseph Wilmot would have given us the slip as neatly as ever a man did yet. But if Mr. Thomas Tibbles is true, we shall nab him, and bring him home as quiet as ever any little boy was took to school by his mar and par. If Mr. Tibbles is true,—and as he don't know too much about the business, and don't know anything about the extra reward, or the evidence that's turned up at Winchester,—I dare say Thomas Tibbles will be true. Human nature is a very noble thing," mused the detective; "but I've always remarked that the tighter you tie human nature down, the brighter it comes out."

It was morning, and the sun was shining, when the train that carried

Mr. Carter steamed slowly into the great station at Hull—it was morning, and the sun was shining, and the birds singing, and in the fields about the smoky town there were herds of sweet-breathing cattle sniffing the fresh spring air, and labourers plodding to their work, and loaded wains of odorous hay and dewy garden-stuff were lumbering along the quiet country roads, and the new-born day had altogether the innocent look appropriate to its tender youth,—when the detective stepped out on the platform, calm, self-contained, and resolute, as brisk and business-like in his manner as any traveller in that train, and with no distinctive stamp upon him, however slight, that marked him as the hunter of a murderer.

He looked sharply up and down the platform. No, Mr. Tibbles had not betrayed him. That gentleman was standing on the platform, watching the passengers step out of the carriages, and looking more turnip-faced than usual in the early sunlight. He was chewing nothing with more than ordinary energy; and Mr. Carter, who was very familiar with the idiosyncrasies of his assistant, knew from that sign that things had gone amiss.

"Well," he said, tapping Sawney Tom on the shoulder, "he's given you the slip? Out with it; I can see by your face that he has."

"Well, he have, then," answered Mr. Tibbles, in an injured tone; "but if he have, you needn't glare at me like that, for it ain't no fault of mine. If you ever follered a lame eel—and a lame eel as makes no more of its lameness than if lameness was a advantage—you'd know what it is to foller that chap in the furred coat."

The detective hooked his arm through that of his assistant, and led Mr. Tibbles out of the station by a door which opened on a desolate region at the back of that building.

"Now then," said Mr. Carter, "tell me all about it, and look sharp."

"Well, I was waitin' in the Shorncliffe ticket-offis, and about five minutes after two in comes the gent as large as life, and I sees him take his ticket, and I hears him say Derby, on which I waits till he's out of the offis, and I takes my own ticket, same place. Down we comes here with more changes and botheration than ever was; and every time we changes carriages, which we don't seem to do much else the whole time, I spots my gentleman, limpin' awful, and lookin' about him suspicious-like, to see if he was watched. And, of course, he weren't watched—oh, no; nothin' like it. Of all the innercent young men as ever was exposed to the temptations of this wicked world, there never was sech a young inner-cent as that lawyer's clerk, a carryin' a blue bag, and a tellin' a promis-kruous acquaintance, loud enough for the gent in the fur coat to hear, that he'd been telegraphed for by his master, which was down beyond Hull, on electioneerin' business; and a cussin' of his master promis-kruous to the same acquaintance for tele-graphin' for him to go by sech a train. Well, we come to Derby, and the furry gent, he takes a ticket on to Hull; and we come to Normanton, and the furry gent limps about Normanton station, and I sees him comfortable in his carriage; and we comes to Hull, and I sees him get out on the platform, and I sees him into a fly, and I hears him give the order, 'Victorier Hotel,' which by this time it's nigh upon ten o'clock, and dark and windy. Well, I got up behind the fly, and rides a bit, and walks a bit, keepin' the fly in sight until we comes to the Victorier; and there stoops down behind, and watches my gent hobble into the hotel, in awful pain with that lame leg of his, judgin' the faces he makes; and he walks into the coffee-room, and I makes bold to foller him; but there never was sech a young inner-cent as me, and I sees my party sittin' warmin' his poor lame leg, and with a carpet-bag, and railway-rug, and sechlike on the table beside him; and presently he gets up, hobblin' worse than ever, and goes outside, and I hears him makin' inquiries about the best way of gettin' on to Edin-borough by train; and I sat quiet, not more than three minutes at most, becos', you see, I didn't want to *look like* follerin' him; and in three minutes time, out I goes, makin' as sure to find him in the bar as I make sure of your bein' close beside me at this moment; but when I went outside into the hall, and bar and sechlike, there wasn't a mortal vestige of that man to be seen; but the waiter, he tells me, as dignified and cool as yer please, that the lame gentleman has gone out by the door looking towards the water, and has only gone to have a look at the place, and get a few cigars, and will be back in ten minutes to a chop which is bein' cooked for him. Well, I cuts out by the same door, thinkin' my lame friend can't be very far; but when I gets out on to the quay-side, there ain't a vestige of him; and though I cut about here, there, and everywhere, lookin' for him, until I'd nearly walked my legs off in less than half an hour's time, I didn't see a sign of him, and all I could do was to go back to the Victorier, and see if he'd gone back before me.

"Well, there was his carpet-bag and his railway-rug, just as he'd left 'em, and there was a little table near the fire all laid out snug and comfortable ready for him; but there was no more vestige of hisself than there was in the streets where I'd been lookin' for him; and so I went out again, with the prespiration streamin' down my face, and I walked that blessed town till over one o'clock this mornin',' lookin' right and left, and inquirin' at every place where such a gent was likely to try and hide hisself, and playing up Mag's diversions, which if it was diversions to Mag, was oncommon hard work to me; and then I went back to the Victorier, and got a night's lodgin'; and the first thing this mornin' I was on my blessed legs again, and down at the quay inquirin' about vessels, and there's nothin' likely to sail afore to-night, and the vessel as is expected to sail to-night is bound for Copenhagen, and don't carry passengers; but from the looks of her captain, I should say she'd carry anythink, even to a churchyard full of corpuses, if she was paid to do it."

"Humph! a sailing-vessel bound for Copenhagen; and the captain's a villanous-looking fellow, you say?" said the detective, in a thoughtful tone.

"He's about the villanousest I ever set eyes on," answered Mr. Tibbles.

"Well, Sawney, it's a bad job, certainly; but I've no doubt you've done your best."

"Yes, I have done my best," the assistant answered, rather indignantly: "and considerin' the deal of confidence you honoured me with about this here cove, I don't see as I could have done hanythink more."

"Then the best thing you can do is to keep watch here for the starting of the up-trains, while I go and keep my eye upon the station at the other side of the water," said Mr. Carter, "This journey to Hull may have been just a dodge to throw us off the scent, and our man may try and double upon us by going back to London. You'll keep all safe here, Sawney, while I go to the other side of the compass."

Mr. Carter engaged a fly, and made his way to a pier at the end of the town, whence a boat took him across the Humber to a station on the Lincolnshire side of the river.

Here he ascertained all particulars about the starting of the trains for London, and here he kept watch while two or three trains started. Then, as there was an interval of some hours before the starting of another, he re-crossed the water, and set to work to look for his man.

First he loitered about the quays a little, taking stock of the idle vessels, the big steamers that went to London, Antwerp, Rotterdam, and Hamburg—the little steamers that went short voyages up or down the river, and carried troops of Sunday idlers to breezy little villages beside the sea. He found out all about these boats, their destination, and the hours and days on which they were to start, and made himself more familiar with the water-traffic of the place in half an hour than another man could have done in a day. He also made acquaintance with the vessel that was to sail for Copenhagen—a black sulky-looking boat, christened very appropriately the *Crow*, with a black sulky-looking captain, who was lying on a heap of tarpaulin on the deck, smoking a pipe in his sleep. Mr. Carter stood looking over the quay and contemplating this man for some moments with a thoughtful stare.

"He looks a bad 'un," the detective muttered, as he walked away;

"Sawney was right enough there."

He went into the town, and walked about, looking at the jewellers' shops with his accustomed rapid glance—a glance so furtive that it escaped observation—so full of sharp scrutiny that it took in every detail of the object looked at. Mr. Carter looked at the jewellers till he came to one whose proprietor blended the trade of money-lending with his more aristocratic commerce. Here Mr. Carter stopped, and entered by the little alley, within whose sombre shadows the citizens of Hull were wont to skulk, ashamed of the errand that betrayed their impecuniosity. Mr. Carter visited three pawnbrokers, and wasted a good deal of time before he made any discovery likely to be of use to him; but at the third pawnbroker's he found himself on the right track. His manner with these gentlemen was very simple.

"I'm a detective officer," he said, "from Scotland Yard, and I have a warrant for the apprehension of a man who's supposed to be hiding in Hull. He's known to have a quantity of unset diamonds in his possession—they're not stolen, mind you, so you needn't be frightened on that score. I want to know if such a person has been to you to-day?"

"The diamonds are all right?" asked the pawnbroker, rather nervously.

"Quite right. I see the man has been here. I don't want to know anything about the jewels: they're his own, and it's not them we're after. I want to know about *him*. He's been here, I see—the question is, what time?"

"Not above half an hour ago. A man in a dark blue coat with a fur collar—"

"Yes; a man that walks lame."

The pawnbroker shook his head.

"I didn't see that he was lame," he said.

"Ah, you didn't notice; or he might hide it just while he was in here. He sat down, I suppose?"

"Yes; he was sitting all the time."

"Of course. Thank you; that'll do."

With this Mr. Carter departed, much to the relief of the money-lender.

The detective looked at his watch, and found that it was half-past one. At half-past three there was a London train to start from the station on the Lincolnshire side of the water. The other station was safe so long as Mr. Tibbles remained on the watch there; so for two hours Mr. Carter was free to look about him. He went down to the quay, and ascertained that no boat had crossed to the Lincolnshire side of the river within the last hour. Joseph Wilmot was therefore safe on the Yorkshire side; but if so, where was he? A man wearing a dark blue coat lined with sable, and walking very lame, must be a conspicuous object wherever he went; and yet Mr. Carter, with all the aid of his experience in the detective line, could find no clue to the whereabouts of the man he wanted. He spent an hour and a half in walking about the streets, prying into all manner of dingy little bars and tap-rooms, in narrow back streets and down by the water-side; and then was fain to go across to Lincolnshire once more, and watch the departure of the train.

Before crossing the river to do this, he had taken stock of the *Crow* and her master, and had seen the captain lying in exactly the same attitude as before, smoking a dirty black pipe in his sleep.

Mr. Carter made a furtive inspection of every creature who went by the up-train, and saw that conveyance safely off before he turned to leave the station. After doing this he lost no time in re-crossing the water again, and landed on the Yorkshire side of the Humber as the clocks of Hull were striking four.

He was getting tired by this time, but he was not tired of his work. He was accustomed to spending his days very much in this manner; he was used to taking his sleep in railway carriages, and his meals at unusual hours, whenever and wherever he could get time to take his food. He was getting what he called "peckish" now, and was just going to the coffee-room of the Victoria Hotel with the intention of ordering a steak and a glass of brandy-and-water—Mr. Carter never took beer, which is a sleepy beverage, inimical to that perpetual clearness of intellect necessary to a detective—when he changed his mind, and walked back to the edge of the quay, to prowl along once more with his hands in his pockets, looking at the vessels, and to take another inspection of the deck and captain of the *Crow*.

"I shouldn't wonder if my gentleman's gone and hidden himself down below the hatchway of that boat," he thought, as he walked slowly along the quay-side. "I've half a mind to go on board and overhaul her."

- CHAPTER 44 -

CHASING THE "CROW"

Mr. Carter was so familiar with the spot alongside which the *Crow* lay at anchor, that he made straight for that part of the quay and looked down over the side, fully expecting to see the dirty captain still lying on the tarpaulin, smoking his dirty pipe.

But, to his amazement, he saw a strange vessel where he expected to see the *Crow*, and in answer to his eager inquiries amongst the idlers on the quay, and the other idlers on the boats, he was told that the *Crow* had weighed anchor half an hour ago, and was over yonder.

The men pointed to a dingy speck out seaward as they gave Mr. Carter this information—a speck which they assured him was neither more nor less than the *Crow*, bound for Copenhagen.

Mr. Carter asked whether she had been expected to sail so soon.

No, the men told him; she was not expected to have sailed till daybreak next morning, and there wasn't above two-thirds of her cargo aboard her yet.

The detective asked if this wasn't rather a queer proceeding.

Yes, the men said, it was queer; but the master of the *Crow* was a queer chap altogether, and more than one absconding bankrupt had sailed for furrin parts in the *Crow*. One of the men opined that the master had got a swell cove on board to-day, inasmuch as he had seen such a one hanging about the quay-side ten minutes or so before the *Crow* sailed.

"Who'll catch her?" cried Mr. Carter; "which of you will catch her for a couple of sovereigns?"[138]

The men shook their heads. The *Crow* had got too much of a start, they said, considering that the wind was in her favour.

"But there's a chance that the wind may change after dark," returned the detective. "Come, my men, don't hang back. Who'll catch the *Crow* yonder for a fiver, come? Who'll catch her for a fi'-pound note?"

"I will," cried a burly young fellow in a scarlet guernsey,[139] and shiny boots that came nearly to his waist; "me and my mate will do it, won't us, Jim?"

---

[138] Sovereign: a gold coin worth £1.
[139] A guernsey: type of smock made from wool that had many of the natural oils left in, which helped to protect fisherman from the elements.

Jim was another burly young fellow in a blue guernsey, a fisherman, part owner of a little bit of a smack with a brown mainsail. The two stalwart young fishermen ran along the quay, and one of them dropped down into a boat that was chained to an angle in the quay-side, where there was a flight of slimy stone steps leading down to the water. The other young man ran off to get some of the boat's tackle and a couple of shaggy overcoats.

"We'd best take something to eat and drink, sir," the young man said, as he came running back with these things; "we may be out all night, if we try to catch yon vessel."

Mr. Carter gave the man a sovereign, and told him to get what he thought proper.

"You'd best have something to cover you besides what you've got on, sir," the fisherman said; "you'll find it rare and cold on t'water after dark."

Mr. Carter assented to this proposition, and hurried off to buy himself a railway rug; he had left his own at the railway station in Sawney Tom's custody. He bought one at a shop near the quay, and was back to the steps in ten minutes.

The fisherman in the blue guernsey was in the boat, which was a stout-built craft in her way. The fisherman in the scarlet guernsey made his appearance in less than five minutes, carrying a great stone bottle, with a tin drinking-cup tied to the neck of it, and a rush basket filled with some kind of provision. The stone bottle and the basket were speedily stowed away in the bottom of the boat, and Mr. Carter was invited to descend and take the seat pointed out to him.

"Can you steer, sir?" one of the men asked.

Yes, Mr. Carter was able to steer. There was very little that he had not learned more or less in twenty years' knocking about the world.

He took the rudder when they had pushed out into the open water, the two young men dipped their oars, and away the boat shot out towards that seaward horizon on which only the keenest eyes could discover the black speck that represented the *Crow*.

"If it should be a sell, after all," thought Mr. Carter; "and yet that's not likely. If he wanted to double on me and get back to London, he'd have gone by one of the trains we've watched; if he wanted to lie-by and hide himself in the town, he wouldn't have disposed of any of his diamonds yet awhile—and then, on the other hand, why should the *Crow* have sailed before she'd got the whole of her cargo on board? Anyhow, I think I have been wise to risk it, and follow the *Crow*. If this is a wild-goose chase, I've been in wilder than this before to-day, and have caught my man."

The little fishing smack behaved bravely when she got out to sea; but even with the help of the oars, stoutly plied by the two young men, they gained no way upon the *Crow*, for the black speck grew fainter and fainter upon the horizon-line, and at last dropped down behind it altogether.

"We shall never catch her," one of the men said, helping himself to a cupful of spirit out of the stone-bottle, in a sudden access of despondency. "We shall no more catch t' *Crow* than we shall catch t'day before yesterday, unless t' wind changes."

"I doubt t' wind will change after dark," answered the other young man, who had applied himself oftener than his companion to the stone-bottle, and took a more hopeful view of things. "I doubt but we shall have a change come dark."

He was looking out to windward as he spoke. He took the rudder out of Mr. Carter's hands presently, and that gentleman rolled himself in his new railway rug, and lay down in the bottom of the boat, with one of the men's overcoats for a blanket and the other for a pillow, and, hushed by the monotonous plashing of the water against the keel of the boat, fell into a pleasant slumber, whose blissfulness was only marred by the gridiron-like sensation of the hard boards upon which he was lying.

He awoke from this slumber to hear that the wind had changed, and that the *Pretty Polly*—the boat belonging to the two fishermen was called the *Pretty Polly*—was gaining on the *Crow*.

"We shall be alongside of her in an hour," one of the men said.

Mr. Carter shook off the drowsy influence of his long sleep, and scrambled to his feet. It was bright moonlight, and the little boat left a trail of tremulous silver in her wake as she cut through the water. Far away upon the horizon there was a faint speck of shimmering white, to which one of the young men pointed with his brawny finger. It was the dirty mainsail of the *Crow* bleached into silver whiteness under the light of the moon.

"There's scarcely enough wind to puff out a farthing candle," one of the young men said. "I think we're safe to catch her."

Mr. Carter took a cupful of rum at the instigation of one of his companions, and prepared himself for the business that lay before him.

Of all the hazardous ventures in which the detective had been engaged, this was certainly not the least hazardous. He was about to venture on board a strange vessel, with a captain who bore no good name, and with men who most likely closely resembled their master; he was about to trust himself among such fellows as these, in the hope of capturing a criminal whose chances, if once caught, were so desperate that he would not be likely to hesitate at any measures by which he might avoid a capture. But the detective was not unused to encounters where the odds were against him, and he contemplated the chances of being hurled overboard in a hand-to-hand struggle with Joseph Wilmot as calmly as if death by drowning were the legitimate end of a man's existence.

Once, while standing in the prow of the boat, with his face turned steadily towards that speck in the horizon, Mr. Carter thrust his hand into the breast-pocket of his coat, where there lurked the newest and neatest thing in revolvers; but beyond this action, which was almost involuntary, he made no sign that he was thinking of the danger before him.

The moon grew brighter and brighter in a cloudless sky, as the fishing-smack shot through the water, while the steady dip of the oars seemed to keep time to a wordless tune. In that bright moonlight the sails of the *Crow* grew whiter and larger with every dip of the oars that were carrying the *Pretty Polly* so lightly over the blue water.

As the boat gained upon the vessel she was following, Mr. Carter told the two young men his errand, and his authority to capture the runaway.

"I think I may count on your standing by me—eh, my lads?" he asked.

Yes, the young men answered; they would stand by him to the death. Their spirits seemed to rise with the thought of danger, especially as Mr. Carter hinted at a possible reward for each of them if they should assist in the capture of the runaway. They rowed close under the side of the black and wicked-looking vessel, and then Mr. Carter, standing up in the boat gave a "Yo-ho! aboard there!" that resounded over the great expanse of plashing water.

A man with a pipe in his mouth looked over the side.

"Hilloa! what's the row there?" he demanded fiercely.

"I want to see the captain."

"What do you want with him?"

"That's my business."

Another man, with a dingy face, and another pipe in his mouth, looked over the side, and took his pipe from between his lips, to address the detective.

"What the —— do you mean by coming alongside us?" he cried.

"Get out of the way, or we shall run you down."

"Oh, no, you won't, Mr. Spelsand," answered one of the young men from the boat; "you'll think twice before you turn rusty with us. Don't you remember the time you tried to get off John Bowman, the clerk that robbed the Yorkshire Union Assurance Office—don't you remember trying to get him off clear, and gettin' into trouble yourself about it?"

Mr. Spelsand bawled some order to the man at the helm, and the vessel veered round suddenly; so suddenly, that had the two young men in the boat been anything but first-rate watermen, they and Mr. Carter would have become very intimately acquainted with the briny element around and about them. But the young men were very good watermen, and they were also familiar with the manners and customs of Captain Spelsand, of the *Crow*; so, as the black-looking schooner veered round, the little boat shot out into the open water, and the two young oarsmen greeted the captain's manoeuvre with a ringing peal of laughter.

"I'll trouble you to lay-to while I come on board," said the detective, while the boat bobbed up and down on the water, close alongside of the schooner. "You've got a gentleman on board—a gentleman whom I've got a warrant against. It can't much matter to him whether I take him now, or when he gets to Copenhagen; for take him I surely shall; but it'll matter a good deal to you, Captain Spelsand, if you resist my authority."

The captain hesitated for a little, while he gave a few fierce puffs at his dirty pipe.

"Show us your warrant," he said presently, in a sulky tone.

The detective had started from Scotland Yard in the first instance with an open warrant for the arrest of the supposed murderer. He handed this document up to the captain of the *Crow*, and that gentleman, who was by no means an adept in the unseamanlike accomplishments of reading and writing, turned it over, and examined it thoughtfully in the vivid moonlight.

He could see that there were a lot of formidable-looking words and flourishes in it, and he felt pretty well convinced that it was a genuine document, and meant mischief.

"You'd better come aboard," he said; "you don't want *me*; that's certain."

The captain of the *Crow* said this with an air of sublime resignation; and in the next minute the detective was scrambling up the side of the vessel, by the aid of a rope flung out by one of the sailors on board the Crow.

Mr. Carter was followed by one of the fishermen; and with that stalwart ally he felt himself equal to any emergency.

"I'll just throw my eye over your place down below," he said, "if you'll hand me a lantern."

This request was not complied with very willingly; and it was only on a second production of the warrant that Mr. Carter obtained the loan of a wretched spluttering wick, glimmering in a dirty little oil-lamp. With this feeble light he turned his back upon the lovely moonlight, and stumbled down into a low-ceilinged cabin, darksome and dirty, with berths which were as black and dingy, and altogether as uninviting as the shelves made to hold coffins in a noisome underground vault.

There were three men asleep upon these shelves; and Mr. Carter examined these three sleepers as coolly as if they had indeed been the coffined inmates of a vault. Amongst them he found a man whose face was turned towards the cabin-wall, but who wore a blue coat and a traveller's cap of fur, shaped like a Templar's helmet, and tied down over his ears.

The detective seized this gentleman by the fur collar of his coat and shook him roughly.

"Come, Mr. Joseph Wilmot," he said; "get up, my man. You've given me a fine chase for it; but you're nabbed at last."

The man scrambled up out of his berth, and stood in a stooping attitude, for the cabin was not high enough for him, staring at Mr. Carter.

"What are you talking of, you confounded fool!" he said. "What have I got to do with Joseph Wilmot?"

The detective had never loosed his hand from the fur collar of his prisoner's coat. The faces of the two men were opposite to each other, but only faintly visible in the dim light of the spluttering oil-lamp. The man in the fur-lined coat showed two rows of wolfish teeth, bared to the gums in a malicious grin.

"What do you mean by waking me out of sleep?" he asked. "What do you mean by assaulting and ballyragging[140] me in this way? I'll have it out of you for this, my fine gentleman. You're a detective officer, are you?— a knowing card, of course; and you've followed me all the way from Warwickshire, and traced me, step by step, I suppose, and taken no end of trouble, eh? Why didn't you look after the gentleman *who stayed at home*? Why didn't you look after the poor lame gentleman who stayed at Woodbine Cottage, Lisford, and dressed up his pretty daughter as a housemaid, and acted a little play to sell you, you precious clever police-officer in plain clothes. Take me with you, Mr. Detective; stop me in going abroad to improve my mind and manners by foreign travel, do, Mr. Detective; and won't I have a fine action against you for false imprisonment,—that's all?"

There was something in the man's tone of bravado that stamped it genuine. Mr. Carter gnashed his teeth together in a silent fury. Sold by that hazel-eyed housemaid with her face tied up! Sent away on a false trail, while the criminal got off at his leisure! Fooled, duped, and laughed at after twenty years of hard service! It was too bitter.

"Not Joseph Wilmot!" muttered Mr. Carter; "not Joseph Wilmot!"

---

[140] Intimidating, mistreating or bullying.

"No more than you are, my pippin," answered the traveller, insolently.

The two men were still standing face to face. Something in that insolent tone, something that brought back the memory of half-forgotten times, startled the detective. He lifted the lamp suddenly, still looking in the traveller's face, still muttering in the same half-absent tone, "Not Joseph Wilmot!" and brought the light on a level with the other man's eyes.

"No," he cried, with a sudden tone of triumph, "not Joseph Wilmot, but Stephen Vallance—Blackguard Steeve, the forger—the man who escaped from Norfolk Island, after murdering one of the gaolers—beating his brains out with an iron, if I remember right. We've had our eye on you for a long time, Mr. Vallance; but you've contrived to give us the slip. Yours is an old case, yours is; but there's a reward to be got for the taking of you, for all that. So I haven't had my long journey for nothing."

The detective tried to fasten his other hand on Mr. Vallance's shoulder; but Stephen Vallance struck down that uplifted hand with a heavy blow of his fist, and, wresting himself from the detective's grasp, rushed up the cabin-stairs.

Mr. Carter followed close at his heels.

"Stop that man!" he roared to one of the fishermen; "stop him!"

I suppose the instinct of self-preservation inspired Stephen Vallance to make that frantic rush, though there was no possible means of escape out of the vessel, except into the open boat, or the still more open sea. As he receded from the advancing detective, one of the fishermen sprang towards him from another part of the deck. Thus hemmed in by the two, and dazzled, perhaps, by the sudden brilliancy of the moonlight after the darkness of the place below, he reeled back against an opening in the side of the vessel, lost his balance, and fell with a heavy plunge into the water.

There was a sudden commotion on the deck, a simultaneous shout, as the men rushed to the side.

"Save him!" cried the detective. "He's got a belt stuffed with diamonds round his waist!"

Mr. Carter said this at a venture, for he did not know which of the men had the diamond belt.

One of the fishermen threw off his shoes, and took a header into the water. The rest of the men stood by breathless, eagerly watching two heads bobbing up and down among the moonlit waves, two pairs of arms buffeting with the water. The force of the current drifted the two men far away from the schooner.

For an interval that seemed a long one, all was uncertainty. The schooner that had made so little way before seemed now to fly in the faint night-wind. At last there was a shout, and a head appeared above the water advancing steadily towards the vessel.

"I've got him!" shouted the voice of the fisherman. "I've got him by the belt!"

He came nearer to the vessel, striking out vigorously with one arm, and holding some burden with the other.

When he was close under the side, the captain of the *Crow* flung out a rope; but as the fisherman lifted his hand to grasp it, he uttered a sudden cry, and raised the other hand with a splash out of the water.

"The belt's broke, and he's sunk!" he shouted.

The belt had broken. A little ripple of light flashed briefly in the moonlight, and fell like a shower of spray from a fountain. Those glittering drops, that looked like fountain spray, were some of the diamonds bought by Joseph Wilmot; and Stephen Vallance, alias Black-guard Steeve, alias Major Vernon, had gone down to the bottom of the sea, never in this mortal life to rise again.

- CHAPTER 45 -

GIVING IT UP

The *Pretty Polly* went back to the port of Kingston-upon-Hull in the grey morning light, carrying Mr. Carter, very cold and very down-hearted—not to say humiliated—by his failure. To have been hoodwinked by a girl, whose devotion to the unhappy wretch she called her father had transformed her into a heroine—to have fallen so easily into the trap that had been set for him, being all the while profoundly impressed with the sense of his own cleverness—was, to say the least of it, depressing to the spirits of a first-class detective.

"And that fellow Vallance, too," mused Mr. Carter, "to think that he should go and chuck himself into the water just to spite me! There'd have been some credit in taking him back with me. I might have made a bit of character out of that. But, no! he goes and tumbles back'ards into the water, rather than let me have any advantage out of him."

There was nothing for Mr. Carter to do but to go straight back to Lisford, and try his luck again, with everything against him.

"Let me get back as fast as I may, Joseph Wilmot will have had eight-and-forty hours' start of me," he thought; "and what can't he do in that time, if he keeps his wits about him, and don't go wild and foolish like, as some of 'em do, when they've got such a chance as this. Anyhow, I'm after him, and it'll go hard with me if he gives me the slip after all, for my blood's up, and my character's at stake, and I'd think no more of crossing the Atlantic after him than I'd think of going over Waterloo Bridge!"

It was a very chill and miserable time of the morning when the *Pretty Polly* ground her nose against the granite steps of the quay. It was a chill and dismal hour of the morning, and Mr. Carter felt sloppy and dirty and unshaven, as he stepped out of the boat and staggered up the slimy stairs. He gave the two young fishermen the promised five-pound note, and left them very well contented with their night's work, inglorious though it had been.

There were no vehicles to be had at that early hour of the morning, so Mr. Carter was fain to walk from the quay to the station, where he expected to find Mr. Tibbles, or to obtain tidings of that gentleman. He was not disappointed; for, although the station wore its dreariest aspect, having only just begun to throb with a little spasmodic life, in the way of an early goods-train, Mr. Carter found his devoted follower prowling in melancholy loneliness amid a wilderness of empty carriages and smokeless engines, with the turnip whiteness of his complexion relieved by a red nose.

Mr. Thomas Tibbles was by no means in the best possible temper in this chill early morning. He was slapping his long thin arms across his narrow chest, and performing a kind of amateur double-shuffle with his long flat feet, when Mr. Carter approached him; and he kept up the same shuffling and the same slapping while engaged in conversation with his superior, in a disrespectful if not defiant manner.

"A pretty game you've played me," he said, in an injured tone. "You told me to hang about the station and watch the trains, and you'd come back in the course of the day—you would—and we'd dine together comfortable at the Station Hotel; and a deal you come back and dined together comfortable. Oh, yes! I don't think so; very much indeed," exclaimed Mr. Tibbles, vaguely, but with the bitterest derision in his voice and manner.

"Come, Sawney, don't you go to cut up rough about it," said Mr. Carter, coaxingly.

"I should like to know who'd go and cut up smooth about it?" answered the indignant Tibbles. "Why, if you could have a hangel in the detective business—which luckily you can't, for the wings would cut out anything as mean as legs, and be the ruin of the purfession—the temper of that hangel would give way under what I've gone through. Hanging about this windy station, which the number of criss-cross draughts cuttin' in from open doors and winders would lead a hignorant person to believe there was seventeen p'ints of the compass at the very least—hangin' about to watch train after train, till there ain't anything goin' in the way of sarce as yen haven't got to stand from the porters; or sittin' in the coffee-room of the hotel yonder, watchin' and listenin' for the next train, till bein' there to keep an appointment with your master is the hollerest of mockeries."

Mr. Carter took his irate subordinate to the coffee-room of the Station Hotel, where Mr. Tibbles had engaged a bed and taken a few hours' sleep in the dead interval between the starting of the last train at night and the first in the morning. The detective ordered a substantial breakfast, with a couple of glasses of pale brandy, neat, to begin with; and Mr. Tibbles' equanimity was restored, under the influence of ham, eggs, mutton-cutlet, a broiled sole, and a quart or so of boiling coffee.

Mr. Carter told his assistant very briefly that he'd been wasting his time and trouble on a false track, and that he should give the matter up. Sawney Tom received this announcement with a great deal of champing and working of the jaws, and with rather a doubtful expression in his dull red eyes; but he accepted the payment which his employer offered him, and agreed to depart for London by the ten o'clock train.

"And whatever I do henceforth in this business, I do single-handed," Mr. Carter said to himself, as he turned his back upon his companion.

At five o'clock that afternoon the detective found himself at the Shorncliffe station, where he hired a fly and drove on post-haste to Lisford cottage.

The neat little habitation of the late naval commander looked pretty much as Mr. Carter had seen it last, except that in one of the upper windows there was a bill—a large paper placard—announcing that this house was to let, furnished; and that all information respecting the same was to be obtained of Mr. Hogson, grocer, Lisford.

Mr. Carter gave a long whistle.

"The bird's flown," he muttered. "It wasn't likely he'd stop here to be caught."

The detective rang the bell; once, twice, three times; but there was no answer to the summons. He ran round the low garden-fence to the back of the premises, where there was a little wooden gate, padlocked, but so low that he vaulted over it easily, and went in amongst the budding currant-bushes, the neat gravel-paths and strawberry-beds, that had been erst so cherished by the naval commander. Mr. Carter peered in at the back windows of the house, and through the little casement he saw a vista of emptiness. He listened, but there was no sound of voices or footsteps. The blinds were undrawn, and he could see the bare walls of the rooms, the fireless grates, and that cold bleakness of aspect peculiar to an untenanted habitation.

He gave a low groan.

"Gone," he muttered; "gone, as neat as ever a man went yet."

He ran back to the fly, and drove to the establishment of Mr. Hogson, grocer and general dealer—the shop of the village of Lisford.

Here Mr. Carter was informed that the key of Woodbine Cottage had been given up on the evening of that very day on which he had seen Joseph Wilmot sitting in the little parlour.

"Yes, sir, it were the night before the last," Mr. Hogson said; "it were the night before last as a young woman wrapped up about the face like, and dressed very plain, got out of a fly at my door; and, says she, 'Would you please take charge of this here key, and be so kind as to show any one over the cottage as would like to see it, which of course the commission is understood?—for my master is leaving for some time on account of having a son just come home from India, which is married and settled in Devonshire, and my master is going there to see him, not having seen him this many a long year.' She was a very civil-spoken young woman, and Woodbine Cottage has been good customers to us, both with the old tenants and the new; so of course I took the key, willin' to do any service as lay in my power. And if you'd like to see the cottage, sir——"

"You're very good," said Mr. Carter, with something like a groan. "No, I won't see the cottage to-night. What time was it when the fly stopped at your door?"

"Between seven and eight."

"Between seven and eight. Just in time to catch the mail from Rugby. Was it one of the Rose-and-Crown flies, d'ye think?"

"Oh, yes, the fly belonged to Lisford. I'm sure of that, for Tim Baling was drivin' it and wished me good-night."

Mr. Carter left the Lisford emporium, and ran over to the Rose and Crown, where he saw the man who had driven him to Shorncliffe station. This man told the detective that he had been fetched in the evening by the same young woman who fetched him in the morning, and that he had driven another gentleman, who walked lame like the first, and had his head and face wrapped up a deal, not to Shorncliffe station, but to little Petherington station, six miles on the Rugby side of Shorncliffe, where the gentleman and the young woman who was with him got into a second-class carriage in the slow train for Rugby. The gentleman had said, laughing, that the young woman was his housemaid, and he was taking her up to town on purpose to be married to her. He was a very pleasant-spoken gentleman, the flyman added, and paid uncommon liberal.

"I dare say he did," muttered Mr. Carter.

He gave the man a shilling for his information, and went back to the fly that had brought him to the station. It was getting on for seven o'clock by this time, and Joseph Wilmot had had eight-and-forty hours' start of him. The detective was quite down-hearted now.

He went up to London by the same train which he had every reason to suppose had carried Joseph Wilmot and his daughter two nights before, and at the Euston terminus he worked very hard on that night and on the following day to trace the missing man. But Joseph Wilmot was only a drop in the great ocean of London life. The train that was supposed to have brought him to town was a long train, coming through from the north. Half-a-dozen lame men with half-a-dozen young women for their companions might have passed unnoticed in the bustle and confusion of the arrival platform.

Mr. Carter questioned the guards, the ticket-collectors, the porters, the cabmen; but not one among them gave him the least scrap of available information. He went to Scotland Yard despairing, and laid his case before the authorities there.

"There's only one way of having him," he said, "and that's the diamonds. From what I can make out, he had no money with him, and in that case he'll be trying to turn some of those diamonds into cash."

The following advertisement appeared in the Supplement to the *Times* for the next day:

"*To Pawnbrokers and Others.—A liberal reward will be given to any person affording information that may lead to the apprehension of a tall man, walking lame, who is known to have a large quantity of unset diamonds in his possession, and who most likely has attempted to dispose of the same.*"

But this advertisement remained unanswered.

"They're too clever for us, sir," Mr. Carter remarked to one of the Scotland-Yard officials. "Whoever Joseph Wilmot may have sold those diamonds to has got a good bargain, you may depend upon it, and means to stick to it. The pawnbrokers and others think our advertisement a plant, you may depend upon it."

- CHAPTER 46 -

CLEMENT'S STORY – BEFORE THE DAWN

"I went back to my mother's house a broken and a disappointed man. I had solved the mystery of Margaret's conduct, and at the same time had set a barrier between myself and the woman I loved.

"Was there any hope that she would ever be my wife? Reason told me that there was none. In her eyes I must henceforth appear the man who had voluntarily set himself to work to discover her father's guilt, and track him to the gallows.

"*Could* she ever again love me with this knowledge in her mind? Could she ever again look me in the face, and smile at me, remembering this? The very sound of my name must in future be hateful to her.

"I knew the strength of my noble girl's love for her reprobate father. I had seen the force of that affection tested by so many cruel trials. I had witnessed my poor girl's passionate grief at Joseph Wilmot's supposed death: and I had seen all the intensity of her anguish when the secret of his existence, which was at the same time the secret of his guilt, became known to her.

"'She renounced me then, rather than renounce that guilty wretch,' I thought; 'she will hate me now that I have been the means of bringing his most hideous crime to light.'

"Yes, the crime was hideous—almost unparalleled in horror. The treachery which had lured the victim to his death seemed almost less horrible than the diabolical art which had fixed upon the name of the murdered man the black stigma of a suspected crime.

"But I knew too well that, in all the blackness of his guilt, Margaret Wilmot would cling to her father as truly, as tenderly, as she had clung to him in those early days when the suspicion of his worthlessness had been only a dark shadow for ever brooding between the man and his only child. I knew this, and I had no hope that she would ever forgive me for my part in the weaving of that strange chain of evidence which made the condemnation of Joseph Wilmot.

"These were the thoughts that tormented me during the first fortnight after my return from the miserable journey to Winchester; these were the thoughts for ever revolving in my tired brain while I waited for tidings from the detective.

"During all that time it never once occurred to me that there was any chance, however remote, of Joseph Wilmot's escape from his pursuer.

"I had seen the science of the detective police so invariably triumphant over the best-planned schemes of the most audacious criminals, that I should have considered—had I ever debated the question, which I never did—Joseph Wilmot's evasion of justice an actual impossibility. It was most likely that he would be taken at Maudesley Abbey entirely unprepared, in his ignorance of the fatal discovery at Winchester; an easy prey to the experienced detective.

"Indeed, I thought that his immediate arrest was almost a certainty; and every morning, when I took up the papers, I expected to see a prominent announcement to the effect that the long-undiscovered Winchester mystery was at last solved, and that the murderer had been taken by one of the detective police.

"But the papers gave no tidings of Joseph Wilmot; and I was surprised, at the end of a week's time, to read the account of a detective's skirmish on board a schooner some miles off Hull, which had resulted in the drowning of one Stephen Vallance, an old offender. The detective's name was given as Henry Carter. Were there two Henry Carters in the small band of London detective police? or was it possible that my Henry Carter could have given up so profitable a prize as Joseph Wilmot in order to pursue unknown criminals upon the high seas? A week after I had read of this mysterious adventure, Mr. Carter made his appearance at Clapham, very grave of aspect and dejected of manner.

"'It's no use, sir,' he said; 'it's humiliating to an officer of my standing in the force; but I'd better confess it freely. I've been sold, sir—sold by a young woman too, which makes it three times as mortifying, and a kind of insult to the male sex in general!'

"My heart gave a great throb.

"'Do you mean that Joseph Wilmot has escaped? I asked.

"He has, sir; as clean as ever a man escaped yet. He hasn't left this country, not to my belief, for I've been running up and down between the different outports like mad. But what of that? If he hasn't left the country, and if he doesn't mean to leave the country, so much the better for him, and so much the worse for those that want to catch him. It's trying to leave England that brings most of 'em to grief, and Joseph Wilmot's an old enough hand to know that. I'll wager he's living as quiet and respectable as any gentleman ever lived yet.'

"Mr. Carter went on to tell me the whole story of his disappointments and mortifications. I could understand all now: the moonlit figure in the Winchester street, the dusky shadow beneath the dripping branches in the grove. I could understand all now: my poor girl—my poor, brave girl.

"When I was alone, I rendered up my thanks to Heaven for the escape of Joseph Wilmot. I had done nothing to impede the course of justice, though I had known full well that the punishment of the evil-doer would crush the bravest and purest heart that ever beat in an innocent woman's bosom. I had not dared to attempt any interposition between Joseph Wilmot and the punishment of his crime; but I was, nevertheless, most heartily thankful that Providence had suffered him to escape that hideous earthly doom which is supposed to be the wisest means of ridding society of a wretch.

"But for the wretch himself, surely long years of penitence must make a better expiation of his guilt than that one short agony—those few spasmodic throes, which render his death such a pleasant spectacle for a sight-seeing populace.[141]

"I was glad, for the sake of the guilty and miserable creature himself, that Joseph Wilmot had escaped. I was still gladder for the sake of that dear hope which was more to me than any hope on earth—the hope of making Margaret my wife.

"'There will be no hideous recollection interwoven with my image now,' I thought; 'she will forgive me when I tell her the history of my journey to Winchester. She will let me take her away from the companionship that must be loathsome to her, in spite of her devotion. She will let me bring her to a happy home as my cherished wife.'

"I thought this, and then in the next moment I feared that Margaret might cling persistently to the dreadful duty of her life—the duty of shielding and protecting a criminal; the duty of teaching a wicked man to repent of his sins.

"I inserted an advertisement in the *Times* newspaper, assuring Margaret of my unalterable love and devotion, which no circumstances could lessen, and imploring her to write to me. Of course the advertisement was so worded as to give no clue to the identity of the person to whom it was addressed. The acutest official in Scotland Yard could have gathered nothing from the lines 'From C. to M.,' so like other appeals made through the same medium.

"But my advertisement remained unanswered—no letter came from Margaret.

"The weeks and months crept slowly past. The story of the evidence of the clothes found at Winchester was made public, together with the history of Joseph Wilmot's flight and escape. The business created a

---

[141] In 1864, when *Henry Dunbar* was published, public hanging was still practised. It was abolished in 1868 when the government passed the Capital Punishment Amendment Act.

considerable sensation, and Lord Herriston himself went down to Winchester to witness the exhumation of the remains of the man who had been buried under the name of Joseph Wilmot. Only by induction

"The dead man's face was no longer recognizable. Only by induction was the identity of Henry Dunbar ever established: but the evidence of the identity was considered conclusive by all who were interested in the question. Still I doubt whether, in the fabric of circumstantial evidence against Joseph Wilmot, legal sophistry could not have discovered some loophole by which the murderer might have escaped the full penalty of his crime.

"The remains were removed from Winchester to Lisford Church, where Percival Dunbar was buried in a vault beneath the chancel. The murdered man's coffin was placed beside that of his father, and a simple marble tablet recording the untimely death of Henry Dunbar, cruelly and treacherously assassinated in a grove near Winchester, was erected by order of Lady Jocelyn, who was abroad with her husband when the story of her father's death was revealed to her.

"The weeks and months crept by. The revelation of Joseph Wilmot's guilt left me free to return to my old position in the house of Dunbar, Dunbar, and Balderby. But I had no heart to go back to the old business now the hope that had made my commonplace city life so bright seemed for ever broken. I was surprised, however, into a confession of the truth by the good-natured junior partner, who lived near us on Clapham Common, and who dropped in sometimes as he went by my mother's gate, to while away an idle half-hour in some political discussion.

"He insisted upon my returning to the office directly he heard the secret of my resignation. The business was now entirely his; for there had been no one to succeed Henry Dunbar, and Mr. John Lovell had sold the dead man's interest on behalf of his client, Lady Jocelyn. I went back to my old post, but not to remain long in my old position; for a week after my return Mr. Balderby made me an offer which I considered as generous as it was flattering, and which I ultimately and somewhat reluctantly accepted.

"By means of this new and most liberal arrangement, which demanded from me a very moderate amount of capital, I became junior partner in the firm, which was now conducted under the names of Dunbar, Dunbar, Balderby, and Austin. The double Dunbar was still essential to us, though the last of the male Dunbars was dead and buried under the chancel of Lisford Church. The old name was the legitimate stamp of our dignity as one of the oldest Anglo-Indian banking firms in the city of London.

"My new life was smooth enough, and there was so much business to be got through, so much responsibility vested in my hands—for Mr. Balderby was getting fat and lazy, as regarded affairs in the City, though untiring in the production of more forced pine-apples and hothouse grapes than he could consume or give away—that I had not much leisure in which to think of the one sorrow of my life. A City man may break his heart for disappointed love, but he must do it out of business hours if he pretends to be an honourable man: for every sorrowful thought which wanders to the loved and lost is a separate treason against the 'house' he serves.

"Smoking my after-dinner cigar in the narrow pathways and miniature shrubberies of my mother's garden, I could venture to think of my lost Margaret; and I did think of her, and pray for her with as fervent aspirations as ever rose from a man's faithful heart. And in the dusky stillness of the evening, with the faint odour of dewy flowers round me, and distant stars shining dimly in that far-off opal sky; against which the branches of the elms looked so black and dense, I used to beguile myself—or it may be that the influence of the scene and hour beguiled me—into the thought that my separation from Margaret could be only a temporary one. We loved each other so truly! And after all, what under heaven is stronger than love? I thought of my poor girl in some lonely, melancholy place, hiding with her guilty father; in daily companionship with a miserable wretch, whose life must be made hideous to himself by the memory of his crime. I thought of the self-abnegation, the heroic devotion, which made Margaret strong enough to endure such an existence as this: and out of my belief in the justice of Heaven there grew up in my mind the faith in a happier life in store for my noble girl.

"My mother supported me in this faith. She knew all Margaret's story now, and she sympathized with my love and admiration for Joseph Wilmot's daughter. A woman's heart must have been something less than womanly if it could have failed to appreciate my darling's devotion: and my mother was about the last of womankind to be wanting in tenderness and compassion for any one who had need of her pity and was worthy of her love.

"So we both cherished the thought of the absent girl in our minds, talking of her constantly on quiet evenings, when we sat opposite to each other in the snug lamp-lit drawing-room, unhindered by the presence of guests. We did not live by any means a secluded or gloomy life, for my mother was fond of pleasant society: and I was quite as true to Margaret while associating with agreeable people, and hearing cheerful voices buzzing round me, as I could have been in a hermitage whose stillness was only broken by the howling of the storm.

"It was in the dreariest part of the winter which followed Joseph

Wilmot's escape that an incident occurred which gave me a strangely-mingled feeling of pleasure and pain. I was sitting one evening in my mother's breakfast-parlour—a little room situated close to the hall-door—when I heard the ringing of the bell at the garden-gate. It was nine o'clock at night, a bitter wintry night, in which I should least have expected any visitor. So I went on reading my paper, while my mother speculated about the matter.

"Three minutes after the bell had rung, our parlour-maid came into the room, and placed something on the table before me.

"'A parcel, sir,' she said, lingering a little; perhaps in the hope that, in my eager curiosity, I might immediately open the packet, and give her an opportunity of satisfying her own desire for information.

"I put aside my newspaper, and looked down at the object before me.

"Yes, it was a parcel—a small oblong box—about the size of those pasteboard receptacles which are usually associated with Seidlitz powders[142]—an oblong box, neatly packed in white paper, secured with several seals, and addressed to Clement Austin, Esq., Willow Bank, Clapham.

"But the hand, the dear, well-known hand, which had addressed the packet—my blood thrilled through my veins as I recognized the familiar characters.

"'Who brought this parcel?' I asked, starting from my comfortable easy-chair, and going straight out into the hall.

"The astonished parlour-maid told me that the packet had been given her by a lady, 'a lady who was dressed in black, or dark things,' the girl said, 'and whose face was quite hidden by a thick veil.' After leaving the small packet, this lady got into a cab a few paces from our gate, the girl added, 'and the cab had tore off as fast as it could tear!'

"I went out into the open yard, and looked despairingly London-wards. There was no vestige of any cab: of course there had been ample time for the cab in question to get far beyond reach of pursuit. I felt almost maddened with this disappointment and vexation. It was Margaret, Margaret herself most likely, who had come to my door; and I had lost the opportunity of seeing her.

"I stood staring blankly up and down the road for some time, and then went back to the parlour, where my mother, with pardonable weakness, had pounced upon the packet, and was examining it with eyes opened to their widest extent.

"'It is Margaret's hand!' she exclaimed. 'Oh, do open—do, please,

---

[142] Laxatives containing a mixture of sodium bicarbonate, Rochelle salt, and tartaric acid, sold as powders to dissolve in water.

open it directly. What on earth can it be?'

"I tore off the white paper covering, and revealed just such an object as I had expected to see—a box, a common-place pasteboard box, tied securely across and across with thin twine. I cut the twine and opened the box. At the top there was a layer of jewellers' wool, and on that being removed, my mother gave a little shriek of surprise and admiration.

"The box contained a fortune—a fortune in the shape of unset diamonds, lying as close together as their nature would admit—unset diamonds, which glittered and flashed upon us in the lamplight.

"Inside the lid there was a folded paper, upon, which the following lines were written in the dear hand, the never-to-be-forgotten hand:

"'EVER-DEAREST CLEMENT,—*The sad and miserable secret which led to our parting is a secret no longer. You know all, and you have no doubt forgiven, and perhaps in part forgotten, the wretched woman to whom your love was once so dear, and to whom the memory of your love will ever be a consolation and a happiness. If I dared to pray to you to think pitifully of that most unhappy man whose secret is now known to you, I would do so; but I cannot hope for so much mercy from men: I can only hope it from God, who in His supreme wisdom alone can fathom the mysteries of a repentant heart. I beg of you to deliver to Lady Jocelyn the diamonds I place in your hands. They belong of right to her; and I regret to say they only represent a part of the money withdrawn from the funds in the name of Henry Dunbar. Goodbye, dear and generous friend; this it the last you will ever hear of one whose name must sound odious to the ears of honest men. Pity me, and forget me; and may a happier woman be to you that which I can never be! M. W.'*

"This was all. Nothing could be firmer than the tone of this letter, in spite of its pensive gentleness. My poor girl could not be brought to believe that I should hold it no disgrace to make her my wife, in spite of the hideous story connected with her name. In my vexation and disappointment, I appealed once more to the unfailing friend of parted or persecuted lovers, the Jupiter of Printing-House Square.

"'*Margaret,*' I wrote in the advertisement which adorned the second column of the *Times* Supplement on twenty consecutive occasions, '*I hold you to your old promise, and consider the circumstances of our parting as in no manner a release from your old engagement. The greatest wrong you can inflict upon me will be inflicted by your desertion. C. A.*"

"This advertisement was as useless as its predecessor. I looked in vain for any answer.

"I lost no time in fulfilling the commission intrusted to me. I went down to Shorncliffe, and delivered the box of diamonds into the hands of John Lovell, the solicitor; for Lady Jocelyn was still on the Continent. He packed the box in paper, and made me seal it with my signet-ring, in the presence of one of his clerks, before he put it away in an iron safe near his desk.

"When this was done, and when the *Times* advertisement had been inserted for the twentieth time without eliciting any reply, I gave myself up to a kind of despair about Margaret. She had failed to see my advertisement, I thought; for she would scarcely have been so hard-hearted as to leave it unanswered. She had failed to see this advertisement, as well as the previous appeal made to her through the same medium, and she would no doubt fail to see any other. I had reason to know that she was, or had been, in England, for she would scarcely have intrusted the diamonds to strange hands; but it was only too likely that she had chosen the very eve of her own and her father's departure for some distant country as the most fitting time at which to leave the valuable parcel with me.

"'Her influence over her father must be complete,' I thought, 'or he would scarcely have consented to surrender such a treasure as the diamonds. He has most likely retained enough to pay the passage out to America for himself and Margaret; and my poor darling will wander with her wretched father into some remote corner of the United States, where she will be hidden from me for ever.'

"I remembered with unspeakable pain how wide the world was, and how easy it would be for the woman I loved to be for ever lost to me.

"I gave myself up to despair; it was not resignation, for my life was empty and desolate without Margaret; try as I might to carry my burden quietly, and put a brave face upon my sorrow. Up to the time of Margaret's appearance on that bleak winter's night, I had cherished the hope—or even more than hope—the belief that we should be reunited: but after that night the old faith in a happy future crumbled away, and the idea that Joseph Wilmot's daughter had left England grew little by little into conviction.

"I should never see her again. I fully believed this now. There was never to be any more sunshine in my life: and there was nothing for me to do but to resign myself to the even tenor of an existence in which the quiet duties of a business career would leave little time for any idle grief or lamentation. My sorrow was a part of my life: but even those who knew me best failed to fathom the depth of that sorrow. To them I seemed only a grave business man, devoted to the dry details of a business life.

"Eighteen months had passed since the bleak winter's night on which the box of diamonds had been intrusted to me; eighteen months, so slow and quiet in their course that I was beginning to feel myself an old man, older than many old men, inasmuch as I had outlived the wreck of the one bright hope which had made life dear to me. It was midsummer time, and the counting-house in St. Gundolph Lane, and the parlour in which—in virtue of my new position—I had now a right to work, seemed peculiarly hot and frowsy, dusty and obnoxious. My work being especially hard at this time knocked me up; and I was compelled, under pain of solemn threats from my mother's pet medical attendant, to stay at home, and take two or three days' rest. I submitted, very unwillingly; for however dusty and stifling the atmosphere in St. Gundolph Lane might be, it was better to be there, victorious over my sorrow, by means of man's grandest ally in the battle with black care—to wit, hard work—than to be lying on the sofa in my mother's pleasant drawing-room, listening to the cheery click of two knitting-needles, and thinking of my wasted life.

"I submitted, however, to take the three days' holiday; and on the second day, after a couple of hours' penance on the sofa, I got up, languid and tired still, but bent on some employment by which I might escape from the sad monotony of my own thoughts.

"'I think I'll go into the next room and put my papers to rights, mother,' I said.

"My dear indulgent mother remonstrated: I was to rest and keep myself quiet, she said, and not to worry myself about papers and tiresome things of that kind, which appertained only to the office. But I had my own way, and went into the little room, where there were flowers blooming and caged birds singing in the open window.

"This room was a sort of snuggery, half library, half breakfast-parlour, and it was in this room my mother and I had been sitting on the night on which the diamonds had been brought to me.

"On one side of the fireplace stood my mother's work-table, on the other the desk at which I wrote, whenever I wrote any letters at home—a ponderous old-fashioned office desk, with a row of drawers on each side, a deep well in the centre, and under that a large waste-paper basket, full of old envelopes and torn scraps of letters.

"I wheeled a comfortable chair up to the desk, and began my task. It was a very long one, and involved a great deal of folding, sorting, and arranging of documents, which perhaps were scarcely worth the trouble I took with them. At any rate, the work kept my fingers employed, though my mind still brooded over the old trouble.

"I sat for nearly three hours; for it was a very long time since I had had a day's leisure, and the accumulation of letters, bills, and receipts was something very formidable. At last all was done, the letters and bills endorsed and tied into neat packets that would have done credit to a lawyer's office; and I flung myself back in my chair with a sigh of relief.

"But I had not finished my work yet; for I drew out the waste-paper basket presently, and emptied its contents upon the floor, in order that I might make sure of there being no important paper thrown by chance amongst them, before I consigned them to be swept away by the housemaid.

"I tossed over the chaotic fragments, the soiled envelopes, the circulars of enterprising Clapham tradesmen, and all the other rubbish that had accumulated within the last two years. The dust floated up to my face and almost blinded me.

"Yes, there was something of consequence amongst the papers—something, at least, which I should have held it sacrilegious to consign to Molly, the housemaid—the wrapper of the box containing the diamonds; the paper wrapper, directed in the dear hand I loved, the hand of Margaret Wilmot.

"I must have left the wrapper on the table on the night when I received the box, and one of the servants had no doubt put it into the waste-paper basket. I picked up the sheet of paper and folded it neatly; it was a very small treasure for a lover to preserve, perhaps: but then I had so few relics of the woman who was to have been my wife.

"As I folded the paper, I looked, half in absence of mind, at the stamp in the corner. It was an old-fashioned sheet of Bath post, stamped with the name of the stationer who had sold it—Jakins, Kylmington. Kylmington; yes, I remembered there was a town in Hampshire,—a kind of watering-place, I believed,—called Kylmington! And the paper had been bought there—and if so, it was more than likely that Margaret had been there.

"Could it be so? Could it be really possible that in this sheet of paper I had found a clue which would help me to trace my lost love? Could it be so? The new hope sent a thrill of sudden life and energy through my veins. Ill—worn out, knocked up by over-work? Who could dare to say I was any thing of the kind? I was as strong as Hercules.

"I put the folded paper in the breast-pocket of my coat, and took down Bradshaw. [143] Dear Bradshaw, what an interesting writer you seemed to me on that day! Yes, Kylmington was in Hampshire; three hours and a half from London, with due allowance for delays in changing carriages. There was a train would convey me from Waterloo to Kylmington that afternoon—a train that would leave Waterloo at half-past three.

"I looked at my watch. It was half-past two. I had only an hour for all my preparations and the drive to Waterloo. I went to the drawing-room, where my mother was still sitting at work near the open window. She

---

[143] See note 28, p.58 above.

started when she saw my face, for my new hope had given it a strange brightness.

"'Why, Clem,' she said, 'you look as pleased as if you'd found some treasure among your papers.'

"'I hope I have, mother. I hope and believe that I have found a clue that will enable me to trace Margaret.'

"'You don't mean it?'

"'I've found the name of a town which I believe to be the place where she was staying before she brought those diamonds to me. I am going there to try and discover some tidings of her. I am going at once. Don't look anxious, dear mother; the journey to Kylmington, and the hope that takes me there, will do me more good than all the drugs in Mr. Bainham's surgery. Be my own dear indulgent mother, as you have always been, and pack me a couple of clean shirts in a portmanteau. I shall come back to-morrow night, I dare say, as I've only three days' leave of absence from the office.'

"My mother, who had never in her life refused me anything, did not long oppose me to-day. A hansom cab rattled me off to the station; and at five minutes before the half-hour I was on the platform, with my ticket for Kylmington in my pocket."

- CHAPTER 47 -

THE DAWN

"The clock of Kylmington church, which was as much behind any other public timekeeper I had ever encountered as the town of Kylmington was behind any other town I had ever explored, struck eight as I opened the little wooden gate of the church-yard, and went into the shade of an avenue of stunted sycamores, which was supposed to be the chief glory of Kylmington.

"It was twenty minutes past eight by London time, and the summer sun had gone down, leaving all the low western sky bathed in vivid yellow light, which deepened into crimson as I watched it.

"I had been more than an hour and a half in Kylmington. I had taken some slight refreshment at the principal hotel—a queer, old-fashioned place, with a ruinous, weedy appearance pervading it, and the impress of incurable melancholy stamped on the face of every scrap of rickety furniture and lopsided window-blind. I had taken some slight refreshment—to this hour I don't know *what* it was I ate upon that balmy

354

summer evening, so entirely was my mind absorbed by that bright hope, which was growing brighter and brighter every moment. I had been to the stationer's shop, which still bore above its window the faded letters of the name 'Jakins,' though the last of the Jakinses had long left Kylmington. I had been to this shop, and from a good-natured but pensive matron I had heard tidings that made my bright hope a still brighter certainty.

"I began business by asking if there was any lady in Kylmington who gave lessons in music and singing.

"'Yes,' Mr. Jakins's successor told me, 'there were two music-mistresses in the town—one was Madame Carinda, who taught at Grove House, the fashionable ladies' school; the other was Miss Wilson, whose terms were lower than Madame Carinda's—though Madame wasn't a bit a foreigner except by name—and who was much respected in the town. Likewise her papa, which had been quite the gentleman, attending church twice every Sunday as regular as the day came round, and being quite a picture of respectability, with his venerable pious-looking grey hair.'

"I gave a little start as I heard this.

"'Miss Wilson lived with her papa, did she?' I asked.

"'Yes,' the woman told me; 'Miss Wilson had lived with her papa till the poor old gentleman's death.'

"'Oh, he was dead, then?'

"'Yes, Mr. Wilson had died in the previous December, of a kind of decline, fading away like, almost unbeknown; and being, oh, so faithfully nursed and cared for by that blessed daughter of his. And people did say that he had once been very wealthy, and had lost his money in some speculation; and the loss of it had preyed upon his mind, and he had fallen into a settled melancholy like, and was never seen to smile.'

"The woman opened a drawer as she talked to me, and, after turning over some papers, took out a card—a card with embossed edges, fly-spotted, and dusty, and with a little faded blue ribbon attached to it—a card on which there was written, in the hand I knew so well, an announcement that Miss Wilson, of the Hermitage, would give instruction in music and singing for a guinea a quarter.

"I had been about to ask for a description of the young music-mistress, but I had no need to do so now.

"'Miss Wilson *is* the young lady I wish to see,' I said. 'Will you direct me to the Hermitage? I will call there early to-morrow morning.'

"The proprietress of Jakins's, who was, I dare say, something of a matchmaker, after the manner of all good-natured matrons, smiled significantly.

"'I know where you could see Miss Wilson, nearer than the Hermitage,' she said, 'and sooner than to-morrow morning. She works very hard all day,—poor, dear, delicate-looking young thing; but every evening when it's tolerably fine, she goes to the churchyard. It's the only walk I've ever seen her take since her father's death. She goes past my window regular every night, just about when I'm shutting up, and from my door I can see her open the gate and go into the churchyard. It's a doleful walk to take alone at that time of the evening, to be sure, though some folks think it's the pleasantest walk in all Kylmington.'

"It was in consequence of this conversation that I found myself under the shadow of the trees while the Kylmington clock was striking eight.

"The churchyard was a square flat, surrounded on all sides by a low stone wall, beyond which the fields sloped down to the mouth of a river that widened into the sea at a little distance from Kylmington, but which hereabouts had a very dingy melancholy look when the tide was out, as it was to-night.

"There was no living creature except myself in the churchyard as I came out of the shadow of the trees on to the flat, where the grass grew long among the unpretending headstones.

"I looked at all the newest stones till I came at last to one standing in the obscurest corner of the churchyard, almost hidden by the low wall.

"There was a very brief inscription on this modest headstone; but it was enough to tell me whose ashes lay buried under the spot on which I stood.

'To the Memory of
J. W.
Who died December 19, 1853.
'Lord have mercy upon me, a sinner!'

"I was still looking at this brief memorial, when I heard a woman's dress rustling upon the long rank grass, and turning suddenly, saw my darling coming towards me, very pale, very pensive, but with a kind of seraphic resignation upon her face which made her seem to me more beautiful than I had ever seen her before.

"She started at seeing me, but did not faint. She only grew paler than she had been before, and pressed her two hands on her breast, as if to still the sudden tumult of her heart.

"I made her take my arm and lean upon it, and we walked up and down the narrow path talking until the last low line of light faded out of the dusky sky.

"All that I could say to her was scarcely enough to shake her resolution—to uproot her conviction that her father's guilt was an insurmountable barrier between us. But when I told her of my broken life—when, in the earnestness of my pleading, she perceived the proof of a constancy that no time could shake, I could see that she wavered.

"'I only want you to be happy, Clement,' she said. 'My former life has been such an unhappy one, that I tremble at the thought of linking it to yours. The shame, Clement—think of *that*. How will you answer people when they ask you the name of your wife?'

"'I will tell them that she has no name, but that which she has honoured by accepting from me. I will tell them that she is the noblest and dearest of women, and that her history is a story of unparalleled virtue and devotion!'

"I sent a telegraphic message to my mother early the next morning; and in the afternoon the dear soul arrived at Kylmington to embrace her future daughter. We sat late in the little parlour of the Hermitage; a dreary cottage, looking out on the flat shore, half sand, half mud, and the low water lying in greenish pools. Margaret told us of her father's penitence.

"'No repentance was ever more sincere, Clement,' she said, for she seemed afraid we should doubt the possibility of penitence in such a criminal as Joseph Wilmot. 'My poor father—my poor wronged, unhappy father!—yes, wronged, Clement, you must not forget that; you must never forget that in the first instance he was wronged, and deeply wronged, by the man who was murdered. When first we came here, his mind brooded upon that, and he seemed to look upon what he had done as an ignorant savage would look upon the vengeance which his heathenish creed had taught him to consider a justifiable act of retaliation. Little by little I won my poor father away from such thoughts as these: till by-and-by he grew to think of Henry Dunbar as he was when they were young men together, linked by a kind of friendship, before the forging of the bills, and all the trouble that followed. He thought of his old master as he knew him first, and his heart was softened towards the dead man's memory; and from that time his penitence began. He was sorry for what he had done. No words can describe that sorrow, Clement: and may you never have to watch, as I have watched, the anguish of a guilty soul! Heaven is very merciful. If my father had failed to escape, and had been hung, he would have died hardened and impenitent. God had compassion on him, and gave him time to repent.'"

(The end of the story.)

357

THE EPILOGUE – ADDED BY CLEMENT AUSTIN SEVEN YEARS AFTERWARDS

"My wife and I hear sometimes, through my old friend Arthur Lovell, of the new master and mistress of Maudesley Abbey, Sir Philip and Lady Jocelyn, who oscillate between the Rock and the Abbey when they are in Warwickshire. Lady Jocelyn is a beautiful woman, frank, generous, noble-hearted, beloved by every creature within twenty miles' radius of her home, and idolized by her husband. The sad history of her father's death has been softened by the hand of Time; and she is happy with her children and her husband in the grand old home that was so long overshadowed by the sinister presence of the false Henry Dunbar.

"We are very happy. No prying eye would ever read in Margaret's bright face the sad story of her early life. A new existence has begun for her as wife and mother. She has little time to think of that miserable past; but I think that, sound Protestant though she may be in every other article of faith, amidst all her prayers those are not the least fervent which she offers up for the guilty soul of her wretched father.

"We are very happy. The secret of my wife's history is hidden in our own breasts—a dark chapter in the criminal romance of life, never to be revealed upon earth. The Winchester murder is forgotten amongst the many other guilty mysteries which are never entirely solved. If Joseph Wilmot's name is ever mentioned, people suggest that he went to America; indeed, there are people who go farther, and say they have seen him in America.

"My mother keeps house for us; and in very nearly seven years' experience we have never found any disunion to arise from this arrangement. The pretty Clapham villa is gay with the sound of children's voices, and the shrill carol of singing birds, and the joyous barking of Skye terriers. We have added a nursery wing already to one side of the house, and have balanced it on the other by a vinery, built after the model of those which adorn the mansion of my senior. The Misses Balderby have taken what they call a 'great fancy' to my wife, and they swarm over our drawing-room carpets in blue or pink flounces very often, on what they call 'social evenings for a little music.' I find that a little music is only a synonym with the Misses Balderby for a great deal of noise.

"I love my wife's playing best, though they are kind enough to perform twenty-page compositions by Bach and Mendelssohn for my amusement: and I am never happier than on those dusky summer evenings when we sit alone together in the shadowy drawing-room, and talk to each other, while Margaret's skilful fingers glide softly over the keys in wandering snatches of melody that melt and die away like the low breath of the summer wind."

THE END

Appendix A

Contemporary Reviews and Responses

This is a highly-seasoned dish of tainted meat that has been already contrived and served up for a kitchen dinner by the great *chef* of the kitchen maids, and is now brought upstairs for the delectation of coarse appetites in the politer world. The story has been appearing in a penny journal for the kitchen under a title relishable [sic] to the readers of Penny Pirates and Female Highwaymen as 'the Outcast.' It now appears in three volumes as 'Henry Dunbar: the Story of an Outcast.' Before it appeared we received from the publisher a circular, requesting us to announce the excitement it was going to produce. We like to be obliging, and will print—though somewhat after the date—the paragraph supplied to us:

"MISS BRADDON.—Recently announced" (we announced nothing of the sort, but such an announcement had, indeed, been sent us for insertion) "that this popular writer was busily engaged upon a new "sensation" Novel, which would appear early in May, and was rumoured to surpass 'Lady Audley's Secret' in dramatic interest and in strongly developed plot. We are now enabled to state that the new work will be called 'HENRY DUNBAR'—the Story of an Outcast—and that Editions in the English, French, and German languages will be published simultaneously. Subscribers to Circulating Libraries are already on the *qui vive* for early copies.

"** *The Editor will much oblige by inserting the above as a News paragraph which may interest his readers. The publishers will forward the usual Trade advertisement in due course for a series of insertions.*"

Next we were told of the miraculous and immediate exhaustion of the first edition. Then, two or three weeks after the publication of the book, we, doubtless in common with our neighbours of the press, received an appeal for a prompt notice, with information that the publisher of the French edition reports that the work is making a greater sensation in Paris than any novel produced there since "Monte Christo."

The publisher in Paris seems to be under the same curious hallucination as the publisher in London, who now appends to the advertisements of this book his own opinion that, "Beyond all question, *Henry*

Dunbar has excited more genuine public interest than any other work issued this year;" the year, by the way, in which, to say nothing of graver works, Mr Dickens is issuing a new novel that, without any acts of puffing, needs an edition of some forty thousand to meet only the first demand; and the year, too, in which the last work from the hands of Thackeray has issued from the press.

The fact has, nevertheless, already become evident that no labour of puffing, though there were Jupiter himself at the bellows, can ever hoist Miss Braddon's novels into true repute. They are at the head, perhaps, of Kitchen Literature, because a novel of hers tells its story more cleverly and with less would-be-fine writing, than any story by another hand that we have yet met with in such publications as *Reynold's Miscellany* or the *London Journal.* In every other respect we recognize the same appeals from a coarse taste to a taste that cannot in many kitchens of the land be coarser.

The hero of this story, whom Sally the cookmaid [sic] and Tom the knife-boy learnt to pity as "the Outcast" before he was introduced into the drawing-room, is a most mean and brutal murderer and forger, so ingeniously placed that every act of his life during the story is a lie, and he cannot write the commonest note without being therein guilty of forgery. "The author of *Henry Dunbar* has to make the same appeal to the critics which has been made by an eminent novelist on a previous occasion—namely, not to describe the plot." So says the preface. But the quality of a novel depends always in some degree upon the quality of the plot, and how is that to be at the same time concealed and criticized?

[....]

But in this case there is no reason why Miss Braddon should make any appeal. What we suppose to be the secret of her book, namely, that Henry Dunbar is personated by his murderer, is not a secret for a single page. Her arts of construction—addressed to the illiterate and clumsy-minded—are all coarsely and explicitly effective, but by their very coarseness and explicitness are to the practised reader manifest from the beginning.

[....]

We have said, perhaps, too much about this book, which is balanced with no more than an interpolated page or two about Remorse, in the usual style of penny criminal romance, and which is of the worst class of what is called "sensation" literature. It is a bad book, not because it tells of crime,—for the highest poetry may do that,—but because it expresses relish of details of crime for their own sake as matter of adventure, in a narrative enlightened by no subtlety of thought, no charm of style, and wanting throughout the wholesome tone that a commonly healthy, educated mind, even without a spark of genius, would give to the narration of such incidents. There is not a fresh thought or a genuine touch of human pathos, or a single turn of true humour in any of its volumes. We are told—for there are some who will show us points of resemblance, which undoubtedly there are, between Hyperion and a satyr—that we censure in writers like Miss Braddon what is to be found in Shakespeare, whose tragedies are heaped with crime. If that were all one had to say of Shakespeare and his tragedies, his name would have been long since forgotten. Still there are, of course, points of resemblance between Shakespeare and Miss Braddon. Shakespeare had a head, so has Miss B.; eyes in it, so has Miss B.; the same earth sustained them both. And yet for all that, there was such difference between their heads, eyes, tongues, and enjoyment of earth's uses, that one knew how to bring life out of corruption while the other only turns life into rottenness. Shakespeare created where the Braddons kill.

From Anon. 'Kitchen Literature'. Review of *Henry Dunbar. Examiner* (25 June 1864): pp.404-6.

In the preface to her last novel, Miss Braddon awakens a curiosity which the perusal of the three volumes does not tend to diminish. She makes the same appeal to her critics which Mr. Wilkie Collins made on the publication of the *Woman in White*. She beseeches us not to reveal the secret of her tale, lest by so doing we should weaken the interest in it of those for whose amusement it is written. This of course excites our curiosity, but when we have come to the end of the story we are as eager as ever to know what is the secret which should not be divulged, and which if divulged too soon may destroy the interest of the tale. The tale no doubt concerns a secret, but it is a secret only to the personages of the plot; and Miss Braddon labours under an extraordinary delusion if she imagines either that the fact upon which the story hinges is unknown to her readers, or that if known it must mar the interest of the novel. In spite of the author's remonstrance, we mean to speak of this fact without reserve. It is so far similar to that which Mr. Wilkie Collins wished to be kept a secret that in both cases it depends on the substitution of one person for another. Mr. Collins had two women in white like as two peas, and in the style of a skilful thimblerigger he excited our interest in number one; he then secretly changed number one for number two; next he horrified us by what seemed to be the tragical death – the murder of number one; lastly, when the sensation of distress was at its height, he showed us that number one still lived, and that what seemed to be her murder was in reality the natural death of number two. Miss Braddon follows a somewhat similar course, only she does not succeed in concealing from her readers that a substitution has taken place. She brings together two men, the very opposite of each other in worldly circumstances – for whereas Henry Dunbar is of untold wealth, Joseph Wilmot is an outcast with scarcely a penny – but like each other in this, that both are almost unknown in England, Henry Dunbar having been for 35 years absent from his home, and Joseph Wilmot having for a long time lived in concealment under various fictitious names. The poor outcast, who had known the man of wealth in younger days, and who had been irreparably injured by him, met him at Southampton as he arrived from India, strangled him next day, took possession of his property, assumed his name, and played for about a year the part of the wealthy banker, Henry Dunbar. All this time the world imagined that it was Joseph Wilmot, the outcast, who had been murdered, and the police were unable to discover who was the murderer. The murderer and the victim change places. He who is supposed to have been murdered really lives, and he takes the place of the man who is supposed to live but is really murdered.

Now, we honestly think that we pay Miss Braddon a great compliment in refusing to regard her prefatory petition, and in divulging the mystery on which her story depends. We must remind her, in the first place, that we should not care to criticize her novel at all if the chief interest depended on mere thimblerigging. When novelists like Mr. Collins or Miss Braddon come with clasped hands and on bended knees to us critics, and say – "Oh critics, be merciful, and do not announce to the world that there is thimblerigging in our novels, for indeed their chief interest is due to the change of peas, and if you tell this to the world our occupation is gone," we can only say that they take a very mean view of their own prowess and of our vocation. They expect us to criticize seriously their works of art, the supreme interest of which they declare to consist in a change of pea. They expect us to criticize them, too, without letting anybody know what it is that we are criticizing. It is not, however, for the honour of criticizing alone that we refuse to attend to Miss Braddon's request. In point of fact, as we have already said, there is no secret in the novel that requires to be kept from the reader. The murder occurs about the middle of the first volume, and the authoress appears to assume that her numerous readers are as much mystified with regard to the facts as were the people of Winchester, where the tragedy was enacted. All the world believed that Joseph Wilmot was murdered, and that Henry Dunbar was Henry Dunbar. Every reader of the story who has sense enough to take an interest in it can see that it is Henry Dunbar who is murdered, and that Joseph Wilmot, having committed the murder, changes names with his victim. Nor, as we understand these matters, does it heighten the interest which readers take in such a story as we have here related to keep them in ignorance of the facts. We all know with what intense eagerness the public receive the report of a trial, let us say, for murder. For weeks, it may be months, beforehand, all the facts of the case are thoroughly well known. In report after report every detail has been well sifted; whatever can be said for and against the prisoner is a thrice-told tale, and we have all made up our minds that he is guilty. One morning there appears in the papers an account of his trial and condemnation. Are the public content to hear that the jury has found him guilty, and that the judge has condemned him to death? So far from that, they will read a dozen columns of small print, and if we could afford the space they would gladly accept two dozen columns, containing every tittle of evidence – evidence with which they are perfectly familiar, but which they are anxious to see marshalled in proper form, first as analyzed by the prosecution, then as analyzed by the judge. There could not be clearer proof than this, which occurs several times every year, that the interest which the public take in the machinery of detection is not dependent of their ignorance of the result. We may state the result from the outset, and still they will hang over the feverish tale of crime, calculate motives, live over the event, and watch with curious satisfaction the slow advances of discovery.

It is difficult to believe that Miss Braddon is serious in supposing that the interest of her three volumes rests on an unexpected catastrophe which it is injurious for us to reveal. The truth is that some of the most effective situations in the novel would be thrown away if the reader is to be kept in ignorance of the facts. Let us specify, for example, that chapter which is called "Looking for the Portrait." Henry Dunbar has a daughter who left India when she was a babe – too young, therefore, to remember the features of her father. She laments that there is no portrait of her father as he appeared in all the pride and beauty of his youth. She cannot bring herself to love the father who has come home to her from India, and wonders what he could have been in his youth, when he was much admired. Being in Paris, she hears of an English artist there named Kerstall. We need not too curiously analyze the circumstances which led to her discovery of the painter; else we might ask how it came to pass that he, a living artist, had his pictures in the galleries of the Louvre, where students and amateurs went to copy them? Never mind these details. Let us now dwell only on the fact that Henry Dunbar's daughter, hearing of Kerstall, suddenly remembers that his was the name of a portrait painter who drew her father's likeness when he was a young man. The artist was requested to make some alteration in the portrait; he took it with him to Italy, and it had never since been heard of. Is there a chance of recovering the long-lost treasure? The daughter determines to go and see. Now observe here that if we are ignorant of the fact that the supposed is not the real Henry Dunbar, then the whole force and meaning of this search for the portrait is lost upon us. It seems to be an idle episode, that has no relation to the current of events, and especially since, as afterwards appears, the search is in vain, and ends in nothing. On the other hand, a reader who knows that Henry Dunbar is really dead, and that the bearer of the name is an imposter, sees in a moment that the existence of a portrait of the real man is of vital importance to the progress of events, and he begins to tremble for the fate of those personages in whom he is most interested. It turns out that Kerstall is an old man with a very bad memory. He makes the most outrageous mistakes of memory; he declares, in the first instance, that he never knew a person named Henry Dunbar; and when afterwards, with the portrait of Henry Dunbar in his hands, he declares that it is his portrait, no one believes him, because it is impossible to trace the resemblance. Here we repeat that a reader who has not penetrated the secret of the tale must be sadly at a loss to know what can be the object of this chapter. A portrait is sought for, it is pointed out, it is not recognized, the non-recognition of it is easily explained, and the chapter seems to have been written for the mere purpose of filling a certain number of pages. The chapter is really written for the purpose of tantalizing the reader, and making him feel how precarious is the position of the supposed Henry Dunbar. Accident leads his supposed daughter to the verge of a great discovery. She has the portrait of her actual parent in her hands, and is told that it is his portrait. Accident dashes the discovery out of her hands, and she does not believe that the portrait is genuine. The whole moral influence of this is lost if we are, as the authoress professes to believe, in ignorance of the facts which gave it significance.

Not only in a definite incident like that which we have referred to is the superiority of the mode of treatment which supposes knowledge, not ignorance in the reader, evident; it is evident also in the general tone of the description and course of the reflections. We know that Henry Dunbar is an impostor who has murdered the man whom he personates. Knowing this, a hundred sources of interest arise in the progress of the story for which we could have no perception, and could find no adequate substitute, if the discovery of his real character and position were postponed to the end of the tale. We are in the first place interested in the audacity of the man, his amazing assurance, his remarkable ingenuity. Then, in each new sphere of life into which he passes after having done the deed, we are curious to see how he will conduct himself, and to guess what is working in his mind. Miss Braddon has devoted several pages to show how carefully and methodically Joseph Wilmot, when he took possession of Henry Dunbar's property and assumed his name, overhauled his boxes and arranged his papers. The whole of our interest in that description depends on our knowing that here is a new man in a new situation, feeling his way. What interest should we take in learning that Henry Dunbar, believing him the genuine Henry Dunbar, when he arrived in England examined all his boxes and papers most carefully, but also to all appearance without any purpose? So, when the false Dunbar comes into the presence of his supposed daughter, all that is peculiar in his conduct and repels the girl is interesting so long as we know the true relationship; it is uninteresting and unintelligible without that key. So, again, there is a terrible interest in the situation created by the relationship of the supposed Henry Dunbar to Margaret Wilmot, which is not, indeed wholly lost, but is rendered comparatively tame if that relationship is concealed. Joseph Wilmot has a daughter Margaret, who believes that her father has been murdered, and that Henry Dunbar is the culprit. Miss Braddon seems to think that we are all equally deceived, and will be satisfied with the interest which the situation as so understood is fitted to awaken. Doubtless a girl grieving for the loss of her father (though a reprobate) may well excite our sympathies, and especially when she fixes upon the murderer and calls for vengeance on his head. But is not the interest in such a situation tame in comparison with that which the true state of affairs is calculated to excite? The position is this. Margaret vows vengeance and works might and main against Henry Dunbar – that is, against her own father, who personates Henry Dunbar. To avenge the murder of her father, as she supposes, she sets the bloodhounds of the law on the track of her father, and in the end exposes him. The daughter, in love for her father, brings that father to punishment for murdering himself. Here is a singular complication that leads to situations of the highest interest, the whole force of which would be lost upon us if we were indeed ignorant of the secret upon which the story turns.

We hope that we have said enough to show that in choosing to disregard Miss Braddon's injunction, and to divulge her secret, we have some reason on our side. We hope, also, that the analysis on which we have ventured, imperfect though it may be, may lead her seriously to examine the two paths of art which now lie before her. Shall she go on dealing with secrets, and seek to interest her readers by powers of mystification, throwing in a little light here and a little light there, until towards the end of the third volume she thinks it necessary to undo the know and to explain the puzzle? Or will she boldly venture on a more open, perhaps a more difficult but also a more fascinating, style of art – that which, dispensing with the aid of melodramatic surprises and wonderful secrets, trusts rather to the force of situations and to our sympathy in the passions for the sources of power? In Henry Dunbar there appears to be something like a crisis in Miss Braddon's style. She has well nigh exhausted the old style. All the machinery of detection and mystification she has worn out, and in this last novel she appears still to imagine that she is in the region of secrets and detectives, when, as we have attempted to show, her secret is as clear as day, and the chief interest of her novel depends on the fact that from the very first her secret is known. She imagines, as we learn from her preface, that her success depends, as of old, upon a secret, and we have shown that it depends upon her secret being known – upon there being no secret. This is the first of her novels, we believe, in which she proclaims to the world in a preface that she has a secret to be carefully guarded – that her art is of such a melodramatic, sensational order, as requires mystery and profound silence for its due appreciation. She proclaims an over-whelming consciousness of secrecy. We, on the other hand, proclaim that here there is less of a secret than in any of her novels – that the chief interest of her work, in fact, depends on there being no secret in it. May we hope that this contrariety between the fact and her consciousness of it indicates a real advance in Miss Braddon's career as a novelist?

Henry Dunbar has been more exposed to criticism than, perhaps, any of the same writer's works, and it has evidently been written in much haste. We could point out in it some very extraordinary blunders, contradictions, and extravagances. In the middle of the first volume, for example, Mr. Balderly,[1] partner of Henry Dunbar, rushes down to Winchester to see him after his arrival at Southampton, and spends some time with him there. When next he sees him, some months appear to have elapsed, and they meet as strangers. Mr. Balderly said, "Mr. Henry Dunbar, I believe;" and the reply is, "Yes, I am Henry Dunbar," as if they had never met before. "It seems late in the day," Mr. Balderly, after they were seated, "it seems late in the day to bid you welcome to England, Mr. Dunbar, but I do so, nevertheless, most heartily." Surely this is an odd mode of address, when Mr. Dunbar has been in England

---

[1] *The Times* reviewer mistakenly refers to "Mr. Balderly" throughout. Braddon's character is called Mr. Balderby.

several months, and when Mr. Balderly has seen him two days after his arrival. The story, too, is full of improbabilities when we come to look into it closely. Nevertheless, improbabilities of detail are overlooked in the general merit of the plot, and in the real interest which we are led to take in the characters. Margaret Wilmot, for example, is an admirably drawn character, and she gives an elevation to the novel which Miss Braddon has hitherto failed to reach in the company of the heroines whom it has been her pleasure hitherto to introduce to our notice. In spite of haste, and in spite of mistakes, we are inclined to think that this last novel is not in any respect inferior to the same author's previous works, while in method of treatment and in moral elevation it belongs to a higher style of art than she has yet approached.

From Anon. "Henry Dunbar", *The Times*, Tuesday, August 9, 1864, p.4.

In our opinion, the story of "Henry Dunbar" is superior to "Lady Audley's Secret," or any other novel that we have seen from the pen of its author. She has retained all her excellence of plot, her strength, her animal vivacity and boldness of incidents; and she has lost much crudeness and other defects likely to appear in early writings. The deep and secret workings of the human heart, a delicate conception of character shown in nice traits, high philosophy and heroic sentiment do not belong to the mind which creates these popular stories. They attract, nevertheless, and closely fix the reader's attention. They do not make him think, but they make him feel. They are essentially melodramatic, as distinguished from high tragedy, and we know that on the stage the lower style is full as popular as the higher.

Henry Dunbar is a very powerful tale. The old East India City house, with its dingy outside and wealthy interior, the partner brothers, their clerks and dependents, the last heir to all their riches, his miserable fall, and implication of a subordinate clerk, which fact gives the whole interest to the story, are all most graphically described. Then the reappearance of Henry Dunbar, the young rake who had brought ruin on himself and disgrace to the family, after a supposed expiation of his fault by a long exile in India – the mystery which hangs over this nabob after his reinstatement as a member of the Dunbar family, and heir of the Dunbar wealth – all this is well told. The murder, too, at Winchester, and the *something* always arising to show that all had not been discovered and settled, these are points skilfully handled by the writer, who knows well how to hold her readers in breathless interest.

The female characters are of a type, and that not very distinguishable or marked, but they are nice; and a faithful daughter to a bad father is well portrayed. But the crowning jewel of the book is the account given of the detective's run after the murderer. In this description Miss Braddon is thoroughly at home. Mr. Carter, with appetite whetted by the offer of a handsome reward from the Home Secretary, goes to his work like a glutton. He has his subordinate, or "agent in advance," who keeps watch ahead, whilst the principal is busy at leaving no stone unturned before he quit one inch of the way by which, like a blood-hound, he is tracking his game. The night train from the South down to Derby, and on to Hull via Normanton, with all its discomforts; and at Hull the scent suddenly lost, but recovered, and the spirited pursuit in an open boat of the vessel which is carrying to a northern port the object of Mr. Carter's search – his boarding the overtaken vessel – his face-to-face meeting with his slippery chase giver – his proving him not to be the one he wanted, but another equally valuable, and the failure at last, are all incomparable sketches – life-like, real, and good.

This novel having attained its third edition within a month, after appearing in a periodical, can require no praise from us. Its success is as brilliant as the wing of the summer butterfly. Let us hope it will be more enduring.

From Anon. "Literature", *The Era*, Sunday 12 June 1864. 9.

… a story of the sensational school in which circumstantial evidence and a detective are the chief agents, is a poor excitement, and the sense of tragedy is lost on the multitude of every-day details and the constant reference to "Bradshaw." A fourth edition of "Henry Dunbar" attests the unabated popularity of Miss Braddon's works. As in its predecessors, there is in this story infinite skill in the management of an intricate, improbable plot, great cleverness in the manifold contrivances for startling and telling situations, and much mechanical ingenuity in working them up into a highly-coloured effective whole. It is a new, and not altogether a gratifying, feature to see a lady-writer chief among the caterers for strong excitement, and foremost among those who would degrade fiction to the level of inferior melodrama. If it be good to stimulate our predatory instincts and keep them on the stretch while we trace the dodges and doublings of an accomplished scoundrel matched with an adroit detective, then let all praise be given to Miss Braddon, for she understands her work and does it thoroughly, with a never-failing supply of expedients and an inexhaustible stock of disguises. There seems to be but one thing positively essential to her besides the central crime – she must have plenty of money. She can do nothing without heaps of gold, and seems positively to bask in her own gorgeous descriptions of the splendour of wealth. Her heroine's rich dresses are dwelt upon with the unctuous delight of a dressmaker's apprentice, and she writes of upholstery – satin curtains, gilded mouldings, chairs covered with velvet, and "the rich thickness of the sombre Turkey carpet," like one to whom those articles of furniture were subjects of blissful reverie. But perhaps in this as in other things she understands her public, and is well aware that next to its enjoyment of a barbarous murder or a gigantic fraud, is its delight in golden visions of untold wealth.

From Anon. "Belles Lettres", *Westminster Review* 82 (1865). pp.539-54: 547-8.

Appendix B

Parody

How To Make A Novel
   A Sensational Song.   (Air – "Bob and Joan")

Try with me and mix
What will make a Novel,
All folks to transfix
In house or hall or hovel.
Put the caldron on,
Set the bellows blowing;
We'll produce anon
Something worth the showing.
Toora-loora loo,
Toora-loora leddy;

Something neat and new,
Not produced already.
Throw into the pot
What will boil and bubble;
Never mind a plot,
Tisn't worth the trouble.
Character's a jest,
Where's the use of study?
This will stand the test
If only black and bloody.
Toora-loora, &c.

Here's the 'Newgate Guide',
Here's the 'Causes Celebres';
Tumble in beside
Poison, gun, and sabre.
These Police reports,
Those Old Bailey trials,
Horrors of all sorts,
To match the Seven Vials.
Toora-loora, &c.

Down into a well,
Lady thrust your lover,
Truth as some folks tell,
There he may discover.
Stepdames, sure though slow,
Rivals of your daughters,
Bring us from below
Styx and all its waters.
Toora-loora, &c.

Crime that knows no bounds,
Bigamy and arson;
Murder, blood, and wounds,
Will carry well the farce on.
Now it's just in shape;
But with fire and murder,
Treason too, or rape,
Might help it on the further.
Toora-loora, &c.

Tame is Virtue's school;
Paint, as more effective,
Villain, knave, and fool,
And always a Detective.
Hate instead of love,
Gloom instead of Gladness;
Wit and Sense remove,
And dash in lots of Madness.
Toora-loora, &c.

Stir the broth about;
Keep the flame up steady:
Now we'll pour it out;
Now the Novel's ready.
Some may jeer and jibe.
We know where the shop is,
Ready to subscribe
For a thousand copies!
Toora-loora loo,

Toora-loora leddy;

Now the dish will do,
Now the Novel's ready!

[*The Examiner*, 30April, 1864: 279.]

Recipes for Authors

As everything is now worked by machinery, it is not surprising that a "Hand-book to Literary Success" should be talked about. Having been favoured with a glance at the pages of the coming volume, we have much pleasure in making a few extracts for the benefit of those of our readers who are fond of "writing."
How to Write a Sensation Novel.—Take two breaches of the seventh commandment, and one breach of the eighth, and mix well together. Throw in a few dolls, a *soupçon* of sermon, and serve up with a handful of (well-paid-for) allusions to expensive shop-keepers.
…

From "Recipes for Authors", *The Tomahawk: A Saturday Journal of Satire* 1, ed. Arthur William A'Beckett. 11 May, 1867: p.159.

Appendix C

Dramatic Adaptations

Enter Henry Dunbar, R., *evidently agitated, Margaret's card in his hand.*

DUNBAR. Mar—the young person who sent in this card, where is she?

LAURA. In my boudoir—waiting to see you. Yes, you needn't stare, she's my dear friend, Margaret Wentworth.

DUNBAR. *Your* friend!

LAURA. Yes, she used to give me music lessons. She's the dearest creature. (DUNBAR *turns away*) But she has lately lost her father.

DUNBAR. What do you mean by all this? (*fiercely*) As if I didn't know enough—too much about her.

LAURA. What do you know?

DUNBAR. That she's the daughter of that poor wretch, Wilmot; the man—the man—

LAURA. Who received you at Southampton, and was so cruelly murdered!

DUNBAR. Girl, how dare you? Don't you know I can't bear to think of it, to hear of it, that it well nigh crazes me to look back?

LAURA. I beg your pardon, papa, but her name is Wentworth.

DUNBAR. One of Wilmot's many aliases, he told me so. I cannot see her.

LAURA. Not see her, papa?

DUNBAR. No, the sight of her would shake me too much. I should have to live that miserable week over again. I tell you, child, I could not answer for the consequences.

LAURA. Must *I* tell her?

DUNBAR. Tell her what you will, so that she goes, now and for ever. More than this, your acquaintance with her must end.

LAURA. Oh, papa, I love her so—she is so fond of me!

DUNBAR. She is not a proper acquaintance for you. Her father was a dishonoured man, an outcast; who knows what *she* may be. (*checking himself*) No, no, Heaven help me! I know nothing but good of her! Would I could say as much of her miserable father, (*he turns away.*)

LAURA. How am I to give her such a message?

DUNBAR. Your love will find you words, words that will spare her pain—tell her that I will *never* see her; that she must cease to seek it—that I will make her an allowance of two hundred pounds a-year. Here is the first fifty pounds: make her take it: poor girl, I owe it to her Heaven knows, though he was not much of a father to her.

LAURA. Yet she loved him so dearly.

DUNBAR. As if *I* did not know that! *(impetuously)* Go to her, I say, get her away, let me never hear of her again! *(Exit R., in a state of strong excitement.)*

LAURA. Pale, quite pale, and scared! I have never seen him look so before, *(at door* L.) Margaret!

Enter MARGARET WENTWORTH, L. U. E.

MARG. *(eagerly)* Well?

LAURA. I'm so sorry, dear, papa refuses to see you.

MARG. Then he knows who I am—Margaret Wilmot?

LAURA. Yes, he cannot bear the shock.

MARG. I understand.

LAURA. He fears to call up the horrors of that week again.

MARG. He may well fear!

LAURA. And—and—he says our acquaintance must end too!

MARG. Better it should, oh, so much better! Goodbye, my darling.

LAURA. *(embraces her passionately)* Oh, Margaret! It breaks my heart to leave you, in your unhappiness too.

MARG. It is not your fault, *(aside—going)* I will bide my time.

LAURA. Stay, darling, he told me to give you this. *(gives envelope with note)* You will receive the same every quarter.

MARG. *(tearing up and throwing down the envelope)* I would sooner crawl from door to door begging my bread of the hardest stranger in this cruel world—I would sooner die of starvation, pulse by pulse, and limb by limb—than I would accept help from his hands!

LAURA. Margaret! Why, why is this?

MARG. I cannot tell you, Laura. May you never know! Now, for the last time, good-bye, and Heaven bless you!

LAURA. *(sadly)* Stay a moment, I will tell my father. *(going R., turns)* Oh, Margaret! (MARGARET *signals her in passionately.)* *(Exit LAURA. R.)*

MARG. Another broken, of the few ties that linked my life with love! But he shall not escape me. I will dog his steps—I will haunt his goings-out and his comings-in, but I *will* see him, and *he* shall see *me*, if I wait till I drop down dead! *(going,* c.)

From *Henry Dunbar: Or, A Daughter's Trial.* A Drama in Four Acts. Founded on Miss Braddon's novel of the same name. By Tom Taylor (1865). From Act II, Scene 1.

Olympic Theatre

A new drama in four acts, founded upon Miss Braddon's famous novel of "Henry Dunbar, or, The Outcast;" and bearing the same title, was produced at this theatre on Saturday evening in the presence of a numerous audience whose judgment on the performance was enthusiastically favourable. It is worthy of remark that this is not the first occasion on which Miss Braddon's highly-wrought fiction has appeared in a theatrical guise. It has already been dramatised for the French stage by M. Hippolyte Hostein, and, under the title of "L'Ouvriere de Loudres," it was played last winter with brilliant success at the Ambigu Comique, where M. Just and Madlle. Laurent achieved great celebrity as the two most important personages. That the work of an English novelist should have found such favour in Paris as to have suggested this unusual game of reprisal in the very quarter from which British playwrights have for generations been accustomed to derive their supply of "plots," is a curious fact in the annals of international literature, and one of which Miss Braddon may assuredly well feel proud. The novel of "Henry Dunbar" is so extensively known, that in noticing the present version of the work it were superfluous to describe in detail the leading incidents of a story with which all who claim even a cursory acquaintance with the most popular publications of the day, may fairly be presumed to be familiar. It will be remembered that the plot is founded upon a circumstance ingenious in conception, and singularly capable of dramatic development—the audacious assumption by a murderer of the character, the estate, and the position in society of the very man he had slain. By taking his name, wearing his clothes, and quietly gliding into possession of his property—acts which the absence of the murdered man from England for many years, and the consequent ignorance of his friends respecting his personal appearance rendered easy of accomplishment—the murderer disarms suspicion, deludes a jury, and escapes the punishment due to his crime. How this crafty device prospers for a time, and how it comes at last to confusion—how the murderer's daughter, mistaking the assassin for his victim, tracks the guilty man from phase to phase of his perilous career—how like Eleanor Vane, though with a somewhat gentler purpose (her object being not vengeance, but the honour of her family), she relentlessly pursues him, only to discover the murderer in her own father—how she thenceforward devotes herself to the filial task of protecting the man whom she had before so eagerly hunted down ... are problems which live in the memories of Miss Braddon's multitudinous readers with too vivid a sense of vitality to need recapitulation. Though there is no mention of Mr. Tom Taylor's name in the playbill, it is understood that to that accomplished gentleman has been assigned the duty of condensing within the limits of a dramatic represent-ation the manifold incidents which occupy three octavos in the narration. He has on the whole preformed his task as well as could reasonably be expected, regard being had to the essential difference between a play and a novel, and the amazing difficulty of transforming the one into the other. He has reproduced with as much fidelity as was possible under the circumstances all the more important characters and events of the story; but, with a view no doubt to make the play less painfully tragic than it might otherwise be, he has ventured to diverge in some incidental matters from the course and tenor of the original narrative. Thus, for instance, the death of Wilmot is ascribed to no deliberate assassination, but simply to a chance blow struck in a sudden and unpremeditated quarrel. There is also a variation towards the close of the drama, which is made to take place in the major's rural villa in Hampshire, where Margaret Wentworth, disguised as a rustic servant, throws the detectives off the scent, and fools them to the top of their bent. This scene, though introduced at the most critical period of the action, is the most comic in the play, and in its farcical humour contrasts rather too forcibly with the tragic sentiment of the following scene, in which the death of Henry Dunbar brings the piece to a melancholy conclusion. These modifications, however, may pass muster; but in the first act of the play the dramatist appears to us to have fallen into an error, which ought certainly to be rectified. The death of Wilmot might assuredly be left to the imagination of the audience. It was all very well for the novelist to describe that calamity with the graphic eloquence characteristic of her style; but the visible and tangible representation upon the stage of the subject she so vividly depicts is another matter. "Sensation," in a legitimate sense of the word, so far from being opprobrious, is most desirable. A play that creates no dramatic sensation must be a dull, commonplace affair, and wholly destitute of interest; but on the stage, as in everyday life, excitement should not be bought at the expense of good taste and good feeling. To introduce the body of a murdered man upon a shutter, with a white sheet spread over the corpse, is doubtless to produce a "sensation," but to purchase it also at too dear a cost. The rectification of this blunder, together with such a vigorous retrenchment of the dialogue as would give swifter and more lucid action to the plot, would sensibly improve the general effect of the drama.

[....]

The play—for which Mr. Hawes Craven has furnished some good scenic pictures, chiefly interiors—occupied more than three hours in the representation, but it did not appear to tax the patience of the audience, whose applause, on the contrary, was frequent and fervid. Some latitude, however, is conceded as a matter of course on a first night, and to render the play permanently attractive the adapter will unquestionably have to prune the dialogue and accelerate the action.

"Olympic Theatre", *The Morning Post*, Monday, 11 December 1865: p.3.

Victorian Secrets

www.victoriansecrets.co.uk

Victorian Secrets revives neglected nineteenth-century works and makes them available to both scholars and general readers.

New titles are under development all the time. An up-to-date catalogue can be found on the website.

If you would like to suggest a title for publication, please contact us at suggestions@victoriansecrets.co.uk

Should you find any major errors in this book, please let us know at feedback@victoriansecrets.co.uk

Lightning Source UK Ltd.
Milton Keynes UK
26 June 2010

156117UK00001B/58/P